RAIDER'S
Vendetta

Written by
Karen Arnpriester

RAIDER'S Vendetta

Reviews

A surprising twist for this new and rising author, Karen Arnpriester, Raider's Vendetta has all the action and edge-of-your-seat suspense required to captivate and hold its audience to its spectacular and unexpected ending. I loved, hated and will not soon forget the main character, Raider. Is there hope for Raider? Is anyone beyond God's reach? Will Charley survive? This book I could not put down until I had the answers I craved. I was hooked from the beginning and am hooked on this author! I'm already anticipating her next release that I hear is pending. Put me on the waiting list!!!
Pam Rich

A Christian drama with twists and turns, two people's journeys of self discovery and life lessons through a harrowing event. Rich characters, action, and deep Christian experiences.
J. Locke

After reading Karen Arnpriester's first book, and heard another was released, I had to give it a read since the first book. I could not put down. Now, with Raiders Revenge, it picks up more velocity with a fascinating character study that had me hooked. There were many twists and surprises and the writing style had me hooked again. I highly recommend this book to any reader who wants to be lost into the story, and delve deep into the mind of her characters. Bravo Karen.
Tom Allen

RAIDER'S Vendetta

Introduction

I am thrilled to present my second book. Only the Lord knows how I ended up on this journey of telling stories. Stories about the pain life presents and the healing that can come from Heaven's grace.

As the writer of this story, I was able to step into the heart and mind of a very angry, vindictive person. Raider could easily be the type of person that we throw away, but the journey allows us to see how he became a man filled with fury. A man who could have been a loving, kind husband and father, but succumbed to a life of hardship and regret.

Charley, a faithful woman who would be tested and pushed to the ultimate limits. Could she follow God's directives and put her own pride, safety and fears aside?

The questions brought up in the book are and were my questions. Questions that kept me separate from God for many years. Some have been answered, but others have not, not yet. The story contains miracles, some fictional but others are actual Heavenly encounters that I was cherished enough by God to experience.

I would love to hear about your reactions and thoughts.

karnpriester@gmail.com
www.facebook.com/karen.slimickarnpriester
twitter.com/KarenArnpriester
amazon.com/author/karenarnpriester
Blog: http://karenskoncepts.com/mythoughts

raidersvendetta.com

RAIDER'S Vendetta

Long Ago

He tried many times to escape, but Itchy couldn't figure out how to undo the latch from the inside. *How long will she keep me in here this time?* he wondered.

It was a simple mistake; he hadn't meant to see Mrs. Anton naked. Itchy was just hanging out with his best friend, Marty Anton. When he threw open the unlocked bathroom door to relieve himself, he saw her standing in the tub. She hadn't removed the towel from the bar yet and Itchy saw all of her nakedness. Itchy quickly looked down and fell backwards as he scrambled to get away. The screams from Mrs. Anton blasted his ears as he peed his pants. The uncontrolled release was horrific for a fourteen-year-old boy.

Mrs. Anton was enraged. She threw on her robe and telephoned his Aunt Rose, screaming that Itchy was a pervert and Rose needed to keep him away from her son. She insisted that he would corrupt Marty and turn him into a "Peeping Tom." Itchy panicked and ran from the house as Marty's mom shrieked at him to never come back.

Itchy was afraid to go home. He knew that his Aunt Rose would use his latest misfortune to punish and shame him, but if he didn't go home right away, the punishment would be even harsher. She had a way of stacking sins on top of each other. He could already hear her screeches in his head. "It wasn't bad enough that you lusted after a grown woman, but then you refused to face your foul sin and suffer the consequences. God sees your filthy heart. You can't run away from Him!"

When Itchy slunk into the house through the back door, Aunt Rose was waiting for him. She looked at his soiled crotch and clucked with distain. Itchy didn't understand that his Aunt had mistakenly assumed the worst. The wooden paddle that she used for pulling bread from the oven was spinning in her hands. He knew what was coming next – he unzipped his pants and they, along with his boxers, fell around his ankles. She nodded toward the kitchen table and he placed both hands flat on the surface.

The beating was vicious this time. He tried not to cry, but the repeated swings of the paddle became unbearable. The tears rolled down his cheeks and puddles formed on the table.

While he endured her wrath, she quoted scripture to him. She always pulled scriptures out of context and Itchy was convinced that God expected him to suffer to be worthy of forgiveness and salvation. Aunt Rose would alternate scripture with demeaning statements, telling him that his pain was only a small measure of what he deserved. He was born a bastard to a mother who was cheap and easy with filthy men. Aunt Rose would do whatever it took to save him from himself.

After Aunt Rose felt the punishment had suited the crime, she stopped and opened the cabinet door to the vegetable bin, an outdated storage area for fresh produce. It was the cell Itchy must endure until he repented for his wrongdoings. Itchy carefully pulled up his pants. There was no longer enough room to sit, as there had been when he was smaller. He had to squat, bend over, and squeeze in to fit. The blisters on his backside were on fire and wet. Itchy was sure they were bleeding. This was typical when she suspected his punishable infraction was sexually motivated, which was more frequent as he became older.

The door closed and latched from the outside. There was no air circulation except for small holes drilled into the cabinet door. Originally, they had been drilled to keep the produce from rotting as quickly. Now, the holes were small windows into a kitchen filled with pain and horror.

Each time Aunt Rose walked past the bin, she would kick the door and scream at him to pray louder for forgiveness. This was the angriest she had ever been. It was quite evident to Itchy that she felt he had crossed over to a new level of depravity. When he was young, his prayers were heartfelt. He wanted to be clean, but after years of belittlement and reinforcement of his undeserving and vile nature, his prayers were hollow and solely to pacify this enraged woman. His knees and legs began to ache and his muscles throbbed.

Aunt Rose's rantings over the years filled in the holes of Itchy's history. His mother, June, had become pregnant at the age of sixteen. She was the youngest and the wild child in her family of staunch believers. She had run off to California with Itchy's daddy, Arthur, who was seventeen. They didn't have the decency to get married and lived in lustful sin. His father was blonde, handsome, and charming, like all demons were, and he'd tempted June beyond her strength to resist.

When Itchy was only six years old, his mother escaped and left Itchy to survive his father's brutality alone. No one heard from June again and Itchy didn't know if she was alive or dead. Most days, he hoped she was dead, a long, painful, lonely death.

Itchy had earned his name by contracting a severe case of head lice when he was young. His father's abuse included extreme neglect. When he did go to school, the kids were relentless with their taunting. Itchy hated the nickname, but hated his real name even more. His real name, Arthur, was his father's name.

Eventually, his father was arrested for manslaughter, a bar fight gone bad, and the police officers took Itchy to Langston Hall. Most kids would be scared in a children's home, but Itchy felt safe there. He had three meals a day, a clean bed, and clean clothes. He didn't make many friends but there was one girl who touched him deeply. Her name was Pagne. He didn't know her for long, but she would always be in his heart, one of the three females he would ever trust.

The county eventually located his widowed Aunt Rose and she begrudgingly agreed to take Itchy to live with her. "It is the Christian thing to do," she told the social worker. He was flown back to Boston to live with her and her son, Darrell. Itchy was excited to have a new home and an older brother. Darrell, however, was indifferent. He was too busy avoiding his mother's wrath and quickly learned that having Itchy around proved to be an advantage. If he lay low, Itchy caught most of the hell.

Before arriving, Itchy had no idea of the loathing his aunt harbored or the horror that awaited him.

RAIDER'S Vendetta

Chapter 1

When Charley Abrams pulled into the bank's parking lot, Charley was relieved to find it empty. There was no one at the ATM. When she walked up to the machine, she saw an electronic message on the screen announcing that the ATM was offline for programming updates and would be offline for several hours. Charley was annoyed. She hated going into the bank for simple transactions. There was always a wait, but she needed to deposit a large check today. When she approached the reflective doors, Charley stared at her reflection. She had become her mother over the years. There were wrinkles, but they weren't deeply etched like a lot of women her age. Her body build was always meaty, gradually heavier as she got older. She liked to say that she wasn't overweight, just too short. When asked how tall she wasn't, Charley would smile and say, "four-twelve."

Charley kept her hair in a spiky short style and had recently allowed it to remain gray. This was a big adjustment in her appearance. Though she had watched the face of an old woman slowly appear as the years passed, she still admired her eyes. They were large and gray. They weren't as bright as they used to be, but still unique. Charley had never liked her mouth. She had thin lips and always envied women with pouty, full mouths. She had entertained the idea of Botox injections when younger, but it required needles and that was a definite deal breaker. When she pulled open the mirror of herself, she was glad to see that she was the only customer in the bank.

When her transaction was complete, Charley tucked her receipt into her pocket. As she turned toward the door to leave, she heard a loud commotion and looked up. Charley saw two men with ball caps pulled down low, bandanas over their mouths and noses, pushing a young woman through the doors. One of the men shoved the woman and she fell to the floor, landing on her hands and knees. Charley grimaced with sympathy pain. She had fallen recently and remembered how it had jarred her whole body. The second man, who was quite tall and had a large build, turned the dead bolt, pointed a gun at the group of tellers, and bellowed, "Everyone behind the counter, take three steps back with your hands over your head! Now!" The shorter man grabbed the fallen woman's arm and drug her further into the bank, then snarled at her to lay down flat on the floor.

"You," the larger man said, glaring at Charley, "get down on the floor." Charley slid down the front of the counter and sat down. "Down flat, face on the floor," the man screamed at her. Charley quickly lay down, staring at the floor

The shorter man, thin but muscular, moved behind the counter and raised his gun so everyone saw it. He also had a large, open black garbage bag. He swiftly moved from station to station, making each of the tellers step up and open their drawer. The money moved quickly from the drawers into the bag.

Once the drawers were emptied, the robber behind the counter herded all the tellers around to the front. Charley hoped that someone had triggered the silent alarm. She sensed the movement of bodies close to her as the tellers were told to lie flat on the floor. She was curious, but didn't look up. She wondered why the bank didn't have an armed security guard. Weren't all banks supposed to have a guard? If she survived this, she would find a new bank with big guards and big guns.

The shorter man made his way to the doors while pointing the gun at the group of people on the floor. "Let's get going!" he hollered at his companion.

No response.

"Man, we gotta go. Now!"

"We got time... wanna check the vault," the taller man threw back as he knelt by the teller closest to Charley.

"Who can open the vault?" he sputtered as he grabbed the young woman by her hair. His other hand held the gun next to her skull and tapped it hard. Charley heard her yelp in pain.

"The manager, Mr. Mitchell." Since there was only one man working in the bank, it was obvious who he was. Charley heard the masked man jump up and move to her right. She positioned her head slightly so she was able to see where the manager was lying. The robber grabbed him and pulled him up, holding the gun next to his chest. The tension was building as the shorter man continued to scream and curse at his partner who was dragging the manager back to the vault.

"Shut up! We're almost done here," the taller man yelled back.

Charley slowly shifted herself to get a better view of the room. The woman next to her looked like she was going to pass out. Charley smiled, hoping it would reassure her. Charley saw the man closest to the door. She had time to take in details now. Muscular, but not big, jeans, Nike tennis shoes, long sleeved blue shirt, red print bandana, and an Oakland Raiders cap. It was too hot to be wearing a long sleeved shirt. Charley assumed he had tattoos he was covering, but enough skin was showing to know that he was Caucasian. His hair was tucked under the hat, but a little blonde still showed. She decided to label that one Raider.

Once the vault was opened, the manager turned to face the bank robber. In that moment, the bandana slipped down off the robber's face. The two men locked eyes and the realization that the robber could now be identified registered with both men. The robber's eyes narrowed with an evil determination. Mr. Mitchell had only one option, to take the gun.

Charley jerked as she heard struggling and then the blast of the gun as it went off. She saw Raider move to the center of the bank and lift his gun. She squeezed her eyes shut, a natural reaction, as another shot rang through the bank. She heard the loud wail of a man and then the thud as he went down. "Darrell!" Raider bellowed. Charley heard another man cursing and moaning. "Damn it, Darrell, what did you do?"

Raider demanded that they all slide to the left wall and sit with their hands on their heads as he made his way to the counter. He kicked the young woman he'd pushed down earlier and screamed at her to move over with the others. She managed to make it to the wall without throwing up. Raider kept his gun pointed at the stricken group of women.

He looked over the counter and saw the manager in a crumpled heap and Darrell sitting on the floor. His hand clutched his chest as the blood oozed between his fingers.

"Holy crap, Darrell. How bad is it?"

"Bad enough to kill me I expect," Darrell managed to say with sarcasm. Darrell tried to stand but fell onto his back. "Get the hell outta here, I'm done."

"You ass, I should leave you," Raider snarled.

Raider moved around the end of the counter to get to Darrell, still trying to keep all the hostages in view. His partner lay on his back, unblinking eyes staring at the ceiling. He was obviously dead. Raider looked at the front doors, his expression frantic, like that of a trapped animal looking for a way to escape.

Charley, trying to make sense of what happened, assumed that Mr. Mitchell had grabbed the gun, killed the robber in the scuffle, and was shot by Raider before he got off another round. The coppery smell of blood filled the bank.

When Raider came around to the front of the counter, he saw several cars pulling in. They appeared to be customers. Charley could see that he had no idea what to do now. "In and out quick, you stupid idiot," he mumbled under his breath.

Chapter 2

As Charley scanned the room with her limited view, she saw an elderly man walk up to the bank entrance and try to open the door. The bank doors were tinted almost black, since they faced west, and she knew the man only saw his reflection in the doors, even though the people inside saw him. He looked confused, then looked at his watch and tried the door once more. He stood there, not knowing what to do next, baffled by the locked door.

It appeared to Charley, that Raider would rush the old man and get past him before he could react; might even shoot him. As Raider moved toward the doors, four construction workers moved in behind the old man. They tried the door, also looking confused. One of them knocked and waited. The conversation among the group was accented with shrugs and searching looks, seeking a sign or someone with an explanation. Several of the men pressed their faces against the glass, trying to see into the bank. They all stood there, waiting, discussing the situation. More people joined the group. A woman pulled out a cell phone and dialed. Charley heard the phone ringing from behind the counter. Each ring made the room vibrate as if a gong had been hit. Everyone held their breath. The woman hung up and tried again. The ringing continued. Raider appeared to be calm, but Charley was close enough to see his hand twitching as he held the gun. She feared the outcome for all of them. Charley silently began praying to God. The woman with the phone hung up again and dialed a short number. Charley assumed it was 911.

Charley heard Raider quietly repeating, "Leave." The

young woman on her cell phone became more animated, then suddenly became still, staring at the locked doors. She slowly began stepping back, instructing the others to do the same, keeping her eyes glued on the doors. Obviously, the police had warned them to move back for their safety. The construction workers hesitated but finally moved a short distance away. Charley identified the body language; the group of strong men were primed for a fight. They were ready to be heroes. She knew Raider would not be exiting through the front doors. The rest of the group moved to the far side of the parking lot and appeared to be waiting for the show to begin. Raider squatted on the floor, keeping the gun turned on the group, as he tried to use the bandana to wipe the sweat away from his eyes. This was difficult to do while keeping his face hidden. Charley thought how hot it must be in that disguise. By now, he would have been racing away in a fast car, air conditioner blasting, counting the money, if his partner had not gotten greedy.

They didn't have to wait long. A black and white cruiser pulled into the lot and several officers got out. They stayed on the far side of their cruiser. One officer took out a phone and dialed the bank's number.

The hostages were startled when they heard the phone begin to ring again. Raider jumped up and paced some more.

"Should we answer it?" one of the teller's asked. The bank robber seemed to be searching his brain for an idea.

"Yeah," he finally said. "Tell them the electricity is off and you had to close down for awhile." The teller, whose nametag said Anne, slowly got up and picked up the phone. Raider was pointing his gun at the young lady who had been pushed into the bank. He jerked the gun at her to remind Anne that he would shoot if she didn't do what he said.

"Hello, Ellisville Bank," she managed to say. Charley was impressed. She didn't know if she would be able to speak. "Everything is fine, Officer. Our power went out and it is procedure to lock the doors until everything is back up and running." Pause. "I assure you, we are all fine." Pause again. "I realize you have a job to do, but Mr. Mitchell is not here. Only he can authorize us to unlock the doors." Another pause. "I'm sorry, sir. Soon, sir," then she was quiet, listening to the other end of the line. From her facial expression, it was obvious to Charley that the officer was not buying her explanation.

Anne hesitated and looked at Raider. "They want to talk to you, sir. They know something is wrong." Raider began pacing and cursing again.

"Hang up you moron" he said through clenched teeth. Anne hung up the phone. She stood there, scared to move or speak. Raider walked over to her and smacked her across the face with the gun. She fell to the floor, whimpering. He pointed the gun at her and pulled back the hammer.

She managed to whisper between her sobs, "He knew. I didn't tell him, he already knew. You heard me. I tried to send them away." Charley felt her heart in her throat. She thought about trying to knock him off his feet with her legs, but he was too far away.

Dear God, please don't let him kill her! she screamed in her head. She heard the hammer slip back into position.

"All of you get behind the counter." They half crawled, half slid to the new location. Charley was able to get next to Anne and put her arm around her shoulder. She looked at the damage to her face and saw that, in spite of all the blood, the injuries were not serious. She would be bruised and swollen, but she would be okay. She felt Anne move in tighter next to her. Charley felt her whole body quivering.

They jumped when the phone began ringing again. No one moved to answer it. Raider squatted across from them, aiming the gun from one frantic face to another. The ringing kept going and going. It felt warmer inside the bank. Was it the closeness of the group, the sweat that comes with fear, or had they shut off the air conditioning? Charley had seen that happen in cop shows; make the criminals as uncomfortable as possible. She always felt bad for the hostages and now she would be the one sweating it out. The phone finally stopped ringing.

~

Now that they were behind the counter, they couldn't see anything outside, but Raider would stand periodically to check on things. More police cars had pulled in. Raider wasn't sure what to do now. He had to think quickly. They had always done hit and run robberies; gas stations, convenience stores, or drunks trying to find their cars. This was their first bank robbery and Darrell had said he had it all worked out. "Don't worry, it'll be a breeze. The drawers will have plenty. It's payday for most slobs and they load the drawers up just before lunch. We'll hit them hard and fast."

Darrell, you fool, you didn't say anything about the vault, he thought. Even Raider knew the vault required too much time, especially with just two guys.

Chapter 3

A voice boomed through a bullhorn, "This is the police. We want to talk to whoever is in charge. We'll be calling you." After what felt like an eternity, the phone rang. Raider picked it up on the tenth ring. He held the phone to his ear, but didn't speak. Agent Morris was on the other end. "I'm Agent Megan Morris, with the FBI, and I want to help you help us resolve this situation. We don't want anyone hurt. What can we do for you?" After a few minutes of hesitation, he moved the receiver under the bandana.

"Look, I don't want anyone else killed. Just clear out and I'll leave."

"Anyone else? People have been killed? Wounded?"

"I'm not telling you anything. I just need you all to leave and no one will get hurt. If you don't, I will shoot someone."

"Can you tell me who is in there with you?" Raider slammed the phone down, hoping he burst the wanna-be cop's eardrum. Women with badges, just as bad as soldiers with boobs. Raider got up and looked around the bank. He needed to find a way to control the hostages while he searched the bank for a way out. He glanced over to the vault and saw that the metal bar door was standing open; the keys were still in the lock. "All of you, move into the vault, stay low."

They crawled past Mr. Mitchell's body and tried not to look into his shocked face, frozen in death. Then they crawled past the second body. It had been many years since this fifty-seven year old woman had been on her knees, let alone traveled on them. Blood had drained onto the floor from both bodies and their hands and knees were covered with the warm stickiness.

Charley made it into the vault first. The rest of the hostages followed her in and huddled in the far corner. Raider pulled the phone in the vault out of the wall and stepped out to shut the gate. Raider tested it with a hard tug. Once the hostages were locked in and no longer a threat, he knelt down and looked into Darrell's glazed over eyes. *What the hell did you get me into Darrell?* he thought. He saw the gun lying between his cousin's thighs. Raider picked it up and wiped the blood onto his jeans. He pocketed the keys, stuck the second gun in his waistband, and moved back into the bank to locate the cameras.

Raider entered each office and room looking for other employees or an exit. If a door was locked, he forced it open. He found the room with the recording boxes and surveillance equipment. He saw there were two screens. One was positioned to cover the front doors and the second would show the faces of people in line at the teller windows. He went back into the bank and smashed both cameras. He jumped when the phone rang. Raider decided to pick it up and see what they were offering.

"Thank you for picking up. I'd like to help," Agent Morris offered. Raider thought for a minute,

"Okay" he said with a smirk.

"How would you like for me to address you?" she asked.

"Sir will be just fine."

"I'm here to work with you. Tell me what you need."

"I want a helicopter and a pilot. If you provide that, I won't kill anyone. So you do what you gotta do to work that out." Raider slammed the phone down. He pulled the scarf off his face and the air, even though warm, felt good on his skin.

He continued to search for another way out. He knew he wasn't going out those front doors. He knew they would string him along, promise him anything, and wait for a sniper to get a clear shot. Raider figured he would find a way to slip out and be long gone before anyone knew he wasn't there. He checked the ducts, the windows, and the service doors. He saw that cruisers had surrounded the bank. He kicked himself for being disappointed. What did he think they would do? He checked for trap doors that would lead to the roof or under the building.

~

Charley knelt next to Anne to offer whatever comfort she could. She felt the bulk of her cell phone in her pocket. She looked out the vault gate bars, and didn't see or hear anything. She prayed that Raider wasn't on his way back. Charley looked at the huddled mass of women. "Is there anyone else in the bank, in any of the offices?"

"No," Geena answered. "We all come behind the counter for the lunch crowd."

Charley only had two bars on her phone and hoped it was enough to send a text. She texted her daughter, Mari, and told her where she was. When her daughter's return text flashed on the screen, Charley felt connected to the outside world again. She then entered the other hostages' names and phone numbers. There were a total of seven women: Charley; Angie, the lady they had pushed in the door; Anne, the teller hit with the gun; Lenore, the supervisor; Geena, the loan officer; Brittany, a teller; and Iris, another teller. Next, she texted that one of the robbers and the bank manager had been killed. She also told her to tell the police there was only one robber in the bank and all the hostages were locked in the vault. After assuring her daughter she was fine, she turned the volume off and hid the phone in the vault so she wouldn't be found with it. After getting the message from Mari, Angie's husband texted her to tell her that he loved her and he would be at the bank soon. Angie texted him back and told him they were all safe in the vault.

Charley saw the fear in the women's eyes. "I'd like to pray for our safety," Charley suggested.

Angie quickly straightened up and said, "Absolutely, we pray all the time; me, my husband and my three little ones.

The other women looked at Charley in disbelief. Lenore even snickered at the suggestion. "If God is so wonderful, why are we sitting in here? Why is Mr. Mitchell dead? He was a Christian. Just pray silently if you're going to pray. I don't want to hear it. The police will get us out of here."

Charley was surprised that the severity of their situation didn't lead them to want God's protection. Charley prayed silently while holding

21

Angie's hand. She felt Angie squeeze her hand several times. She felt blessed to know that they were united in their prayer. The Holy Spirit touched Charlie's soul with the understanding that she was needed in this crisis.

Chapter 4

Raider couldn't find a way out that wouldn't put him face to face with the police. He had been frantically searching for the last hour, no exit. He had found a pile of white tablecloths used for the bank's display tables and several boxes of promotional t-shirts. These could come in handy.

Raider pulled the bandana back up. He got to the vault door and then he heard the distinct vibration of a cell phone. No one is without a cell phone these days. He began cursing the women, unlocked the door, and pushed it open. "I want your phones, all of them." He pointed the gun at Lenore, "I'll blow her head off." Angie slid her phone over to his feet. The other ladies had been working, so no phones were on their person. He looked at Charley and she stared back. "I don't have a phone on me," she finally said. She wasn't lying; it certainly wasn't on her. He told her to stand up. He patted her down and when he was convinced she wasn't concealing a phone, he pushed her back to the floor.

It was a deranged sight, this man with a gun, looming over them, covered in blood. Charley knew this vision would terrorize any sane person. Raider picked up Angie's phone and checked her outgoing calls and then texts. Angie cringed with fear, realizing she should have deleted the message to her husband when she had the chance. He saw her last text sent and didn't bother to read any further. Raider glared at her through narrowed eyes. Without hesitation, he lifted the gun and shot her. He didn't shoot to kill, but hit her in the thigh. "You stupid, stupid woman," he muttered as she wailed in pain. Charley moved toward her and he lifted the gun to her face. Her nose was inches from the end of the barrel. She smelled the hot metal and the spent bullet. "Stay put or you're next," he growled. Charley wasn't a nurse, but she knew, if left unattended, Angie would bleed out.

"She's worth more to you alive," Charley stated calmly, even though she was terrified on the inside. "You may have hit a major artery. Just let me get a tourniquet on it so she doesn't die." Raider looked at the blood gushing from Angie's leg. He didn't respond but lowered the gun and stepped back. Charley pulled off Angie's t-shirt and wrapped it tightly around Angie's thigh above the bullet hole. She saw the mixture of terror, shock, and anguish in Angie's eyes. "God is with us," she mouthed to Angie. Angie seemed to relax a little.

The bank phone began to ring. Raider pointed the gun at Geena, "You answer it and tell them time is ticking. They now have a wounded hostage." Geena stood up slowly and Raider shoved her to the nearest phone, just outside the vault. She answered the phone and relayed his message word for word. They wanted to know details and Geena looked at Raider. "Hang up!" he screamed. He pushed Geena toward the storage closet and demanded, "Grab those T-shirts and take them into the vault." Geena obeyed. The women were instructed to rip the shirts into strips. Charley took one of them and helped Angie put it on. She knew Angie wouldn't want to be sitting there in just her bra. Raider started to stop her but found it curious that this old woman would worry about modesty. Charley also took several of the shirts and folded them into a compress for Angie's wound.

Raider then had all the women tie themselves together, just a few inches apart, with their arms extended. He looked at Angie and realized she wasn't mobile. To move her, they would have to drag her. She would have to be left in the vault. He had the remaining women at each end of the shredded T-shirt rope tie themselves together to make a circle. He looked at his shield and was pleased. Raider ducked under the rope and into the center of the circle. Now he would have their bodies as a shield. Any attempts to subdue him would jeopardize the women.

Raider kept his gun pointed in Geena's side. "Anyone try anything and I won't miss. At this range, the bullet will tear her in half." Charley

24

was directly in front of Raider, face to face. She hadn't known what he was planning or she would have turned around before tying herself in. She walked backward as they moved into the bank. She could see the details of his eyes, deep green with gold veining. How did such beautiful eyes contain such hate? She found herself praying that she wouldn't trip. If she went down, the whole group would go down. The gun could easily go off and kill one of them.

Trying to walk past the bodies and maneuver across the blood-covered floor was difficult. The women could smell the mixture of their sweat as they shuffled together. It was soured and musty. Raider's was the strongest. His anxiety level combined with the heat in the bank made it ooze from his pores. The bank was warm and uncomfortable, but at least they were no longer sitting in the vault. It felt too much like a tomb. They were tied so close together, there was no airflow to help dissipate their body heat. Charley felt like she was suffocating.

The phone rang again. They shuffled their way to the desk and Raider picked up the receiver and waited.

"Sir," Agent Morris said. "We are working on getting your chopper. We can land it in the field just behind the bank, but we need to know that the ladies are safe and that you have not hurt them. We heard a shot."

"Well, one got shot for blabbing her mouth. She's alive but not for long."

"Sir, please allow her to leave the bank. You don't want a murder against you, especially of an innocent woman. Juries won't show mercy to a man who shoots an unarmed woman." Raider considered what she was saying.

"You're assuming that I will get caught and face a jury," Raider replied.

"It would show good faith with us if you let her go so she can get medical attention. We will see that you are a man of character."

Raider knew the routine. They were stalling, looking for an opportunity to take him out. He wasn't ready to make a move yet. He had worked out a plan now and needed to drag things out. "What about a trade?" he suggested. "The woman for some food and cold drinks."

"We can do that Sir. Give us twenty minutes. We will put the food at the front door. Just let her slip out and we can work out the rest of your demands once we have a show of good faith. How many people are there with you? We want to make sure we get enough food."

"You mean alive? Of course you do." Raider looked around him and there were six women in his circle of protection. "Seven including the wounded snitch," he supplied.

"Okay Sir, have the wounded lady come to the door. We will have the food shortly." Agent Morris quickly hung up and Raider suspected she had intentionally cut him off before he could protest. The group moved back to the vault and Raider unlocked the gate. Angie was unconscious and wouldn't wake up when Raider slapped her. He tried several times, using more force with each strike. In frustration, anger, and total disregard for her, he punched her hard in the face. She didn't stir. Charley saw how pale Angie was. The wound wasn't gushing, but the makeshift bandage was soaked through with her precious blood.

"Sir, we need to get her out now, she doesn't have long." Raider turned and Charley saw him searching their faces to see who had spoken. Charley took a deep breath, "Sir, please, let's get her to the door." Raider kept his gun in one hand and grabbed Angie's good leg with the other. He pulled until she slid down the wall and lay flat on her back. With the help of several of the women, they drug Angie into the main foyer of the bank, ten feet from the door. Raider knew that if they all struggled to get her out the door, the cops would pick him off even while surrounded by his shield. He instructed everyone to pull back into the center of the bank. He looked at Lenore who appeared to be the strongest of the women.

"Untie yourself. You will drag her through the door and bring in the food." He nodded toward Angie, still unconscious on the floor. "Remember, I have the gun shoved into your buddy's back," he had grabbed Iris. "You try to run and she's dead. Her blood is on your hands." Lenore looked into Iris's pleading eyes. Lenore nodded agreement and slowly untied herself from the shield of women. She moved over to Angie and saw the officers setting bags of food just outside the door. She slipped her arms under Angie's and backed over to the door, struggling to drag Angie by herself. She set Angie down and turned to unlock and open the door. Lenore pushed it open a few inches and blocked it from closing with her foot. She then reached down to pick up Angie. When her trembling hands were only an inch from Angie's dying body she lurched to her right and pushed through the doors, leaving Angie on the floor and Iris's fate up to Raider. By the time her escape registered with Raider, she was gone.

"Dammit!" he screamed. Iris body tightened. Suddenly, an officer dressed in full SWAT gear pulled open the door, grabbed Angie by the shoulders, and drug her out of the bank. Raider pulled the women tight around him, blocking any access.

~

The officer pulled Angie around the corner of the bank and to a waiting ambulance. She was rushed to the hospital with her husband sobbing at her side. Agent Morris asked what he could see.

"Well, there are five more women. Everyone is covered with blood, but they all look okay. Must have been a massacre in there. I only saw one suspect, but he had the women tied together as a human shield around him. Very clever," the officer observed.

"Yes, yes, it is. I think he's in over his head, but he's quick on his feet. That's not good." Agent Morris replied.

~

Raider picked up the ringing phone. "Sir," Agent Morris said, "Don't think things went the way you planned. Food is still out here and you're down two hostages." Raider was still reeling from Lenore's cowardly betrayal. He wasn't sure what to do about Iris. He should shoot her, but that hadn't worked out so well with the blonde in the vault. Did he want to kill her? No, he needed her; he needed all of the hostages.

"No, not at all how I planned. Didn't think she was a heartless bitch, but guess you all are down deep."

"Well, we're going to give you this one, tell the press you released two hostages. Looks good for you, Sir. Want to make sure those ladies get some food, been a rough day for them. I'll have the officer bring the food inside the door."

"No, *Megan*, no one is starving in here. Keep your food."

Raider slammed down the phone and moved his party back behind the counter. He had to regroup. The door was unlocked and he was a sitting duck. Raider found himself looking into the face of Charley. He thought he saw something in her eyes. Gratitude? "What's up with you?" he asked.

"Thank you for not shooting Iris," she said softly.

"If you care about these women, you'll go lock that door. If you take off, I will shoot her this time." He put the gun up to Iris's temple. There were several moments of intense eye contact between Raider and Charley. She untied her bindings and walked with determination to the door. She looked back at Iris and smiled a reassuring smile. Charley obviously decided to collect the food. She knelt down then opened the door a few inches. Raider saw an officer crouched on the far side of the food, reaching to grab Charley's arm to pull her out, but he pulled back. Charley pulled the food in, locked the door, moved back to the group, and retied her bindings. This woman intrigued Raider. *Why didn't she run? She could have escaped. Why didn't the officer try to grab her?*

Chapter 5

Their appetites surprised the ladies. The events of the morning had drained them and their bodies begged for nourishment. Raider refrained from eating, even though the burritos smelled incredible. He didn't trust that they hadn't laced the food with something. He would wait to see if the ladies reacted and then eat later if they were okay. He took one of the sealed water bottles and searched for pinpricks before downing it. The cold water brought his body temperature down several degrees. The group sat on the floor, legs crossed, with Raider still in the center. He kept the bandana over his face, even with the sweltering heat.

Iris ate her burrito slowly, like a timid little bird picking at the edges. Raider watched her, wondering how someone so frail survived life. She caught his gaze and jerked when he said, "Boo." Her distress was obvious and she was ready to crumble.

Raider noticed that Charley didn't eat, and was suspicious and confused by Charley. He stared at her and when she looked up, they made eye contact. He nodded toward the burritos and she said, "No thanks, beans do not like me."

After everyone else had finished eating, they sat and waited. The phone rang. Geena was closest and answered when Raider nodded his head. She handed him the receiver. "Sir, Agent Morris here," Megan said.

"Yes, hello *Megan*," Raider responded with mock familiarity.

"Everyone get enough to eat?" she asked, feigning sincerity.

"Yes, yes we did," he said with sarcasm.

"Well, we are working on that chopper, and it should be here any time. Since this is wrapping up soon, think you can spare a hostage? Maybe someone older, someone with health issues?" Raider looked at the ladies. Charley was the only one he would consider as older. "Would go a long way with my bosses if I can show them you are willing to work with me."

"What do I get out of this? Why should I work with you? Going to get my chopper either way." Raider enjoyed toying with her, this woman with a badge – thinking she was more than any other tramp out there.

"What do you want, Sir?" She waited without breathing.

"You turn the air back on and I'll send someone out." It was dreadfully hot in the bank and Raider was having trouble thinking. He knew the cool air would revive him.

"We have to see a hostage released first; that's how it works."

"No, Megan, that's not how it works, air first. You can always shut it off if I don't deliver. I can't do a thing if you lie on your end. Oh, that's right, I can shoot someone. The advantage of having multiple hostages. Cushion."

Agent Morris hesitated and then responded, "Okay, Sir, we'll do it your way. Air, then you release a hostage."

"Great, I'll be waiting. Don't take too long though, you understand?"

"Yes, Sir, I do." Within ten minutes, they felt the cool air flowing into the bank. Everyone breathed a sigh of relief, but only for a moment. Raider wasn't ready to give up a hostage quite yet. He wanted the bank to cool down first, in case they shut off the air again once the hostage was released. He knew that this was a game of wits and deception. He couldn't count on anything they said. He had to rely on his military training and skills. He also knew he had to stall until sunset if his only option was going to work.

Iris spoke so quietly they almost didn't hear her. "How long will you keep us here?" she asked. Raider looked in the direction of the doors.

"I don't know," he lied.

Iris spoke again, an embarrassed tone in her voice. "I *really* need to use the restroom now." Raider had wondered when this would present itself. Raider wasn't surprised that Iris needed to relieve herself, but he had no idea how urgent the need was. They all stood and moved as a group to the restroom. During his earlier search of the bank, Raider had found a small bathroom that didn't have a window. They would not be able to escape. When they reached the bathroom, Iris untied herself and rushed in.

"If anyone else needs to go, do it now. I'm not going to be taking potty breaks all afternoon," snapped Raider. Panic began to creep up in Raider's mind. He realized that he also needed to use the restroom, and not just to pee. He tried to push down the urge, but this was not going to pass.

After the rest of the ladies had used the toilet, his own need had become urgent. He had not thought this part out. The ladies would be tied up tight, but he was concerned that the cops might have eyes inside the bank. A small wire with a camera could be pushed through small openings or vents. He could not be in the bathroom alone for any amount of time. The cops would rush in while he had his pants down. This presented an awkward situation, but he had no choice. He looked at the women and decided to have Charley and Iris tie up the other ladies. Charley was older and Iris was frail. He knew they weren't a threat if they decided to attack, he would easily kill them. He told them to tie the other hostages tight and threatened to kill them if anyone worked loose. Charley and Iris did their best not to hurt the ladies, but did not want to test him either. Once the ladies were tied up, he motioned for Charley and Iris to move into the bathroom with him. Iris's eyes showed panic. She was a young, attractive woman and Raider knew she thought he was going to violate them. Raider would have laughed if he had not felt such humiliation since his aunt was alive.

~

Once Raider positioned himself by the toilet and unzipped his pants, Charley knew that this was going to be awkward. The embarrassment was minimized when they were told to face the wall, shut their eyes, and not say a word. Charley considered making a run for it while he was indisposed, but she didn't know where the gun was pointed. It would be aimed at one of them and she knew she couldn't outrun a bullet. Once Raider was finished, they joined the others, and sat on the floor. No one had escaped.

Charley was distracted, staring at the clock, playing out all the ways this could end. She began praying silently and was surprised to get a word from the Holy Spirit. It was "Stay." No sooner than she heard this direction, Raider told her to untie herself from the other ladies.

"You'll be leaving us, Granny," Raider shared. Charley was relieved and quickly began to untie herself.

Again she heard the voice of the Holy Spirit say, "Stay." Charley sat back on her heels and tried to make sense of this direction. She wanted to argue, to plead for her release, but the Holy Spirit spoke again, firmly, and she knew the plan and purpose.

"Get moving you stupid woman, I'm telling you that you get to leave." Just as he finished speaking, Iris covered her mouth but could not stop the flow of vomit. "Are you kidding me?" Raider yelled as he moved back to avoid the gush of stinking bile mixed with burrito, releasing a flood of obscenities as he glared at her. Iris drew back as far as possible, terrified, waiting to see what he was going to do. Would he shoot her? Several ladies began to weep, which agitated him even more.

Charley had to do something before someone got shot, even if she brought his wrath on her. She lightly touched his shoulder and whispered, "Raider, please let Iris leave instead. Obviously, she is very ill." Charley suspected that Iris's frail demeanor was unable to withstand the terror of being held hostage.

"Why are you calling me Raider?"

"It's just a name. I don't know your real one." He looked confused. Charley pointed at his head, "Your hat, the Raiders?" Raider began laughing hysterically, not because of the name, but the insanity of his circumstance. "What's your name?"

Charley hesitated, she didn't want to stand out from the rest, but he was waiting. "Charley," she said quietly. He didn't react, she wasn't even sure he heard her. It didn't seem to matter any longer.

Raider stayed in the center of the women. When Iris wasn't in the bathroom, she was balled up on the floor, crying from the cramps that twisted her gut. "Please Raider, please let her go. She isn't getting any better," Charley pleaded. Raider looked at the quivering Iris and gagged at the smell of the vomit covering her clothes. Getting rid of that smell wasn't a terrible idea. "We don't want the air turned off, sir." Raider looked at Charley again, seeing the concern in her eyes.

"Can I get her to the door? She can't get there herself and I promise I won't run."

Raider knew she wouldn't. She could've escaped earlier and didn't. "Okay, but if you do run, I will shoot." He looked around at the remaining women, "What's your name?" Raider asked, looking at Geena.

"Geena," she said meekly.

"Okay Geena, you better hope Charley here is on the up and up." This threat was to scare the hostages, but he already knew Charley would be back. He was drained and losing his edge. He wanted them to know he was tough and mean, so he pulled the gun up to Geena's head and tapped several times. Not enough to hurt her but menacing none the less. Charley rolled her eyes and then caught herself. She didn't want to upset him. Raider caught her reaction but decided to pretend he hadn't. He was getting low on hostages and didn't want to shoot one unnecessarily. He had to stretch them out until the time was right.

~

Charley helped Iris to her feet and they slowly walked away from the others. When Charley got Iris to the doors, she set her down. "Now, when I open the doors, you crawl out. They will come grab you."

Iris looked up at Charley. "Why are you doing this? You could have left."

"You have a family at home?"

"Yes," said Iris.

"This is God's gift to them and you. He loves you Iris. Please take this opportunity to find Him."

Iris looked at her, confused, and then smiled. Charley saw several officers moving near the door. Once she opened the door and they saw two hostages, they would make a grab for both of them. She knew if she didn't step back, they would drag her out, too. She couldn't let that happen. "Okay Iris, after I unlock the door, you gotta push it open with your shoulder and just crawl." Iris positioned herself. Charley turned the lock and as she stepped back the two officers pulled open the doors, startling Charley. One officer grabbed Iris's arms and yanked her through the doors like a ragdoll. The second officer grabbed Charley's arm. She felt the tug and dropped to the floor. She heard Geena scream "No." Charley braced her feet on the doorjamb and prevented herself from being pulled out the door. The officer had to let go and pull back quickly, before Raider had time to react and shoot. As soon as the officer let go, Charley rolled back into the bank.

Charley lay there, breathing deep panting breaths. She knew they wouldn't expect her back at the door. She jumped up, ran over, and locked it, then ran back to the others. Raider looked at her in total disbelief. She winked at Geena and began tying herself back into the circle.

~

Raider hated women. They lied, connived, cheated, humiliated, and sucked the life out of men. Charley didn't make sense in his world.

The phone rang. Raider looked forward to this call. They moved as a group to the closest phone and Raider picked it up. "Yes, Megan?"

"Thanks for sending out Iris. You got your mom in there with you?" Agent Morris asked. Raider grinned at Charley. "Nope, just a loyal hostage. Guess she didn't want Geena's brains splattered on the walls."

"Do the ladies need anything?"

"They'll be just fine when I'm on that chopper and they can go home to their families. When is that gonna be *Megan*? Do I need to shoot another one to show you I'm getting irritated? I won't kill her, just a good wound, and one that bleeds fast. Do you work well under pressure, Megan? Would that help move things along? I got plenty of bullets left, got my partner's gun. I can spare another one if it will help motivate you."

"I'm on it Sir. You should hear it coming in soon." Raider heard Agent Morris slam her fist as she hung up. This triggered a satisfying grin.

~

Charley felt real hatred for this man. He was cruel and would do everything he threatened. She tried to give everyone the benefit of the doubt, but this is one time that she needed to remember that a snake is a snake and it doesn't think twice about biting.

RAIDER'S Vendetta

Chapter 6

They could hear the constant hum of the air conditioner and Charley was thankful that they hadn't turned if off again. Brittany and Geena drifted in and out of a light doze. She looked over at Raider, who stared at the glass doors. Who was he and why was he so indifferent to life? He showed no remorse for killing the manager and he'd shot Angie without hesitation or emotion. How does a baby grow into such a monster?

Raider instructed them to return to the vault, bringing the tablecloths with them, and he moved out of the center. He took one of the t-shirts and tore eyeholes, then tied off the top of the shirt and, with his back turned, took off his bandana and hat. Next, he pulled the shirt over his head, pushing the sleeves into the shirt. He looked like a scarecrow when he turned around. He began to work on the tablecloths using a stapler.

It seemed like hours before the phone rang again and when Charley checked the clock, it had been. Why was Raider being so patient? She would have expected him to push for a quick escape. He seemed eerily calm, like a man with a plan.

Before entering the vault again, they had drug a phone close to the door. Raider picked up the phone and opened with, "I don't hear any blades whirling. Where is my chopper?"

"I'm sorry, Sir, my boss is stalling on me. He just doesn't think that you will keep your end of the bargain and let all of the hostages go. He wants to see another one come through those doors before he'll release the chopper."

"Well, Megan, I never said I'd let all the hostages go.

Now that would be foolish of me, wouldn't it? But, I'll tell you what. If your boss wants to see my intentions, have him listen to this." Raider set the receiver down and ignored Agent Morris's pleas and lies. Raider looked at Geena and spoke without any emotion in his voice, calm, like a stranger on the street giving you directions. "I'm going to have to shoot you. I'll be careful and aim for your thigh. I hope I don't hit an artery. Don't think they can move fast enough to save you if that happens." Geena jerked out of her exhausted stupor and began screaming. Raider had the look of someone determined and detached. Charley knew he would do this.

"Wait," yelled Charley. "Shoot me." Raider turned his head toward her.

"You're crazy! Are you out of the loony bin on a two-day pass?"

"No, just listen to me, please. I'm old, kids are grown, husband is dead. I've only got an old cat at home." Charley looked at Geena. "Geena, you got kids?"

"Yes, two little girls," she managed to whisper.

"How old are you, hon?" Charley kept switching her eyes from Geena to Raider, watching his finger on the trigger.

"I'm twenty-seven."

"Raider, she could be crippled for life or dead. I've lived a good, long life. Shoot me."

"You're screwing with me. Don't think I won't do it."

"I know you will. I know you have to. This is survival for you. I get that. But, does it matter who? Can just as easily be me, right? Let me do this for Geena and her kids." Raider's confusion was obvious, and then Charley heard the gun go off as she felt a fist punch her in the face. She screamed from the pain in her jaw and nose. Raider hung up the phone.

Charley saw stars. Her head had snapped back with the punch. Blood gushed from her nose. With tears rolling down her cheeks, she tenderly examined her jaw and nose with her fingers. Her nose felt like it was broken.

Once she could think clearly, she looked at Geena, relieved that she was not shot. Charley then looked at Raider. She saw a flicker of regret in his eyes when he saw the blood pouring from her nose, but it dissolved as soon as their eyes met. He glared at her and his words were an ominous whisper. "Next time, I will shoot you. Maybe I should anyway, put you out of your stinkin' misery. You are freakin' crazy." Geena was a mass of jelly, crying and shaking. Raider couldn't take it. "Shut up!" he screamed. Geena brought her hand to her mouth to smother her cries. The remaining ladies all sat there in silence, not wanting to draw Raider's attention.

~

It wasn't long before they heard the distinctive wop of a helicopter. Sunset was quickly approaching. The phone rang and it was Agent Morris. "Well, Sir, you hear that?"

"Yep, music to my ears."

"How's Charley. It was Charley you shot?"

"I don't know their names, not like we're ever going to hang out again."

"Well, is she okay?"

"Bleeding bad. Think she'll be okay if you guys follow directions."

"Let her come out, Sir. We need to get her to the hospital, right now."

"We put a tourniquet on her leg. I'll leave her in here. When we leave, you can come in and get her. Gotta apply pressure, Megan, you appear to work best under pressure."

"Okay, Sir. We'll do it your way. You need to come through the front and around to the right of the building." Raider hung up.

In a low whisper, "Geena, take these," Raider threw her several of the t-shirts, "soak them with blood from the bodies. If the blood on the floor has dried, you'll have to push on one of the bodies. It has to look like Charley is bleeding. Stay low, below the counter. I'm sure they have cameras hooked in and probably microphones." Geena obeyed. She had to push on the dead robber's body to force more blood onto the floor.

Raider looked at Charley. "If you tip off the cops when they come in, you'll get these women killed. You understand me?" he said just barely loud enough for Charley to hear. He then spoke in a much louder voice, hoping the police would hear, "The rest of you are coming with me. We'll move out to the chopper. I'm only taking one of you with me. The rest of you can run when I say. Got it?" They all nodded. Raider knew that dangling the carrot of freedom would buy compliance from the hostages and possibly the police if they were listening. They may refrain from any heroics if they thought most of the hostages would be released soon.

~

Charley felt a moment of relief that she would be rescued, but then the will of the Holy Spirit replayed in her head. She had to go to the helicopter. Charley wasn't clear what would come next, the Holy Spirit hadn't given her anymore, just that she was supposed to go to the helicopter with Raider. Charley looked into Geena's frantic face. She was clearly thinking *What if he takes me on the chopper?*

"Raider?" Charley said in a whisper.

"What now old lady?"

"Look, they won't know who's in here since you didn't give them a name. They'll just whisk whoever it is into the ambulance. Let Geena stay. Let her go home to her babies," she said quietly.

Raider looked at Charley in disbelief. "Who do you think you are? You runnin' some scam? You an old lady ninja who's going to take me down? You're up to something!" Raider whispered through clenched teeth.

Charley had to press, there wasn't much time. "Look Raider, you owe me one. I have done everything you said and I have done everything I promised. If you do this, I won't run. I will be the perfect hostage."

Raider looked in her eyes. She didn't blink or look away. He looked at Geena, and it was clear that she was barely functioning. "Okay, not because you asked, but because she is useless. Sit down." Raider instructed Geena. Charley wrapped Geena's leg in the bloody t-shirts and tied a strip around her thigh to look like a tourniquet.

"Not too tight is it?" she whispered to Geena.

"No, it's fine." Geena looked into Charley's determined face as she adjusted the deception to look real. "Just hold it and cry when they get

40

to you. Don't talk to the police. You're in too much pain, okay? You can answer all their questions once we're off the ground. You don't want them to figure out you're not hurt before we get to the chopper. If they don't think he's a lunatic, they might kill us by trying to take him. Once Raider and I are up, the rest will be safe, too." Geena looked at Charley, bewildered.

"You and Raider?" she barely spoke.

"Yes, hon, me and Raider. I'm not letting him take one of these girls if I can stop it."

"But what about you? Don't you want this over? Why take my place?" Charley looked into her sweet face.

"This is a gift from God. Seek Him out once this is over. He wants to help you have an incredible life with your family. I'll be fine. He's looking out for me. Please tell Brittany and Anne that God loves them and He protected them today."

Geena was sitting in front of the spot where Charley had hidden her phone, so she quickly slipped it out of hiding and into her pocket. Luckily, she had turned it off before she hid it. Last thing Charley needed was to receive a call.

"Get over here." Raider barked. "We gotta go." Charley patted the top of Geena's head and joined the group. Charley tied herself into the shield circle and moved as Raider led. He tried dragging the garbage bag full of money from the registers, then stood for a moment, considering the logistics of holding two guns, maneuvering in a tight group, and bringing the money, before moving on again. On the way out of the vault, he grabbed the stapled tablecloths. Raider maneuvered them behind the counter, where he found a zippered cash bag, then had Anne fill the bag up with as much of the stolen money as she could hold before stuffing it into his shirt.

"I'm going to give you guys your directions. Don't screw with me and you'll be home tonight in your little beds. If you mess up, you'll be in the morgue. I will have a gun on two of you at all times," Raider threatened.

Agent Morris stood outside the bank, watching for any movement at the door. She had her best gunmen in position. They planned to shoot him in the head even though the hostages surrounded him. He would drop instantly. She would do everything possible to keep him from getting to the chopper.

The bank door slowly opened and, to Agent Morris's dismay, a huge white ghost slowly moved out. A large mass of white cloth covered the group. Using the stapler, Raider had converted the tablecloths into a large tent, cutting small slits in the sheet so they could see. The police couldn't even see their legs. Without a clear shot, the cops could not shoot.

Agent Morris considered rushing them, their visibility had to be horrible, but she wasn't dealing with a dummy. He had to have considered that possibility and his guns would be pointed at someone. Any attempt to take him down would result in the injury or death of one or more of the hostages. They could not be sure of getting to him before he pulled the trigger and, grouped so tightly together, he wouldn't miss his shot. Agent Morris signaled for everyone to back off and for the snipers to stand down.

"Anne, yell out and tell them to cut the engine," Raider instructed. Anne did as she was told.

Agent Morris bit her lip in frustration. She hadn't known he would come out covered, but had quickly realized the swirling air from the blades was to their advantage. They would get a break when the blades blew the sheet up, revealing the prize underneath. The white ghost stopped, waiting for her to comply. Agent Morris yelled, "Sir, you can't stand there all day. Give yourself up."

One of the ladies yelled out, "If you don't turn off that engine, he will shoot as many of us in the head as he can before you take him down. He is a dead man and he doesn't mind taking us with him. He has nothing to lose and he thinks you do."

There was no alternative; Agent Morris gave the signal to turn off the engine. The ghost continued its slow march to the field. It was the most bizarre picture – a circle of armed officers moving along with the huge white ghost, husbands and family members held back by more officers, and a lone helicopter sitting a short distance away.

When they got close to the helicopter, Charley slowly positioned herself to be the first one to reach their destination. When they made it to the open door of the cabin, she was where she needed to be. She knew that Raider had been watching her with a curious look on his face. She hoped that he wouldn't insist on one of the other women going.

"Charley, you're going with me," he said with authority. She heard the other hostages exhale with relief. It was then that Charley realized they had all been holding their breaths. "Drop down and crawl, then up into the chopper." Once Charley was in the helicopter, Raider slipped in next to her, still under the tent. The two remaining hostages were standing on the ground still under the drape and Raider had his gun pointed at Brittany. "Charley," he said in a low voice, "tell the pilot to get out of the cockpit."

"What?" Charley asked in disbelief.

"Tell him I have one gun on the hostages and one at the back of his seat." Charley repeated his instructions.

"I need to fly you out of here," the pilot argued, refusing to leave. Raider fired a shot through the back of the seat. The pilot was hit in his shoulder. Raider had missed the bulletproof vest and ripped a hole in the man's flesh. The SWAT pilot could not get a clear shot at Raider. He was losing blood quickly and was forced to abort the mission. He jumped from the cockpit. Charley's ears were still ringing from the gunshot.

"Charley, get up to the cockpit and shut the door." He then barked orders telling her how to start the engine. She could feel the vibration of the main rotor beginning to turn. Raider shoved the remaining hostages away from the copter, and slammed the door shut. He moved up to the cockpit and pushed Charley against the pilot's door. She shielded him from the officer's line of fire. He sat on the edge of her seat, and grabbed the controls. Charley could see the officers running toward the helicopter, shooting at the main rotor, and then felt the copter lifting off the ground. She assumed that the woman stomping the ground was Agent Morris.

"You've flown one of these before?" Charley asked with her heart in her throat.

"Yep, for Uncle Sam. I was in Iraq until my discharge." Once they were in the air and the field was behind them, Raider moved between the seats and ordered Charley to slide over to the other chair. The helicopter pitched as she struggled to obey.

"Dammit, be careful."

They sat quietly as they flew through the darkening sky. So many questions and fears raced through Charley's mind. Her journey to this seat, next to this criminal, felt surreal. Finally she dared to ask, "So, what are you going to do with me?"

"Do you really care?"

"Of course I care."

"You don't act like someone who cares. I can't figure out your game."

"I don't have a game," Charley responded.

"Everyone has a game," Raider said with conviction.

Chapter 7

Charley turned to look out the window. In the reflection, she saw Raider pull off his mask. She froze. Did this mean he was going to kill her? He seemed to sense her fear. "They will figure out who I am once they have Darrell's body." Charley looked at him, confused. "He's my cousin. Don't talk any more – this thing is probably bugged. You're safe for now. You are my insurance." This gave Charley a small amount of hope that she would live. She prayed that God's plan included her survival.

Raider looked like your average nice guy. He had white, straight teeth and a chiseled jaw line. Charley braved a glimpse of her own face in the window's reflection. She saw the bruising under her eyes and her swollen jaw. The pain was subsiding, reduced to a dull throb.

It was almost dark and Raider didn't turn on any lights to guide their way. He seemed to have a destination in mind and wasn't flying randomly, as someone panicked would do. She watched him search the control panel and he abruptly pulled out some hardware and ripped the wires. "Ahhhhh, they just lost their ears," he announced proudly.

When the sky was fully dark and filled with stars, Raider explained that they would be jumping from the helicopter.

"No way," Charlie exclaimed. Her friends had tried to convince her to skydive over the years and she wouldn't even discuss it. She was in total panic mode.

"You have three choices, old woman. Jump with me, have me shoot you so you die quickly or you can crash with the chopper. Up to you, but I'm jumping."

Raider opened a storage bin and pulled out two parachutes. He handed her one. "Put this on," he instructed as he slipped on the other one.

"I'm sure we're hooked up with a tracker. We're going to jump out and let them follow the chopper. We have to get down to the skids before we jump, so the rotor blades don't suck us up. We're going to be over a lake soon. If we don't go now, we'll land in the trees. I will hold on to you until it's time to pull this cord." Raider indicated what she was to pull. Charley nodded. "This one on the other side is your backup chute. Keep your feet down. When you see the water coming up, bring your legs up under you, like you're doing a cannonball. If you land straight legged, you can break them and I'll have to leave you to die. As long as you don't panic, you'll be fine, or dead, which seems to be your wish anyway. A few feet above the water take a deep breath and release this buckle. The parachute floats so if you come up under it, dive back down and swim until you're clear."

Raider appeared to be adjusting the controls. "Move toward the back, Charley." He slid off his seat and seemed to be tinkering with something. He stood up quickly and moved toward the center of the chopper. Charley watched as he slid the door open. Charley was sick to her stomach and barely held down the bile.

"I can't do this!" she whined.

"We only have a few minutes before this bird starts to drop," he warned. Since there was no autopilot, he improvised the best he could. It would only buy them a little time before the copter went down.

Raider shoved the guns into his pants. Charley thought about pushing him out, but how would she land the helicopter? She remembered her phone. The police would talk her down. Raider saw her face light up and her hand go subconsciously to her back pocket. He grabbed her and spun her around before she could react. He pulled the phone out of her pocket and grinned at her, "Nice try." He threw the phone out of the chopper. "Guess you'll have to jump now." He slipped out the door and squatted on the skid.

Charley was so angry. She would survive just so she could kill him. She carefully slid down to the skid and felt Raider's arms wrap around her. The helicopter lurched. "Dear God, please give me wings," she prayed. The next thing she knew she was plummeting toward the earth. In a flash, Raider's arms let go and he floated away. She opened her eyes and saw him pull his cord. She did the same. She felt a strong upward jerk and then she was floating. This wasn't nearly as scary as the free falling. She saw the lake surface below, the star's reflections shimmering like diamonds on the water. Even in her fear, the view was incredibly beautiful. She savored the moment in case it was her last.

Charley was able to remember most of his instructions and she hit the water not nearly as hard as she expected. She felt herself tumbling, like a gymnast rolling across hard mats. She was relieved that she was still alive. When she stopped, she was under water and under the parachute. She freaked out and began flailing as she felt herself getting caught up in the fabric. Panic overtook her. The wet material stuck to her, wrapping around her face. She wasn't getting any air. Suddenly, hands grabbed her ankles and yanked her down. She was breathing water before she realized it, and she felt herself fading.

The next thing she was aware of was retching and vomiting up bile and water. She was lying on the bank of the lake. Raider jumped up and swam out to the parachutes. He drug them back to the shore and was back before Charley realized she could have escaped, though she didn't know where to. "Get up now!" he growled. "We need to roll up these chutes and hide them. It will buy us time if they don't know exactly where we jumped."

Raider moved quickly with his and helped Charley with hers. She half carried and half drug her chute while she followed Raider to a small cave. They had hiked at least a mile from the lake. He knew this area and that comforted Charley. He wasn't a mad man, running scared. He had a plan. Charley was wet, cold, and exhausted. "We'll stay in here till there's light. Even though these chutes are wet, they will help keep us warm." He motioned for Charley to go in first. She had to bend over to clear her head. She hoped she wouldn't meet an animal coming out. She assumed that he wanted to be at the front of the cave to keep her from slipping past. His concern was unnecessary because she wasn't about to try and face this wilderness alone.

While in the helicopter, Charley had searched the ground for any sign of civilization, but saw nothing – no lights for miles and miles. In fact, she was worried that he would leave her there so he could move faster. *Was she still his hostage or not? Would he make sure she was safe before disappearing? She knew he wasn't going to kill her. He could've left her in the helicopter or drowning in the lake.* "Crawl into the folds so that you're laying on several and have the rest over you. The layers will keep in your body heat."

Charley needed some answers, but she couldn't stay awake long enough to ask him anything. She was in the middle of a wonderful dream; she had wings and was flying over a shimmering lake. The sun was above her and birds were flitting around on all sides. She heard God speaking to her. "You have heard me well, my child. Your journey is not yet done. I am with you always."

Chapter 8

Charley felt a stick stabbing at her. "Wake up. We gotta move." Charley opened her eyes, happy that she was still alive and that Raider had not abandoned her. As she climbed out of the cave, she saw how beautiful the forest was. "Well, I'm glad no bear came back to claim his cave," Charley said under her breath.

Raider chuckled, "Even if one had, the snoring coming out of there would have scared him off. Lady, you put my cousin to shame, even after he's drunk himself blind." Charley felt herself blush. She had started snoring years ago and hated it. She was sure the cave had amplified the noise coming from her. She couldn't be that loud. Raider continued, "I was worried about being able to stay awake, but you made it impossible to sleep."

"It kept us safe," she said dully.

"Well, hope you got on comfortable shoes. We got some walking to do."

Charley looked around. "This is probably the stupidest thing I've done in the last twenty hours, but I have to ask. What exactly are we doing? I don't know if I'm still a hostage, if you're going to strand me if I can't keep up, or if you'll get me somewhere safe."

Raider looked at her with no expression. "I don't know, to tell you the truth. I didn't sort that part out. The smart thing would be to keep you with me for a while, 'til things calm down. If the cops find us, I'll have some leverage. If they don't, guess I'll figure that out as we go. Nowhere for you to run to out here. You'll just get yourself eaten or starve. Let's get moving and make sure you keep up old woman. I don't need you as much as you need me."

RAIDER'S Vendetta

Chapter 9

Agent Morris paced in her office. The phone rang and she snatched it. "Give me some news. I'm dying here," she said to Officer Burns, who was on the other end.

"They didn't say anything helpful before the equipment was ripped out. Apparently, they jumped before the helicopter crashed. We're figuring they could've jumped out any time after the last conversation was recorded."

"The woman jumped too?"

" Well, didn't find any bodies at the crash site, so that's our best guess. He may have pushed her out once he was clear of the bank."

"Get the different precincts along their flight path to check for bodies that have fallen from the sky."

"I would think she was in on this whole thing, but after debriefing the other hostages, it doesn't seem to fit. They all describe her as this angel that protected them."

Agent Morris knew this woman wasn't involved in the robbery. She'd heard the pleading while on the phone. She hadn't seen this much strength or character since her father was alive.

"Well, have some choppers fly their course and see if there are any likely spots for jumping out of a helicopter, in the dark, with an old woman." Morris directed before she hung up. It took a very experienced pilot to know how to keep an unoccupied helicopter in the air, but how long would it stay up? she wondered.

Officer Brennan tapped on Agent Morris's door. "I've got the file." He handed it to Agent Morris. They had discovered who the bank robbers were. The dead accomplice was found with his wallet and drivers license in his pocket. Darrell Anderson. Darrell's cousin, Arthur Myers, had been a helicopter pilot in the Air Force up until three years ago. Four years of honored service and then a dishonorable discharge. Darrell had several previous charges for robbery and assault. Arthur only had the discharge against him. Agent Morris had requested his military file last night and was anxious to review it. They certainly could use some helpful information about this man. Once she knew who she was dealing with, Agent Morris felt confident that she could find him no matter where he hid. She knew he was in the Sierra Mountains. He wouldn't be moving unencumbered, dragging his hostage with him. But, she also knew that he had survival training and had survived Iraq for four years.

Chapter 10

"What's your real name?" asked Charley as they pushed through bushes and vegetation.

Raider looked at the back of her head, debating whether he wanted to answer. "Arthur, but you can still call me Raider."

"Okay, Raider? You got any family?"

Raider was still trying to size up Charley and her agenda. He played along, for the moment. "Not any more. Mom died when I was young, dad died in prison, aunt raised me, but she's dead, and now my cousin Darrell is dead. Last relative I know about."

Heavy silence again. Charley didn't know where to go from there. She mumbled, "Sorry." Charley felt her heart pounding and her breathing was labored. She desperately wanted to stop and rest, but feared that Raider would keep moving and leave her alone in the wilderness.

"Let's stop here," he announced. "I hear water close by." They moved a few more feet and arrived at a small stream. The water was clear and refreshing. Charley lay on the ground and sucked in the cold water. Raider squatted down and scooped handfuls into his mouth. "Don't drink too much or your stomach will cramp up," he instructed. "I don't want to be held up cuz you're puking your guts out."

Held up? Charley was relieved to know he had a plan. Everything he was doing felt intentional. "Where are we going?" she asked, cautiously.

"You'll know when we get there. Until then, just shut up and keep up." With that, he stood and began to move quickly through the shrubbery, still heading south.

Charley was struggling to keep up with him. She was

glad when the terrain became flat and open, but Raider could also move faster, which put more distance between them. Several times, she lost sight of him and felt herself panic. At one point, she sat down and cried. Charley knew she couldn't catch up. She was exhausted and starving. She felt scared and lost. "Dear Lord, please don't forsake me now. I've done all you've asked. Please Lord, get me home alive," she prayed.

Suddenly, Charley heard a sarcastic laugh. Raider had doubled back and she didn't realize she had been praying aloud. "You're wasting your breath. There is no loving God, you stupid woman. I am your salvation out here. I am your Lord. Beg me old woman. Maybe I'll save you, maybe I won't."

Charley was shocked at his level of animosity. "Well, we have a difference of opinion," she shot back.

"I should have known. You're a Bible thumper! I thought you were gutsy, but you're just another naive, idiot woman who thinks she's on God's mission. I'm guessing that all your antics came from a twisted brain that believes God is talking to you? I should have shot you, not in the leg, but in the head. Put you out of your misery. You could be having tea right now with Jesus."

He was enraged. Charley was concerned that he would shoot her and leave her body for the animals to clean up. She decided not to respond. She stood and began walking in the direction he had gone when he first disappeared. He followed her, cursing and bemoaning his luck. Charley felt his gaze on the back of her head. She cringed and waited to feel her brains explode inside her head. She didn't understand the fury her prayer had unleashed.

She suddenly felt his hand on her arm and he snapped her around. She was facing a man with absolute hatred in his eyes. "How can you be so ignorant and believe the lies? You're just a puppet with no mind of your own. You want it all wrapped up in a pretty package with a big bow. Well, life isn't pretty. It's bloody ugly and you don't get to bypass hell. Hell is now." Charley was at a loss for how to respond. She knew that he was irrational and would lash out at whatever she said, but he was demanding a response.

She shook her arm free from his grasp. "Why do you care what I believe? You've got it all figured out. There is nothing I can say that will be good enough for you," she said, quietly, without attitude. She continued to walk, hoping he would back off if she didn't argue.

"Don't you dare walk away from me!" Raider screamed. Charley felt his fist come down hard on her upper back. Her knees buckled with the blow and she fell to the ground. She pulled herself into a ball and cried. The pain was intense.

Raider looked at her and hatred spewed from his mouth, "Let's see if your God shows up, if He protects you. Get up and get moving or I'll leave you on your own. The bears will deliver you to your God!"

Charley almost thought she would be better on her own, but slowly obeyed. She struggled to keep up, but found renewed strength. She believed Her God was moving through her.

Raider disappeared through a group of trees. When Charley came to the center of the grove, she saw a canvas cabin. It reminded her of the cabins she'd stayed in as a child at summer camp. The floor and lower walls were wood. The rest of the structure was camouflage canvas. It was faded and tattered at the edges, but appeared to be sound enough to keep out any rain. Raider popped out of the cabin with a big grin. This was obviously his destination.

"We'll be holed up here for a few days. Make yourself comfortable," he said without any sincerity. Raider moved past her and headed into the trees carrying an empty water jug, the kind used in offices. It looked disgusting and Charley hoped he would rinse it out before using it to get water, but she didn't want to ask or suggest anything. The blow to her back was still throbbing and she wanted to be as invisible as possible. Charley looked inside the cabin and was alarmed at how dirty and disgusting everything was. There were several cots, but only one that wasn't torn and rotted through. She smelled the distinct odor of urine. It was unclear how many animals had nested and used this tent for shelter. Other than protection from moisture and rain, this cabin offered no comfort or value. How long did he plan to hide here?

She heard Raider returning with water sloshing in the bottle. She was relieved to see that he had cleaned out the jug before filling it up. He must have seen her relief. "Don't get too excited old girl. It's going to cost you! If you don't like the rules, then get God to provide." What was up with him and God? Charley was thinking she would just find water herself and bypass his garbage. "Ahhhhh, I know what you're thinking. Well, you can try to find the water source, but we hid it well. It's a tap on an underground spring. Hope you don't die of thirst before you find it."

"I'm taking the cabin. You can figure out where you'll sleep. Just make sure it's far enough away that your snoring doesn't keep me awake."

Charley knew from his tone that he was punishing her and she didn't understand why. It was as if something snapped in him and she was now a captive for him to torment. Charley wasn't disappointed that she'd have to sleep outside the foul cabin, but she did need to find some protection from the cold night while it was still light. Her stomach growled from hunger and she worried about what she would eat, but she didn't dare ask Raider about food. She hoped that, with some time, his mood would mellow out. She was sure he had things worked out. He had to eat, too.

The woods were thick with trees and, even though it was summer, Charley knew that once the sun began to drop, the temperature would become quite chilly. She tried to remember all the survival shows that her husband Archie had watched, hoping for an idea as she looked around. There were leaves and needles covering the ground and the best plan she could come up with was to make a nest to cushion the ground, and then use leaves to cover herself. She found a cluster of trees that made a bowl of sorts at the bases of their trunks, just the right size for her to curl up in and padded the ground with piles of vegetation. Stepping back, she felt proud of her efforts.

The shade was darkening the sun-filled pockets and there was a noticeable drop in temperature. Charley worked quickly to collect a large pile of leaves next to the nest. She would pull these on top of herself to insulate her from the cold. She considered trying to start a fire, like they did on the TV show Survivor that she watched every season, but she knew that Raider would trample it out if she succeeded, or worse. He'd warned her that the forest rangers would see the smoke from miles away during the day. They won't see the smoke at night, but their surveying planes could possibly see the flames.

Charley quietly went back to the cabin area to see what Raider was up to. She was hoping there would be some food hidden at the site. She found him sitting on the front step of the cabin, looking up from a weathered can of kidney beans. He had opened it with his pocketknife and let the beans slide down his throat. He gave Charley a nasty grin. "Sorry, didn't save you any, figured your God dropped some manna out there in the woods." Charley bit her tongue and sat down a few yards away from him. She didn't want to get within striking distance. "Well, gonna get some sleep. You have a good night out there with all God's creatures. I'm sure He's got your back." Raider stood up and Charley realized that he not only had hidden food, but he was also sitting on a folded blanket. Her face must have shown her frustration, because he gave her a sly smile and began to laugh hysterically as he walked into the cabin. Her anger began to build. She hadn't done a thing to deserve this. Raider tossed the can out the door and she heard the clang of the empty container hit the ground by her feet.

At first Charley was determined not to subject herself to humiliation, but the cramping in her gut was a strong incentive. She picked up the can and carefully slid her finger around the inside, trying to salvage anything that was left. She tried to avoid the jagged metal, where the can had been ripped open, but she was not so lucky. A yelp escaped from her as the deep gash began to bleed. She didn't see Raider, but she was sure that he was just inside, watching her. The few remaining beans and sauce did nothing for the hunger she felt, and she regretted giving him the satisfaction of seeing her desperate. Maybe she would find some berries tomorrow, or chew on some bark. Charley was sure that the survivors had eaten bark, at least on one of the seasons.

Charley slipped away to her nest. She realized that she had tiptoed, a sad effort to conceal her sleeping place from Raider. He probably already knew exactly where she was or at least he would know when she began to snore.

The nest was comfortable at first. Charley wiggled in and plumped up a pile of leaves for a pillow. She then pulled another pile of leaves on top of her. Only her head was exposed to the night air. Her cotton blouse, lightweight jeans, and canvas tennies were not going to provide much protection. She prayed that the leaves would keep her toasty warm and dry as she drifted off. Charley remembered to ask God to keep bears and any other of His creatures away from her nest. She also asked that He share Raider's cabin with a few bears. She drifted off with a smile, picturing Raider waking up to a bear licking his face before it ate him.

As the night passed, Charley tossed and turned, trying to get comfortable. The leaves were brittle and crumbled to powder beneath her. The ground was hard and cold. She hadn't thought to remove the small rocks or twigs before piling up the leaves. These small items became large, painful lumps under her weight. The layer of leaves covering her moved and shifted until there was nothing protecting her. She got colder and colder. Charley's exhaustion was the only thing that allowed her to doze. Then the itching started.

First, it was as a tickling sensation, not enough to wake her fully, but then pain replaced the itching and she was suddenly wide-awake. She realized something was biting her. She jumped up and began swatting at the large red ants that seemed to be everywhere. She had to pull off her clothing to wipe off the ants that had crawled in while she lay on the ground. Once she was sure they were all off, she dressed. Her frustration increased when she realized they were still in her clothing. Charley did her best to squash and remove the last of the ants. Her body and face were covered with the burning, itching wounds left by the powerful jaws of these ferocious insects. Charley wasn't sure what to do. It was still dark and she knew sleeping on the ground was not an option. Her exhaustion wouldn't allow her to stand much longer. She didn't want to admit it, but the cabin was looking better and better. She wasn't sure what Raider would do if she tried to slip in, but she had no other options.

Charley tried to be quiet as she crept into the camp area, but in the dark, she stepped on every twig and tripped over every rock. By the time she reached the cabin steps, she was sure every creature was awake for miles around. She hoped Raider wasn't. Her feet found the steps and she moved as silently as a wood nymph until the second step creaked loudly, as if in pain under her girth. Charley froze. She didn't hear anything in the cabin. It felt like an hour passed as she held her breath. No yelling, no snoring, nothing. Maybe Raider was out in the woods. Maybe nature had called or he'd gone for more food.

Finally, deciding that she couldn't stand on the steps all night, she slipped into the cabin. She attempted to sit down in the front corner without making any more noise, but heard a loud clattering sound as she bumped something in the dark. She held her breath again. "Ants?" was all Raider said.

"Yes," she said, humiliated. Raider laughed and then she heard something coming at her just before it made contact with her face. She grabbed at it and realized it was rough, reeking of mildew and urine. Her best guess was an old burlap bag. Charley wrapped the nasty bag around herself, hoping it would offer some warmth.

Her humiliation and disgust were only surpassed by her confusion about where God was. Why wasn't He protecting her? He should snap this horrible man in half and get her out of here. It appeared that the best she could hope for was some rest. The scratching, the hunger, the stench, and the anger made it impossible for her to get any real sleep.

~

He was in the storage bin. The waves of anger, shame, and hopelessness rippled over him. The prayers spewed out of his mouth. He no longer controlled the useless, empty words. Then the banging, the constant shattering of sound that vibrated through his brain. "Louder, pray louder," the banshee screamed.

Raider jerked out of his nightmare. He hadn't dreamed about the bin in many years. It used to be every night, but he had buried it, gotten it out of his head. Charley was dredging up the insanity that he had struggled so long to suppress. He was angry. She would pay for having her God, the same God that had unleashed Aunt Rose on a powerless little boy.

Light was starting to filter into the cabin. Raider could just make out the shape of Charley in the corner. She was curled up, wrapped in the rotting burlap bag he had thrown at her. He thought about how poisonous this woman with her God was. His dream brought back all the hatred that was stored up from the years of hell, all endured in God's name. *He should just shoot her, but what if he needed her?* He would enjoy the torment until he hastened her departure to her Jesus.

Chapter 11

Charley woke to unbearable itching all over her body. She finally focused her eyes on her arms. They were covered with large, red pustules. She ran her hands over her face and felt more swollen bumps from the nasty ant bites. Her back ached. Her cut finger was swollen, red, and hot. It took several minutes for Charley to get herself up from the cabin floor. She shuddered when she saw the burlap bag in the daylight. It was far worse than she had suspected.

The smell of coffee and, possibly, oatmeal finally registered in her brain. She slowly made her way to the cabin entrance. Raider sat on a campstool, sipping from a tin cup. There was a small camp stove on the ground in front of him. Her nose hadn't betrayed her; she did smell oatmeal. Charley knew she was in enemy territory. She was not only a hostage; she was now a prisoner of war. She had to test the waters carefully. "Thank you for the blanket, ahh, bag," she said cautiously.

"You thought I gave you that? Nahhh, just coughed up some crap in my throat and tossed it as far as I could. Didn't want that filthy thing anywhere around me." He looked at her with such disdain. "But, you're welcome, any time!"

Charley didn't know how to respond. She was smart enough to know that she was not dealing with a rational situation. Nothing had been rational since she went into the bank two days ago. Charley decided not to react or comment. She looked longingly at the oatmeal bubbling on the camp stove. "You want some?" he asked. *Damn,* she thought, her face betrayed her. "Well, if there's any left over, you can have it. But I'm sure God has a wonderful meal prepared for you." Raider dramatically looked around. "Guess He's running a little late."

Charley was unable to ignore the raging itch all over her body. She began to rub and lightly scratch. She didn't want Raider to have the satisfaction of seeing her in discomfort. "Man oh man, did you ever get chewed up. Don't be scratch'n, you'll make it worse," Raider replied with mock concern.

The bottle of water was sitting next to the cabin and Charley was extremely thirsty. She nodded to the water and waited for Raider's response. "You thirsty? Well, pour yourself a glass," he said sarcastically. Charley looked around, but there were no cups or glasses except for his coffee mug. She heard him snickering. Charley tried to tilt the jug to get a drink, but the water sloshed out on to the ground. She finally managed to get her hand under the neck while her other hand, arm, and leg balanced the jug. She licked the water from her hand and felt the cool liquid quenching her parched mouth and throat. She wanted more, but she sensed that the less desperate she seemed, the less she would fuel his wrath. She reluctantly set the jug back down. The spilled water had created mud and Charley thought she remembered something about mud helping with bites and itching. She scooped up the wet soil and smeared it all over her face and arms. The cool mud soothed the bites at first, but then a burning began to build. Her eyes teared up.

Raider looked smug from his little stool. "It's the pine pitch in the dirt that causes the stinging. You'd think it would stop eventually, but nope, nasty stuff. Stupid, stupid woman." Charley wanted to scream at him, curse at him, throw something at him, but she stood up and just glared at him. She had hoped he was lying, but the stinging was not subsiding.

Charley realized that he was eating the oatmeal from the pot. He was dipping his fingers in and licking off the sticky goo. He grinned at Charley, an evil 'screw you' grin. She salivated and licked her lips before she could stop herself. *Damn, damn* she thought again. He grinned even bigger. She stood there, mesmerized with each finger full. She didn't want to watch, but she was no longer in control. Hunger and the need to survive took over. He stopped and looked into the pan. "Oh dear, I must have been hungrier than I thought. I sure didn't leave much." He had said much, not that he didn't leave any. He clearly said much. She felt her tongue slide over her lips again. *Damn!*

Raider stood up and walked toward her, stretching out his arm with the glorious pot. As Charley reached to pluck the tasty treat from his hand, her fingertips felt the lingering heat of the metal. Then she heard herself screaming, "Nooooooo!" Raider had shot her a nasty grin and intentionally let go of the pot. The pot was falling to the ground, flipping over, oatmeal flying out to land in the dirt. It appeared to happen in slow motion, but it was only moments before the pot bounced on the ground. Charley dropped to her knees, sobbing. It wasn't just the oatmeal anymore; it brought back the memory of the loss of her sweet husband, Archie, and the practical jokes he had once played on her. She needed him now more than ever.

Archie had showed up for a date and held out a wrapped gift for Charley. "Happy Anniversary!" he said with way too much enthusiasm. Charley was unexpectedly touched that he remembered their one-month dating anniversary, but she was also annoyed. She was too old for this goofy stuff and hadn't even considered getting him a gift. If they survived a year, maybe a card. She stepped back with a hollow apology for not getting him anything, but Archie insisted that she take his gift. She didn't want to hurt his feelings since he was grinning like a baboon. He was so pleased with himself. Charley reached out for the garishly wrapped tribute and, as her fingertips touched the cool surface of the magenta foil sprinkled with huge daisies, Archie let go. The audible shout of his "Careful!" and her "No!" filled the kitchen. Next was the sudden shot of bile that climbed up her throat. She saw the horror in his eyes as the package hit the floor and the sound of shattering glass was deafening. What the heck had he bought her? It sounded like a chandelier had plummeted to the floor. Archie stood there; arms limp at his sides, shaking his head. "Charley, I can't believe you dropped it. I spent a fortune on that custom blown-glass fairy."

Charley's emotions were flying everywhere, regret, embarrassment, disappointment, and finally anger. "I dropped it? Me? You didn't even hand it to me. You let go! Don't blame me!" Charley picked up the box, still looking perfectly fine on the outside, but a testing shake made her cringe at the sound of the shattered gift. Charley set the box on the kitchen counter and slowly untied the ribbon, then pulled away the obnoxious wrapping paper. She expected to see a traditional white gift box used by boutiques, but instead it was a hot chocolate box. Charley looked at Archie confused, but he just looked away, shaking his head.

When she opened the box to view the devastated glass fairy, she found instead a large glass mayonnaise jar. When she picked up the jar, she saw that it contained broken light bulb glass and a very large metal bolt. As her brain tried to sort out the contradiction between her eyes and her expectations, she realized Archie was howling with laughter. Then revelation... "You brat!" she said with venom. "That was so not cool!" Archie tried to stifle his wails, which converted to chuckles, tears running down his cheeks. He moved in closer to hug Charley as she brought her hands up to his chest, holding him back. She glared at him, but then felt the anger melting away. Charley realized that she was laughing, quietly at first, and then deep, joyful peals. She pulled Archie in close to her and held on.

"You should have seen your face!" Archie said through his own laughter.

"I'm still mad at you! That was mean!" Charley said without any conviction. "You owe me big time now. You thought that fairy was expensive, just wait till you see the dinner bill."

"Okay, doll. Get all gussied up and we'll head over to McDonalds," Archie cooed with a huge grin.

"Dream on baby, you're taking me to Stuart Anderson's! I'm having appetizers and dessert! Hope your entertainment was worth it!"

"Dang, baby, I think the fairy would have been cheaper," Charley heard Archie mutter as she headed into her room to discard the jeans and T-shirt for an outfit more appropriate for an expensive dinner.

Charley saw the oatmeal scattered all over the dirt. Raider knelt down next to her and said in a hateful, low voice. "You clumsy, stupid old woman. Better eat it before the bugs show up." He paused and, with all the venom possible, asked her, "Where is your God?" As he stood up and stepped away, he purposely kicked dirt onto the oatmeal.

Charley let the sobs escape. She didn't care what he thought. She didn't care if he hit her again. It wasn't possible to feel any more pain anyway. Maybe he would shoot her. That worked for her. She would check out and move on to Heaven, a place of love, joy, and food. Yes, food. She was sure that people ate in Heaven. God would not let humans suffer for eternity without chocolate. After the crying subsided, Charley rocked herself with her eyes closed. She felt better in a strange way, but exhausted. She opened her eyes and saw scouting ants dangerously close to her oatmeal. She took a deep breath and decided to be strong, strong until she died. She bowed her head and loudly thanked God for the oatmeal. She scooped up what she could and ate it dirt and all. She checked out the pan and repeated the task she had used with the bean can. She managed to get some oatmeal minus the dirt. She was glad that she had saved the pan for last. It cleared the taste of the dirt and she had delicious oatmeal to savor.

~

Raider leaned against a tree and watched the show. He wasn't sure what Charley would do. He knew she was breaking, but he also knew she was tough. She'd proven that over and over again. He was impressed when she ate the oatmeal, but was furious that she thanked God for the filth he left her. Not only had she prayed, but out loud, so he would hear. Ballsy! Raider wasn't sure if he should respond or just wait and pace his attacks, so they did the most damage. He decided to wait.

RAIDER'S Vendetta

Chapter 12

Charley walked away from the cabin, found some sunlight, and sat down. She enjoyed the warmth as she tried not to scratch. Raider was wrong; the burning did stop after a while. The mud soothed the itch. She was still covered with bites under her clothing and there was not enough mud to cover them all. She wasn't going to test Raider by trying to make more. Not right now anyway. Raider was clearly a violent and desperate man. But since her prayer, he had become hateful and filled with rage. She couldn't imagine why her prayer would trigger this behavior. Charley relaxed in the warmth of the sun and felt herself becoming peaceful. "Lord, I have no idea what the plan is. I don't know how long I will be here or what I will be required to do. I want to do your will, but Lord I'm tired, hungry, and in such physical pain. I need to know that you have not forsaken me. I know I'm not supposed to think that, but it's hard when you're up to your neck in crap alongside a maniac. I know he's your kid, but he is a maniac! I pray for your guidance and protection, God. Please give me strength and peace to know that You are always in charge."

Charley heard some birds chirping and fluttering a short distance away. She felt that they were talking to her. She got up and followed the sound. There were several apple trees in a sun-filled opening of the forest. Charley didn't want to get too excited. If the apples were green, they would only cause more discomfort. She got close enough to see that the birds were eating their fill. The apples were beautiful, small but plump and deep red. Charley pulled one off and bit into it. It was juicy and sweet. The tears rolled down her face as she thanked God for this gift. After eating her fill, she lay down under the trees and looked up through the branches into the sunlight. She felt at peace.

As she drifted in and out, a brain flash hit her. She knew that the Holy Spirit was speaking to her. It wasn't audible, but it was not her thought. "Take apples to my son." Charley jumped out of her stupor and literally yelled out, "No way!" She was shaking with anger. How could she be asked to reward that animal? He will pick them all and not let her have any more. She prayed under her breath. "Lead him to the apples if you want him to have them. I can't do this." She waited, nothing. She tried to convince herself that she'd misunderstood the request from God. He would want this man to suffer, not reward him, wouldn't He?

Shame began to slip in. He had just led her to nourishment. He clearly requested something from her. Did she trust Him or not? Why would she listen and stay in the bank, but question Him now? Its just apples, not her life. A pang of realization hit her. She hated this man. She couldn't see him as God's kid. She let her own fear and anger blind her vision, her faith. "Okay God, I'll do it." She thought she would feel His grace by her obedience, but she didn't feel any better. The guilt remained. Then it became clear to her, "Please forgive me, God. I will do my best to love him and see him as your son. I am sorry for questioning your wisdom." Charley then felt the Holy Spirit swirl within her, filling her with love and renewed strength.

~

When Raider saw Charley coming back into camp, her shirt filled with apples, he almost fell over. She poured the apples out onto the ground by the camp stove. "Take as many as you'd like," she said. She wanted to say, "God's gift to us," but refrained. She knew that she would be challenging him, and God clearly wanted this to be a gesture from her. Raider walked over to the apples and picked one up. He inspected it carefully. Charley picked up another and sat on the step of the cabin. She bit in and let the juice run down her chin. The look of satisfaction was clear on her face.

Raider took a bite and chewed slowly while looking at her

suspiciously. She ignored him and continued to enjoy her apple. Raider had almost finished his sixth apple when he threw it to the ground. He wiped the juice from his hands on his pants and sat down on the stool. He would glance into the woods, at Charley, and then to the apples. She remained quiet and just waited.

Finally he asked, "Why?"

Charley understood his question, but she wanted to open dialogue. "Why what?"

"Why did you share the apples? You could have kept them hidden, at least until I followed you to figure out why you weren't drooling over my oatmeal anymore."

Charley started to tell him about the Holy Spirit but she got a clear check in her spirit that she was not to share that yet. "We are both stuck out here, hungry. Figured you knew about the trees anyway."

~

Raider hadn't. He would've snagged the apples the first day if he knew they were there. He hated oatmeal. It was Darrell's idea to stash oatmeal. The perfect food he said. You can live on oatmeal and beans for years. Darrel had read that somewhere. Raider got up and left the site, heading the opposite way from the trees. He looped around and headed into the forest in the direction that Charley had come from with the apples. He had to find the apple trees and didn't want her to know he was searching. There should not be any apple trees with ripe fruit in this area of the forest. He gave up after several hours, and decided to follow her the next time she went out. It didn't make any sense. She was old and out of shape. She couldn't have walked far or into any remote areas.

~

Charley wasn't sure where he went or how long he'd be gone. *That was it, God?* she thought. She made the huge gesture to share and she didn't even get a thank you?

Charley decided to take advantage of her energy and the daylight.

69

She went into the cabin and cringed when she clearly saw the area where she had slept. She tossed the burlap bag out. It didn't provide any warmth anyway. She would have preferred to sleep outside, but didn't want to be bait for insects or animals. Raider was in the cabin at night and armed. If anything decided to eat them for a midnight snack, he would shoot it.

After clearing and cleaning her corner the best she could, she searched the outside area around the cabin for anything that would cushion the floor, anything that wasn't infested with insects. There were plenty of pine needles, but she didn't see any advantage to hauling them into the cabin. They would only poke and jab her already tender skin. More mudpacks had been applied to the bites, but she was still fighting the urge to scratch. The cut on her hand was swelling at an alarming rate. She used some of the water to rinse the wound and wrapped it with a torn strip from her shirt. She sat in the corner, head on her knees, and cried. There was nothing to buffer the extreme conditions she was forced to deal with.

Charley managed to doze on and off, jumping with every unfamiliar sound in the forest. The air was muggy and Charley's arthritis screamed rain. As the storm moved in, the wind made eerie melodies in the trees. She dreaded the night. She knew that she would be cold, in pain, and miserable in her corner of the cabin. Hunger pains were beginning to creep in again and Charley decided to bring some of the apples into the cabin before the rain started. As she collected the fruit, Raider came back into camp. Even he looked annoyed as he looked up into the sky. Charley didn't say anything. She didn't want to cause his anger to flare. She didn't want to be outside in this weather, either. At least the roof and walls would keep out the rain.

Raider grabbed the camp stove, pan, stool, and cup and brought them into the cabin. Without any comment, he left the area again. Charley considered following him, but she realized that she didn't care. She would eat her apples, huddle up in her corner, and try to sleep. Suddenly, the cabin glowed brightly as lightening flashed across the sky. Her dread began to manifest into fear. The smell of electricity was strong and menacing.

A short time later, Raider came bursting into the cabin, just as a peal of thunder ripped through the mountains. He missed the downpour that pounded the ground outside by seconds. Charley looked up and was shocked to see that he was carrying another blanket and several cans of soup. Hoping for some of the food was just too risky and she put her head back down on her knees. She was sure the second blanket was to protect him from the cold and dampness. She allowed herself a small prayer that he would take pity on her, even if only for the duration of the storm.

~

Raider had intended to taunt Charley, to let her think he was going to be generous, and then snatch it away. That's what he wanted to do. This stupid woman who believed in a God that cared. He wanted her to cry out and find that she was alone. No one would come saving the day. She had shared the apples, which did surprise him, but not enough to show her mercy.

Once the camp stove was lit, he dumped the soup into a pan to heat. The smell filled the cabin and Raider knew she was hungry for something more filling than apples. His plan of torment would begin.

"Charley, so I'm confused. You're sitting there covered in bites, cold, and miserable. Why hasn't God saved you? Doesn't it make you mad, just a little?"

Charley didn't take the bait. No response.

"Just what I thought. You don't have anything to say because you know I'm right. You're mad as hell. You figured he would have brought in the cavalry by now. I'd be in the back of a squad car and you'd be on your way home to a nice warm bed. You've figured out that He's just a story to keep everyone in line." He watched her out of the corner of his eye to see if she was biting. He stirred the soup and took a taste, letting the slurping sound fill the cabin.

~

Charley was mad, not at God, but at this moron. She knew if she spoke, they would be into it and she didn't want to risk making him mad. She wouldn't make him mad, not tonight, but she knew if she ignored him, he would kick her out anyway. Obviously, he wanted a fight. She whispered a prayer for wisdom and began. "Well, as I see it, God is providing. I survived the bank, I survived the jump into the lake. I haven't been eaten, and I found lovely apples today. I would say that God is all around me."

Raider began to laugh hysterically. "You ignorant hag. I kept you safe in that bank. I carried you down to the water and still had to save you from drowning. You're so old and rank, no animal would want you unless they were starving, and you lucked out on the apples. As I see it, you should be kneeling to me. I'm the reason you're still alive!"

"Just goes to show you that God can do miracles. He can use anyone to do His will." Charley realized too late that this was not a wise comeback. She looked up briefly to see if he was going to attack, but Raider remained seated. In fact, he was staring at her with curiosity.

"You believe He used me? Like I'm some puppet that can be controlled?"

"No, not like that. But, He can speak to hearts, plant grace when it's needed."

Raider was quiet, and then spoke with sarcasm. "You believe this crap. You tell me how you know God is real. If I like your answer, I might share my soup."

"You aren't going to accept anything I say. I don't know who hurt you or how, but you want to humiliate me and it goes way past me being a stupid, old, Christian woman. This is personal."

~

Raider was fuming. He knew it was personal. He had dreamed about the bin last night for the first time in years. This woman dredged up all the pain and shame he suffered at the hands of a devout Christian woman. He felt himself getting mean and he looked forward to making her pay.

"Maybe not, but worth a try, right? You could convert me. Wouldn't that be a real blessing? You could brag to all your churchy friends when you encourage them to come visit me in prison. Cuz you know once I found the Lord, I'd turn myself in and do the time. Then I would have salvation and live for eternity in Heaven with all the pretty angels."

~

Charley was shocked. This guy had been exposed to church at some point. His sarcasm revealed understanding of Biblical teaching. But, he was angry, furious. He had tried to lighten his words with feigned humor, but the hatred had seethed under the surface. "Look, why do you care why I believe. You don't and that's your right. We both know I'm not going to convert you to anything."

"What happened to miracles, Charley? Bible says no man is hopeless. You saying you don't believe I can be saved?"

"Not here, not now, not by me. This is all a game. You want me to set myself up and then you're just going to rip apart anything I say. No thank you!"

"So sad, Charley. You can't even defend your God. You won't even try. Guess I'm stronger than your faith or understanding if you're so afraid of what I'll say. You afraid I'll convert you?"

"It's not what you'll say, you ass. It's you getting angry and throwing me out in the storm. Just leave me alone and let me huddle in this damn corner." Charley knew as soon as she spoke the truth, she was screwed. His face lit up in satisfaction.

"Ohhhhhhh, Charley does have some fight left in her." Raider shifted on his stool, like someone settling in for a long encounter.

Damn, damn, damn, thought Charley.

"Make you a deal. For every question you answer, I'll give you a bite of soup." Raider seemed almost giddy with the prospect of shattering this woman's reality.

Charley knew he was not going to leave her alone and she didn't want to go out in the storm. If she got a few bites of soup, that was better than being hammered by him all night for nothing. She gave in.

RAIDER'S Vendetta

Chapter 13

"Okay," Raider said as he rubbed his hands together in excitement. "Let's get this show started."

Charley rolled her eyes and shifted so that her legs were stretched out in front of her. She felt her body stiffening as the humidity filled her bones.

"How do you know God is real? You've seen Him, heard Him, felt Him? People claim all of these ridiculous experiences. What's your story Charley?"

Charley remembered his bartering in the bank. "First a bite of soup, then I'll answer."

Raider looked at her with mock disappointment. "You don't trust me. That *really* hurts."

"You want me to cooperate? I want the soup first."

The soup was hot, full of vegetables and chunks of beef. The kind of soup that is thick and doesn't require water to thin it down. It tasted better than a steak dinner in a five star restaurant. Charley let the flavors explode in her mouth. The warmth down her throat seemed to reach every part of her shivering body. She couldn't be sure there would be any more coming, so she made this bite count. She saw that Raider was losing patience.

"I've never seen God."

"But you've heard Him and felt Him? Oh this is priceless," Raider said with joy.

"Yes."

Raider urged her on. "And?"

"That was an answered question."

"Oh, hell no. You can't just say yes or no for an answer."

"You just said I had to answer. You didn't say how I had to answer." Charley tensed up, waiting to see if she'd pushed too far, if he would strike her. She could see the decision develop through his eyes, he wanted to punch her, but refrained. Charley supposed that he was enjoying the cat and mouse game.

Raider scooped up another spoonful and held it out, just beyond her lips. "These are the ground rules: no 'yes' or 'no' answers. I'll give you this one, but I eat the soup and you sleep outside if you don't play by my rules."

Charley knew if she took the bite, she was agreeing. She only hesitated a second. The smell was overwhelming. She took the bite and the soup made its way down to her waiting stomach.

"I have heard God, not audibly like I hear you. It comes through like a rogue thought. Sometimes, it's a whisper and once, He yelled at me." Charley had made a point of not looking at Raider. She knew his look of amusement would aggravate her. This was pointless; the verse about casting pearls to swine crossed her mind. Charley hoped that God would understand the pull of hot soup and a dry shelter.

"So, how many times did God speak to you? Once? Lots? Is He whispering in your ear now?" Raider could barely suppress his wicked delight.

Charley glared at him and opened her mouth. "Oh, no, that's part of the same question." She shook her head in disagreement.

"Fine, here," he said as he put another spoonful in her mouth. It was noticeably less soup, but Charley didn't argue.

"Lots of times. First time, I was a teenager. I was yelling at Him while I was driving. I wanted him to show His face and talk to me. I had questions. He told me that He answered all my questions. I, of course, was insistent that He hadn't. He said that He had, I just had to read the Bible. I was quite upset with Him. Not the answer I wanted to hear."

Raider looked at her with a smug grin on his face. "So, that didn't strike you as odd, that He would talk to you? Think I'd run off the road if I started hearing voices."

"No, I don't know why. Felt totally natural. Still confuses me."

"Okay, so you say He yelled at you. I gotta hear this one."

Charley looked at him and opened her mouth.

Raider almost subconsciously slipped the spoon in. Someone on the outside would think he was a son, caring for his invalid mother.

"I had left my husband –"

"Whoa! Left your husband? Thought you Christian ladies married for life and all that crap. How many times you been married?"

Charley almost opened her mouth for another bite, but thought better of it. "Two times. One divorce and then widowed."

"So there's a wild side to you, Grannie?"

This time Charley did open her mouth with a pained expression.

Raider gave her a small bite. She knew that he intended to drag this out and wanted to make the soup last. She hoped he would get bored before the soup got cold.

"Which question do you want me to answer? You've asked several."

"I wanna hear the dirt."

Charley looked at him and decided how much to share. It was her life and God already knew, so this guy couldn't hurt her with truth. "I married my high school sweetheart just after I turned nineteen. After we got married, I realized that I cared about him, but I wasn't in love with him and eventually told him I wanted a divorce."

"That sucks. What kind of Christian are you? What kind of woman are you? Why did you marry him if you didn't love him? He could have found someone that truly loved him. How much of his life did you waste?"

Charley felt the sting of his words, but it wasn't anything she hadn't beaten herself up with. "Twenty-five years." The memories of the years of dysfunction and pain began to swirl to the surface. Her decisions were filled with shame and regret

"Holy crap, lady. You are a real piece of work. I hope he dumped your ass."

"No, I left him. Many times. He would always take me back."

~

Raider noticed that she had forgotten about the soup. That wasn't good. He didn't want her to shut down and not care if he put her out. He was enjoying this – watching the noose slowly tighten around her neck.

RAIDER'S Vendetta

Raider liked that she was showing the attitude that he saw in the bank. No, he would play nice. Get her relaxed, so when he swooped in to shred everything she believed, she wouldn't see it coming.

"Okay, so now you're with number two and you kept him till he died." Raider held up a spoonful of soup. Charley took the bite.

"You put it so eloquently," she said, annoyed. "Yes, he was a good man and we were married for ten years. He died unexpectedly last year."

Raider didn't offer any condolences. He figured the guy was better off dead than with this selfish excuse for a woman. "Well, that was painfully boring, so back to how you've convinced yourself that God talks to you."

"You're asking the questions. Maybe you want to think them through better if my answers are boring." Her glare was challenging. "And the soup is cold."

Raider's first reaction was to throw it in her face. Not only was she a blind-mindless-zombie-church-radical, she was also every woman he'd gotten used by. His hatred for this woman was growing with each answer she spewed out of her foul mouth. He would have to think of a good finale for this one. A fake mugging in an alley was too good for her. He calmed himself down and explained to her that her stupidity was not worth the effort to reheat the soup.

~

"I'm done. I don't want any more of your soup anyway. God provided me with apples today, I'm sure he'll provide tomorrow." Charley was wallowing in her memories and without thinking, asked, "How long are we staying here? Do you have a plan? You definitely had a plan when we left the bank. Now, I think you are a trapped rat and don't know what to do next."

Charley realized that her weariness and the painful memories had allowed her to get sloppy. Raider was on her, pulling her to her feet. She felt his fist make contact with her stomach and then the uncontrollable urge to vomit robbed her of the soup she had worked so hard to earn. His strong hands were pushing and lifting her out the front door of the

78

cabin. She landed in the mud on all fours. The rain beat down on her. Charley managed to get up and finally found some partial shelter among some rocks and fallen logs. She hoped the ants hated rain as much as she did.

"Lord, please don't abandon me. This is beyond me and I just don't know what I'm supposed to do, God. Please help me. I don't want to die here."

Charley couldn't explain it, but the rain was warm. She felt bathed in love and peace. She slept.

RAIDER'S Vendetta

Chapter 14

The next morning brought sunshine and clear blue skies. Charley woke and crawled out of her makeshift shelter. She saw that Raider was outside on his stool, coffee cup in hand and eating her apples. The rage she felt made her stomach sour. She moved as quietly as possible, away from the cabin and into the woods. She wasn't sure where she was going, but she was led by instinct or something more powerful. She heard the songs of birds. When she had only gone fifty yards, she came upon a cluster of fruit trees. There were pears, oranges, and peaches. The branches hung low and heavy with the ripe fruit. Charley was in awe. She knew that these trees were not native to the area and this was too remote and desolate to have been planted by a homesteader. This was absolutely not the season for tree-ripe oranges. Charley dropped to her knees and thanked God for his kindness and blessing for her. She selected several of each, lay in the warm sun, and enjoyed the sweetest fruit she had ever tasted. As each bite slipped down her throat, she was filled with such joy and strength. The tears rolled down both sides of her face. God was good, oh so good.

After Charley had filled her belly with the goodness, she dozed in the warm sun. She lay on her side to relieve the weight on her back. The sun seemed to be warming the stiffness out of her body, but her back ached terribly. As she lay there, trying to get comfortable, she suddenly felt pressure on her neck. It felt like a fingertip pressing in. As the pressure lifted, the pain in that part of her spine diminished. Next, she felt another fingertip press a few inches lower and, once again, the pain was gone. This continued down the length of her back until all the pain had disappeared. Charley laid there, frozen in awe by this miracle. The tears began, sweet, submitting tears. She didn't know if it was her guardian angel, Christ, or God Himself, but she knew it was of Heaven.

Charley lay in the sweet grass and listened to the music of the birds, not wanting to move from this celestial spot. She had never felt such peace and love. Then everything shattered.

"Take fruit to my son," the jolt in her brain said.

"Oh dear God, no. You can't ask me to do this again. It's not fair. You saw how he hurt me. Lord, you say you won't give us more than we can bear. I can't bear this. He is vile, vicious, and he hates me because I follow you. You can't expect me to reach out and forgive him. He doesn't deserve it." Charley waited, nothing. She was sure that God wasn't serious. He knew how horrible she had been treated, His daughter.

Then it all came rushing in and she wept in shame. Christ had been God's son and He was hated and tormented. So much worse than what she had endured. She had been willing to disobey God out of her false sense of entitlement. She got up on her knees and asked God to forgive her.

As Charley collected fruit to take back, she heard the Heavenly voice again. "Answer his questions. Tell him about us, you and Me." She didn't want to obey, but the encounter and the gifts He had bestowed on her would not let her challenge or disobey.

"Yes, Father."

Charley headed back with as much fruit as she was able to carry. When she had walked a few yards, she turned, and the fruit trees were gone, replaced with native pine trees. She began to laugh, quietly at first, then uncontrolled and full of amazement.

A short distance ahead of her, she saw Raider coming toward her. He must have heard her laughing and came to see what was going on. When he got close enough to see what she was carrying, he was dumbfounded. He looked beyond her into the forest. She continued past him, toward the cabin. As she set the fruit down on the ground, he moved up behind her. "Where did you get this?" he asked accusingly.

She smiled, "A gift from God."

Raider lashed back, "Bull. Someone is out there, giving you food. How many, Charley? Why haven't they tried to arrest me?"

"If there was someone out there, do you think I would still be here? You think they would send me back to a deranged maniac? That is just stupid. I would be swept away, far from you."

"Show me the trees then."

"I can't, they're gone. They were just behind me when you found me. God sent them and then He took them back." All the bites were gone and her finger wasn't swollen. Even her face was almost healed from the punch she had received in the bank. She looked refreshed.

Raider looked at her with confusion and then suspicion.
"Here, try some. They are delicious."

He picked up a peach. He smelled it and then squashed it in his hand. The juice ran through his fingers and down his arm. He threw the pulverized fruit at Charley. She didn't flinch. He licked the juice from his fingers and pleasure crossed his face, but only briefly.

"I don't know what you're up to, but I'll figure it out."

"I hope you do," she said with all sincerity.

Charley took an orange, sat on the cabin step, and began to peel it slowly. Once the insides of the orange were exposed, she pulled the sections apart and sucked the delicious juice. Raider eventually selected one of each. She watched him enjoying the pure perfection that God provided. Unexpectedly, he asked, "Why do you share the fruit when I've made it my mission to make your life miserable?"

"Oh, trust me, it's not my idea! God tells me to. Take fruit to my son, He says."

"His son? You expect me to believe you?"

"No, in fact I think anything I say will be a waste of time and breath," Charley admitted. "But for some reason God doesn't think it is. He told me to answer your questions, so fire away."

"You know I hate you right? I won't believe anything you have to say about God." And don't think I believe for a moment that Heaven sent the fruit.

"Yes, I know, but you still want to ask your questions. It's driving you crazy. I don't know why you hate me, but it doesn't matter."

RAIDER'S Vendetta

Chapter 15

Agent Morris was irritated that there seemed to be no leads or clues on her case. They had not received any reports of a dead body dropping from the sky. The detectives on the case were talking with men from Arthur's unit. They hoped that he might have mentioned a cabin or history in the Sierras, something to give them a real break in their search. They researched the family of Arthur and Darrell. There wasn't anyone left. Darrell's mother, Rose, had died fourteen years ago, killed in a senseless mugging while walking home from a local church after a Bible study. Arthur's father had died in prison in a fight over cigarettes and his mother had never been located.

Charley's family was here and waiting to meet with the detective. A phone call would have provided them with the update of no news, but families always wanted to see your face. They have to have something tangible. She hated these encounters. There was absolutely no news and they would want answers. Their beloved mother was missing, held by a ruthless killer. Agent Morris would assure the family of their commitment to finding Charley and tell them about the wonderful technology available to help them do so. The world had become a small place or, at least, that is what she would tell them. The Sierras with a trained survivalist might as well be Mars. She hoped that having Charley along would complicate his ability to remain invisible.

~

Agent Morris called the CSI department next. "Anything on the truck?" After the excitement of the helicopter liftoff, the routine work had started. They ran the plates of all vehicles in a three-block radius of the bank. The bank robbers probably wouldn't have parked further than that, not when they would be running and carrying bags of money. The found an old truck with a non-op registration and stolen plates. The owner had been refurbishing the old clunker for his son. They found Darrell's fingerprints on the steering wheel and his saliva on the cigarette butts in the ashtray. Arthur's prints were on the passenger side of the car.

There hadn't found any butts with Arthur's saliva and Agent Morris was disappointed. She had hoped he was a smoker. Many perps had been found by following the discarded butts. A path of bread crumbs so to speak. Others were caught stealing or buying cigarettes from a gas station or convenience store. A nicotine addiction could undo even the smartest criminals.

"Anything we can use? Any camping gear?" Agent Morris was beginning to think the Sierras had been Arthur's plan the whole time. The chopper just got him there faster.

"Nope, everything looks like it belonged to the owner."

"Damn! Be sure to call me if you find anything. I don't care how big of a stretch it is."

"You got it, boss."

Agent Morris hung up and sat with her head in her hands. She hadn't gotten much sleep and she felt her thoughts beginning to dull. Coffee, she needed coffee.

Chapter 16

"So, God yelled at you," Raider continued. "Doesn't sound loving to me."

"He whispered first. I ignored Him, so He yelled."

Raider looked at her, clearly amazed. "I don't understand how you can have God talking to you and you don't freak out."

"Like I said, it started when I was young and it just felt normal."

"What did He say?"

"Ezekiel 1:28."

"A verse? He could say anything, tell you anything, and He gives you a verse? How disappointing. You would think He would tell you how He created the world in seven days, or why He killed His kid on a cross, or who shot John Kennedy. Ahhh, Charley, if you're going to spread these lies, you need to come up with something a lot more interesting."

Charley felt the uselessness of having this discussion, but knew she had to obey. God had made Himself crystal clear.

"It was the anchor that kept me connected to God. I wanted to be an atheist. I didn't want God messing in my life. But, every time I would convince myself that God wasn't real, I would remember Him yelling at me. Kinda hard to ignore."

Raider sipped some of his coffee. "You, trying to be an atheist? Isn't that just how a normal brain is wired? It's like trying to learn to breathe. The belief in a loving God is brainwashing. Some hope that even though life sucks, there is some big prize at the end if you follow this invisible Lord." Raider stood up, stretched his back, and rolled his shoulders. "So, if this scripture was so profound it kept you chained down to a belief in God, what did it say? Surely it's burned into your brain."

"Like the appearance of a rainbow in the clouds on a rainy day, so was the radiance around him. This was the appearance of the likeness of the glory of the LORD. When I saw it, I fell facedown, and I heard the voice of one speaking." Charley repeated the verse, inwardly ashamed that it had taken her many years to understand it, let alone memorize it.

"What does that mean? Sounds like gibberish to me."

"Basically it told me that the voice I heard was the voice of God, the likeness of His glory. The next chapter was about this guy, Ezekiel. He was told to go back home to his family and be an example to them. Show them God. When I got this verse, I was separated from my husband. He wanted me to come back."

"I doubt that," Raider said, insultingly.

"He wanted me back, and I didn't want to."

"Did you go back?"

"No, not for a long time. And when I finally did, I didn't go back with the intent God wanted. We didn't stay together."

"So if you didn't do what God said, what was the point of Him talking to you? Sounds like it should have been life altering."

Charley groaned to herself. This whole conversation was pointless. "God knew I wouldn't go back then, but He also knew it would stay with me, keep me connected to Him. Years later, I understood the importance. It never let me forget He was real or that the Bible is reliable."

"Whoa, wait a minute. You accept the Bible as truth because of this experience you think you had?" Raider had the most ludicrous grin on his face. "This just gets better and better. The Bible, in case you didn't know, was written by men and has been revised and translated so many times, who knows what the original said. It is the most useless book ever printed."

"You even said, yourself, He could have told me who shot Kennedy. He could have said, 'Go home to your husband,' but no, He gave me a scripture to read from the Bible to get my answer. Why would He do that if the Bible doesn't speak for Him?"

"Okay, I see your logic, but that's only valid if a god said it. Considering you are one crazy old woman, I'm not jumping on the wagon because of your fantasies."

"That's fine. I'm not here to convert you, remember? I'm just doing what God instructed me to do."

"Demanded you mean. If you don't, then you'll burn in hell."

"I have a choice to be obedient or not. If I don't, He'll accomplish what is necessary another way, even if it is a total waste of time!" Charley looked at Raider, hate in her eyes.

Raider laughed, "So if I walk away now, you will be disobeying God's will?"

Charley knew she just had to say 'yes' and this stupid debate would be done. He would walk away to spite her, not realizing it was exactly what she hoped he would do. Charley hesitated. She knew what God wanted, but "Yes," slipped out of her mouth.

"If I can help fry you in hell, then I'm outta here." Raider took a few steps and then whirled around. "Wait a minute, you're trying to manipulate me. You figured I'd walk away if you said 'yes'. You *really* don't want to talk about God."

"Ya think?" she replied with contempt.

"Oh, this is good. You do have to answer my questions!" He sat on the stool, picked up several oranges, and began peeling them.

Damn, Charley thought. *He's settling in and going to milk this. Please God; don't make me suffer him any longer.* She waited for a response, anything she would interpret as a sign. Nothing.

"Well missy, this is gonna take some time," Raider said with a slow southern drawl. Charley grimaced.

"Then I'm going to find a bush. I have to pee."

"Take your time darlin', we ain't got nothing but time," he said in the same dramatic drawl.

~

Charley looked for an appropriate place to squat. Not having toiletries required creative problem solving. She also kept her eye out for a 'burning bush' and continued to pray for God to release her from this humiliation. But, when she came back into camp, she knew she was doomed to endure this idiot's barrage of questions. She resigned herself to the knowledge that God was smiling down at her.

"You ready?" Raider asked, as she sat back down on the cabin step.

"I suppose," she responded.

Raider threw her a peach and she nibbled on its sweet, cool flesh.

"Got my first one all ready for you."

"Fine."

"You guys are always saying that each of us is special, that God would leave all others to find and rescue one lost sucker, the sheep story. Right?"

"Well, I wouldn't use those words, but yes."

"Okay, what about all the humans slaughtered before Christ came. Many were killed under God's orders! Didn't they matter? Were they just collateral? Won't they all burn in hell now? Makes it hard to believe that each of us, me, is so damn important to this God above."

This was one of the biggest issues that had kept Charley removed from God for so long. She knew exactly what Raider was talking about. The hardest part of the Old Testament for Charley was when the Jews were told to kill everyone, including women and children, when they got their land back. God told them to wipe out everyone and this went against everything Charley believed to be Christ-like in the New Testament.

"I understand what you're asking. This was a big issue for me for a long time."

"So you just put on the rosy blinders and followed the moron in front of you?"

"No, I prayed about it, asked people I trusted, and was able to find resolution."

"Oh, please share, wise one," he said, his voice dripping sarcasm.

Charley's jaw tightened and she thought to God, *What is the point of this? He's not hearing.*

"They were not forgotten for eternity. When Christ was crucified, He went into Hades and preached to the souls there. They were given a chance to receive Christ and have an eternity in Heaven."

"A little too late don't you think?"

"No, I was angry that God would toss them away without a chance of salvation. This helped me to believe that we all matter, each one of us."

"And that makes the slaughter okay?" Raider asked with anger in his voice.

"No, but I am not God. I can only see things from a human's perspective here on Earth. I chose not to judge Him any longer." *To try not to*, Charley thought.

"Any longer? You used to judge?"

"Yes, when I thought something in the Bible or life was cruel and unfair."

"So, it's all okay with you now? The cruelty?"

"No, but I have decided to trust that God is good and that his actions are in the best interests of mankind, for me."

"Wow, sounds pretty naive to me."

"I suppose so, but if you can't dismiss God, you have to find a way to accept God."

"That's right. You've bought in because He yelled at you once. So stupid, Charley."

"It's not just based on that, you idiot. I have a lifetime of God's relationship. This was just the anchor that kept me from writing him off." She wanted this to be over. Charley hadn't resolved everything, or every question, and she felt like she was taking a final after missing half of the class time.

"Let's back up then. What was your first encounter with God?"

"My dad was healed instantly while a group from our church prayed over him. I was eight."

"A sore back, a headache, something totally lame that could be explained by aspirin he took earlier, I'm guessing."

"No," she snapped. "He had rheumatic fever when he was a kid and he got better. When my dad was thirty, we were on our way to California and he got sick again. We had to stop in Ohio and live there for a while. He would work, but crawled up the stairs every night to go to bed. The day after the prayer, he came home from work and ran up the stairs. He was cured and we moved on to California. He was fine after that. It never came back."

"That's bull, Charley. You were just a kid. It was a fantasy you made up."

"My parents weren't kids. You could ask them for yourself, but they're dead."

"I don't believe you."

"I don't give a rat's ass if you do or not."

"Nice language from a Christian."

Charley rolled over all the things she wanted to say and thought to herself that he would be shocked.

Raider picked up more fruit and began to nibble, as if deep in thought. "So, okay, let's say it really happened. Why him? Why do so many people suffer? Where is your God for them? Doesn't He love us all the same?"

Charley was tired. She didn't have answers for all of his questions, or hers. "I don't know," she said quietly. She thought about explaining the devil and his power over the earth, but decided he'd probably already heard all of that.

"There are so many children out there – hurt, abused. Let's give God a break and say that most adults make their own mess, but what about the kids? They can't change anything; no matter how hard they try. They can't make people love them – treat them right. They are stuck in a nightmare that never stops. Where is He for them, Charley? Why would He abandon me if He gave a damn?" He threw an orange at Charley, barely missing her.

Charley looked closely at Raider. She saw the anger in his tensed body. She didn't think he realized he had said ME. It was beginning to make sense now. This anger for the children was anger for himself. He must have been abused and abandoned by everyone.

"What about that, Charley? Where is their God? You Christians like to spew out this nonsense that all you gotta do is pray and God will save you. It doesn't work, Charley." Raider stood up and paced. He looked at her with absolute disdain, "You are like so many stupid people. You've been brainwashed into thinking if you believe hard enough, you can make the lies real." He released a loud, obnoxious fart. "I gotta go take a dump – now that's real!"

Charley watched him head into the forest and realized that she had been holding her breath. She breathed deeply and stood to stretch. The tension she was under made her body tight. She twisted and stretched her body to loosen up. "Lord, I feel like I'm on a carnival ride and can't get off. Please give me wisdom and peace, peace about the point of this craziness."

His question about the kids had been a tough one for Charley. This had been a huge stumbling block for her. It was one of the areas that she judged God the harshest for. There was no simple answer and, when she decided to trust God again, it went into the "Hopefully-I'll-Understand-Someday" category. When she'd asked the questions he was asking, well-meaning people would give her the "free will of man" and "Satan has domain over the earth" speech. They had meant well, but it didn't satisfy her. The children still suffered and it brought up the question of why God allowed Satan to have dominion? He was the boss, right? Charley didn't like having these feelings bubbling back to the surface. She hated not having a clear understanding of how things worked. Charley wanted to be able to defend God, to bring resolve for Raider. No Charley, don't get sucked in. He is mean and would hurt you in a second. *Don't think there is a heart in there!* she told herself sternly.

Charley waited to see if Raider was coming back to continue his attack, but he appeared to need a break or had just lost interest. She decided to explore the area and see what was nearby. She didn't want to stumble into him, so she headed in the opposite direction. The area was breathtaking. She saw her nest from the first night and, upon closer inspection, realized there was a huge anthill on the backside. "How stupid was that?" she asked herself. She moved further away from the cabin, in a circle, not wanting to go too far into the wilderness. Last thing she needed was to get lost. She was sure Raider wouldn't come looking for her.

She heard water running and thought she had found a stream. When she got closer, she saw Raider, shirtless, splashing water over his head and onto his chest. Obviously, the water was cold from the way he shivered. Charley didn't care. A bath looked so refreshing. He turned off the faucet that he and Darrell had hooked up to the spring months earlier and shook like a dog coming out of a lake. Water sprayed around him, the sun making the drops look like tiny jewels. If she had been younger and he had been kinder, it could have been a great scene in a romance movie. Charley waited to see how he hid the spigot. She felt relief knowing how to find water.

The bushes concealed her, but without covering the spring access, Raider walked right toward her. She pressed into the shrubs and he passed only inches from her. She couldn't tell if he didn't see her or just chose to ignore her. Charley was confused. Why didn't he hide the spring? She waited several long minutes to see if he would return, but he didn't. It was so frustrating. The water was right there, but she was sure he was hidden nearby, waiting for her to get close to it and then he would pounce. Her mouth began to salivate and she longed for the cold, refreshing water.

Suddenly she heard a whisper in her head. "The fruit Charley, the fruit brings grace." Now she understood. God wanted her to share the fruit so that Raider would also be touched by Heaven's grace, which had brought grace for her. She felt tears rolling down her cheeks. God was with her, protecting her. Charley, still concerned about how much grace Raider would require, slowly left the bushes and headed to the water. She turned the spigot and allowed the water to trickle into her mouth. It was clean, pure, and delicious. Charley drank her fill. She thought about bathing, but didn't want to show up at the cabin wet and suffer his wrath. She settled on washing her face and rinsing the residue of mud from her arms and chest.

Charley decided not to return right away so her blouse would have time to dry. She found some sun and sat. She slipped into a quiet conversation with the Lord. She felt the warmth of the sun and began to relax. It wasn't long before she reclined with her arms under her head, dozing. She was having such delightful dreams. She was on a tropical beach watching her children, as toddlers, playing in the waves. Her beloved husband, Archie, was next to her telling silly stories about his antics. She missed them all terribly, but even so; she felt utter peace until

Archie poked her. She laughingly asked him to stop, but he kept poking her. It was irritating and ruining her mood. She finally swatted at him and yelled, "Stop it!" Another deep poke that was painful. This jarred her out of her dream and she looked into the face of Raider, grinning his nasty grin at her. He was holding a stick.

"Heard you snoring and decided you would attract every bear and cougar within five miles." He sat back and stretched out his legs. "Don't think I'm worried about you. I don't want them in the area. Can't risk someone hearing a gunshot if I have to save myself. You're on your own."

Any thought of him having a heart disappeared from Charley's imagination.

"Besides, I might still need you at some point. No good to me if you're all ripped up."

"Good thing, I suppose," she said, sarcastically. Charley hoped her shirt had dried before he showed up.

"Thought you'd at least wash up, you stink. Maybe when you get old your nose doesn't work so good. Maybe you don't smell yourself."

So, he had known she was there in the bushes. She silently thanked God again for making her share the fruit. "I thought I should ask you for permission first," she lied.

"Didn't ask for permission before you drank it."

"No, you're right, I didn't. I should have," she said with all the remorse she could muster, which wasn't much.

Charley knew that he was enjoying the power. He thought he was in control, but she knew that God was the final power. Raider was no match for Him.

"I am showing you grace since you shared the fruit. This doesn't change the fact that I still find you stupid and disgusting."

Charley smiled to herself. She found it wonderfully appropriate that he used the word grace. "I understand," she said with a tone of respect.

Raider got up and headed back toward the cabin. Charley got up quickly and returned to the spring. She had intended on a leisurely washing but as soon as the ice-cold water hit her sun-warmed skin, she decided to wash quickly. She trusted that Raider had given her privacy, so she removed her blouse. Once done, she dressed and moved back into the sun to dry. She did not want her hair or clothing damp when the sun dropped from the sky.

When she was dry, Charley headed back to the cabin. The fruit was wonderful, but didn't fill the need for protein. She was hungry and not sure if Raider's grace would extend to beans or soup. The soup game had been disastrous and she didn't want a repeat. Charley heard a chirp. She looked toward the sound and saw a large, fat bird sitting on the ground. She wondered if she could catch it, but then realized she would have to kill it and, as hungry as she was, she knew that it would break her heart. The bird closed its eyes and fell over. Charley went over and tried to revive it. The bird was dead. Again, she heard another chirp, another bird. It also died. This happened four times.

~

Back at the cabin, Raider looked up from his can of beans. He was struggling to open it with his knife and wishing for a can opener. He cursed himself for not double-checking when Darrell had packed everything they would need several months ago. The stockpile and the cabin had been Darrell's idea. Raider had thought it was overkill. They wouldn't need all this stuff if they had a huge stash of money, but Darrell had insisted. They were going to get rich off the backs of the working schmucks some day. Darrell watched a lot of movies and he had a plan, but Raider hadn't been so sure. He'd been right about not getting rich. Most of the money had been left at the bank and he'd barely managed to keep twenty grand, now hidden with the beans and oatmeal.

There was no link between Raider and this cabin. It was a remote federal forest. Two years ago, he and Darrell had hiked for several weeks and picked the site. Actually, it had picked them. It must have been a miner's site, but the underbrush and the state of the cabin clearly indicated that no one had been there for many, many years. They'd found the cabin fairly intact and locating the spring had sealed the deal. They made several trips back, carrying in food and supplies, and storing enough food to feed them both for a month. They had also planned to replace the worn canvas, but never got around to it.

Raider had considered getting rid of Charley the first night at the cabin. It would make the supplies last longer and buy him some extra time. Certainly, he would be able to slip into Mexico after two months. His trail would be cold by then. He didn't really need her now that he'd made it to the cabin. He'd only needed her in the chopper and during the hike to the cabin. He'd needed the leverage in case the cops found him. Now, she was a liability. But, when he'd heard her praying, his rage exploded. His desire to even an old score convinced him to keep her alive. He just wouldn't feed her. He would have more food for himself and the pleasure of tormenting her.

Normally, he wouldn't have been so cruel. He would have put a bullet in her head while she slept, but she brought God back into his life. This was his opportunity to get even, to satisfy his vendetta against God and His sanctimonious converts.

He saw Charley's arms full of feathers. "What the hell?" he asked more to himself than her.

"Know how to cook birds?" she asked with a smile.

"How? Where?" he asked, amazed.

Charley just looked up and shrugged. She came over to the stove and set them on the ground. Neither of them had seen birds like these. They were brown with white specks, large like a crow but fat like a chicken.

Raider just stared at them in disbelief.

"Well, you gonna keep gawking or show me how to fix them?" Charley asked.

"You killed them? How? They look perfect."

"I didn't kill them. They landed on the ground and keeled over, dead."

"Oh crap, they have that bird flu. I'm not eating them."

"Up to you, but I'm eating them. They winked at me before they fell over. I know God provided them for us," said Charley with a smile.

Raider stood up and ran his hands through his hair. "I'm not buying this supernatural voodoo stuff." He headed into the cabin with his can of beans.

Charley released a sigh of disappointment. She'd never cooked birds with feathers and guts before. "Well, it can't be that tough." The stove and pot were sitting out, so she dared to use them. She started pulling the feathers out, but it was difficult. An old movie came to mind and she remembered them dropping doves in boiling water to make the feathers come out easier. She filled the pot with water from the bottle and got it boiling. She dropped the first bird in and let it stay for just a few minutes. She grabbed the bird by a wing tip and pulled it out. Luckily, the bird just fit in the pot. She tried to pull the feathers out, but the bird was too hot to handle. She hated to lay the bird back onto the ground but needed to let it cool. She dropped the second bird in, hoping this wasn't all pointless.

After a few minutes she tried the first bird again. The feathers came out easily. She shouted with excitement. She worked on each until she had a pile of feathers and four pink, naked birds sitting on them. She didn't see Raider, but she was sure he was watching her progress. Once done removing the feathers, she went to the cabin doorway and asked Raider if she could use his knife.

"You're not serious? Like I'm gonna hand you my knife?" he responded from his cot.

"Well, I can't cook these birds with their guts inside."

After a few minutes, Charley stepped back as Raider came out of the cabin. He went over to the featherless birds and had them cleaned out, wings removed and heads cut off in short order. He looked longingly at the birds and asked, "How are you cooking these?"

"Since I'm using the camp stove, I'm planning on boiling them."

Raider knew that grilled over an open flame would be the most delicious way to cook them, but he couldn't risk the smoke being spotted.

Charley wasn't a chef, but she was an experienced cook. After examining the naked birds, she added, "There are pockets of substantial fat on the birds. I wonder if we should try frying one and see if works. Wish you had a skillet. That would work better than this pan."

Raider stood and walked into the woods, returning with an old skillet and some salt. He threw them at Charley, just missing her. She bit her tongue, wanting to say all the hateful things she was feeling. Once the skillet was hot, Raider cut one of the birds in smaller pieces and dropped them in. The smell of the bird searing on the hot surface of the skillet made their mouths water and their stomachs growl. The scent filled the area and increased their appetites to the point of aching. The fat on the birds made them sizzle and turn a glorious brown.

Once Charley was sure the meat was thoroughly cooked, she pulled off a piece. As she put it in her mouth, Raider watched her face with the anticipation of a kid. She moaned with delight and chewed deliberately. Suddenly Raider grabbed a large piece out of the skillet and tried to salt it without burning his fingers. He shifted the piece between his hands while blowing on it. Before long, he was ripping away at it with his teeth. The satisfaction was evident on his face. Charley put the cooked pieces in the pot so she could start the next bird.

Once the second bird was cooking, Charley took a piece and let the sweet, hot meat fill her mouth, and then her stomach. It was better than chicken, turkey, or even squab. She'd had that once when a date had tried to impress her.

Raider was eating the cooked pieces as quickly as she could cook them. Charley wanted to let the meat cool, but she wasn't sure he would leave her any. She felt the hot meat burning her fingers as she tried to hold on. While the third bird was cooking, Raider finally slowed down. While the fourth cooked, the third cooled, and Charley was able to leisurely enjoy the meat. Raider continued eating, but slowly. He licked his fingers and moaned in pleasure. She wondered if he'd even tasted the first bird.

Once they had their fill, there was almost a whole bird left over. Charley wanted to take it into the cabin for later. Raider looked at her like she was an idiot. "You want to bring every animal within smelling distance into the cabin tonight? We either eat it or dump it in the woods." Charley picked up another piece and took a bite. She realized that she was stuffing herself out of fear, rather than relying on God to provide. The bite reinforced that she was full to the point of discomfort.

"I'm done. Do with it as you will."

Charley got up and cleaned the skillet with plain hot water. Raider nibbled on another piece as he headed out to the woods with the pot of delicious meat. She overheard him mumbling to himself, "Some of you will eat good tonight."

Cooking the birds took up most of the afternoon and it was well into the evening before they were through eating. The sun was beginning to drop and as the evening air wrapped around Charley, she held herself tightly, trying to keep what little heat her body was creating. Once she was in the cabin, she stared at the hard floor, wishing she had a pile of feathers to make a soft nest. She offered a moment of silence for the birds and thanked God again for His gift. Charley looked for something to give her warmth, but there wasn't anything useful, only Raider's blankets. She just wanted to get to sleep and end this day. It would mean she was one day closer to the end – whatever that would be.

Raider came into the cabin a short time later. "That was some good eatin'," he said with contentment. "I am stuffed!" He lay down on his cot.

"Me too," Charley offered. She so wished to be warm and curled up with her full belly on a soft chaise or bed. Sitting against the wall, growing colder only made her gorged stomach more uncomfortable.

"Sure hoping they didn't die from the bird flu."

"They didn't."

"So you say. Where did you get them Charley? And don't give me your bull about falling from Heaven."

"Okay," was all she said.

He decided that she wasn't going to reveal her source, not yet anyway, so he moved on to the entertainment for the evening. "I was thinking about my questions and I've got some good ones for ya. I'm curious to see what fantasies you'll come up with next."

"Raider, not tonight. I'm not feeling so good and I just want to sleep."

"Crap, you got the bird flu. I should've known."

"No, not like that. I'm cold, the floor is hard, and sitting up is uncomfortable after all I ate."

Before she realized what happened, she was hit in the face with a blanket. It wasn't soft and snuggly like her blankets at home, but it wasn't burlap either. It was the most wonderful thing she had felt in days. She started to comment but decided against it. Instead, she wrapped herself in the blanket and let it warm her.

"So, now you're not cold. I plan on continuing our debate. If you don't cooperate, you're back outside without the blanket."

Charley rolled her eyes in the darkening cabin. She was thankful for the blanket and understood that the birds had been saturated with God's grace. She figured it was too much to pray for a sedative, too. She just wanted him to shut up and sleep.

RAIDER'S Vendetta

Chapter 17

Agent Morris still hadn't come up with anything useful. Her detectives talked with members of Arthur's squadron, but no one remembered him mentioning the Sierra Mountains. Arthur had been a good airman, but not well liked. He was moody and antisocial, spending most of his off time alone. They mentioned that he spent his money and free time with the prostitutes in Baghdad.

Arthur had been awarded multiple medals during his career in the Air Force: A Commendation, Aerial Achievement, Cross, and Airman's Medal for Heroism. Then, he had been dishonorably discharged for desertion. Why, after so many years of exemplary service, did he run? wondered Agent Morris. She went through the trial records and noted that he had plead guilty and offered no defense for his actions.

Since he wasn't in combat, his behavior hadn't resulted in a prison sentence. He'd been on an approved leave and just didn't show up at his airbase when it was over. He was eventually found drunk and holed up in one of the roughest neighborhoods in Baghdad, a strip of apartment buildings a few blocks from the Palestine and Sheraton hotels. Several of the prostitutes had provided him with sleeping quarters until his money ran out. When one of the women told him he had to leave, he became abusive and she reported him to the airbase authorities. He was shipped home, tried, and discharged.

Agent Morris also requested police reports for all inhabited areas along the flight path of the helicopter, beginning with the day of the robbery. There was nothing unusual in any of the police reports. Agent Morris scrutinized every one, looking for something, anything that would give them a place to start looking. There were assault charges, public intoxications, vandalism, domestic violence, and several bungled robberies.

When Officer Burns knocked on her door as she put a check next to the last item she'd read. A woman had reported that someone shattered her greenhouse. How sad, she thought. Agent Morris had always wanted a greenhouse.

"The captain is calling everyone in for a briefing on those murders over in Montague," said Officer Burns.

"Okay, I'll be right in," she responded.

Chapter 18

Obviously, Raider was not going to give Charley any peace, not until he was through for the evening. He had lit a small lantern. "Okay, the biggie. If God loves us, why does He threaten hell if we don't obey? Would you tell your kids to love and adore you or they would fry? No, you wouldn't. You'd give them the choice. We are told we have a choice to love God or not, but that's not true if you believe in hell. Is that why you buckled under, Charley? You don't want to fry for eternity?"

Charley didn't have this one figured out either, but remembered an answer she received from her sister years ago. Here goes, she thought to herself. "Let's say you live in the wilderness with your children and there was a rabid bear running around, killing anything it found. You might ..."

"I'd never live in the wilderness with kids. That's just stupid."

"Are you going to let me answer or would you rather hear yourself rant?" she asked, annoyed. He nodded for her to continue.

"So, you might dig a huge hole and put sharpened, poisoned spikes in the bottom – a hole for the rabid bear. You build a fence around the area where the hole is and you tell your children not to climb the fence. There is a deep hole with spikes to contain the bear. You provide them with what they need so they don't need to climb the fence. You remind them and explain to them that you don't want them to fall into the hole. It isn't for them, but for the bear."

"I'm assuming the bear is Satan and the hole is hell," asked Raider.

"Correct. Let's say one of your kids climbs the fence, goes to the hole to look, and falls in. Didn't you do everything you could to protect your child? Wasn't it their disobedience to the truth that landed them in the hole?"

"Ahhhhhhh, I see what you mean, except one small thing. Why would I create the bear and then try to protect my kids from it?"

Damn, thought Charley. She had asked her sister the same thing. "Okay, I get your point. This is how I resolved it. I know there is a God, the Bible speaks for Him and it refers to hell repeatedly. I have to accept that there are two teams. I even wished there was a third option, but there isn't. I can ignore the truth and suffer later if I choose Satan's team or I can choose God and have the promise of eternal life in Heaven. I chose Heaven."

"What if it isn't real, Charley? What if it's just over when you die? Look at what you missed out on by being a goody-two-shoes."

Charley thought about her life, the pain she caused herself and others by walking away from God. "I can say this with all honestly. Without God in my life, it sucked. I was miserable, felt useless, didn't trust anyone, and screwed it up royally. With God in my life, I have purpose. I have peace. It's not all wonderful. I'm sitting in this nasty cabin with you, right? But, I know that there is hope and grace beyond my ability or yours – which as much as you'd like to think you are in control, you're not. God has the final say." Charley stopped abruptly, fearing she'd triggered the rage that would put her out in the cold. She wrapped the blanket tighter around her, deciding he would have to fight her for it.

Charley waited for Raider to take offense to her outspoken challenge and throw her out, but he didn't react. His breathing became deep and slow, almost as if he was in a relaxed stupor.

Charley held her breath and to her amazement, she heard him snoring, a silly whistling snore that made her giggle. She knew he would be mortified if he heard himself. "Thank you Lord for hearing my prayers about the sedative and if you brought the snore, thank You for that, too." Charley tried to get comfortable and finally drifted into a deep, glorious sleep. She was laying on soft, billowy clouds, watching birds glide by and higher clouds drifting overhead. The sunlight was warm and soothing. Several birds like the ones she had eaten earlier landed next to her and nuzzled in. She petted the feathery creatures and scratched their necks. "I'm so sorry about your friends, but they were delicious."

RAIDER'S Vendetta

Chapter 19

Charley was startled awake by a loud banging next to her ear. She jumped up in a panic to see Raider's face grinning at her. He was holding the pan and skillet. "Damn girl, you're quick." She was surprised at how limber she felt. No aches or pains in any joints. Her back felt wonderful. Maybe she did sleep on clouds last night. "It's getting late, almost noon. I'm hungry and I don't want oatmeal. Go get your fruit, your birds, or whatever you can find."

"It doesn't work like that. I can't make anything magically appear. Besides, I'm still stuffed from all the meat last night. You've got your beans and soup."

Raider glared at her. "I know you found a stash out there, Charley. I want you to take me to it. Your explanation of gifts from God is bull and I want to know what's going on. You take me now or you'll regret it." Charley stepped out into the sunlight and tried to figure out what to do. She didn't think God would take kindly to Raider's demands, but He wouldn't abandon her now and allow Raider to hurt her, not after everything He'd done to protect her.

"I guess we can walk around and see what we find. That's how I found everything else." Raider pushed her down the steps and gave her another hard shove toward the trees. Charley moved slowly, trying to think her way out of this mess. She knew Raider wasn't starving. It was a showdown; her, God, and him. He was going to prove to himself that there was another explanation for the fruit and birds. She felt real concern that Raider might kill her. She tried to remember if she had seen a bulge in his pocket. Did he bring the gun on this walk?

RAIDER'S Vendetta

Charley was looking everywhere, praying that God would rescue her once again. She didn't see anything in the area that had provided the fruit trees before. Raider began taunting her, belittling God, and threatening bodily harm if she didn't quit wasting time. "You better take me to your stash, Charley, and I mean now." She felt a strong shove again and fell to the ground. She tried to break her fall, but landed with her face in the dirt. Raider then placed his foot on her back and pressed. She felt the unmistakable cold metal of a gun to her temple. "I'm through screwing around. There ain't no God and you know something. I want to know what it is."

Charley began to cry, a soft suppressed cry. She didn't want to give Raider the satisfaction of knowing she was scared. He removed his foot and pulled her up by her hair. "I swear I'll kill you, Charley. You serve no purpose to me."

Charley was at a loss for what to do, so she prayed aloud, "Dear God, I pray for your protection." As Raider brought the gun up to her nose, Charley saw a look of bewilderment cross his face. He was staring behind her. Charley turned and saw a tree, a tree that was not there before. The tree was loaded with nectarines, swollen with sweetness and juice. Raider lowered the gun and pushed Charley toward the tree. She moved under the branches and stared up at all the luscious fruit above her. The tears, uncontrollable now, flowed. She was crying tears of joy, not fear, and didn't care if Raider saw. She pulled off one of the nectarines and bit into it. Her mouth tingled with sheer delight. Raider stood there with his mouth gaping open, not able to speak.

Charley watched him while she continued to eat the fruit. They both noticed movement under the brush nearby and two large brown rabbits hopped over to Charley. They sat with their backs to her and seemed to be staring at Raider. He was rubbing his eyes, as if his vision was distorted. The rabbits then lay down and closed their eyes. Charley knew they had died for her.

"What the hell?" Raider was finally able to spit out.

"Do you want to collect fruit or carry the rabbits? We need to take what we want; the tree won't be here for long." She waited for Raider to respond. He continued to stand there, frozen and confused. Charley picked up the rabbits and headed back toward the cabin. Eventually, Raider followed her with his arms full of nectarines.

~

Raider didn't speak to Charley. He just paced, muttering to himself. His hands were raking through his hair. Charley put water on to boil. She figured if dipping in boiling water worked for feathers, it would work for fur. She had no clue how to dress a rabbit. Once the water was at a full boil, she lifted the first rabbit with the intention of submerging it. "Wait," Raider yelled. "It is skinned with a knife, not plucked."

Charley stood up and handed him the rabbit. "I don't have a knife and no clue how to skin one anyway, so you get to do it if you want to eat them." She wanted to follow with something smug like "Told ya sucker," but the experience of the gun at her temple and in her face kept her attitude in check. Raider took the rabbit and stared at it as if waiting to see if it was really dead. Charley grabbed a few nectarines and moved away from him, the rabbits, and the cabin. She decided to give him some space and get herself out of shooting range. She didn't want to take the chance that he would totally lose it and go on a rampage. She understood the gifts, but it must seem like a twilight zone to Raider.

Charley came to a ridge overlooking a deep ravine. It was beautiful down there, maybe two hundred feet or so deep. She was guessing since she had no clue how to judge distances. A streamed ran down the middle. In early spring, it probably flowed with melting winter snow, but now, in the latter part of summer, it was dry. The edge jutted out and she was unable to see the entire bottom of the ravine. She realized that she was on an overhang with no idea of how stable it was and moved back.

Her stomach was still full from the birds eaten last night, so she decided to remain scarce as long as she could. The area was lovely with shade trees, so she settled in. Charley enjoyed the fresh air and the smells for the first time. She loved the wilderness and, under different circumstances, would have enjoyed her stay here. The afternoon was warm and, even though she had slept until nearly noon, her body began

111

to relax and she dozed off and on. The memories of her kids, grandkids, and Archie began to float in and out. Sometimes like a video, but mostly snapshots, captured moments of great joy.

Charley had been hiding out for several hours while Raider skinned, cleaned, and cooked the rabbits. He was going to try frying the meat again, but the lack of fat would mean a much drier meal this time. When the rabbit began sticking to the pan, he added some water. It was now a blend of fried and stewed rabbit. He was thankful that he had salt.

The scent of cooking meat filled the area around the cabin. The scent was faint, but enough to create hunger rumblings. "No," she thought. "I don't want to be hungry. I want to stay here until the cavalry arrives." Charley had nectarines with her; they would provide food and water. She could hold out a long time if she ignored the smell of cooking meat. Charley was determined to stay put and enjoy her time alone and she drifted off to sleep.

Charley woke to the eerie feeling that someone was staring at her. She figured Raider had found her and was going to poke her with a stick or worse. She opened her eyes and looked into the face of a large, gray wolf with piercing blue eyes. She didn't know what to do, so she froze. The wolf was right next to her. There was no way to get up and run without his teeth snagging her throat. "Lord, Lord, Dear Merciful Jesus, please help me," she prayed with urgency. The wolf licked his lips slowly, as if directed in a movie for dramatic effect. The wolf seemed to be searching her eyes. She looked away, remembering that if you make eye contact with a dog, they see it as a challenge. She decided to let him be the alpha. She heard the wolf whine and, when she looked up, he definitely focused on her eyes again. She smiled, thinking it would help make the wolf feel more comfortable. *How absurd*, she thought. *Either he is going to eat me or he's not. Don't think the expression on my face matters much.* Charley was stuck. She was afraid to move and afraid not to. Just as her heart reached the point of bursting, the wolf turned and walked back into the forest.

When Charley was confident that the wolf wasn't lurking nearby, waiting for his prey to run and make the game more interesting, she ran back to the cabin. Raider was sitting on his stool, gnawing the cooked rabbit. It was charred and wet at the same time. "Have a nice vacation?" he asked her. "Hope you didn't want any." Charley picked up another nectarine and chewed thoughtfully.

"Have you seen any large wild life? I thought that there would have been a bear, cougar, or wolf by now."

"Nope, you hoping to get eaten up? Take you away from this misery? I can shoot you if you want."

"No, thank you. Just wondering is all." Charley sat on the cabin steps. She tried to look over her shoulder now and then, watching, without Raider getting suspicious.

The air was tense. Ignoring a huge, paisley elephant sipping a cup of tea would have been less conspicuous. Charley wanted to gloat, to make him admit what happened, but everything in her spirit said not to, to leave it alone. God didn't need to be defended or explained. She knew that Raider knew and that would have to be enough. He was not going to acknowledge the event they both had witnessed. It seemed outrageous at first, but then she thought about the Jews when they had escaped Egypt. They were there for all the plagues and the parting of the sea and still they would not trust that God was real. Guess some fruit and rabbits paled next to those miracles. She did notice, however, that Raider wasn't tormenting her about her stash.

"I haven't heard any praising coming out of you. Don't you worship your God?"

"I do, but not in front of you."

"Embarrassed? You probably sing like a twisted cat in heat."

Lovely picture, she thought.

"Thought that it was a requirement. God loves His adoration."

"He does, but not the way you make it sound."

"It's the only way to take it. I always wondered though. If man wanted to be worshiped, he'd be called egotistical. What does that make your God? Does He need our pitiful adorations to feel important? It's like telling someone to say they love you. Does it have any value if you demand it?"

Charley had to think before she spoke. This was a tough one. If you looked at his example, a man would be considered egotistical, a tyrant, and self-centered. This had been a question brought to her by a teenage girl when she was a youth leader. She believed God revealed His heart to her when she answered the young woman. "The best way I can explain it is that a relationship takes two. God provides so much for us, but He doesn't need anything from us. How do we share a relationship with Him if we can't do anything for Him? We can praise Him and show Him our love. You don't get it because you don't love Him or have a relationship with Him. Hasn't there ever been anyone you adored? Someone that you would do anything for?" She waited for him to answer.

Raider looked down, "Twice, once when I was a boy and one other time."

"Didn't you want to love them and express your emotions so that they felt loved and connected to you?" she asked softly.

"You're comparing your imagined relationship with God to real love?"

"Yes, God created love. It was the best gift he gave mankind."

~

Raider abruptly got up and left Charley to wonder what their exchange had touched. He moved through the woods, walking faster and faster, until he was running. He ran until he was out of breath. He was fighting the memories of her, the woman that had captured his heart. Badria had been the most beautiful woman Raider had ever seen. She was born in Afghanistan and escaped to Iraq when the Taliban invaded her village. Badria was one of many women who needed to support herself and her family after the invasion of Iraq by the United States. Against all of her beliefs, she'd finally resorted to prostitution to feed herself, her elderly father, and her young brother.

Raider dropped to the ground and fought the tears that began to well up. He should have saved her. He should have fought harder to get permission to marry her. He could have gotten her out of that hellhole if she had been his wife. She loved him, but she wouldn't disobey her father. It had been instilled in her since childhood to be obedient to him. Her father spent the money she earned, but he would not protect her, would not allow her to marry an American, to escape. Raider knew she had been targeted. He saw the threatening words painted on her front door. She was trapped; let her family starve or continue to sell her body. He pleaded with every officer at the base to get her a visa to leave Iraq, but they didn't care. They wouldn't be bothered. Raider requested leave. He was going to convince her to leave the country with him, but it was too late. He found her battered body in a back alley and the bloody rocks that surrounded her. Raider was through with the Air Force. The military had abandoned her and left her at the mercy of the barbaric laws of the country. He kept himself blind drunk so he wouldn't feel the horror of the brutality. Once his leave was over and he was considered AWOL, Raider was glad that they had found him and discharged him from the Air Force.

It had been a long time since he cried for Badria. It was Charley's fault. She dredged up everything he had struggled to forget. He would make her suffer. She would not come into his life and rip him open without paying a penalty.

RAIDER'S Vendetta

Chapter 20

Charley wasn't sure what was happening, but she instinctively knew she should hide. She grabbed her blanket and some more fruit and slipped into the woods. She searched for a safe place while she still had light. She would wait out the night. She found an opening in a tight thicket that led to a chamber, similar to a cave. She was in deep and invisible from the outside. She broke several branches and hid the opening. Charley needed to stay awake so her snoring would not betray her. The sky was overcast, concealing the stars and the moon, which made the forest pitch black.

Almost as if on cue, she heard Raider walking through the woods. She saw a shimmer of light. Raider had the lantern.

"Charley, come out, come out, wherever you are. Let's play hide 'n seek. Be sure to stay awake, Charley. I wouldn't want your snoring to cut our game short." Raider was quiet, listening, Charley supposed. "You're just like her, Charley, my Aunt Rose. You two will get along real good. She's in Heaven now, waiting for you."

Charley held her breath. The light was just outside of her thicket. Why did he want her dead? What did she touch on that angered him to the point of murder? She'd done what God asked. She'd played Raider's stupid games.

She pulled back when the light became brighter. He was just outside. Did he see her? Was he toying with her? Playing another sick game at her expense?

"Charley, I can smell your fear. I know you are here somewhere close. I've got all night to find you."

Pending doom was crushing her breathing. She

feared she would die that night. She pulled back even further and heard the dry branches behind her shift. It wasn't loud, but it shrieked in the dead quiet of the forest.

"Charley, I knew you were here, close. You should have stayed still. I figure you're only a few feet away."

She heard a deep growl and thought that Raider was stepping up his game of hide and kill, trying to freak her out, but the next sound was Raider. "What the hell! You trying to scare me off, Charley? Won't work." A deeper growl this time, coming from the front of her thicket. Raider turned to position the lantern toward the source of the sound. Charley saw the silhouette of a huge animal. Raider cursed and dropped the lantern. The light faded to solid black. It must be the wolf from earlier in the day, thought Charley.

~

Raider slowly backed away and pulled out his gun. The wolf didn't move or make a sound. Raider debated whether to shoot into the darkness, but he couldn't see enough detail to make a clean kill in one shot, and he would not have time to get off a second before the wolf was on him. Raider decided to get to the cabin where he had some protection and backed away slowly. Once he reached the security of the camp, he yelled out, "Good luck, Charley, you're not alone out there! Maybe you're already dead," he muttered under his breath. No, he would have heard her scream if she'd been attacked.

~

Charley wasn't sure what to think or how to feel. The wolf didn't attack her before, but maybe he hadn't been hungry enough yet. Maybe he scared Raider off to protect his prey. She couldn't see the wolf, but she smelled him. He was just outside the thicket. "Dear God, I don't know how much more I can handle. Please release me from this nightmare. Let this wolf be a blessing from You to me."

The wolf whined, yawned, and then she heard him lie down. He wasn't going anywhere, but he wasn't trying to come into the thicket either. "Is he my protector, God? Did You send him?" No audible answer, but she was filled with an internal peace and smiled. He was her protector. Even though Charley tried not to go to sleep, she drifted off. Several times through the night, she woke to the sound of the wolf growling. She didn't know if Raider was lurking about or if she was just being protected from other predators.

RAIDER'S Vendetta

Chapter 21

The morning light filtered into the thicket. Charley woke up and had no clue what to do. Was Raider's rage exhausted or was she still in danger? She looked through the thicket and saw that the wolf was gone. She removed the branches and climbed out. She decided to leave her blanket hidden in case she had to spend another night in hiding. She concealed the opening with more branches. She was thirsty and decided to see if the spring was clear. The plan was to stay low, in the shadows, and quiet. When she approached the spring faucet she drank until her thirst was quenched. She realized that she didn't smell coffee. Raider must still be asleep.

Charley walked softly into camp and peered into the cabin. She didn't hear anything. The back of the cabin was dark and she didn't know if he was on his cot or not. She backed down the steps and avoided the section that creaked. She took another step and bumped against a warm wall. Raider was behind her. She turned, praying that he didn't have a gun pointed at her, a club raised to strike, or the knife to slit her throat. He was just standing there, no weapon.

"You see that wolf last night?" he asked.

"A wolf? No, I was up in a tree. One come into camp?"

"No, I was out looking for you. Thought I found you, but it was a huge wolf."

"I didn't hear a gunshot. Did he run away when he saw you?"

"No, he just stood his ground and growled. I came back into camp and he didn't follow. Damndest thing. Thought you would have seen him."

"No, thank goodness. I don't know what I'd have done."

"So, you were up in a tree? You climbed a tree?" Raider asked with a lift to his voice.

Charley felt apprehension. "Well, it was low to the ground and I didn't go up far. You seemed to need some time alone."

"Hmmmmm, yeah, guess I did. Well, found this under some scrub. You must have dropped it out of that tree you were in."

Charley looked down, and Raider was holding her blanket. Damn, he knew she was lying.

"Yeah, kinda weird. I went back out this morning to look for signs of the wolf or a trail. Looks like he slept on the ground, right by that scrub. Don't remember seeing a tree though, Charley."

"Okay, you caught me. I was in the forest with my friend, the wolf, having tea in the bushes with a forest elf."

Raider smacked her hard across the face. Charley fell back against the cabin, her eyes tearing from the pain.

"Don't screw with me old woman. You a witch? There are too many unexplained events that surround you. I want an explanation right now. What are you?" He raised his hand, balled into a fist this time, and pulled back to punch her. As his arm began to move forward, an ominous growl pierced the silence. The wolf had returned and leaped up, sinking his teeth into Raider's shoulder. Raider went down on his knees and screamed in agony. The wolf shook his head and bit down harder. Raider howled in pain and the wolf released him. Raider dropped to the ground and clutched at his shoulder. The wolf moved in front of Charley and herded her away from Raider. Charley was dumbfounded.

Raider got up on his knees again and stared at the wolf in disbelief. He looked at Charley and realized that she was as shocked as he was. The wolf put his head down and growled a deep, threatening growl. Raider slowly stood, holding his hands up, hoping the wolf would see that he wasn't a threat. Raider stepped away from the wolf and Charley. "What the hell, Charley?"

"Not hell, Heaven. This is God's love for me, protecting me."

Raider didn't show any anger, just confusion as he looked from Charley, to the wolf, and back to Charley.

Raider grimaced as he sat on the stool. He was turning pale as the pain and blood loss took their toll on his body. He swayed and then slipped over onto the ground, unconscious.

RAIDER'S Vendetta

Chapter 22

Agent Morris was thrilled. When the lady with the greenhouse had started to clean up the mess, she found a cell phone in the shattered glass. She thought it might belong to the vandals and turned it in to the police. When they checked the number, it turned out to be Charley's phone. The police already knew the helicopter's flight path, so the phone alone was not that significant, but it did give them a starting point. Something happened for the phone to be thrown out of the helicopter there. Maybe that's when Charley found out she was going to be jumping. The residence was isolated and one of the few homes before the mountainous terrain took a steep climb.

The team that investigated the greenhouse site called Agent Morris with some more details. Several miles beyond the residence, they found a substantial lake. "Wondering if they would have aimed for the water, Detective?" the agent suggested.

"Isn't that a difficult landing?" asked Agent Morris.

"Not for a trained military pilot," he replied.

"I'm thinking about Charley. She'd die on impact."

"Well, if I had to jump out of a helicopter at night, I'd go for the water. The trees would hide all kinds of risks."

Agent Morris thought it was worth checking out. "Get a team of dogs up there, see if anything turns up along the bank."

"You got it, already have them on alert."

"Thanks. Let me know if we get a hit."

~

Finally, a break. The dogs picked up their trail at the

lake. It wasn't strong. The storm had washed most of it away. The dogs circled, whined, and seemed to be confused. There wasn't any physical evidence left and no footprints, but the dogs were gradually leading the officers away from the lake and into the forest. They were also finding some disturbances in the vegetation, broken branches and moss scraped from trunks. Finally, they came to a small cave. Inside were two parachutes.

"You think they both survived the jump?" asked Agent Morris.

"Yes, Detective. Looks like it. The intensity of the storm they had up here is making it difficult for the dogs, but we think we can get some idea of which way they went. You heading up?"

"Not quite yet. It could prove to be a dead-end. Keep me posted. I can get a chopper up there if you think you can track them."

"Sure, boss. Hey, this is some old dame. Talking to some jumpers and they said that water landing is tricky. I figure we'll find her with him, and he'll be tied up to a tree."

"Wouldn't that be a great ending? Hope you're right." Agent Morris meant it. She wanted a happy ending. "Hey, see if there are any old-timers that know some history about the area. You might turn up something useful."

~

Agent Morris decided to head up to meet with her team. The flight was turbulent; another storm was coming in. The air was heavy and smelled of copper. The dogs were working hard and seemed to be pulling some scents. They kept moving higher into the mountains. The chopper landed in an open area not far from the lake.

The drive into the forest was on rough dirt roads. Agent Morris's stomach hadn't settled from the flight and these bumpy, curved roads were not helping. It was obvious that they had not been used for quite some time. The officers that had gone ahead had cleared several fallen logs off the roads. One team of officers was on foot with the dogs and the support officers were traveling the fire roads as well as they could. These teams brought water, tents, and anything else they would need as they followed the dogs. Usually the handlers had to struggle to keep up with the dogs, but this was slow work. The heavy rain had compromised any trace their prey would have left.

Once Agent Morris caught up with the support team, she was taken to the dogs' location. "Any history we can use?" she asked the agents.

"Well, there was a time when miners worked the area. They didn't find much gold and eventually left. There are stories about mining sites that would provide shelter, but nothing specific. They may be holed up or they may have kept moving south into Mexico," an agent volunteered.

"We've got the border patrol on alert," Agent Morris replied. "Would be tough for him to get through, especially if he's got her with him. Looks like he kept her alive, so we gotta figure they are still together."

"Think we should bring in some choppers to start searching?"

"Not with this storm coming in. Let's give the dogs a little more time. Lot of ground to cover, and nothing looks obvious for a destination. Let's see where the dogs take us."

The dogs were trying so hard. They moved in circles, whining when they found the trail, but would lose it again quickly. They fanned out in large sweeping circles to find it again. The officers were getting frustrated and suggested aerial searching again. Agent Morris was tired and wanted to speed things up, but she knew that there was too much land to cover and a storm moving in. Arthur wasn't stupid. He wouldn't be out in the open. There were no reports from forestry planes that routinely covered the area in search of fires. No non-permit campfires, no smoke. He was lying low, under the radar. No mistakes yet. Yet, was the important word. She had to stay hopeful that he would screw up. "Not yet, let's give the dogs another day. I think they will be our best option."

"What if they didn't hole up? What if they just kept moving?"

"My sense is that Charley wouldn't be pressed that hard. Either we will catch up to them or we will find her dead. He'll have shot her because she was slowing him down."

They heard an excited howl as a one of the hounds picked up the scent. They rushed over to find a pile of excrement at a makeshift bathroom. The dogs were energized. They barked, growled, and ran around the area with their noses flush to the ground.

RAIDER'S Vendetta

Chapter 23

When Raider woke up, he was lying on the ground. His shirt had been torn and used as bandaging for his shoulder. It ached terribly. He smelled meat cooking and his stomach growled. The shadows revealed that it was late afternoon, almost evening. He tried to sit up, but his head was reeling.

"Let me help you," he heard Charley say. She was at his side and supported him while he got up onto his knees. He was then able to stand. She pulled over the stool for him to sit on. He looked around as if in a dream. Charley was frying more of the brown birds, and the wolf was laying close by, watching Raider carefully.

"He's still here, I see," Raider managed.

"I did the best I could with your shoulder. It's pretty bad, Raider. I think you need to think about Step B of your plan. You need a doctor to stitch you up and some antibiotics. He doesn't appear to be rabid though, so I don't think you need any shots." Charley flipped the bird sections in the pan and Raider realized she had his knife. His gun, where was his gun?

"You need to know that I've hidden your gun. I only found one, so I realize you still have another somewhere. That does leave you some leverage, but my friend, Bulwark here, has settled in and I believe will follow your every move. I don't think you want to lose an arm next time." She patted the large wolf on the head. He didn't break his focus on Raider.

Raider felt like he had just fallen down the rabbit hole and he was in Wonderland. He half expected the wolf to fade out, leaving his grinning fangs.

"Are you hungry or thirsty?" She held out a piece of fried bird and his tin cup. Raider slowly accepted the items from Charley, without moving his body from the stool. He didn't want Bulwark to see any of his movements as aggression. He bit into the meat. "There's plenty, but we only got three this time."

"Why didn't you shoot me or take off? If this is God's wolf, won't he lead you out?"

"I tried to coax him, but he wouldn't leave the camp. He wouldn't leave you. Guess he knew you needed protection too – that you would be vulnerable, hurt and unconscious like that."

Raider guffawed at that. "Yeah, right. God would protect me?"

"Yes, Raider. Haven't you understood that the gifts have been for you, too? Why else would God tell me to share?"

Raider chewed his meat slowly and he appeared to be thinking. "I realize you've tied this all up with a big bow, but I'm not buying it. God was never there when I needed him the most. If He is real, then He abandoned me a long time ago."

"Obviously, you have a lot of anger and pain. I wasn't there, but I doubt that God abandoned you."

"Oh really, Charley? You think I'm just overreacting?" His body tensed and he leaned forward. Bulwark growled in warning. Raider pulled back, watching the wolf. "Someone who just didn't get a cushy life? How's this, Charley? My mom deserted me as a small boy and left me with a monster for a father. He finally killed someone and ended up in prison where he died in a fight for cigarettes. I was shipped off to my only living relative, my Aunt Rose. Her idea of taking in a lost, scared kid was to beat me into submission – submission to her precious God - a God that found me vile and a product of sin, a Christian woman who locked a beaten kid in a dark, stinking box for any infraction of her many rules. She kept me there for hours, until she thought I'd pleaded to her God long enough. Years, Charley. He could have stepped in for years. Where was my Bulwark? My protector, Charley?" Raider's rage was building, his hands curled into fists. He wanted so badly to beat God out of her. Raider heard a low growl from the huge wolf. He knew the wolf was watching his every move and probably detected the rage that filled every fiber of his body. He let his hands relax. He had to pacify this mongrel until he could take him down. Raider wanted to shatter Charley's make-believe world, a world with a loving heavenly Daddy, so he continued.

"After surviving the demented beliefs of this woman, I truly found love. An incredible woman who loved me, but she was stoned to death because of religious men. They didn't approve of how she had to support her family. She was an angel and they trapped her in an alley and pummeled her body with rocks until she lay there broken and dead - left for the rats and birds to eat. If He didn't abandon me Charley, then it sickens me that He was present and just watched."

~

Charley didn't know what to say. She looked into his tortured face and felt the tears rolling down her cheeks. Raider looked up from his hands and met her eyes. He couldn't control it; the tears welled up in his eyes, too. Charley instinctually moved to comfort him, but when she got close, he barked at her to stay away.

"You're her, Charley. You represent everything Aunt Rose stood for."

"No, Raider, I don't," Charley whispered. "Your aunt missed the whole point of God. He is love, not condemnation. It isn't supposed to be what she showed you. That was a distortion, a horrible misrepresentation of what God intended for His kids."

"That sounds great, but Charley, he made food appear, he gave you a freakin' wolf to keep you safe. If He loved me, where was He? Where was He?" Raider looked down and she saw his whole body slump with exhaustion.

Charley sat back down, not knowing how to resolve any of this. Where was God in this man's life? It all made so much sense now. What would her beliefs be if she had endured all that he had?

They both saw the wolf stand up and stretch. He moved slowly to Raider and sat in front of him. He laid his head on Raider's lap. Raider raised his hand to push him away, but sat motionless for a few minutes; he then put his hand on Bulwark's head and slowly stroked the thick fur.

The wolf began to lick his other hand. "Why do you call him Bulwark? That's an odd name."

"I know. It means protection. I read it in a story once, and it suits him." *He is your Bulwark, too, Raider,* Charley thought, *maybe it feels too late, but He's here.*

~

Raider agreed to let Charley check his shoulder after they finished eating. She unwrapped the bandages and used some heated water to clean the wounds. They were deep and gaping. "Raider, we gotta get you to a doctor. If these bites get infected, they can kill you. We don't have clean bandages or even topical disinfectant. You didn't pack a first aid kit with the food did you?"

"No, we didn't. This is the perfect solution for you. I'll be dead and the wolf can lead you out."

"Don't think that's God intent. He would have had Bulwark kill you straight out," she said matter-of-factly, without emotion.

Raider glared at her and then at Bulwark, who had positioned himself a distance away while Charley worked on his shoulder. He was still was close enough to attack quickly, if needed. Charley boiled the bloody bandages in a pot of water and added some of the salt. After a few minutes, she wrung them out and rebandaged Raiders wounds. Raider made his way slowly to the cabin without a word.

"Raider, don't be stubborn. We gotta clear out in the morning, before you get too weak to travel. I can't carry you out of here."

Raider tried to get comfortable on the narrow cot, but the wood framing pressed into the injured shoulder. He shifted to his side, but this was an unnatural position for him. He knew he was in for a long, uncomfortable night. Charley was right; they had to leave. It hadn't been a long enough stay for him to slip across the border unnoticed. The police would still be on alert and guards on both sides would want to be a hero and make a capture. He would have to deal with Charley soon. He couldn't cross into Mexico with her and he couldn't leave her alive to tell anyone he was hurt or where he was headed. This would be his first official murder.

The military didn't count. He got paid to kill then. Raider had been present for his Aunt Rose's mugging, but he wasn't the one who killed her. He had ripped up her Bible and tossed it, but Darrell was the one who took her life. She didn't beat Darrell and stuff him in a wooden cell, but she did pound him with God's wrath and told him how disgusting he was. She accused him of terrible thoughts and behaviors that would drag him straight to hell. Darrell hated his mother. For years, he would share his plans for her death with Raider. They would lie in their beds at night and Darrell would try to think of the most embarrassing, disgusting ways he would take her out. Raider considered warning her many times, but there would be another beating and torture in the box. He finally decided that she deserved anything Darrell would dish out.

Raider drifted into a fitful sleep, a sleep filled with the nightmare of his Aunt Rose's death.

~

Darrell, now eighteen, was out again, drinking with his buddies. Itchy knew his aunt would be home soon from one of her many Bible studies and all hell would break loose if Darrell came in drunk. She had threatened to kick him out if it happened again. Itchy was only sixteen and couldn't bear being in that house without Darrell. Darrell didn't protect him, but Itchy was smart enough to know that with Darrell gone, his hell would get worse. He would have all of her focus. He was too big to be put in the box any longer, and the beatings had stopped, but she still had the ability to make his life miserable.

Itchy went looking for Darrell and finally found him. They were almost home. Darrell was sober enough to walk, but drunk enough to be physically maneuvered. He weaved and staggered as Itchy pushed him along. They were almost through the alley when Itchy heard his Aunt Rose screeching at the top of her lungs behind them. "You filthy drunkards. May God cast his wrath on your vile carcasses. You are putrid in His eyes. I cast you away from me. I am done. There is no salvation for either of you. God has found you worthless and so do I." She was moving quickly toward them. They stood frozen, absorbing her words.

She held up her Bible with one arm, swinging her purse around and around with the other as she came closer, preparing to strike them.

Itchy started to run, but felt Darrell tense up, stiff, as he rushed toward his mother. His first punch went into her gut and then his fists pounded her again and again. The rage overtook his drunkenness and he directed all his strength and rage at her body, her face. She went down without a sound as the first punch left her breathless and unable to scream. Itchy watched in horror as Darrell stood over her, unzipping his pants to urinate on her battered body. "No, Darrell, stop! They will know it was you if you pee on her." Darrell looked at Itchy and the realization of what he had done began to show on his face. He zipped his pants back up and, using the corners of his shirt to prevent fingerprints, opened his mother's purse and dumped the contents onto the ground. He picked up the twenty that fluttered out and stuffed it in his pocket. "Thanks Mom," is all he said as he walked toward home.

Itchy was shocked and walked over to the body, careful not to step in any blood. He loved CSI programs and knew there were many ways to leave evidence at a crime scene. The many years of abuse began to rise to the surface and push aside the horror of Aunt Rose's beating. It was almost primal. Itchy felt such a sense of justice and power. He wanted to pee on her himself, at least spit on her, but it would be a stupid thing to do. Then he saw her Bible. He followed Darrell's lead and used his shirt corner to pick it up. He would have his revenge with the one thing she loved the most. He ran home. After hiding the Bible where no one would find it, he went to look for Darrell.

He found him standing in the doorway of his mother's bedroom. "Think I'll sleep in a big fluffy bed tonight, Itchy. I will be on a hard pad for a long time once they figure out what I did."

"No Darrell. They don't have to find out. Don't change your pattern. You gotta sleep in your own bed. Give me your clothes and shoes. I'm going to get rid of them in case there is any blood. Go take a shower and dry your hair with the blow dryer. It can't be wet. Put on the dirty jeans and t-shirt you left on the floor. You don't want to put on clean clothes. Then crash on your own bed. When the cops come, cuz they will, you gotta look like you came home from drinking and flopped on your bed.

If they think you cleaned up, you'll be a suspect for sure. And Darrell, don't brush your teeth! Oh yeah, and if they ask you, you guys argued some, but you love her." Itchy then looked at Darrell's knuckles. Awesome, he thought, no scrapes or scratches. Darrell did everything Itchy told him and fell asleep as soon as his head hit the pillow.

When Itchy was young and trying to find a way out of the vegetable bin, he had worked the backboard loose at the top. There wasn't enough room when he was in the bin to pull it down, so he'd waited for an opportunity when his Aunt Rose wasn't close by to check it out. He pulled the wood panel down and found a hollow space between the house studs. His first thought was to punch a hole through the wall to the outside, but the outside brick facade prevented any break-through. He'd used this cubby for years to hide his treasures from Aunt Rose. It had started with things he found that she would find useless or dirty; Rocks, bird skulls, things boys found priceless. It graduated to girlie magazines and a partial pack of cigarettes, in case he ever wanted to take up smoking. He pushed Darrell's bloody clothes and shoes in next to the Bible and closed it up.

Itchy watched the clock. Aunt Rose was always home by 8:15. Bible study was over at 8:00. He waited until 8:45 before he called 911. "My Aunt Rose is late and I'm getting worried. She's always home by 8:15. Her Bible study was over at 8:00."

"How old are you?"

"Sixteen."

"She's only half an hour late, hon. I'm sure she's fine. Maybe she went for a cup of coffee with friends afterwards."

"She doesn't have any friends."

"Well, we can't do much for forty-eight hours. She's an adult. You have anyone else there with you?"

"Yeah, my cousin, he's eighteen. He got home about an hour ago. He's asleep. "I'm worried that something bad happened," Itchy said, making his best attempt to sound young and pitiful.

The woman on the line paused, "If she's not home by midnight, give us a call, hon. We'll alert the police to keep an eye out."

"Okay. You think she's okay, right?" Itchy used the most innocent

voice he was able to muster.

"I'm sure she is. People change plans all the time."

"Okay, thank you ma'am.

"What we're here for."

Okay, Itchy thought, we're all set. Darrell has an alibi and a concerned family member has missed her. Itchy figured he wouldn't have to wait for midnight. Someone would find her body and the police would be there at any time. Itchy turned on the TV and balled up in the corner of the couch. It was a warm evening and he purposely left the front door open, leaving only the transparent screen closed. The police would see him huddled on the couch when they came up on the porch. He had to wrap his mind around being a worried nephew, waiting for his aunt to get home.

~

At 9:15, Itchy heard a car pull up out front and waited. He wanted the police to see him on the couch. He heard the officers at the door and before they knocked, he jumped up and yelled out, "Aunt Rose, you're finally home!" When he came around the couch and faced the screened door, he stopped. Panic spread over his face. Itchy had practiced this response while waiting for the police to come. "Where's my aunt?" he asked with his lip quivering.

"Can we come in son?" the officer reached for the doorknob.

Itchy stepped back, "I guess. Do you know where my Aunt Rose is?" he asked quietly.

"You here alone, son? Are there any adults home?"

"My cousin, Darrell, is here. He's asleep."

"Can you show us where he is? We need to speak to both of you."

Itchy took one of the officers toward their shared bedroom. The other officer stayed behind, scrutinizing each room as he moved through the house. When they got to the bedroom door, the officer asked Itchy to open the door.

"Darrell, this is the police. We need you to step out here," the officer said firmly. Snoring poured out the open door. "Please wake your

cousin," he instructed Itchy.

"I'll try, but he's been snoring like that since he got back."

"Back? When did he get back?"

"Around 7:30."

"You sure about the time?" the officer asked, glancing at the other cop.

"Yeah, I asked him if he wanted to watch South Park with me, but he said he was tired and was going to bed. I figure he was drunk. He wasn't walking very good."

"Does he drink a lot?"

"Sometimes."

"South Park starts at 7:30 I'm guessing? Well, try and wake him up. We need to talk to him."

Itchy turned on the bedroom light and moved next to Darrell on the bed. He hoped that Darrell wouldn't say anything stupid when he woke up. He shook him lightly at first. "Darrell, you gotta wake up. The police are here. Wake up!" Itchy shook him harder. "Darrell, wake up, I think something bad happened!"

Darrell opened his eyes and looked into Itchy's panicked face. "What's going on, Itchy?"

"The police are here and your mom's not home yet. They want to talk to you."

Darrell shot up and stared at the police. "Where's my mom? Is she alright?"

"We'll talk to you out here, sir."

The officer stepped back into the kitchen and watched as Darrell came in to the light. Itchy was sure they were looking for blood or evidence that Darrell was involved in the murder of his mother.

"Please tell us what's going on," Darrell said to the officer. He looked at the clock. "Mom's not home?" he asked Itchy.

"No, I called 911, but they said she was okay."

"Why didn't you wake me, Itchy?"

"The woman on the phone said she was okay and I should just wait." Itchy was impressed with Darrell's performance.

The officers directed them to sit down at the table and told them that

137

their Aunt Rose had been found beaten to death in the alley nearby. It appeared to be a mugging. Darrell didn't cry out loud, but his eyes teared up. He was so convincing. Itchy, being younger would be expected to show more emotion. He grabbed onto Darrell and cried. Not sobbing, but it was quite touching just the same.

"In any violent crime, we have to first eliminate all family as suspects. We have an investigative team coming over to run some tests and get your statements. Do we have your permission to search the house?"

"Yes, of course, but shouldn't you be looking for evidence where she was mugged?" Darrell was careful not to say murdered. He had to maintain his charade as a grieving son.

"It is procedure to check the victim's home as well as the crime scene. We will wait with you until the team arrives. You are not allowed to discuss the details of the evening between yourselves until we've taken your statements. Once the CSI team is finished, you will be taken to your mother if you choose. We don't recommend it, especially for minors," the officer looked at Itchy, "There has been extensive physical trauma."

Itchy began to tear up again. He wished he had never mentioned South Park to the police. There wouldn't be an opportunity to give Darrell a head's up.

"Whatever you need us to do, sir. I want you to find the animal that did this to my mom."

It was hours before the police left their house. They tested both of the boys for blood on their clothes, under their nails, and in their hair. They went through the house, focusing primarily on the bedrooms. Itchy was thankful that he had stopped Darrell from lying on Aunt Rose's bed. Surely, they would have found his hair. That would be difficult to explain. They checked out Darrell's alibi and his friends were so drunk, they had no idea when Darrell left. When asked what his conversation was with Itchy when he returned home, he was clever enough to say he was so drunk he didn't remember what was said. There was no way to prove or disprove anything. The tests came up clean on everything except his blood alcohol level. He was drunk by legal standards, which reinforced his statement to the police. They couldn't find any evidence to link

Darrell to the crime scene.

The day after Rose was killed, Itchy took Rose's Bible from the hiding space. He sat for some time, flipping through it. Reading all of her notations and the highlighted verses. Most of them were pounded into his memory from the sessions in the cell. He then ripped the Bible to shreds. He used Aunt Rose's dishwashing gloves to be sure there were no prints. He had expected a real rush of revenge, but it was hollow. Itchy found a dumpster some distance away to discard the shredded book.

The church Rose attended covered the cost of her funeral and the house was paid for, so the boys lived comfortably with help from a victim's fund provided by the county until Darrell got a job and social security benefits for Itchy. Itchy was on his own most of the time, which he liked. Darrell introduced him to beer, girls, and petty crime. When Itchy turned eighteen, Darrell was arrested for pushing over a drunk and taking his wallet. He was caught in the act by security cameras. That's when Itchy decided to join the Air Force and left Darrell and his past behind.

~

Raider and Charley didn't hear the howl, but Bulwark did. He whined and paced. The rain soon started and Charley moved into the cabin with Bulwark by her side. She wrapped her blanket around herself and sat on the floor, anticipating another miserable night. Bulwark finally calmed down and lay down next to her. Charley snuggled in and was soon sound asleep. The wolf provided warmth and a soft pillow for her head. Bulwark rested, his breathing slow and rhythmic, but he never slept. He watched Raider on his cot throughout the night.

RAIDER'S Vendetta

Chapter 24

A relief shift came in with a fresh team of dogs. Agent Morris filled them in on the details.

"This guy killed the bank manager?" they asked her.

"No, his partner did. Apparently, the bank manager went for the gun after he opened the vault. In the scuffle, he shot Darrell Anderson while trying to take his gun and then Darrell shot the manager when he tried to run. Don't think Arthur isn't dangerous though. He shot an unarmed female hostage, our pilot and was physically violent with several others. He has extensive military training and should not be underestimated."

It was early evening and the dogs had been quiet, focusing on the task assigned to them. The sweeping patterns and educated guesses by the trainers kept the dogs moving up the mountain. Suddenly, a hound bayed loudly, startling everyone. She had picked up the scent and was pulling her trainer hard. The other dogs began barking excitedly. Agent Morris felt the adrenaline rushing. She was hopeful that they would soon have their target in sight.

They moved quickly, watching the dogs pulling at their leashes. Everyone was so focused on the dogs they didn't notice the storm clouds quickly rolling in. They didn't see the rain coming until the drops started to fall. Lightly at first, but within minutes they were in a downpour. Agent Morris cursed, frustrated and dreading another night huddled in a wet tent. The tents were popped up quickly and Agent Morris crawled into hers, angrier than she'd been in a long time. The rain would hinder their progress.

RAIDER'S Vendetta

Chapter 25

When they woke the next morning, Raider was disappointed to see that the rain was still heavy. He did not look forward to traveling during a downpour, but knew they were running out of time. He was getting weaker and struggled to pull himself off the cot. "Raider, we gotta go," Charley insisted.

"I know, just back off, I need to get the money, I'm not leaving without the money." *The money and the gun* he thought to himself. He wasn't sure how he would get around Bulwark yet, but he would figure something out. He had to. At some point he would kill Charley.

Raider left the cabin and headed to his stash knowing that Charley and the mongrel were following, but he had no choice. His considered shooting her when he was able to get to the gun hidden in the moneybag, but he knew the wolf would be on him in a second and finish him off. He had to keep Charley calm so the wolf wouldn't attack again. Raider considered shooting Bulwark and then go for Charley, but she also had a gun. His odds were not good either way. He still didn't understand how she communicated with the wolf, but he knew that God certainly didn't send him. He had decided that Charley was a witch. Nothing else made sense.

~

Charley had considered taking the blanket but knew that once it was wet, it would weigh a ton and make traveling even more difficult. Once the rain stopped, it would take a long time to dry out enough to be useful. She decided to leave it. Charley didn't know how long

143

they would have to hike before finding a doctor or food. She had to trust that God had a plan.

When they reached Raider's stash, Charley was disappointed to find that a plastic storage tub had been buried in the dirt. Shrubs and rocks protected it from view. She had expected a labyrinth of caves, something more intriguing than a plastic tub. Raider pulled out the moneybag and slipped it under what was left of his shirt. They had agreed earlier that neither of them would be able to manage the terrain in this weather carrying heavy cans of food. They would have to leave everything else behind.

They headed south and made their way slowly through the forest. Charley didn't recognize anything in the downpour. Raider led, followed by Bulwark, and then Charley. Several times Raider had to stop and catch his breath. Charley worried about how she would get help if he collapsed. She certainly had no affection for him, but she had come to respect that God loved him. God provided food and Bulwark; He would see this through. Charley didn't know how, but knew she could trust that it would all work out for the best.

~

At one point, Raider had to wrestle with some undergrowth and felt the bag of money with the gun slip out from under his shirt. He bent over to pick it up and saw that Bulwark had put a huge paw on it. When he tried to touch it, Bulwark growled a clear warning. Raider looked at Charley. "Tell your mutt to give me the bag. I'm not giving up the money."

"I don't tell him what to do. He's his own wolf," she answered.

Raider reached for the bag again and Bulwark snapped at him, grazing his fingers with the sharp teeth. Raider pulled back and before he could react, the wolf grabbed the bag in his teeth and disappeared into the forest.

"Damn it, Charley, call that mangy overgrown dog back here."

She looked at him like he was an idiot. "You still think I control that wolf?"

"I know you do! It's your spirit or familiar or whatever you witches call the poor creatures you embody."

~

Charley laughed in Raider's face. She felt a strong check in her spirit, but had had enough. She didn't care if she wasn't being a good Christian. She was entitled to have her say. What could he do to her, injured and without a gun? She could finally say what she was thinking. She ignored every warning that pulsed through her brain. "You are so blind, Raider. How did you get so stupid? What does God have to do? Step up, shake your hand, and give you his business card? Unbelievable! He sent us food and a protector!" she said with an arrogance that mimicked his Aunt Rose. She continued with all the frustration and anger that had built up since she first saw him push through the bank doors. "God, you are wasting your time on this idiot!"

The next thing Charley knew, Raider had come at her with both fists. She hadn't anticipated his anger overriding his disability. She moved back quickly and began to run. Charley didn't get far before she realized that she was on the ridge she had seen yesterday, the one that dropped hundreds of feet. She stopped and turned to see if Raider was behind her. He was coming, slow, but steady and irate. Charley realized that her mouth had once again gotten her into a situation that was not going to play out well. She knew she had the upper hand, but could she use it? The gun she took from Raider was shoved in her waistband. Charley pulled it out and pointed it at him. He stopped a few feet away.

"Damn, you gonna shoot me with my own gun? Commandment says THOU SHALT NOT KILL, Charley."

"Who says I'll kill you, maybe I'll just cripple you."

"You that good of a shot? What if you hit me in the heart or hit a major artery. You gonna be able to drag me out of here, bleeding, with a bullet in me? What if I die, Charley? God is telling you to feed me, love me. How's he gonna feel if you kill me so close to my salvation?"

"Just stay back and we won't have to see how good a shot I am," she said, mocking him. "And you're nowhere near salvation. Everything God revealed to you was pointless. You are too stubborn to see the grace and compassion you've been given."

Raider moved still closer. Charley shook the gun as if she could scare him into thinking she was capable of pulling the trigger. He laughed at her and took another step toward her. The dense rain, coupled with her poor vision, left her wondering if she could even hit him, let alone where. "Please Raider, I don't want to shoot you, but I will."

Just as the words left her lips, the ground began to slip under her. She was on a thin area of the overhang and the pounding rain had saturated the soil. As she began to fall through, she saw Raider lunge for her. Charley dropped the gun and tried to grab at anything to stop her descent through the ground she stood on. She felt him grab the collar of her shirt as she slipped through the mud and roots. When she stopped falling, she hung suspended over the deep ravine, at the mercy of her captor. Raider was trying to clutch at plants, rocks, anything he found with his bad arm. He finally found a sturdy branch, part of a large tree, rooted deeply away from the ridge.

It took a few seconds for reality to sink in. Raider was belly down in mud, holding onto a branch with his wounded arm and holding onto Charley with his good arm. Charley was dangling over the ravine. Why didn't he just let her slip through and plummet to her death? She was smart enough to know that he wasn't going to let her walk away alive. He had planned to kill her when the time was right.

Charley's weight was dragging him deeper into the mud. *Why had he grabbed her? He should have let her fall. It would solve everything,* she thought. But, here he was, holding her life in his hands. She heard him grunt and groan each time they slid. "Damn it, Charley, you're pulling me with you."

Charley was screaming in her head but nothing came out of her mouth. She felt herself dropping. The realization that Raider was unable to pull her back up made her gut seize in fear. She grabbed at roots and small branches, but nothing was stable enough to support her. She began to cry, close to sobbing.

"Stop it. You're shaking and I'm losing my grip," Raider said through clenched teeth.

Charley pulled herself together and realized that Raider was trying to save her and it confused her. "You gotta let me go Raider. You can't save me and I won't let you go down with me."

"Shut up, Charley. I'll figure something out."

Charley felt herself drop a few more inches. "Raider, you gotta let go," she said, resigning herself to her fate.

~

Raider knew it was hopeless, but could he let go? He would have been able to shoot her, put her out of her misery quick, but could he let her fall to her death – maybe taking hours to die?" He tightened his grip. The burn in his damaged shoulder was turning into a ripping pain. His good arm had a strong grip on her collar, but he felt himself sliding in the mud. Even if he didn't drop her, how would he get her up? The slippery mud provided no traction to pull either of them back up. Still, he held on.

~

Charley felt herself drop again, maybe six inches this time. She couldn't let Raider die. He needed to find God. She tried again. "Let go Raider, it's useless."

"Where's your God, Charley? Tell Him to fix this. I'm not dropping you off a cliff. If you go, then I go too. You want my soul, God? Then you better get down here quick." Charley knew her mouth had put her here. This wasn't God's plan. If only she had listened to the Holy Spirit's warning.

Charley waited a moment to see if God would show up, but more of the wet bank slipped away and, with the next drop, at least a foot, she knew what she had to do. "Last chance Raider, let go." She reached up and dug her nails into Raider's arm. They weren't terribly effective, broken and soft from the humidity.

"Ouch, you stupid old hag. I'm not letting go."

Charley knew she only had one option. "Raider, God loves you. He has peace and healing for you. Promise me that you'll talk to Him, just

147

you and Him. Your aunt was wrong. She did not hear God."

"Knock it off, Charley. I don't want to hear your crap. Do you know where you are? You are without a God, hanging off a cliff. You're going to fall and be smashed on the ground, broken in little pieces!"

She saw the top of Raider's head now. He was slipping and coming through the gaping hole she'd made. She had to do something before it was too late. Charley prayed quietly to herself, and then took a moment to picture her children and grandchildren. With tearful eyes, she said firmly, "Bye, Raider. Find Him." With those last words, Charley unbuttoned her shirt, starting from the bottom. The last few buttons tore loose from her weight and she slipped out.

"Noooooo!" Raider screamed.

~

Raider lay in the mud, not moving. His sliding had stopped, but he felt the ground below him shift. He pulled up his arm and stared at the shirt. He let go and watched it flutter and float in the wind as it made its way down to Charley. He knew he had to get off the overhang before it collapsed on top of her, carrying him with it. With some effort, he was able to pull the gun from the mud and slide back on stable ground. Raider stood up and, with intense rage, confusion, and frustration, he shook his fist at the sky and cursed God. He heard a rumbling and the ledge crumbled and fell down on Charley. Raider hoped she'd died on impact. The thought of her hurt and buried alive was too much, even for him. He knew this area, and there was no way to get to her from where he was. He yelled "Charley!" at the top of his lungs, hoping for a response. He heard nothing but the wind.

Chapter 26

Charley felt herself fall. She thought she would splat at the bottom in the blink of an eye, but she seemed to be falling in slow motion. She could see the far side of the ravine as she dropped. Lord, I am at your mercy, do as You see fit, repeated over and over in her head. She didn't have a clean plunge straight down. The ledge overhang hid the trees jutting out, as well as the rocks. She felt herself hit the branches of a tree. It hurt, but seemed to slow her down. Then another smack, this one hard, and she felt the bone in her leg snap. She was tumbling now. Hitting branches and rolling, falling, then another slam to her right arm. The pain was intense. Charley's head made contact with one of the boulders and it was the last thing she remembered. Her limp body tumbled down the face of the ravine, landed on an incline of mud, and slid the remainder of the distance, coming to a stop at the bottom. She would have been frantic when the ledge above broke loose and slid down on top of her, but she was no longer aware of anything except the deep realms of her unconscious brain.

~

Her wolf waited at the bottom of the ravine and positioned his body over her face to protect her from the avalanche of mud. Once it was safe, he pulled himself out of the sludge and carefully licked the mud from her face, which allowed her to breathe. She didn't move, but the wolf sensed that she was still alive. Bulwark positioned himself to block her face from the rain and water running down the ragged furrow her body had carved out. He constantly licked her face to keep her mouth and nose clear. The rest of her body was covered in mud, which provided protection and warmth.

By afternoon, the rains had stopped. Bulwark pushed Charley's face with his snout, trying to wake her. He howled a deep, aching plea to the heavens, but she slept, unaware of her predicament or her injuries. The wolf quietly whined and stood guard by her body.

~

"Where was it?" Charley wondered. She heard it, but was unable to find her way to the crying infant. She was in a hospital with many halls and rooms. Charley would lumber, trying to maneuver with her broken limbs. The pain was intense and pounding. Just when she thought she was close, the sad wails of the baby clear and distinct, she would see another hallway or stairwell telescope out in front of her, pulling her further and further away. Her heart ached to find and comfort the baby, to end the sad cries. Just as she reached her destination, and heard the infant on the other side of the door, the floor opened up beneath her. She fell through mud, roots, and rocks. She felt herself suffocating and clawing at the muck that encased her.

As her breath left her body, she felt a strong tug on her wrist, and saw daylight. Once her eyes focused, she was looking into the face of Archie. "Hello darlin', you ready to come?"

"Ready to come where?" she asked in confusion.

"With me silly, an eternity with me."

Charley looked down and she was in a beautiful dress with sparkling high heels. The dress was shades of purple melting in to each other. Her shoes were a deep plum covered in glitter. She saw a mirrored wall behind Archie and stepped around him so she could see her reflection. She was breathtaking, even to herself. She was younger, thinner, and glowing. Archie stood beside her, looking into the mirror and grinning from ear to ear. He was handsome, sporting a dramatic black tuxedo.

"You will like it here. It's a new adventure every day."

"Here? Where are we Archie?"

Archie held her close and whispered lovingly how much he missed her and adored her. Charley melted into Archie and felt the joy that surrounded him. "Am I dead, Archie? Am I in Heaven with you?" Before Archie answered, she felt him evaporating in her arms – his sweet murmurings of "Not yet my love" were replaced with the howl of a wolf. She was suffocating in the slime again, sliding deeper and deeper, then into empty darkness.

~

Hours passed as the wolf continued to provide shelter from the elements and ward off hungry, curious wildlife. Bulwark's presence and formidable growl kept the hungry animals a safe distance away. He guarded her while she drifted through the desires and fears of her soul.

~

The wind was warm on her face. The lake was a swirling mass of diamonds. She leapt from the helicopter and drifted down. As she hovered over the surface of the water, she began flapping her arms. Charley's body lifted up and she was flying. It was an incredible sensation. She pulled herself up and soared over the forest until she came to the cabin. She landed softly on the ground, tiptoeing, looking for Raider. If he was still here, she would fly away. But, what if he was able to fly also? She knew she had to be careful. She also knew she had to find him. It was an unexplainable obsession.

Charley was swept into the cabin, knowing it was dangerous. She was just inside when a door slammed shut behind her. It startled her because there had been no door when she entered. She heard Raider's cruel laughter in the pitch-black room. There was a red glow building at the far end of the cabin and she saw the silhouette of Raider. His eyes, which must have been closed before, suddenly burned fiery red as he glared at her. His laughter subsided and he began to speak in a deep, hateful voice. "Charley, where is your God, you stupid woman? He has left you to die in the wilderness. Your body is broken and will be ravaged by the creatures He created. When will you admit that you are nothing to Him but a toy He can play with and destroy at will?"

A sense of hopelessness overtook Charley. She looked down and saw the blood and broken bones protruding through her flesh. The pain began to swell within her, making her drop to the floor in agony. Where was her God? He had forsaken her. Maybe Raider was right. Maybe she had bought into the fantasy and now she had to face that she was all alone. Alone except for this berserk man who hated her. The wallowing of self-pity swirled around her, permeating her mind. She was an old, stupid woman. Raider had been moving closer, watching the devastation he had unleashed. His face showed cruel delight in his handiwork. He reached Charley, placed a scaled hand below her chin, and lifted her face up. She looked into the burning eyes and felt herself melting into them, melting into the fire. It was the core of Raider's hatred, the demon that tormented him.

She heard an ear-shattering howl and then the cabin canvas ripped open. Bulwark lunged into the cabin through the canvas wall. Raider pulled back with terror on his face as the wolf sank his teeth into the throbbing flesh of Raider's neck. Scarlet blood gushed over Charley as Bulwark pushed Raider to the floor and devoured him. She plunged into a place of peace and the pain left her body.

Chapter 27

Donald, seventy-nine years old, called himself an 'Old Fart.' He'd spent his summers in the mountains ever since he'd retired from his position as a geologist for the University of San Diego ten years ago. His life was rocks, geodes, gems, fossils, and his wife, Loraine. Loraine loved their summers in the Sierra Mountains, but she was always ready to return to their small apartment in San Diego for the cold weather. Loraine had died last year and Donald had moved out of the apartment, planning to brave his first winter at the cabin. If he died, he died, but at least he would live or die surrounded by his beloved rocks and his precious memories of Loraine. They'd never had any children and Donald was ready to join her wherever she was.

They had made the perfect homestead, a small, but adequate home for two. There was a well on the property and they were set up with propane and pellet burning stoves for heat, no wood chopping or woodpiles to keep dry. The Department of Forestry insisted that they have a short-wave radio, since they couldn't get a phone line this far out and cell phones didn't work. Donald checked in every few days, so someone knew he was okay.

Today would be his last long hike for the season. The temperatures were cooling already and his joints ached from the cold. Donald knew his limits and he would be sticking close to the cabin until spring.

The rain continued most of the day. He was dying to get out and hit his favorite spot. He didn't resent the rain; it was actually his friend. Many wonderful discoveries were made after a good rain. The soil was washed away to expose new crevices and the ground was soft for digging. It was especially helpful when it cleared dirt and debris from the rocky terrain. He just hoped that it would stop soon. Winter was approaching quickly and he didn't want to miss out on his last hike of the season.

~

By late afternoon, the skies were clear and Donald had packed his equipment. That evening, Donald settled into his recliner and drifted off to sleep. He dreamed of Loraine and their life here at the cabin.

Donald acted surprised that she had provided a meal he loved. It was silly, a game they played. He was in the house all day and smelled the ground turkey, vegetables, and broth simmering. He knew exactly what she was cooking, but gave her the joy of pleasing him by letting it appear to be a surprise. After a good, hot meal of thick soup, green salad, and garlic bread, Donald got comfortable in his recliner. Loraine laid a warm knitted throw over his legs to keep the damp air from invading his bones. Loraine was close by, reading her current romance novel, and Donald made some notes in his journal and planned his route for the next day. The pellet stove radiated waves of heat to take away the chill of the evening. Soon, Loraine was urging him to wake up and go to bed. He slept better in the recliner, but obeyed and followed her into the bedroom.

Now that Loraine was gone, he slept most nights in his chair. He missed her the most when he lay in the bed, alone. He set his alarm for an early rise, but knew he wouldn't need it.

The surrounding mountains had become his backyard. He knew every ravine, every creek-bed, every cave. Many areas had looked promising, but after years of searching, they offered no treasures, while other spots had proven themselves, concealing incredible discoveries. If he got an early start, he would have enough time and daylight to visit his favorite one before he surrendered to nature and his age.

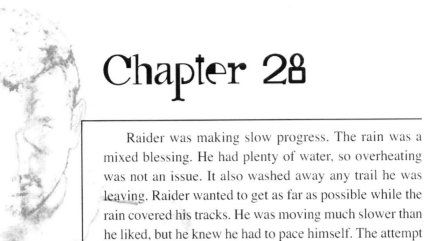

Chapter 28

Raider was making slow progress. The rain was a mixed blessing. He had plenty of water, so overheating was not an issue. It also washed away any trail he was leaving. Raider wanted to get as far as possible while the rain covered his tracks. He was moving much slower than he liked, but he knew he had to pace himself. The attempt to save Charley had pumped him up with adrenaline, but once it left his system, he felt drained. So many thoughts ran through his head. Was Charley dead or suffering? Would the wolf show up to avenge her? Would he survive the long hike out of the mountains? Why had he tried to save her? That last one haunted him. He had been convinced that he was a man of survival. Emotions, obligations, and empathy did not cloud his judgment. Raider was confused by his reaction to grab her. Where did that come from? Was it primal humanity? He tried not to dwell on it. It felt like a crack in his thick wall of indifference.

The ache in his shoulder was increasing. Raider felt a warm flush over his upper torso. He knew that infection was his biggest concern right now. The will to live overtook his pain and exhaustion and he pressed on.

RAIDER'S Vendetta

Chapter 29

Agent Morris endured a miserable night in the tent. It was cold and damp as the storm raged through the night. She woke to more rain and finally moved to the large tent that was set up with coffee and tables. She sipped hot coffee, warming herself from the inside out, and nibbled on gooey sweet rolls, packaged in plastic. Agent Morris watched the rain and hoped that it was just as debilitating to Raider's situation. The dogs were useless in this downpour and they knew it was washing away any scent left from the newly discovered trail they were following. They would have to stumble onto a fresh trail and pray that there was enough scent left to follow. The team asked if they should remain or pack it up. Agent Morris wasn't ready to give up. She had to wait it out, at least for a few more hours. The fighter in her just wouldn't give up the chase, not when they were so close. Agent Morris felt it.

~

About four o'clock in the afternoon, the rain stopped. They looked at the soaked landscape and felt hopeless. Again, Agent Morris was asked what she wanted to do. "Let's just head straight up for a few miles. See if anything grabs us. I can't shake the feeling that we are close to something." The team loaded up on hot coffee and put on their warm gear. The air was damp and cold. The dogs were eager to get moving again. No one talked as the dogs attempted to pick up a scent, but they whined and stayed in the heeled position next to their trainers most of the time. The terrain was steep and slippery and they were soaked from pushing through the wet vegetation. Agent Morris could see the apathy building in the group. She was beginning to look like a fool. How long was she going to chase after a ghost?

Suddenly, they broke through some trees and found a canvas cabin. Agent Morris and the other officers pulled out their guns and took a defensive position. The dogs went crazy, howling and straining toward the cabin. The treasure the dogs had sought was right there. The smell of their prey filled their senses.

Agent Morris yelled out, "The area is surrounded, come out with your hands over your head." She waited. Nothing. Several officers slowly moved toward the cabin and then looked inside. No one was there. They motioned for Agent Morris to come closer. The inside was disgusting. Everything was there, just as Arthur and Charley had left it. Blankets, camp stove, and blood. The cot and blanket at the back of the tent was stained with a substantial amount of blood. Agent Morris hoped that it was Arthur's blood and not Charley's. They would know soon enough. The dogs confirmed that Arthur's and Charley's scents were present in the cabin. She was still alive, or had been recently.

The team was searching the immediate area to see if Arthur and Charley were still in the vicinity. It was a stretch, since the dogs could be heard for at least a mile. Arthur would be on the run, but maybe Charley was close by. They found the spring and the plastic bin. Arthur hadn't worried about burying it when they left. The location was called in and crime scene investigators were on their way. The nearest clearing flat enough for a helicopter was at least three miles away. The team and their equipment would have to be transported to the cabin. It was an involved process. Luckily, there was an old, overgrown fire road, too arduous for vehicles, but easy enough for quad runners. They would be set up in four to six hours.

The dog teams split up and began canvassing the area around the cabin. Tents and provisions from base camp arrived and Agent Morris could smell coffee brewing and food cooking. She realized she was ravenous.

The search teams returned and reported the location of areas used for bathrooms and trash. They were amazed to find shriveled apple cores, nectarine pits, and orange peels. Agent Morris wondered how they could have had fresh produce available to them.

The dogs were fed and ready to go back out, but they quickly became frustrated. The scents in the cabin were overpowering, but a short distance away left them with nothing. The officers looked for obvious paths that someone might take if they were heading south, but the terrain was pristine, without any indication of trails or easy passage. They came to a deep ravine when they headed due south. There was no way that anyone would have scaled these steep walls. This meant that Arthur had to go east or west to get around. Their team would split up to cover both directions. Maps of the area revealed a long ravine that Arthur wouldn't be able to cross for many miles. They didn't know how much of a head start he had yet, but the investigation team might be able to give an estimate once they examined the cabin and any evidence they found.

Agent Morris was encouraged that Arthur's escape route was limited. This was a big advantage for them. If he was heading south, he only had two options, not hundreds, with only a few degrees between them. They would head out at first light. The terrain was treacherous in the dark.

RAIDER'S Vendetta

Chapter 30

The rain stopped and Raider was exhausted. He had covered a lot of ground under the blanket of rain. He found some rocks to curl up in. The ground was soaking wet and cold, but the rocks had dried quickly. His shoulder was on fire and throbbed with pain. *I need to rest, just a little while,* he thought to himself. As sleep overtook him, Raider entered the mixed blessing of much needed rest and the torture of memories.

~

He was bored; being on base with so many idiots was taking its toll. Arthur liked to have a drink and relax, but these guys obsessed over it. They weren't happy until they were all staggering, vomiting piles of stupidity. There were a few that didn't drink, but they were Bible thumpers. When they saw he wasn't partying like the others, they assumed God was in control of his life, that he needed a higher authority to keep him sober and make his decisions. He made it quite clear what he thought of their God and they left him alone. Arthur suspected he was on their prayer list, which annoyed him, but it was their time they were wasting.

Arthur enjoyed flying helicopters. He was a bird, a bug, whatever he wanted to pretend. The freedom of leaving the ground and being able to soar through the sky was the closest he had ever come to true joy. It got sticky at times, being the target of the enemy's artillery, but it was also a rush. Knowing that it was you or them amped him up. He was a good pilot, but everyone had a time to check out. Arthur had thought that was how he'd go out;

getting hit and crashing suited him.

One evening, however, the boredom was intolerable. He heard about a section of Baghdad that offered prostitutes. A real contradiction for such a religious country, but there they were. Guess man's desire always makes a way. He enjoyed sex and that was his goal, but his deeper need was companionship. He would never admit it, but Arthur had felt the drain of loneliness all of his life. He had tried dating women and having relationships, but the smart ones wanted to control you. Tell you what to wear, what to say, how to think. The dumb ones got boring. He tried a few barflies, but they disgusted him after a short time. They needed the alcohol to loosen up – laughing like hyenas and trying to be seductive with slurred speech and bloodshot eyes. There didn't seem to be a middle ground, so he gave up and resorted to buying sex when the urges overtook him. He got what he wanted and didn't have to humor them, pretend to care about their emotional needs, romance them, or put up with their families. He would satisfy himself and be done with them.

He found the apartments he was looking for and saw several women in the shadows. It was eerie and felt dangerous. He was used to brazen, half-naked women flaunting their wares, not ghost-like women shifting in the darkness.

The language was another barrier. He had picked up a few words in the local dialect but it was minimal at best. As he moved closer, hoping that these truly were women and not radicals waiting to cut his throat, they seemed to slip out of the darkness, many more than he'd first suspected. One woman pushed her way through and laid her hand on his arm, an extremely bold move for this culture. She had a shawl over her head, which covered most of her face. He pulled the shawl up and saw an average looking woman of about thirty-five. She could have been anyone's mother. She grinned at him and revealed missing teeth. Arthur shuddered.

Another woman pushed herself in front of him, and pulled back her head covering enough for him to see her face. She was much younger and quite lovely. She had an aggressive expression, which excited him. Arthur didn't know what the going rate was. He had converted some American money into Dinar. He held the money out. This prostitute took all the money and, as she attempted to stuff it in a small bag she carried, another woman moved up and grabbed her arm. She said something in Arabic and the woman backed away. Arthur found himself looking into the face of an angel. "She was cheating you. She took three times what is usual," she said in English as she handed Arthur his money.

Arthur was looking at the most beautiful woman he had ever seen. Her eyes were a deep brown, almost black. Her nose turned up at the tip and she had full, natural red lips. Her skin was a beautiful taupe that glowed. She wore no makeup and her beauty was breathtaking. "Thank you," was all he would say.

He wanted her, but he didn't know if she was also a prostitute and he didn't want to insult her by asking. What if she wasn't?

"You have to be careful out here. Not all of us are honest. Some will take you off to their husbands, brothers, or fathers. Your body will end up out in the desert, carved and beheaded. Many people are thankful for the Americans, but many are not."

She had said us, not them. Us. It implied that she was also looking for customers. "Would you drag me off to have me carved up?" he asked with a hint of humor. He wanted to confirm her profession without insulting her.

"No, it would be stupid to kill off my customers," she said, quite seriously.

Arthur grinned. "Well, I would like to enjoy your company if you are available," he said sincerely. She smiled back and took his hand. She led him into the maze of apartments until they reached her door. As they entered, she asked him to be quiet. Her brother and father were asleep in the back room. This reminded him of when he was a teenage boy, sneaking around a girl's parents. He felt himself becoming aroused.

He was all about his release, his pleasure. He was drawn to this woman, but wasn't looking for a relationship, not here, not with a whore. But, the intimacy connected her to him in a way he could not explain. This was different from any encounter he'd had with other professional women. The others were flirty, nasty, and crude. She was tender and kind and when Arthur entered her, he saw shame and sadness on her face. He couldn't complete the act. He moved off of her and stared at the ceiling.

"Why do you do this? Obviously, it is not what you want to do," he said softly. She was on the verge of tears.

"I'm so sorry. Please give me another chance. I can do better."

Arthur rolled over and looked into her doe eyes. He felt the contradiction. She didn't want to be here, but needed to pretend that she did. "Isn't there something else you can do to earn money?"

She seemed drained when she realized he was not going to use her services; she was not going to earn the money she desperately needed. She needed him to leave so she could find another customer. She would do it right - be happy and sexy, fool the next man into thinking she wanted him. Her culture trained women not to show anger, but his question made her want to punch him in the face. Did he think she would choose this if there was another choice?

"I am so sorry that I displease you. I am sure one of the other women will take good care of you. I will take you back to the courtyard." She started to get up and Arthur grabbed her wrist.

"What is your name?" he asked.

"Badria" she answered.

"I want you, Badria, just you," Arthur said and meant it.

She lay back down and waited for him to continue. He turned on his side and looked into her face. The moonlight was filtering down and she looked incredible.

"How many men do you see each night?" he asked.

"One, maybe two," she answered, blushing with shame.

"Okay, I will pay for two if you relax and talk to me."

Badria looked at him, confused. "You just want me to talk to you? You will pay me to do this?" she asked.

"Yes, just talk to me. First, I want to know, where did you learn to speak English so well?"

Badria relaxed and they talked deep into the night. She explained about her mother's passion for all things American. Her mother was a doctor in Afghanistan before the Taliban took over. She was a brilliant woman who educated her children. Once under the rule of the Taliban, she was broken – her spirit and then her body. She was not allowed to practice medicine and was under the total rule of her husband. She was crushed that her husband so easily assumed the position of master. They had always had a loving, equal partnership. She thought that it was out of fear at first, but then she realized that he liked the power his twisted beliefs gave him. She died and left Badria alone with her brother and father. They discussed her early years when life was good and then how everything had turned dark and scary when the Taliban entered their world.

Arthur didn't touch her in a sexual way, but tenderly. He would stoke her face, her hair. At one point, she lay with her back nestled into him and he held her while she described the dreams she once had. She'd wanted to travel the world, study art, and open her own gallery. Eventually, Arthur drifted off to sleep and was awakened by Badria gently shaking him. "You can't be here when my family wakes up. You must leave." Another shake and then blinding sunlight pierced his eyes.

Arthur jerked back to the present, on the rocks again. The sun, which had gently warmed him, was now roasting him. The rocks were hot to the touch when he attempted to get up. He was dazed and still between dream and reality. Arthur moved into the trees and continued his escape. He was disoriented and his thinking was numbed by pain. Luckily, for him, his military training put him on autopilot and he traveled east. He would soon come to a place where he would cross over. Since the rain had stopped, the ground was drying and he would be leaving a scent trail again soon. He wasn't sure why, but he felt the need to travel quickly, to take advantage of the saturated soil.

Arthur was moving through the underbrush, staying away from open areas. With each sound he heard, his paranoia increased. He was sure he was being followed or that silent, stealth helicopters above were searching for him. When Arthur came into a small clearing, he was shocked to see Charley. She was standing there, bloody and broken, smiling at him. The bones jutted out from her thighs. She reached her hand out to her right and Aunt Rose stepped out of the trees and joined her. They held hands like schoolgirls who were best friends. They swung their arms and grinned at him as if they had a secret. His Aunt Rose looked the way she had that night in the alley, battered to hell. Then the laughing started. The two women began a shrill, high-pitched squeal of delight. They released their hands and began clapping with excitement. Arthur kept blinking his eyes. They were dead, yet they stood before him – mocking him. What did they know?

Suddenly Arthur felt the teeth of the wolf clamp down on his injured shoulder. Blood and infection spurted up on his face. He dropped to his knees and they watched with sheer joy as the wolf mauled him. Arthur turned his head and stared into the blue eye of the beast biting him, then passed out. The fever had induced torturous hallucinations.

Chapter 31

Raider woke in the early hours before sunrise to a terrible ache in his shoulder and head. He was coherent enough to remember that he was in the wilderness and dying. He had to keep moving. He wasn't far from the bridge, the bridge that would get him across the ravine and heading south again. Raider knew he needed medical help, but that would have to wait until he crossed the border. Raider pulled himself up and managed to cover the last two miles to the rickety, wooden bridge. He sat down and rested. His strength was drained and he felt his circumstances closing in around him. Raider truly feared that he would die in these forsaken mountains just as Charley had.

Raider drifted off, hoping his body would recharge and allow him to continue. The hallucinations started to churn and swirl in his fever-ravaged brain. He jumped from the vegetable bin to a tree with Pagne at Langston Hall. Then just as quickly, he was in the bank screaming at Darrell to leave. Next, cute fluffy rabbits circled him, grinned, and then dropped dead. The pile of rabbits continued to build until he was buried alive in the soft fur.

Raider heard a deep growl. He was startled when he realized the sound wasn't in his head. He opened his eyes to see a large black bear staring down at him. Raider froze; there was no way for him to escape. The bear was sniffing and licking its lips. The smell of Raider's blood filled the bear's nostrils. His gun was useless. He could not take the bear down before it ripped him apart, but he couldn't lay there frozen indefinitely either. Raider decided to go down fighting and began screaming as he reached for his gun. His quick movement summoned a deep, menacing growl and the bear attacked him. Raider pulled the gun out, but it was knocked out of his hand as the claws tore at him with incredible force. He wrapped his bloody arms over his chest and gut, protecting his vital organs.

In the frenzy of fur, claws, and roars, Raider thought he saw a flash of gray. He passed out from the pain and escaped into unconsciousness.

Chapter 32

Donald was up early. His backpack contained his digging tools, strong nylon cord, a flashlight, a knife, trail mix, a water bottle, a small first aid kit and a rain slicker, just in case. There was also a roll of biodegradable toilet paper and a large mesh bag for holding his treasures. Donald blew a kiss to the cabin, as he had done on every trip as Loraine watched him head out. His excitement was building as he headed north, to the deep, long ravine that was his favorite place to dig. The joy of the birds singing and the smell of clean air filled his spirit with peace. If there was a God, Donald would be thanking Him for this gift, but being a man of science, he couldn't buy into an all loving Father in the sky. He believed in evolution. It wasn't as romantic as creation, but it made sense to him.

Donald had grown up in a loving family where education was the focus. Both of his parents had been teachers, his father a science teacher, his mother an English professor. His mother had loved books with a passion that melted over onto her children. Donald was the eldest, followed by his sister Kaithlyn who was two years younger, and his brother Sam, the youngest, who had come to their family when his parents were in their early forties. Sam had been a surprise and He had joined the Marines and died in Desert Storm. It broke their hearts. He was the sweet clown that everyone adored. Donald still felt a twinge of regret that he would never see Sam again. He had entertained the thought of Heaven when Sam died, thinking he would love to have eternity with him, but science had prevailed and Donald had to say farewell. Sam had been the only family member who believed in Heaven and had a relationship with Jesus.

RAIDER'S Vendetta

It took Donald several hours to reach the mouth of the ravine. It split off in two directions. He headed to his left, which led to the area that was productive and held treasures. The direction to the right had been useless. He had spent hundreds of hours in backbreaking digging and found nothing substantial. He wouldn't waste his precious time on this last trip out. He moved into the ravine and turned to his left, but then stopped. He felt a pull to go to the right. It confused him. His pride? He wanted to challenge what he already knew? No, this was stupid. He knew exactly where he wanted to go. He had been there only days ago and found several large gold chunks. Donald believed he had found the edge of a large deposit. His steps continued to the left. As he made his way into the ravine, he felt a longing to go to the right. It made no sense. "You're getting senile old man," he said aloud. "You've given that blasted area too much of your time. You might only have today."

Donald pushed down the impulse to go to the right and headed to his favorite spot. He was excited to see what was hiding there. The rain would make his digging much easier. As Donald came around the first curve, his heart sank. Fallen trees and a landslide had filled the narrow passage. "Damn it!" He didn't need a difficult journey. The site of his last dig was several miles beyond the barricade and he didn't want to use up his strength crawling through this maze. "You gotta try, can't be that bad," he said. Donald loved his time alone, but he had started talking to himself out loud. He supposed that it offered some sense of companionship.

Donald approached the pile of debris. He looked at it from several viewpoints and was a little discouraged. It was a mess. He pushed and pulled on several of the smaller branches, but nothing shifted. It appeared to be tightly compacted. "Looks like the only option is to climb over this mess. Certainly not getting through here," Donald said, disappointed. Donald was in good shape for his age, but the idea of trying to maneuver over this barrier created anxiety. He knew the dangers of twisting an ankle or worse. Breaking a leg would be suicide out here. He had checked in with the forest rangers that morning, so they wouldn't miss him for days.

"You can do it, Donald. Just be slow and careful. Make sure your footing is secure before you move on." As Donald made his way to the top of the barricade, his confidence soared. He was moving slowly, but successfully. His anxiety began to build again when he realized that he didn't know if he could scale the other side. "You'll have to decide once you get to the top, old man. You've come this far, don't give up now."

When Donald reached the summit of rock, dirt, branches, and vegetation, he felt like he'd won a contest. He put both arms up and yelled. He felt foolish immediately after, but grinned anyway. He looked down and was relieved to see an easy descent. He turned to position himself and heard a low growl. He froze. Slowly he turned his head to see a huge gray wolf with piercing blue eyes sitting on the ground below him. Donald hadn't seen him when he looked just moments ago. The wolf growled again.

Donald knew he couldn't outrun this powerful animal and he hadn't thought to pack his gun. He hadn't seen any predatory wildlife in years. "Oh, you stupid, stupid man. You're going to die here today," he whispered. There were only two choices. Freeze and wait for the wolf to come up or get down as quickly as he could and run. Donald chose the second and got down quicker than he ever thought he could. The adrenaline rush gave him strength and the courage to flee. Once off the barricade, Donald ran toward the mouth of the ravine. He would keep running until he couldn't. He had to get as far as possible from the wolf. Donald glanced back and didn't see the wolf chasing him. He thought it was odd, but kept running, his heart and lungs struggling to keep up with his fear.

Once he got to the mouth of the ravine, panting and aching in every joint, he stopped dead in his tracks. The wolf was in front of him, blocking his passage out of the ravine. "How? This makes no sense. These walls are too high and steep for you to come around ahead of me," Donald said, more to himself than the wolf. The wolf didn't growl but moved closer to Donald. Donald began to back up. The wolf circled around him, to the left, and moved closer, keeping his head low, his blue eyes staring into Donald's. Donald backed up again and realized that the wolf was herding him into the right arm of the ravine. Maybe other wolves were waiting. Maybe they would rip into his flesh and he would spend his last day feeding the wild animals of his beloved mountains. There was some poetry to it. He would live on forever. "No Donald, you'll just be dead, and it will hurt. Do you want them chomping into you? You have to do something!" Donald said aloud as he pulled his backpack off and began swinging it, screaming at the top of his lungs. He took a step closer to the wolf. The wolf didn't move. Donald took another step closer, but the wolf still didn't move.

In the blink of an eye, the backpack swung in front of the wolf and the wolf grabbed it with his teeth and pulled. Donald lunged toward the wolf and dropped the pack. He turned and ran into the ravine, in the very direction the wolf had wanted him to go. Donald stopped and looked ahead, waiting to see a ferocious pack of crazed wolves, salivating for his old, wrinkled flesh. Nothing. He looked back at the wolf. The wolf was walking slowly toward him, still holding the pack in his teeth. Donald felt a strange sense of relief. If the wolf kept the pack in his mouth, then he couldn't bite him. The wolf was only a few feet away and he growled a deep warning growl. Donald kept backing into the belly of the ravine. The reality of his situation began to sink in. He was being herded by a huge wolf that could take him down in a matter of seconds, rip out his throat, and feed on his still pulsing flesh. His heart was beating out of his chest. What did this animal want with him? The wolf's size suggested he was a male, but if he was a female, it was too late in the season for pups. Thankfully, he wasn't being led to feed a litter of pups. The thought of being gnawed to death by cute, fluffy puppies was just too disturbing to consider. He wouldn't rule out a pack of crazed wolves, but that seemed less viable the longer they traveled.

Donald heard the wolf growl behind him. When he stopped and turned around, the wolf had dropped the backpack. The wolf stepped back and stared at the pack, then back at Donald. Donald had the distinct impression that he was supposed to pick up the pack. He moved slowly toward it and with each step he took, the wolf took another step back. It was a strange dance. When he picked up the pack, he heard the water bottle slosh. He opened the flap and pulled out the bottle. He showed it to the wolf. What odd behavior, he thought, but he knew the wolf was in charge and he needed to treat him with respect. The wolf sat down and waited. Donald took a long drink of the refreshing water. The wolf suddenly growled and looked at the backpack. Donald replaced the cap and slid the bottle back in. The wolf had apparently decided he'd had enough. The wolf stood up and took a step toward Donald. It was time to move on. "Where are you taking me?" he asked, fascinated. Donald relaxed a little when he realized the wolf was not going to attack him from behind. The wolf seemed to have a destination in mind so, until they arrived, Donald felt somewhat safe.

~

Donald wove his way through the rocky crevice. The wolf kept his distance behind, but pushed him nonetheless. The fear of death had faded. The wolf had the ability to end his life at any time, but didn't. He needed Donald for something.

His old legs were beginning to throb and he was thirsty. He stopped and opened his pack. He pulled out the water bottle and trail mix. The wolf growled viciously and Donald shoved the items back into his pack. The wolf took several steps closer, indicating that he was to continue.

When they rounded the next curve, the wolf ran past Donald to an area piled with debris from a mudslide. The wolf whined and paced. Donald walked over and saw what appeared to be the body of a woman covered in mud. Her face was the only part of her that wasn't buried. He looked at the wolf, shocked that this animal had led him to the woman. He must be her pet, Donald thought. Donald moved quickly to her side and felt for a pulse, nothing. She appeared to be dead, killed by the avalanche. Donald stood up and looked at the wolf with sorrow. "She's gone, boy," he said with compassion.

The wolf growled deep and fierce. He nudged and licked Charley's face while staring at Donald. Donald saw her eyelashes flutter. She was alive! The wolf locked eyes with him, barked, and disappeared into the forest.

RAIDER'S Vendetta

Chapter 33

When Raider woke, he was in so much pain; he wanted to pass out again. But, he felt something warm and wet lapping at his face. He opened his eyes and saw Bulwark lying next to him. He wasn't as beautiful as Raider remembered, but matted and red with blood. Bulwark's eyes were dull and flat, but his tongue continued to lick Raider's face. Raider slid away and stared at the torn up wolf. He looked around for the bear, but only saw a bloody trail heading into the forest.

Raider looked back at Bulwark and the reality of what had happened began to sink in. This wolf, the very same wolf that had ripped him open only days before, had protected him from the bear. Raider was flooded with mixed emotions. One minute he thought it served him right, the next he wondered why the wolf would do this for him. Raider took inventory. His arms and legs were torn up, but the bear had missed any major arteries and there was no gushing blood. He turned his attention back to the wolf. Bulwark's gaze was milky. He was dead.

"You stupid wolf. You were too late. I'm going to die anyway. What was the point?"

Raider lay back down and stared at the sky. "God, if you're up there, you are one jacked up..." he said as he passed out again.

RAIDER'S Vendetta

Chapter 34

Melinda Johnson was headstrong. Her parents could never contain her energy or stubbornness. They had protested when she announced she was taking up sky-diving, and again when she chose to explore rock climbing and scuba diving. Melinda was determined to discover every part of the world she lived in. Her parents had gone ballistic when she announced at her high school graduation party that she had joined the Air Force so she could travel the world. Her second passion was helping people, so nursing suited her perfectly, and the Air Force had provided her education. She had recently returned to the states after completing her military commitment and was making a cross-country trip before settling in at her new job in San Diego. She was in the final phase of her adventure - four weeks of camping in the Sierras. She had finally made it to Yosemite and spent a glorious week drinking in the beauty. She was now heading south through the mountains. Melinda was confident and decided to take the old mining roads. She wanted to see the pristine beauty of the forest. Most women would have been scared to travel these desolate roads alone, but Melinda had grown tough while serving as a nurse in Afghanistan. Her military training, her jeep, and her rifle gave her the confidence to embark on this journey.

The roads had been a challenge in sections, especially with the recent rains, and she was several days behind schedule. She knew she was cutting it close and might be late in starting her new job, but decided to continue on the back roads anyway. She should have cut over to the main highway the day before, but felt that God was urging her to stick to her plan. Melinda believed that all things serve a purpose and she trusted her relationship with God.

The map showed a bridge that crossed over a deep ravine and she hoped it was still intact. She didn't want to backtrack if it was no longer open to vehicles. She rolled down her windows. The early afternoon air was warm on her face.

When Melinda reached the corner, she was relieved to see there were no blockages and the bridge was still functioning. As she drove up to the entrance, she noticed the body of a large wolf. She slowed down to look and saw that there was also a man lying in the shadows. Melinda grabbed her rifle and jumped out of the jeep. She cautiously approached the wolf first. Using the end of the rifle, she poked him. There was no response and she was relieved that the wolf was dead. She didn't want to be attending to the man and have the wolf attack her. She then used the rifle to nudge the man. He moaned as she pressed into his side. Alive, he is still alive, she thought. At first, she thought the wolf had attacked the man, then realized the gashes on his arms and legs were made by something much larger. Possibly a bear?

Melinda ran back to the jeep and returned with the first aid kit. While examining him, she noticed his Air Force tattoos. She felt an instant connection with this injured man. They were part of a brotherhood, sisterhood, whatever-hood. Upon closer inspection, Melinda saw the injured shoulder. "Oh my God," she said aloud. "How has this man survived?"

Melinda had packed a well-stocked first-aid kit and she had both antibiotics and a stitch kit. She decided to do as much repair as possible while he was unconscious. She sterilized, stitched, and bandaged the oozing wounds. She cleaned out the infected shoulder and wrapped it in sterile bandaging, but didn't stitch it up because she wanted to be sure any fluid and infection would drain. She was relieved that there didn't appear to be any broken bones. While she worked on Raider, she checked for weapons and removed his pocketknife. She needed to be careful. She had no clue who this guy was or why he was out in the wilderness, chewed up. She dropped the knife into her first-aid kit.

The wolf was massive and had been ripped apart by a much larger animal. It would have taken a large bear to fight a wolf of this size. Did the wolf protect the man? she wondered. It must have been tamed. His pet? But, the shoulder injuries were different and definitely inflicted prior to the bear clawing. He had been bitten. Melinda saw the trail of blood leading into the woods and decided she needed to work quickly. An injured bear could return at any time. Melinda considered looking around for a campsite or other victims, but decided that she needed to get this man to a hospital right away. Family or friends would be dealt with once he was safe. She considered calling out and honking the horn to see if anyone would respond, but also knew it could draw unwanted attention from the bear.

Melinda grabbed some gauze and soaked it in water. She placed the gauze on Raider's lips. His mouth instinctively tasted the water and began to suck. She kept adding more water to the gauze, giving him a little at a time rather than trying to pour it down his throat. She wanted to get on the road quickly, but she wasn't a big girl and didn't think she could get her patient into the jeep on her own. She would give it a little time and see if he regained consciousness. Melinda began wiping his feverish brow with a cool, wet compress and prayed for God's protection and assistance. He began moaning, low at first and then louder.

~

Raider felt the coolness of the compress on his skin. Was he imagining the water on his lips? He slowly opened his eyes and saw a lovely young woman leaning over him. She was about twenty-eight or so, large, chestnut brown eyes, and dark brown hair pulled back into a ponytail. She was wearing a goofy grin, like a kid who has just put the last puzzle piece in. "Hey there, glad to see you came back," she said. "You're pretty messed up, but I think you'll survive." When he was able to swallow, she gave him a dose of pain medicine and antibiotics. Melinda helped Raider sit up and he saw the jeep. He was trying to remember where he was and why. He looked over and saw Bulwark laying there. Just a shell of the force of nature he had been.

"Can you talk? My name is Melinda Johnson. I'm an Air Force nurse. Well, I was."

179

Raider looked at her in disbelief. How did she find him? What on earth was she doing way out here? "What? How?"

"You probably have a lot of questions and I'll do my best to answer them. But, right now, we have to get you into the jeep and to a doctor. I fixed you up the best I could, but you need some serious treatment on those injuries." Melinda stood up. "I'll pull the jeep closer."

Melinda climbed into the jeep, started it up, and slowly drove over to Raider. Raider saw his gun under Bulwark's neck and quickly stuck it in his pocket. When she came back over, she helped him to stand up. His legs buckled and he almost fell. Melinda slipped her arm around his waist and brought his good arm over her shoulder. She struggled to get him into the back of the jeep where he could lay down and rest more comfortably.

"What do you want to do about the wolf? Was he a pet?"

"No," mumbled Raider. "He bit my shoulder."

Melinda looked at him, confused.

"I'll take it as slow as I can, but you're going to get bounced around some. Try to get comfortable. It's gonna hurt.

Raider wasn't thinking about the pain. That he could handle. The fact that a nurse had found him in the wilderness was beyond his understanding. He ignored what his heart knew and he chose to write it off as coincidence.

Melinda drove the jeep across the bridge, heading south toward freedom for Raider. He hunkered down and settled into the soft camping gear. He closed his eyes and tried to rest, but the picture of Bulwark was seared into his brain. Why would the wolf die for him? He was Charley's protector, not his. He didn't want to admit it, but had God sent him? That bear would have killed him. He did owe Bulwark his life. That angered Raider. God wasn't playing fair!

Melinda plugged in her iPod and soft, alternative Christian rock filled the air. She sang along, obviously happy that she had saved one of God's kids. Raider felt his rage building. God was not playing fair. Raider was going to take advantage of this stupid woman and use her to get him across the border. He slipped into a deep slumber as Melinda drove him to freedom.

Chapter 35

Agent Morris and her team headed west with several of the tracking dogs. The team heading east also had two tracking dogs. They kept in contact as each team progressed. So far they had found nothing. Someone again suggested an attempt to use search helicopters and Agent Morris finally relented. Two choppers were on their way. Agent Morris was not convinced they would be effective because of the heavy forest cover and they didn't have much daylight left. She believed the dogs were the best chance they had. Raider could hide from the choppers, but the dogs could still track him. It was obvious from the amount of blood found in the cabin that he was hurt badly. He would not be moving quickly. Tests had confirmed that it was his blood on the cot.

RAIDER'S Vendetta

Chapter 36

Donald was at a loss for how to get this woman out of the ravine alive. She was obviously close to death. He thought about heading out alone, back to his home to call the forestry department on his CB radio, but that would take hours. The howling of coyotes indicated they were near and aware of fresh meat. She would not survive while he went for help. He couldn't leave her alone, but if he didn't get her out, she would die.

Donald remembered the large mesh bag he carried in his backpack. If he split one side, it would open into a fairly large piece of netting. Combined with branches and twine, he could make a sling. He could drag her out. Donald was excited and his efforts paid off. He produced a sturdy travois to support the injured woman's body.

Next, he had to unbury her. He worked slowly and carefully. Donald had no idea what her injuries were and he didn't want to cause more damage. It took him over an hour to get her clear of the mud and debris. Once she was accessible, Donald cringed at the extent of her injuries. Her femur had snapped, the bone protruding through the skin, and her arm appeared to be broken in several places. There was no way of knowing if she had internal injuries, but he had no choice. He had to move her. He cautiously slid her onto the sling, expecting her to scream out in agony, but she moaned only slightly. Donald was relieved that she was unconscious. The leg injury alone would cause unbearable pain. After placing her on the sling, Donald saw a huge gash and a lump on the side of her head.

Donald moved to the front of the travois. He had placed the split bag closer to one end of the branches so he had space to fit between the branches and the sling on the other end. This would allow him to hold the branches and drag her behind him. Donald didn't believe in God, but still found himself praying for a higher power to get them back to safety. Maybe Mother Nature was his best bet. It made sense that she controlled the wolf. His experience with the wolf and the wolf's sudden departure perplexed him. He was sure that no one would believe him, especially since he was beginning to doubt his experience himself.

Donald began the long, arduous journey out of the ravine. Hopefully, his heart would not fail him. This was not a frail woman and she presented a substantial burden to drag.

Chapter 37

Both teams traveled along the ravine and, after several hours, Agent Morris got the call she had prayed for. The dogs in the eastbound group had picked up the scent. They were moving quickly now to bridge the gap. Agent Morris was feeling the excitement of capture. She was sure they were close as she climbed into the helicopter that would take them to join the eastbound team.

Landing was difficult. The forest did not offer many clear openings for a safe landing. They could see open sections, but the ground wasn't level amidst the ravines and mountains. They settled on an area several miles from the pursuing team. The challenges of the wilderness frustrated Agent Morris. Her team would have to push hard to catch up to the tracking team.

RAIDER'S Vendetta

Chapter 38

Donald was making progress. Pitifully slow, but progress. He decided to take a breather and check to see how his passenger was doing. He carefully set the end of his sling down on the ground. The woman was still unconscious, but there seemed to be a lot of activity under her eyelids. She must be dreaming. Donald wasn't sure, but decided that it was a good sign. He checked her pulse and was relieved that it wasn't any weaker than an hour ago. He had been dragging her through the ravine for two hours and had only covered half the distance he had traveled with the wolf. At this rate, it would be dark before he would get to the ravine opening. The dry creek-bed was difficult to maneuver. He'd twisted his ankles several times; luckily, not bad enough to disable him.

He didn't know how much longer he could manage dragging the sling. He didn't want to be stuck overnight in the wilderness with this dying woman. She needed medical attention, now, and the cold night air would be extremely dangerous.

Donald stretched his shoulders and rolled them to work out the kinks. He was exhausted and stopping had made it harder to continue. The sling, when picked up again, felt twice as heavy as before. His sweat-soaked clothes were now cold on his exhausted body. Donald cursed himself for taking a break. The exertion he forced on his body felt overwhelming, but he had no choice. He had to push through. They were able to travel another forty-five minutes with some daylight. After that, the ravine quickly became shadowed and foreboding. Donald had a flashlight, but couldn't hold it and support the sling at the same time. He regretted getting the large, super industrial version that held eight batteries. There was no way he could carry it in his mouth. If he needed a beacon, it was perfect, but it didn't help with the task at hand.

Donald continued in the darkness, then lost his footing and his ankle buckled beneath him. He couldn't release the sling to break his fall. Her head would have slammed on the ground. He felt the rip in his ankle as he hit the ground hard. The rip was intense and it was obvious that he would not be able to walk out of the ravine. To make matters worse, a thick patch of trees covered them. Donald looked up and barely made out a few pale stars in the dusk filled sky. They would not be found. They were hidden from all sides.

Chapter 39

Melinda maneuvered the jeep carefully to minimize the jarring to her passenger. She heard his deep breathing and was relieved that he was sleeping. This was an adventure that would rival even her war stories. She had been an ER trauma nurse. At first, there were unexpected wounds, stories, and outcomes, but after four years, it all ran together. Few cases stood out and those were marked by horrific wounds. She loved helping the injured, but had had her fill of the devastation that war causes. She was ready to live in the real world, not the world of war and death. She had applied for and been hired as a maternity nurse. The thought of new life, babies, and excited mothers was going to bring positive energy into her life.

They wouldn't clear the mining roads and reach paved roads for several more hours. Melinda stopped to redress the wounds and examine his shoulder. The antibiotics should prevent infection in the gashes, but the shoulder was a serious threat to her patient. She heard his deep voice calling out to someone named Badria. He sounded so sad, it made Melinda tear up. She wondered who Badria was and why he sounded so heartbroken.

~

"Badria, you have to listen. It isn't safe for you here. The men that marked your door will be back. Come with me. I'll make them listen at the base. They have to help us."

"Arthur, I can't. I can't leave. My family will starve."

"We'll take your brother with us. Badria, if you die,

who will feed them then? This doesn't make any sense."

"These men, they visit with us women. They are only pressuring me because I only see you. They are angry that I prefer an American soldier to them. They see it as a betrayal."

"Okay, I won't see you until we can leave. I don't want you sleeping with other men. I will give you money. We can get married and I'll take you back to America."

"My father says no. I cannot marry you."

"Badria, he won't protect you. He treats you with such disrespect, but spends the money you earn."

"If I stop seeing you and continue to service them, they will leave me alone. I will be able to continue to provide for my family."

"You don't know that for sure. What if they still kill you, Badria? Several of the women have already been killed. I love you. I don't want you with other men or dead. Please marry me." Arthur hated begging. It was not in his character, but he loved this woman with every part of his being. She had to listen.

"Arthur, I love you also, but my father will never agree and I cannot disobey my father. Your government is not going to help me and they don't want you to marry me either. I have to accept that we cannot be."

"I don't care what my government thinks or says. We'll go somewhere else. We'll get out of Iraq, go somewhere where they don't know us. Start over. You, me, and your brother. Your father will have his brothers to help him."

"How will you work? You won't have papers. We can't survive."

"Badria, we'll figure it out. Please trust me."

Arthur stroked her hair and kissed her softly on her face, neck, and shoulders. Everything told him to capture this moment with her. He feared it would be his last.

"You must leave. It will be morning soon."

"Okay, but we will make plans tomorrow. You just need to believe in us, Badria."

She kissed him tenderly, longingly. "I never would have taken you for an optimist, Arthur. Your heart is showing," she said affectionately.

"Only for you my love, only for you." As Arthur got up and put on

his clothes, he looked at her in the moonlight. Her face seemed to beam with hope.

"Tomorrow, Badria, I'll be back for you tomorrow."

"Okay Arthur. I will believe in us."

Arthur pulled himself from her apartment. He was excited and fought off the fear of the unknown. He would make his commanding officer listen. They had to let him save Badria. As he headed back to base, he missed the shadows shifting in the darkness.

His superiors wouldn't listen when he pleaded the following morning. They would not intervene for a citizen, especially not for a prostitute. Arthur had to understand that the culture and restrictions placed on them kept them from even considering assistance for her and her brother.

Angry and frustrated, but determined, Arthur went to the brothel area to rescue Badria. He didn't have it all worked out, but he had his money and everything of importance with him. They would leave, go somewhere for a fresh beginning. When Arthur entered the alley, he smelled a foul, rotting smell. He found her, broken and dead. He dropped to his knees and cried "Badria, Badria, my beautiful Badria." She had been pulled from her apartment shortly after Arthur left early that morning and was stoned by the zealots who had paid her for her body only months before.

~

Melinda stopped the jeep at a wide shoulder on the dirt road. The engine shutting off woke Raider. He shifted and felt the effects of his wounds. He was in a lot of pain and felt weak. He groaned as he sat up. "Why are we stopping?" he asked.

"It will be quite awhile before I can get you to a doctor. I want to redress your wounds and check your shoulder. I also have a gas can back there and need to add fuel to the tank."

Raider looked at their location and was relieved to see that they were under a dense canopy of pine trees. He didn't want to be visible from the sky. "Okay, I appreciate your help."

"No problem. Just glad I came by when I did. It's a God thing. So many things could've changed our connection. You have a powerful guardian angel."

Raider cringed. Oh no, he thought, it's starting already. He almost laughed but didn't want to have to explain, so he kept quiet.

Melinda had Raider lie down. She quickly removed the bandages, applied salve to the wounds and re-wrapped the bandages. She worked efficiently as she bombarded Raider with questions he ignored. She wanted to know his name, why he was out there all alone, about the wolf, what attacked him, was anyone looking for him, on and on. Raider had to figure out how to manage the situation. He couldn't let her take him to a doctor. The border was his only hope of staying free. If he pulled the gun on her now, he wouldn't be able to sleep and could pass out. She would then take the gun and shoot him. He wanted to put off that possibility as long as he could. But, if he played nice and fell asleep, he could wake up surrounded by cops if she got him to a hospital before he woke up. He evaluated his pain level, how tired he was, and whether or not he would be able to stay awake for the next ten hours or so. His training would help, but he knew his injuries were serious.

He decided to play nice until he figured things out. "So, you're probably wondering who you scooped up off the road. My name is Isaiah. My dad was a pastor and my mom thought I'd score some points for being named after a saint. I was doing some hiking and camping before the season ended. I was in the Air Force, but decided not to re-enlist. Now I'm going to work with the Peace Corp. Trying to make up for all the warmongering I suppose. Heading over to Africa for a two-year stretch. No family and friends are few."

"Nice to meet you, Isaiah. Well, that makes sense. I'm sure you were praying up a storm and God brought me. Is being a preacher's kid as hard as they say?"

"I had a great dad, so not so bad. People like to judge you, but my folks were cool and knew I wouldn't be perfect."

"That's good. So what was up with the wolf? Were you attacked by a bear? The wounds look like they were made by something big."

"Yeah, black bear. Bigger than most. Rough few days. The wolf came into camp and attacked me. Scared him off with some burning firewood. Tried to walk out for help, guess the bear smelled the blood. He came after me, and then the wolf showed up. Suppose the wolf was following me, waiting to finish me off.

"Wow, that's incredible. What happened next?" she asked, like a kid listening to a bedtime story.

"When the bear attacked me, the wolf rushed in from the forest and attacked the bear. Protecting his prey, I guess. They fought and I passed out. When I woke up, the wolf was dead and the bear was gone. I must have lost consciousness again, 'cause I woke up to you eyeballing me." Raider was good at lying, always had been, but this lie stirred up shame. He knew the wolf had died for him.

"I don't eyeball, I examine," Melinda responded with a flirtatious tone.

Raider realized that she found him attractive and interesting. His story about being a preacher's kid had made him appear safe, a person of character. He used this to his advantage. He grinned at her. "Well, eyeballing or examining, your pretty face was a welcome sight. I do believe you are God's answer to my prayers."

Melinda grinned back. "Me too," she said. "Who's Badria? It's a lovely name."

The hair on Raider's neck bristled. "What do you mean?"

"When you were sleeping, you kept calling her name. I'm assuming it was a woman. You sounded so sad."

Raider was angry and caught off guard. He took a moment to calm down before answering. "Well, I was married. She died." He felt his rage building. Calm down, don't go off on her. "She died in a car crash a week after the wedding. It's been a few years now, but I still feel the loss at times."

"Oh my goodness. I'm so sorry," Melinda replied, embarrassed.

"No, it's okay. I've come to terms with her death, ready to find someone to love again. She was special and was always the one to help me when I was sick or hurt. Makes sense I would think about her." Raider didn't have to fake the emotion.

"Of course, makes perfect sense," Melinda said softly.

RAIDER'S Vendetta

Chapter 40

As they moved through the forest, Agent Morris received a call on the radio. The dogs had hit a dead-end. They were at one end of a bridge that crossed a ravine and the scent stopped abruptly. It was now late evening and they had to investigate the scene with flashlights.

"Agent Morris, you're not going to believe this, but there is blood everywhere. We also have a dead wolf."

"Is he shot? You think Arthur killed him?"

"No, he looks ripped up, like an animal got to him, but there are pools of blood that look like something else was on the ground bleeding as well. The way the hounds are howling, we figure it was our guy."

"Did you check around the area in case he crawled off somewhere? This guy can't have much blood left. He probably bled out close by."

"We found a blood trail into the woods, but the dogs aren't interested, probably from the animal that killed the wolf."

"This isn't making any sense," Agent Morris said.

"I know. We found some fresh tire tracks by the blood. Also, some footprints, but the dogs aren't responding. Thought it was the woman, but dogs indicate no."

"Damn it, somebody picked him up. He's on the road."

"That's how it looks. We've notified the choppers and they are focusing on the road, but they say the trees are dense and the old mining road splits off in many directions. The rains have soaked the dirt roads, so no dust will be visible from above and the gravel and rock make it hard to track."

"We need to get those tracks analyzed as soon as possible to identify the type of vehicle we are looking for. We have to get the information to the border patrol right away. They have pictures of Arthur and Charley, but who knows what they might be hiding in."

"Yes, ma'am, we're on it. See you soon."

~

When Agent Morris got to the bridge, she was shocked at how much blood there was. Now that they had a bigger team, several officers followed the blood trail. It led them to a large black bear that had bled out. His throat was ripped open and he had several other deadly wounds. A human was incapable of this kind of damage. This had to be the work of the wolf they'd found.

Agent Morris knelt next to the wolf and felt a pang of regret for the death of this majestic creature. She marveled at his size and his blue eyes. They were glazed over, but the blue was still striking. It would be hours before a forensic team would be here to determine what happened for sure, but Agent Morris knew that something quite extraordinary had played out.

"Why would you die for such an evil man?" she asked the wolf under her breath. She didn't want the other officers overhearing and thinking she had lost her mind. "He's a bad man. Maybe you were protecting Charley? Is that it boy?" Agent Morris looked for Agent Haug. He had taken the lead on the westbound team. "Have the dogs picked up Charley's scent?"

"We gave them her clothing to prompt them, but they didn't respond. There is no indication that she was here."

"Where could she be? Could the dogs have missed her body along the way?"

"Sure, if we were too far off. The rain wiped out everything. We'd have to be fairly close for the dogs to have picked up her scent, unless she's been dead for several days. The smell of decomposing flesh would carry quite a distance."

"None of this is making sense. I'm afraid she's dead."

"That's what we think, too."

"We gotta get this animal. He can't be allowed to hurt anyone else."

"We're doing our best, but these mountains make it difficult to be effective."

"I know, just thinking out loud."

Agent Morris requested all public bulletins, border alerts, and an update on the arrival of the CSI team. She knew she was working against time and felt the frustration of watching the opportunity to catch Arthur slipping away with each minute.

~

Tents and provisions were dropped at the site of the bridge and a makeshift camp was set up, another night on cot. Agent Morris was not a "happy camper." She grudgingly settled in and was sipping on a hot cup of tea when a call came in from her department, a call she did not expect. This case was getting more and more bizarre. This new information convinced Agent Morris that Charley was very much alive and safe. She updated the border alerts to look for Charley, traveling alone. She'd never anticipated this twist. How could she have been so deceived?

RAIDER'S Vendetta

Chapter 41

Melinda inspected and cleaned the shoulder wounds. "I am relieved to see that the swelling has come down."

Once he was re-bandaged, Melinda gave him another dose of antibiotics. Raider checked out the first-aid kit as she put items away.

"Boy, you came prepared. What is all this stuff?"

"Can't take the nurse outta the girl. With all the primitive hiking and camping I was doing, I needed to make sure I had a way to take care of myself if I was seriously injured. I brought antibiotics and pain relievers. I have lots of bandages and topical ointments. I even have a stitch kit, which I used on those gashes. Luckily, you were unconscious when I did all this repair work. Would have been difficult if you were awake."

"I noticed you didn't stitch up my chest. How come?"

"I'm concerned about infection. Doctors will need to examine it and clean it out well. The wound is a few days old and it's best to have it examined before closing it up. I've given you strong antibiotics so you should be fine. Always best to play on the safe side though."

"Well, Melinda, you impress me. I bet you are an incredible nurse, probably better than most of the doctors."

"Oh don't get me started on doctors. Glory hounds that don't acknowledge how many times nurses bailed their butts out."

Raider grinned at her. He was in good hands. Who needed a doctor? He thought he would have to force a doctor to treat him at gunpoint, but she had everything he needed and the expertise to use it.

"Any chance you have some food with you? I'm

pretty hungry. It's been a few days since I've eaten."

"Of course, all healthy. Hope that's okay."

"Looking at your great figure, I wouldn't have expected anything different."

Melinda blushed and busied herself with preparing a quick meal for them. Raider knew that she found him attractive, the flirtatious smiles, batting of her eyes and the unconscious seductive movements of her hands and body. Once the food was ready, fresh vegetables, peanut butter, wheat crackers, and apples for dessert, they ate. She buzzed on about her family, her new job, and her time in Iraq. Raider politely pretended to listen and nodded his head when appropriate, but he was playing out all possible scenarios in his head.

Option one was to tie her up, leave her in the forest, take the jeep, and drive on alone. This option had one major flaw. If she was found, she would give them a description of her vehicle down to the license plate. He was sure she had that memorized. Second option was to kill her, take the car, and head for the border alone. But, this presented the issue of him trying to drive through the border check. He was positive they would still be on alert for him and his injuries would draw attention. This ruled out both of the first two options.

Option three was to keep moving south, play nice until she pressed to stop at a hospital. Then, he would pull out the gun and force her over the border while he hid with the gun in her back. This would require him to stay awake for the next few hours and he wasn't sure he could do that. The medication and food were already making him feel woozy.

He also wanted to take advantage of her medical skills. If he got his chest stitched up and had all the medical supplies, he wouldn't need to risk a doctor once in Mexico.

"Wouldn't you agree?" Melinda asked with conviction.

"I'm sorry, I must have drifted off. Feeling pretty tired. Wouldn't I agree to what?" Raider asked with forced interest.

"Oh never mind, I was just rattling on. If you're done eating, we need to get going."

"Once we get to the hospital, you think they can stitch me up and release me? I'm concerned about racking up more medical bills. They won't want me to stay overnight will they?"

"You need to be observed for a few days."

"Wouldn't need to stay if I was patched up right. They could send me home to follow up with my own doctor."

"I don't know, Isaiah. You're hurt pretty bad. You've started antibiotics and I've given you something for the fever, but you need tests run. What if the bear or the wolf was carrying a disease? I think you'll need to be hospitalized for a few days."

"Okay, I'm just so in debt for Badria's medical treatment. She was in ICU for seven days before she died. I'm making payments, but still owe thousands of dollars. I thought about filing bankruptcy, but that's against my Christian beliefs. I just thought I would be able to minimize the hospital charges if you patched me up before I went in."

~

"But Isaiah, I can't numb you well enough. It's going to hurt like hell."

"I want to try. If it hurts too bad, we can stop."

Melinda stared at her hands. She wanted to help him out but this would be primal.

"Never mind, Melinda. I can see this is too much to ask. I'll figure it out. Guess it can't be that much more than what I already owe."

Melinda knew how quickly the costs added up. Isaiah was doing remarkably well since she had found him and administered antibiotics. He was in great physical shape overall. She continued to rationalize and finally decided to do what he asked.

"I can't promise you a pretty healing. There will be scarring."

"I'm not worried about that. Makes the telling of my testimony much more interesting if I have obnoxious scars," he responded with a heart-melting smile.

Melinda looked at him and convinced herself that this was no different than stitching up his legs and arms. She was trained for this. "Okay, but if you can't handle the pain, you gotta be honest."

"I promise!"

Raider pulled himself out of the jeep and moved to a flat area. "No Isaiah, we need to do it in the jeep. If you pass out, I can drive you to the hospital."

"I'm too bulky for you to have enough working room. Outside is better. You can put the headlights on me for more light. I'd rather you have space. If I pass out, it won't be long. We can head to the hospital once I wake up. It's been this long, Melinda, what's a short nap gonna do?"

Melinda was beginning to suspect that she was being manipulated. Some things just weren't adding up, but her attraction to him blinded her to the obvious. His reasoning made sense or did she just want it to? The jeep was rather tight and the headlights would give her more light than the interior. It was late evening and the forest was getting dark.

~

The stage was set. Raider was lying on a blanket, medical supplies spread out and ready. Melinda had given Raider a healthy dose of pain reliever. This would relax him and help deaden the pain of what was to come. She also had a washcloth for him to bite on in case it got bad. When she began, Raider went into the mindset he used when he was beaten by his Aunt Rose and shoved in the bin. He shut off his body and took his mind to another place, Badria's bed, wrapped in her arms. He grunted and gritted his teeth when the mental escape didn't take him far enough, but he would endure. He had to. He didn't have any money. Well, that wasn't exactly true. He didn't know how much he would have once he took Melinda's, but he was sure it wasn't enough to pay a doctor in Mexico to fix him up and keep his mouth shut about it. This would buy him some time. He could get through anything if he needed to bad enough. Melinda hit a particularly deep tear with her needle and Raider slipped into unconsciousness to escape from the excruciating pain.

His plotting had worked. He knew he would probably pass out before she was done and Raider didn't want her to be able to drive him to a hospital. This way, she had to wait. She couldn't get him into the jeep on her own.

Chapter 42

Several hours went by and Donald was worried. He tried to stand on his foot, but the ankle would not support him. There was no way he was going to be able to drag the injured woman, let alone himself, out of the ravine and he had no supplies. He'd been distracted and left his backpack where he'd found the woman. At least he had the flashlight. He'd shoved it into his waistband when the wolf first showed up, planning to use it as a weapon if the wolf attacked, and it was still there.

The woman was still unconscious. She made whimpering noises and spoke some in her sleep and Donald took her activity as a good sign. He checked her pulse frequently and felt for any sign of a fever. The helplessness was overwhelming. The wolf had not returned and Donald felt mixed emotions. Having a large, powerful animal to protect them would be helpful, but the unpredictability of a wild animal would also keep him on edge. He believed the wolf had intentionally led him to the injured woman and it did care about her survival. It would be an incredible story, hard to believe, if he lived to share it. Donald periodically shined the flashlight up through the trees, hoping the small beacon of light would be visible by a rescue team if there was one. He knew it was a long shot, but it was all he had.

Donald tried to get comfortable next to the woman. They would stay warmer if they were close together. He was relieved that her breathing seemed stronger and more pronounced than it had been earlier in the day. He intended to stay awake all night to keep any creatures from getting close, but he was struggling not to drift off. His body, mind, and spirit were exhausted. Just as he dipped into sleep, he woke with a jolt of adrenalin. He heard the distinct howl of a coyote, close by, followed by another howl farther out. He sat up and grabbed the sturdy branch he had found before it got dark. The branch and the flashlight were the only weapons he had.

Donald heard the brush rustling nearby and he turned on the flashlight and pointed it in that direction. Glowing eyes startled him. A large coyote was standing a short distance away, staring in his direction. Soon, he watched two more coyotes slide in next to the first. They looked smaller, younger, but not pups. The hungry animals cautiously paced and moved closer with each pass. Even though he didn't believe in God, he found himself praying for the wolf to return. Three full-sized coyotes would be difficult to fight off alone, but he was prepared to give it everything he had.

The coyotes were only ten feet away. They continued to pace, but didn't come in any closer. They moved to the left and right, licking their lips and whining. If Donald didn't know better, he would think there was an invisible force field surrounding him and the woman. Donald watched in amazement. The coyotes paced around them, as if trying to find an opening. The larger of the coyotes, possibly the mother of the other two, sat down and froze. She watched him intently; her only movement an occasional blink. The younger animals whined, sniffed the ground, and disappeared into the forest. In pursuit of other prey, he hoped.

The coyote was still sitting there when Donald finally closed his eyes and passed out from physical and emotional exhaustion. His last conscious thought was that the coyotes would eat them both.

Donald dreamed of his wife, their life together, his joy of discovery, sunny beaches where they had vacationed, and fires crackling in their fireplace as they sipped exotic teas. He felt warm and cozy in this false dream of comfort.

~

Charley, on the other hand, started the night with dreams of terrors. Masked men with guns, screams of anguish, feeling lost and abandoned. She dreamed about standing face to face with her Jesus and asking why he left her to the will of such a vicious man. Charley would cry at times, knowing she was in horrible pain, but not feeling it. It was a dream world that scared her and she wasn't able to get out. Sometimes, the real world would be just within her grasp, but then horrible pain and bitter chill would wrack her very soul. Her mind would escape back into the darkness of her nightmares. As scary as they were, the pain was dull and distant in her dream world.

Archie finally came to her, to comfort her, hold her tightly, and tell her how strong she was, how proud he was. She felt the warmth of his body, his love. The deep aching pain and cold left her broken body. She clung to him and begged him to give her the purple sparkling shoes back – to take her with him. He shushed her like a distraught child and assured her that it was too soon. Archie would be waiting for her, waiting for the right time, and then he slipped away. Charley cried until the baby's cries were loud enough to hear. She stopped and listened, not understanding why the baby haunted her dreams.

Charley found herself in the forest, the forest that had surrounded her these many days. She followed the cries and came to a sunlit, open area filled with wild flowers. The baby's cries transformed into coos. There on the ground was a plump, adorable baby boy. She picked up the baby and cradled him in her arms. Such joy filled her and, as she lifted the baby up so she could look into his eyes, he drained through her fingers like sand in an hourglass. The horror of the vanishing child brought her to heartbroken sobs.

RAIDER'S Vendetta

Chapter 43

Melinda was relieved to see Isaiah stirring. While he was unconscious, she had covered him with a warm blanket and stayed close by with her rifle, wrapped in a sleeping bag. She didn't want either of them attacked by another animal. A fire would have been nice, but the wood in this area was still soaking wet from the storm. It would have taken forever to build a fire large enough to generate any heat.

"I'm alive?" he asked with a parched mouth.

"Yes, I have to say I did a marvelous job once you passed out. It was much easier without the cringing and jerking."

"Melinda, thank you."

"You want some water?"

"Yeah, my mouth feels like moths have taken up residence."

Melinda would have smiled at his description, but she was focused on the burning question in her mind. The question she hadn't thought to ask him earlier, before she agreed to stitch up his shoulder. She moved over to the back of the jeep to get Isaiah a drink. Her training had finally overcome her attraction and she wanted to keep the rifle handy. She tried to pour the water while holding the rifle, but she couldn't manage both at the same time. Melinda thought about it and decided she was overreacting. Besides, he was injured and unarmed. She set the rifle down and poured the water.

~

Raider noticed her hesitation to set down the rifle. He

knew she wasn't as smitten as she had been previously. Something was different. He slipped his hand beneath his body and felt the cold metal of his gun. She hadn't found it. He slid it out and tucked it between his side and arm. Raider didn't want her to carry the rifle back with the water, so he asked for something to eat as well. He was feeling weak and lightheaded. Melinda took the bait and focused on finding the crackers and cheese. She turned back to him while holding the water cup and the plate of food. He tried to sit up and feigned the inability to do so. He wanted her to believe he was helpless and no threat. She held his head up and brought the water cup to his mouth. As he drank, she asked the question that evaded her before. "Isaiah, why would you worry about hospital bills? You're a vet. Your medical is covered for the rest of your life."

Raider knew he could no longer flirt her into cooperation. "You lose all benefits with a dishonorable discharge."

Melinda brought the cup down and looked at Raider with disbelief and then judgment. "Dishonorable discharge? What did you do?" Melinda started to move away, but Raider grabbed her wrist. She stared at the hand gripping her. The strength he applied shocked her. She had bought into his act of weakness. She started to pull her arm back, but saw the gun in his other hand, pointed at her face. "It doesn't matter, Melinda. What matters now is that you do what you're told or I will kill you."

~

Melinda stopped pulling and her mind raced through the details of the day, trying to put it all together and locate the clues she had missed. There were several, but the biggest was his insistence that she do the stitching out here. He wouldn't go to the hospital because he was a wanted man. Her stupidity brought a blush of shame to her face.

"Don't beat yourself up, Melinda, I'm just that good."

Melinda spat in his face.

"Now, now, you don't want to piss me off. I have three options here. First is to keep you alive and allow you to help me get over the border, and then release you. The second and easiest is to kill you and take the jeep and everything in it. The last is to dump you here and hope nothing eats you before you're found. I still get the jeep without worrying about you.

"If you cooperate, I opt for number one. Just remember, I have nothing to lose if I kill you. I'm already looking at life in prison or the death penalty. You're just one more stupid woman who can benefit me or annoy me. It's up to you."

Melinda nodded that she would cooperate. At least she had a chance to escape. Raider released her wrist, but kept the gun in her side. "Now, help me up, please."

The thought of getting him halfway up and then pushing him down entered her mind, but she sensed that he was a good shot and she wouldn't be able to outrun a bullet. She decided to keep her eyes open and take him out when the time was right. She pulled him up and moved toward the jeep and the rifle. "Don't even think about the rifle. I emptied the gun when you took your potty break a few miles back."

Melinda glared at him. She'd thought he was asleep when she stopped and ran into the woods. She climbed into the front seat of the jeep and waited for him to climb in the back. She watched as he picked up the rifle and opened the chamber. The bullets slid out and bounced with a clattering sound on the jeep floor.

A blush of rage overtook her. He hadn't emptied her rifle after all. Why was she being so stupid? This man was obnoxious and vicious. She had no doubt about that.

"Melinda! Melinda! You shouldn't let a six pack and a bulging crotch reduce you to a boy crazy ditz!" Raider said, ridiculing her. "This will all be over soon. Don't get any brave ideas and you'll be fine. I just need to get across the border and then I'm gone, out of your life forever."

Raider climbed into the back of the jeep and pressed the barrel into her back. He wanted to make sure she felt the gun. "This gun will be aimed at your spine until we get into Mexico. I don't want to kill you, but I will, if necessary. Stay calm and get going."

Melinda started up the jeep. Again, she searched her brain, trying to make sense of the situation. He was right. His charm and good looks had sucked her in. She was sure that he had never stepped foot in a church, let alone was a preacher's kid. The jeep headed south.

~

Melinda ran through all of the scenarios in her head. How she would survive? What explanation could there be for Isaiah's dishonorable discharge? Maybe he had taken base food for starving children and got caught. Stop it, Melinda, she scolded herself. This is a bad man, not a misunderstood man, a bad man. You can't fix him. He said he would go to prison or be executed. That's not how they handle a softhearted man who feeds kids.

She wanted to ask. She was curious to know how bad he was, but she kept quiet and drove. She considered crashing the jeep into a tree, but feared she would just hurt herself. Every so often, he would push the barrel of the gun deeper into her back, reminding her that he was fully conscious and would take her out in a split second. She had military training, but it had been eight years ago. Nursing hadn't required her to stay a fine-tuned killing machine, like Isaiah. She decided that she just wanted to get through this, not be a hero. She would drive this vile man to the border.

Chapter 44

Saturday

Raider was feeling much better. He took small doses of pain meds when he couldn't handle the throb of his wounds, but he was in survival mode and had to be alert. Melinda appeared to be cooperative, but Raider knew she was not someone that would easily fold. He had to watch her carefully.

The roads were becoming smoother and better maintained and he knew they would be leaving the mountains soon. The border would be a challenge. He knew they would be looking for a man and an old woman. The border patrol would have his picture memorized. His only chance was to remain hidden. Raider looked at the supplies Melinda had packed in the jeep. The blankets, sleeping bag, and duffle bag with clothes and toiletries would be enough to conceal him in the floor space behind Melinda's seat. He would be able to control her with the gun pressed into her back. The border patrol would not be looking for a young woman traveling alone.

"Look, Melinda, I know you have no reason to believe me, but I don't want to hurt you. I just need to get into Mexico and have a chance to state my case. I want to clear my name with the Air Force, but if they catch me and put me in the stockade, I'll disappear. My situation involves several high-ranking officers and they will make sure I can't implicate them."

"You're right, Isaiah. I have no reason to believe you, but I don't want to die today. I will do what you tell me to do, but don't think for one moment that I buy into your story."

"Works for me. I need you to stop the car."

Melinda did so.

"Hand back the keys, Melinda."

She did.

Raider pulled the gun from the seat and moved it to the back of her head. He tapped hard and she yelped. "Put both hands on the car ceiling." She hesitated, not knowing what he was doing. "Now or I'll take option two." Melinda obeyed. "The gun is pointed at the back of your head, so don't move a muscle."

Raider slipped out the door and stood next to the jeep. He unzipped his pants and relieved himself on the side of the road, then used his good arm to arrange the items in the back seat while using the weaker arm to keep the gun aimed at Melinda's head. She watched him in the rearview mirror, hoping for an opportunity to make a move. He constantly darted his eyes to her reflection in the mirror as he worked. It was as if her eyes revealed her thoughts and he was able to read them. She tried not to show any signs of aggression.

He looked at the rifle and decided to toss it. Hiding him would be tough enough. If the border patrol saw any part of the rifle, it could prompt a pullover and search. He grabbed the rifle and hurled it into some bushes by the road. Melinda wanted to protest, it was her father's gun, but decided he might use it on her, so she didn't say a word.

"Get out of the jeep and put your hands on your head."

"But you said you were taking me—"

"Shut up, Melinda, and just do what I say. You will put the rest of the gas into the tank. We won't be stopping again. If you need to pee, tell me now. Just know I have to watch you."

Melinda blushed and shook her head no. They moved to the back of the jeep and Melinda opened the back hatch. When she pulled the can out, she planted her feet. Raider brought the gun up to the back of her head. "Try to swing that can and the bullet will take you down instantly. You might not die right away but soon, very soon," Raider said with a deadly tone.

Melinda relaxed her stance and completed the task of emptying the gas can into the tank. They had plenty of gas to make it to the border. Melinda returned the empty can and started to close the hatch with Raider close behind her. "Leave it open. I need you to pull out your passport, license, and military ID. I'm watching your every move, so don't pull any crap."

"There's a small bag under the front passenger seat that has all my identification."

"Okay, close the hatch and move slowly to the passenger door." Melinda complied and pulled out the bag. She held it out for him to take. "You open it." Melinda pulled out the IDs and passport. "Okay, put them in the visor and toss the bag in the back." They moved to the driver side of the jeep and she climbed into the front seat and put her hands on the ceiling. Raider climbed into the back seat.

"Stay to the right when you come to any splits in the road. We're about two hours from the border."

Melinda took her hands off the ceiling and waited for Isaiah to hand her the keys. Once she started the engine, they headed for Mexico. "You gonna tell me your real name? I figure it's nothing out of the Bible," she said with sarcasm.

"You can call me Raider. All my Christian friends do," he said coldly. She glanced back at him and saw that he was serious. Melinda focused on the road. Raider noticed a relaxed peace in her eyes and knew she was praying. He started to humiliate her, but decided he was done with the game. The border was all he cared about. Besides, he was getting hungry. Maybe God would drop a pizza into the passenger seat if he played nice. Raider couldn't contain the grin. Melinda caught his reaction in the mirror and shuddered.

RAIDER'S Vendetta

Chapter 45

Donald woke and realized that it was early morning and he was still alive. He was comfortably warm, toasty actually. His body should be stiff and frozen after such a cold night. Next, he noticed pressure on his body and a pungent odor. When his eyes focused in the dim light, he saw two large raccoons lying on him, one on his chest and the other on his groin. There were several more stretched out by his side and between himself and the woman. He shifted his eyes to look at her and saw that she was also covered in raccoons. He froze, not sure what to do. Raccoons could be vicious. Their sharp teeth and claws could tear a person up. The raccoon on his chest stretched and shifted his weight. His eyes lazily opened and closed, then suddenly seemed to realize that Donald was awake and looking at him.

The raccoon, now fully awake, sat up on Donald's chest and brought his snout down to Donald's face, staring into his eyes. Again, Donald smiled. The raccoon's tongue slipped out and licked Donald's face. Then he looked up at the sky and chirped. The other raccoons responded quickly and made their way into the forest, followed by the one that had licked Donald's face. The raccoon turned around before the shadows swallowed him up and looked at Donald. It seemed to smile at him. Then the raccoon was gone. It was the oddest event that Donald had ever experienced, outside of the wolf and the invisible barrier, of course.

After checking the woman's condition, which appeared to be stable, Donald tried to figure out what to do next. His hope was beginning to diminish and then, like a song you can't get out of your head, the smiling raccoon came to mind. It oddly gave him a sense of peace. Nature seemed to be fighting for their survival, well, the woman's anyway. Who was she? What was she? Donald wanted to save her, for herself and for his own curiosity. He had to know how she summoned these wild creatures.

The ravine was slowly filling with warm sunlight. Donald looked at their surroundings in the daylight and realized no one would see them in this spot, but there was an open area about fifteen yards away. He had to get himself over there. He tested his ankle, but it had swollen up like a balloon during the night. It would be impossible for him to walk or hop that distance without falling. He couldn't afford to break a leg or worse. He would have to crawl. His knees were used up and crawling would put incredible demand on them, but there was no choice. Donald began his journey to the clearing. He felt the sharp rocks digging into his thin flesh and calcified knees. The pain in his ankle began to shoot up his leg with each movement. He wished he had something to wrap around the ankle so it wouldn't flop as he moved.

Donald didn't like putting distance between himself and the woman, but there was no other way. The journey seemed to take forever, but with bloody knees and aching shoulders, he made it to the clearing. He lay on his back, staring into the skies, listening carefully for the sound of anything. Donald had no way of knowing how long he would have to wait. He would glance over at the woman, but there was no movement. He thought again about praying, but didn't believe it would change their circumstances. He truly believed each man was on his own to deal with the joys and tragedies of life. That's why you tried to surround yourself with good people, avoid risky choices, and look out for yourself. It was the only way to minimize the dangers in life.

Donald knew he had done everything possible, but the idea of dying out in this ravine with a stranger was too much for him. He couldn't go out this way. He watched the sky and listened, hoping for rescue. Donald finally drifted off. The exhaustion of the crawl and the pain in his ankle took its toll on him.

Chapter 46

Agent Morris was awake before daylight.

"Any word on the tire tracks we found found?" Agent Morris asked the officer on the other end of the radio.

"Several vehicles can use these type of tires, well, quite a few actually. The tread is from a universal off-road tire. Could be on any kind of vehicle."

"At least we know what the vehicle is not," Agent Morris said, frustrated.

Agent Morris disconnected and walked the perimeter of the bridge once again. Looking for anything that might have been missed.

One of the agents brought Agent Morris a hot cup of coffee. "Here detective, this will warm you up." The morning air was cold and damp.

"What is your gut telling you?" she asked.

"This sure is a complicated case. The terrain, the storms, and his head start make it hard to feel productive. My gut says we're too late to catch him in this area. Our only hope is at the border. If he makes a clean getaway, he'll be laughing his butt off when we make a statement to the public."

Agent Morris took a long drink of the hot coffee. "Sure hoping you're wrong. I don't take being duped kindly," she paused and then continued, "They had to be in this together from the beginning."

"I don't know, Agent Morris. I heard those tapes. She should win an Oscar for her performance if she was faking. We've checked her records and there is nothing connecting them other than the report you received yesterday. Makes no sense."

"We confirmed that she truly is Charley Abrams?

Could this woman have stolen her identification?"

"Nahhh, Agent Morris. Her kids confirmed it was her. Like I said, makes no sense."

Agent Morris wasn't accomplishing anything here. A chopper was heading out soon and she would be on it.

~

Agent Morris wasn't particularly fond of flying. She made the best of it and took advantage of the scenery. The view from the sky was breathtaking. The morning light was coming through the clouds and the forest below was shimmery after the heavy rains. They were following a ravine when Agent Morris thought she saw an elderly man lying spread eagle on the ground. She tapped the pilot's shoulder and pointed down. They swung back around and dropped lower for a better view. There was an old man down there. The helicopter was not equipped with medical supplies or the capability to airlift, so the pilot called in the coordinates to the forestry department. As they moved on, Agent Morris hoped the old man was still alive.

Chapter 47

Donald was having a troubled dream. He was in a deep cave, backed against the wall in total darkness. There were sounds of animals moving about. At first, he felt their breath on him, then bumping. It was light at first, almost a teasing, then harder, challenging. Donald didn't know what the animals were, but they were becoming braver and braver. He knew that it was only a matter of time before they were on him, ripping his flesh. Just as he felt one's teeth sink into his leg, a man was screaming from above while the sound of helicopter blades whomped.

When Donald opened his eyes, he saw a man suspended over him, slowly dropping from a helicopter above. Tears of relief and joy flooded Donald's eyes. He sat up, and saw a pack of rats clearing the area. He wouldn't die here. He wouldn't die today.

The medic checked Donald over and examined his ankle. Another medic dropped down to check the injured woman. There was no place for the helicopter to land, so they would have to airlift them out of the ravine. The first basket was sent down and the medics prepared the woman to go up first.

"Any idea who she is?" asked Donald.

"We think her name is Charley, but we'll know more once we get her identified."

"What was she doing out here?"

"If it's her, she was a hostage in a bank robbery days ago," he supplied.

Donald shook his head. How much could one person survive, especially an older woman. "Will she be okay?"

"Hard to know right now. She's suffered a lot of

trauma and the elements have complicated her condition. But sir, if she has any chance at all, it's because of your efforts." The medic patted him on the back.

"How did you find us? I'd given up hope," Donald asked.

"One of the search choppers covering the robbery case flew over and spotted you," the medic explained.

Once she disappeared into the helicopter, Donald felt a huge burden lifted off his chest. Another helicopter was coming for Donald. The woman, Charley, was taken to a hospital with a trauma center. Since his injuries were not life threatening, he was taken to the smaller, local hospital. The doctors wanted to keep Donald overnight for observation and he didn't argue. He felt the drain on his body; his joints ached badly. Usually, he was the "tough guy" and didn't want attention when he was sick or hurt, but not this time.

Chapter 48

Raider was getting tired. He knew he had to hang on a while longer. He needed to be alert when they came to the border. His plans for Melinda were not concrete yet. He didn't intend to kill her or hurt her, but he wasn't sure how he would deal with her once they were across the border. He would need her car and money, but not her. She would slow him down and complicate things. Charley had been a good lesson.

Once they got across the border, if they got across the border, he would have to deal with her then. For now, he had to focus on keeping the gun in position and himself from passing out.

~

Melinda glanced into the mirror periodically, hoping to see her unwanted passenger drifting off or losing focus. She considered swerving the jeep quickly, stopping, and then trying to run. But, to her dismay, he stayed clear-headed and met her eyes each time she looked. The gun barrel never moved other than to press harder each time she looked in the mirror, reminding her that she couldn't react quickly enough to avoid a bullet.

They had dropped out of the mountains and were now on a busy road. It was the weekend and many people were entering Mexico for shopping, fun, relaxation, or other activities not easily found in the states. They were coming to a split, east would take them to a small secondary border crossing and west would take them to Tijuana. Raider debated. The smaller border check would be less armed and closer to where they came out of the mountains, but the advantage of the larger border crossing was the crowd, lots of people. The border staff there would be hurried, trying to get people through as quickly as possible. Raider told her to head west, toward Tijuana. His gut told him it would be the best option. They wouldn't be looking for a young woman and they would probably just wave her through.

The car was quiet. He'd purposely kept the radio off. He didn't want Melinda to have a clue who he was or find out anything about the bank robbery. The less informed she was, the more scared and cooperative she'd be. If she thought there was a manhunt going on, with lots of armed guards, she might risk getting shot to escape. If she thought everything was normal, she wouldn't realize she had backup at the border.

"Pull over here," Raider ordered, instructing her to pull behind a deserted gas station. She stopped the jeep and put her hands on the ceiling. Raider took another small dose of painkiller and used his good arm to shift the items to conceal himself behind the front seats. Once ready, he pushed the gun into Melinda's back and told her to go with the flow and keep both hands on the steering wheel. He instructed Melinda to adjust the rear view mirror until he could see her face in the reflection. He wanted to be sure that she didn't try to attract the attention of other drivers or the border patrol using exaggerated facial expressions. Melinda wished now that she had peed. The pressure was beginning to build, but this would soon be over. She needed a distraction. "Can I turn on some music? It will help keep me calm," she asked quietly.

"Sure, but none of that Christian crap. You got anything else on that iPod?" Melinda located and started her playlist for classic rock. Her hands were back on the wheel and they headed toward their fate at the border.

~

Raider and Melinda pulled up to the checkpoint. Only a few cars were in front of them. Mexican border patrol greeted the cars, but Melinda noticed several American officers wandering around, paying close attention to certain types of vehicles. They seemed to be on alert.

Were they looking for her guy? Maybe she should make a move. He wouldn't be able to react quickly enough if she jumped out of the car, would he? She tried not to tense up or let her eyes reveal that she had a plan. Her heart jumped into her throat when she felt Raider's hand grab her t-shirt and pull tightly as he twisted the fabric. The gun was pressed uncomfortably hard into her back. She was convinced that Raider was capable of reading minds. She felt like a dog tied to a leash.

"Nah, I can't read minds Melinda, but I know what I'd be thinking right now. Relax sweetheart, it will be over soon," Raider whispered in an ominous voice.

When it was their turn, Raider pushed the gun even harder into her back. It was painful and a strong reminder that death was near and would come in the twitch of a finger if he chose. Melinda had no idea what he had done or was capable of. Maybe he would shoot her, even if he got caught. If he didn't have anything to lose, why not? Was he that brutal? She didn't want to find out.

The officer seemed more attentive with her than he had with the previous cars. He asked her for her passport. She pulled her IDs from the visor and handed them to him. Melinda tried to appear calm and even flashed a smile. The officer reviewed her passport carefully. There were quite a few entries. He looked at her again, searching her eyes. He seemed to sense something was off, strained. Instead of giving her back her property, he walked around the Jeep, even squatting to look under it. Melinda could see that he was suspicious, that there was something worth investigating. Maybe it was her prayers. Maybe God was unsettling his spirit. He was heading back to her window and Melinda felt both dread and relief.

Suddenly, there was a flurry of activity at the car next to hers. Several men were trying to get out of their car. The nearby guards swarmed the car and pulled their guns. Her guard quickly handed back her IDs and motioned for her to continue as he headed over to assist his fellow officers.

~

223

RAIDER'S Vendetta

Raider wanted to know what was going on, but he didn't want anyone to see Melinda talking to herself. They hadn't cleared the border area yet. It was a real disadvantage not being able to see what was going on outside of the car. He knew they'd been there too long for a clean pass. Something had caused the officer to delay them. The possibilities ran through Raider's mind. Had they figured out that he'd hijacked a driver in a Jeep? They might have found Bulwark and the bloody scene at the bridge. The Jeep would have left tire tracks in the mud. He needed to get away from her and her vehicle as soon as possible.

Once they passed through the city and were into a rural area, Raider released his hold on Melinda's t-shirt. His arm ached from the strain. He pulled back the gun and pulled himself up and out of the camping gear. When he spotted a deserted warehouse, he instructed Melinda to take a right turn and pull behind it.

~

Melinda knew he didn't need her anymore. He had no reason not to kill her. He could take the vehicle and leave her body to rot. She was determined not to go out this way. Now that Raider had moved, he was no longer able to see her eyes in the rearview mirror. Melinda braced herself. Now was the time. She didn't feel the gun in her spine. She would catch him off guard. She was buckled in, but he wasn't. Melinda stomped on the gas and headed for a large tree next to the road. Raider felt the sudden lunge and saw the tree. He tucked back into his cubbyhole and braced himself for the slam. Even if he shot her, they would still hit the tree and he knew it.

~

Raider was dazed, but otherwise unhurt. They'd hit the tree and the front of the Jeep was crunched against it. The vehicle wasn't going anywhere now. Luckily, Melinda hadn't clipped the tree and rolled the vehicle. Raider was able to get out and view the devastation. Melinda was unconscious in the front seat. Blood covered her face, but when he checked her pulse, it was strong. Raider couldn't stay here and help her. He knew someone would come along soon and help her. The money and the medical kit were his biggest concern right now. He checked himself for injuries, but he looked fine. As he ran away from the accident scene, he felt a twinge of concern for Melinda, but survival was all he knew. He found himself speaking to God. "She's your responsibility, not mine. You better send someone right away if you care about her." When he was a short distance away, he heard several cars arrive and felt a sense of relief. She was found and would get help.

RAIDER'S Vendetta

Chapter 49

Agent Morris was ecstatic when she got the call. A medic had taken Charley's picture with his phone at the rescue scene and sent it to the local police department. They forwarded the photo to her when they realized she matched the description of the missing bank hostage. Agent Morris was on her way to the hospital and would arrive just after Charley.

When Agent Morris arrived at the trauma center, she heard the prognosis. Charley had compound breaks and a concussion. The mud had protected her from hypothermia, but bacteria and insects had also caused a serious infection to develop. Agent Morris was able to confirm that the patient was Charley Abrams just before they took her into surgery for her leg. They needed to remove the bone fragments and dead tissue and repair the leg with rods and pins. She would be in traction for a while.

Her other injuries were also treated and she was given powerful antibiotics to fight the infection. The doctors couldn't predict when she would regain consciousness. Agent Morris wanted answers, but knew she would have to wait.

Agent Morris's feelings were mixed. She thought she knew who this woman was - a solid, loving woman who would sacrifice herself for others. But now, that was all under suspicion. The evidence she had received suggested that Charley might be a criminal, an actress playing a role. Maybe that was the plan from the beginning. If things went bad, she would walk away clear. Was she the mastermind or just a puppet? Apparently, things didn't happen as planned. She was lying in a hospital.

Agent Morris was pulled from her thoughts when she heard frantic voices coming into the ICU ward. Charley's children were here. She would give them time with their mother, but then she had some questions for them. She stepped out of Charley's room and saw the heartbreak on their faces. They reacted as any family would when the threat of death hovers over a loved one.

They thanked her for finding their mother and she told them she would need to speak with them as soon as possible. They would need to come down to the station after they visited their mother. Agent Morris would get her questions answered then. She knew their focus was on their mom and trying to question them now would be useless.

Since Charley was still unconscious, Agent Morris headed back to her office. There was no point in hanging around, wasting time. If she showed any improvement, they would notify Agent Morris immediately. She had placed an officer just outside the ICU. Charley wasn't a flight risk, hardly breathing, let alone able to move or be moved, but Arthur might show up.

~

Agent Morris ushered Charley's kids into her office. Mari and Michael were full of questions. Since Charley was unconscious, most of their questions were left unanswered. Agent Morris told them about the cabin and their assumption that Charley fell or was pushed off the ravine edge. Agent Morris guessed she had fallen. It made no sense for Arthur to push her. After the fall, he must have left her for dead and moved on.

Agent Morris began asking them about their family history and their mother's past relationships. The kids were cooperative, but didn't have much to offer. Charley had married her high school sweetheart at the age of nineteen. They had two children and were separate more than they were together. They finally divorced after twenty-five years of marriage. Charley then met Archie and they were married ten years before he died.

The kids described her life as normal. She was a great mother and worked hard at her graphic art business. She had no criminal history other than an occasional speeding ticket. Her parents were deceased and her remaining family members lived in the Midwest.

Agent Morris started to pin things down. "Has she ever talked about knowing a man named Arthur Myers?"

"The bank robber?" asked Mari.

"Well, yes. We have found some indications that your mother may have known him prior to the robbery. We are curious why they ended up at the same bank on the same day."

Michael became cautious. "Are you suggesting that our mother was involved in the robbery?"

"We're not suggesting anything. It is just surprising that they may have a history. We need to investigate all details regarding the robbery and the people involved." Michael and Mari looked concerned. "We just have some unanswered questions that will remain that way until your mother wakes up. Then we can clear this all up." She walked both of Charley's children out of her office.

~

When Agent Morris checked her phone, she saw that she had a message marked urgent. "Yeah Steve, what's up?"

"The woman Arthur carjacked was found early this morning. She's alive, but ran herself into a tree. They got into Mexico."

"Did they find Arthur?"

"Nope, the dogs picked up his scent at the scene but then lost it several miles away, near the highway. Apparently, he was picked up by a passing motorist."

Agent Morris's high from finding Charley was quickly crashing to earth.

"You get anything useful out of the woman? What's her name?"

"Melinda Evans. She's a military nurse and just returned back to the states."

"Holy crap! How many breaks can this guy get?"

"Well, not as many as you think. Apparently, the wolf we found ripped out his shoulder, and the bear ripped up his legs and arms. He was almost dead when Melinda found him by the bridge."

"But a nurse? What are the chances? She have a surgical team with her?"

"No, but she did stitch him up. He also has pain meds and antibiotics."

"When we found so much of his blood, I was counting on him ending up in an ER somewhere. That's shot to hell. Is she well enough to come back with you?"

"They want to keep her overnight for observation. She hit her head pretty bad. She purposely crashed the Jeep. She was afraid he didn't need her any longer and would kill her and take the car. I can stay over and bring her up with me tomorrow morning. This guy is a piece of crap."

"Do you think I need to come down?"

"No. She didn't know anything about the bank robbery or where he was going in Mexico. She thought he was a camper that got attacked by wild animals until he pulled a gun on her."

"Still armed, not surprised. Okay, let me know if anything useful comes up."

Chapter 50

Sunday

Donald was back at his mountain home, sitting in front of the stove and sipping chamomile tea. Loraine thought this tea healed every affliction. He wasn't a fan, but he knew that it was what she would prepare if she was still alive.

"How did the wolf get ahead of me, Loraine? There wasn't any physical way he could have scaled the side of the ravine and made it ahead of me."

He heard her sweet response in his head. *"Sweet-heart, I know you believe what you're telling me is true, but it sounds like something out of a science fiction novel. Maybe you were suffering from heat or dehydration. You were hallucinating?"*

"No, Loraine, I'm telling you, he pushed me up that ravine until I found the woman, Charley. Turns out, she is the victim of that terrible bank robbery last week. You have to believe me, dear. It was early, not even hot yet. I was perfectly sane, then. Not so sure about now."

"Okay, so let's say you're right. Where did he go? Why did he leave you?"

"No idea. Just seemed like he had somewhere important to be and he left."

"Forgive me for asking again, but how many raccoons were piled on the two of you?"

"I don't know dear, I didn't count them. Had to be at least ten."

"I'm not sure which is harder to imagine, the wolf or the raccoons," she would have said with a questioning smile.

"I know it all sounds like the ranting of a crazy man, but Loraine, I swear to you, it is all true. This woman has some way of connecting to animals. Maybe she's a witch?"

"I'm sorry dear. Just know that I believe that you believe. That's enough for me," she would have said with conviction.

"But it's not enough for me. What am I supposed to do with this, Loraine? How do I pretend it didn't happen and if I accept that it did, then I will be admitting that I am crazy."

He imagined Loraine rubbing his shoulders, *"You'll figure it out. You always manage to spring back whenever something knocks you down. No matter how it happened, Donald, you saved that woman's life. I am so proud of you."* She would have kissed him on the cheek and then headed to the kitchen. *"You hungry? I can make some soup."*

Donald leaned back in the recliner. He knew that no one would believe his story. If someone else were trying to convince him, he'd think they were loony, but he was there. He saw it, felt it, and smelled it. Charley was the answer. She would be the one who could explain what happened. He was glad he was well enough to travel soon. He wanted to visit Charley when she woke up. He wanted, no, he needed answers to his questions.

Chapter 51

Charley was sitting on a blanket in a field full of beautiful flowers. There was a picnic basket filled with all of her favorite foods. Soft, lilting music was playing somewhere in the distance. She laid back and looked up into the sky. It was familiar, but odd. The air closest to the ground was blue and filled with beautiful clouds, but higher up, the space was filled with stars. The higher she looked, the darker and farther away things were. She saw shooting stars and swirls of colors and light. It reminded her of the photos taken of outer space. The smells were sweet and intoxicating. Butterflies and birds began to fly around and hovered as if they were looking at her.

Suddenly, Archie's face was over hers. As she sat up, he pulled his head back so they wouldn't slam into each other. "Archie, how'd you get here?"

"Better question, how'd you get here?"

"I must have died. I'm in Heaven with you, right? Oh Archie, I'm so glad to be with you again."

Archie sat down with her and held her tightly. "This is a visit, hon, just a visit."

"No, I don't want to be there anymore. I want to be with you. I want to be with Jesus."

"I know dear, I know, but there are some things left for you to do. People there need you. You have the best chance of reaching them. You want to finish out your destiny, right?"

"No, I'm done. I don't care about anything on Earth. I want to be here, now, with you. I'm tired, Archie. I'm lonely and just waiting to come here."

"I don't believe you, Charley. You have Mari, Michael, and the grandkids. There are also others you

will touch profoundly. Don't you want to help bring as many of your family and friends as possible here with you when it's time?"

Charley knew he was right, but she didn't want to admit it. "Here, let's enjoy our lunch and you can fill me in on all the latest." Archie pulled out a warm chocolate chip cookie and bent it in half. The chocolate stretched until it broke apart. He held it to her lips. Charley took a bite and moaned.

"It's Heavenly," she said with her mouth full. Then she giggled and Archie joined in. They hugged, ate, and talked. Charley told Archie all about her adventure and about Raider. She shared the dreams she had while delirious. Charley asked Archie if he would tell her how she survived after the fall.

"It's not supposed to come from me, sweetheart, but you will meet the man who saved you. He can tell you all the miracles that transpired while God protected you. This is something that you shared with him and it was as much for him as you."

Charley and Archie spent an unmeasured amount of time together. She didn't know if it was minutes, months, or years. It was unrushed, playful, but surrounded by an unspoken sadness. The basket never emptied. Each time she reached in, there was another favorite treat. At one point, she asked Archie about calories in Heaven and he grinned and assured her that there were none.

Archie's mood became serious. It would be time for her to leave soon.

"Charley, your journey is not over yet. You will be facing some unexpected things when you return to Earth. You must remember our time here. This will ultimately be ours. You will see your parents and your Christ the next time you arrive. It will be your home, no going back."

"You're scaring me, Archie. What more is expected of me?"

"I don't know the details, but I know this. You are loved beyond any Earthly measure. You are not alone and there is grace and goodness that can come from pain and darkness. Trust in God, Charley. Trust with all your heart! Don't forget who you are and who He is."

Charley clung to Archie and cried. She knew she would be leaving him and knew that she would be entering into a painful portion of her life.

"Dance with me, Charley. Let me hold you close."

Charley stood up and their favorite song began to swirl around them. "I Finally Found Someone" by Barbra Streisand filled their hearts and minds with their memories, their love, and their longing for an eternity together.

Archie spun her around and she saw him disappear as she whirled back to her hospital room.

She felt the weight of her body on the bed, the ache of her injuries, and the sounds of the equipment around her. Tears rolled down her cheeks and she heard her own sobs trying to escape around the breathing tube.

"Mom, Mom, are you awake? Open your eyes, Mom!" she heard Mari calling.

Charley opened her eyes and saw the exhausted face of her daughter and the hopeful face of her son pop up next to her. Mari immediately squealed with joy and ordered Michael to go get the nurse. He was already running out of the room. She felt Mari wipe away her tears and kiss her face. "Oh Mom, you had us so scared." Charley was unable to speak but squeezed her daughter's hand with surprising strength. She was back, whether she wanted to be or not.

RAIDER'S Vendetta

Chapter 52

When the call came, Agent Morris was elated. Charley was awake. The ICU was bubbling with energy. Obviously, the news had traveled fast and the staff was thrilled. A patient waking up from a coma was always good news. Agent Morris saw Mari and Michael in the family waiting area. They were both engrossed in phone calls. Agent Morris was glad that cell phones were not allowed in the ICU, otherwise she would not have time alone with Charley. She saw excitement and relief in their body language as they shared the news of Charley's improvement. It saddened her to know there was another hurdle awaiting them.

Agent Morris slipped into Charley's room and saw that she was awake. The breathing tube had been removed. "Hello, Charley, I am Agent Megan Morris. I am the agent that is investigating the bank robbery. It is so good to see you safe and awake. You had a lot of people worried about you. Especially your children," Agent Morris said,

"Hello Agent Morris. Were you the one on the phone with Raider?"

"Raider?" asked Agent Morris.

"That's what I called him. I didn't know his name. He was wearing a Raiders cap, so it just stuck. He approved anyway."

"We know him as Arthur Myers."

"He did tell me his real name when we were in the mountains, but Raider was locked in. Hard to change names once they're burned into your brain." Charley smiled, but Agent Morris didn't. "I wanted to thank you for everything you did for us while in the bank. I know he was difficult to deal with. Lot's of issues with that man," said Charley.

"Ahhh, yes, he certainly was difficult. A smart man though. He thinks quickly. Most people get flustered and mess up, especially when they lose their partner during the crime. Panic sets in, plans change. He almost appeared to be too calm. Like maybe someone else was helping him."

"No, he was in there alone. I saw military tattoos when we were holed up. Probably his military training kept him calm."

"You know much about this guy? You had a lot of time together."

"Not much. He wasn't the sharing type." Charley grimaced in pain. "I know he was dishonorably discharged and it sounds like he had a rough childhood."

Agent Morris knew the nurses or her children would be in soon, so she needed to get a reaction quickly. "Did you know Arthur prior to the robbery, Charley?"

"No, of course not. Why would you ask that?"

"It just seems odd that you both would be in the bank on that day, at that time."

Charley was confused. "What are you talking about? I went to the bank, he happened to rob it at that time. What is odd about that?"

Agent Morris chose her words carefully as she watched for any sign of guilt. That look of "I'm caught" spreading slowly over the criminal's face. "Well, it wouldn't be odd except for the fact that you are Arthur's grandmother." Here it comes, wait for it.

Charley looked confused at first and then started to giggle. "Are you nuts? He's not my grandson."

"We tested all the blood samples from the bank and the cabin. Arthur's blood and your blood had similar characteristics. Enough that we reviewed the DNA test results from his father's prison records. His father's DNA matched yours and Arthur's. He is your grandson, Charley. These tests were redone several times to rule out any mistake."

Charley's face froze in shock, not exactly what Agent Morris imagined.

"Raider is my grandson? I had a son in prison?" she finally managed. Agent Morris almost believed her. "Get out, get out now. I want my children. You leave right now. I haven't been through enough? You come in here creating these lies." Charley's breathing and anxiety set off the alarms and nurses pushed in as Agent Morris backed out. She stepped back into the hall and felt bodies behind her. She turned and faced Mari and Michael. "I'm sorry, but your mother has some explaining to do."

Agent Morris pushed past them and headed out to her car. She was troubled. This was not the reaction of a woman hiding a robbery plot. This was the reaction of a woman who was truly shocked. Agent Morris could only guess what dark secrets she had ripped open. If she didn't know about Arthur, she *was* an innocent victim.

RAIDER'S Vendetta

Chapter 53

Charley sat in silence. "Mom, what did she say to you?" Michael asked.

Charley looked at him with such sadness. How could she explain something that she had hidden for most of her life, something that only she and her dead family members knew? "Give me some time son. I'll explain everything soon."

"Sure Mom, when you're ready."

Mari and Michael gave each other concerned looks.

"We will call a lawyer. Don't talk to anyone about the robbery or your time as a hostage," Mari said firmly. "The police think they know something and we need to be careful not to give them something they can twist. No one, Mom, not even the nurses."

"I know you both have a lot of questions, but I'm feeling drained right now. Go home, get some rest, and hug your kids. I would like some time alone. We can talk this afternoon."

"Okay, Mom, we'll be back at three o'clock. You're in Scripps Mercy Hospital in San Diego, so we're at a hotel. It's too far to drive back and forth."

"Oh dear, how long I have been unconscious?"

"Only a few days. We're fine, Mom. We're just glad we were here when you woke up," Michael insisted.

"Me too, Hon," she said as she smiled at both of her children. She hoped that they would still love her after she told them her secrets.

"The kids are worried, Mom," Michael said. "Can I take a picture of you with my phone so they can see you're alive and okay?"

"Good idea, Michael. Me too, Mom?" asked Mari.

241

"I'm sure I look terrible. You're not worried I'll scare them?"

"Nah, you look great Mom, just great!" Michael assured her.

Charley reached up with her good arm to smooth her hair, but felt bandages. She smiled, a strained smile at best. Michael and Mari took their photos and quickly put away their phones. No one wanted to be chastised by the nurses. They would send their prized photos once they left the ICU.

Charley laid still, just listening to her breathing. More than ever, she wished she had stayed in Heaven with Archie. She was smart and knew that life was going to be painfully complicated for some time to come. She was worn out and not up to the journey she was beginning. She remembered Archie's words. Trust in God, Charley, trust with all your heart! Don't forget who you are and who He is.

This should have given her peace, but it felt more like a warning for her to brace herself for a difficult ride. She drifted back to that day, the day that started a chain of events that were slamming her today.

~

Charley had such a crush on the preacher's son. His name was Andrew Lee Whalings. He was sixteen, almost seventeen, but she knew he liked her, too. Andy would always watch to see where she sat in church and then sit behind her. He would poke her at times, slip her stupid notes, and tease her every chance he got. Another boy would have annoyed her, but his attention filled her fourteen-year-old heart with such joy. She couldn't focus on the message or the worship. She only felt his eyes focused on the back of her head.

Summer camp was coming up. Charley was so excited. It would be her first time away from home and for a whole week. The camp was co-ed, but they took every precaution to keep the kids separated and safe from inappropriate contact. The cabins were rustic and filled the kids with a sense of adventure. Charley was having the best time of her life. The games, activities and evening fires were everything she anticipated.

She would see Andy during the shared activities and they would grin at each other or stare longingly. Some of the girls would tease her and she would quickly deny any feelings for him. Being close, but separated, was torturous for her. She dreamed about kissing him and feeling his arms around her.

It was their last night at camp. The bonfire had been lit and they were going to make s'mores. The youth pastor asked Andy to go get the sticks for the marshmallows. Charley happened to walk by. "Can Charley help me? I almost dropped them last time."

The pastor glanced at Charley, who seemed willing, and nodded. He trusted Andy, the pastor's son, and didn't think twice. When they left the light of the fire, Andy grabbed her hand and they ran to the storage building where supplies were kept.

Once inside, Andy grinned at her. He was rather confident for his age and waited for her to blush. It was clear that she liked him. He liked her, too, but he liked a lot of girls. She was his choice from the church congregation. "Is it okay if I kiss you, Charley?"

Charley was shocked. She had thought about this moment for so long and here it was. "Yes," she said shyly. She closed her eyes, leaned forward and gave him her cheek. Andy struggled not to laugh.

"Not like that. Here, let me show you." Andy moved in close and put his hands on her face. She saw his face moving toward hers with his eyes closed. She closed her eyes, too. Next, she felt his soft lips on hers. Lightly, at first, then firmer. Charley was confused by the sensations her body was feeling. She was warm and tingling in areas that were so very private. This was so much better than she ever dreamed.

Andy pulled his face back and smiled at her. "Man, you're a good kisser. Is this your first time?"

"Yes," she answered shyly.

"I'd like to kiss you again." Andy didn't wait for her to respond, but leaned in for a much longer, more passionate kiss. The feelings and emotions began to swirl as she felt his hand slip down to her breast. She knew she should stop him, but it triggered even more reaction from her body. Andy pulled her down to the floor and continued to kiss and nibble her mouth, face, and ears. His breath in her ear sent chills down her spine. This all felt so right, but her mind kept saying, "Stop!" She rationalized that they only had minutes, they were dressed, and he was

243

the preacher's son. He would know when to stop.

Andy climbed on top of her and she felt his groin rubbing against her. He gradually moved her legs apart. All the warning lights were flashing in her head, but the waves of physical desire kept her from stopping him. In a wave of excitement, she felt his hand fumbling, and then she felt excruciating pain. Charley was in shock. She tried to push him away, but he was too heavy. He shuddered on top of her and then rolled off. Charley sat up and saw the blood on her shorts. She was still dressed. Charley had only been alone with Andy for five minutes. How did it happen so quickly?

Andy looked at her and a look of guilt spread over his face. "We better get back. They'll be wondering what took so long." He jumped up and arranged his clothing. He didn't even help her up, just grabbed the sticks, and headed toward the door. He stopped and turned back to her. Charley thought he would say something sweet, something loving to show how much he cared for her. "You can't tell anyone, Charley. We will both be in a lot of trouble." Then he left.

Charley knew she couldn't stay there, but she couldn't face the other kids either. Her friends would know something was wrong. She got up, wiped the blood from her thighs, and slowly headed back to her cabin with tears rolling down her cheeks. Her counselor, Annie, came running up behind her. "Hey Charley, you okay, hon? You look like you're in pain." Luckily, they were in the dark and she couldn't see Charley's face clearly.

"I'm fine, just cramping. Started my period."

"Okay hon. You need to get to the infirmary for pads?"

"No thank you. I have some pads in my suitcase. Is it okay if I go lay down for awhile?"

It was against the rules to let the students stay in the cabins alone, but Charley looked like she was uncomfortable. "Sure, I have some paperwork I can do while you rest. Maybe you'll be up to joining the others in a little while."

Annie put her arm around Charley's shoulder and tried to cheer her up "Good thing you didn't start until today. It would have sucked if you started at the beginning of the week."

"Yeah, it would have," agreed Charley. When they got to the cabin, Charley made a dash for the bathroom. She didn't want Annie to see that she had been crying when the light was turned on. It would have created more questions and Charley didn't know if she would be able to resist Annie's sweet persistence.

Charley closed the door and locked it. She stood facing the mirror and turned on the light. She didn't look any different. There were lots of stories about when a girl became a woman, a glow or something like that. Now that she thought about it, the glow was when you were pregnant. Next, she checked her neck for marks. Andy had bitten her lightly several times and she wanted to be sure he didn't leave any signs that she had had sex. She removed her clothing and stepped into the shower. She wanted everything from their encounter washed off. The pain she felt was physical, but her heart also ached. How did he go from being so sweet and romantic to being so cold and mean? Charley felt foolish and betrayed. He had tricked her, just as her dad had warned her. The flirting and attention had been to sucker her in and then take what he wanted. She sat on the floor of the shower and let the hot water pound her. She wept quietly so that Annie would not hear and demand to know what was wrong. No one could know how gullible she'd been. She wouldn't tell anyone what happened that night and Andy was dead to her. He would no longer stir thrills in her heart just by brushing past her.

~

Three months later, Charley was frantic. She still hadn't started her period and she was sick all the time. Her breasts were tender and sore. She couldn't accept that she might be pregnant. It was the first time and only one time. Everyone knows you can't get pregnant the first time. Charley came down to breakfast and immediately turned green when she smelled bacon cooking. Her mother, Kayla, looked at her with concern. "Charley, you're staying home today. I'm going to get you in to see Dr. Williams. You've been feeling sick for too long to be just a virus."

Charley groaned. "I'll be fine mom. I have a test today."

"Don't argue, young lady. I will feel better if the doctor checks you out."

RAIDER'S Vendetta

Charley realized there was no way to get out of this and, once they were in the doctor's office, Charley thought she would pass out. What would her mother do if the doctor figured out she'd had sex, or worse, was pregnant? Her parents would be so disappointed that she wasn't a virgin anymore. The doctor asked some questions, listened to her heart and lungs, and checked her ears and throat. Next she was asked to lie down on the table and he began pressing and feeling her stomach. It was uncomfortable and she yelped when his fingers pressed in deep. The doctor stood up, helped Charley sit up, and made some notes in her chart.

Next, he sat down on a stool and rolled up close to Charley. Kayla looked concerned from her spot in the corner. "Charley, I need to ask you some personal questions. It is important that you are honest with me."

"Yes sir," she answered quietly.

"Have you become sexually active?"

Her mother gasped and Charley shook her head violently.

The doctor realized that this was not the way to approach her. "I am not asking you if you are having sex on a regular basis, but if you have had sex in the last few months?"

Charley looked down at her hands and began to sob. The doctor rolled back to allow Kayla to move in next to her. Her mother put her arm around Charley and held her tight. She whispered so only Charley heard. "I love you sweetheart. Nothing will ever change that. You need to tell us everything, so we can make sure you are okay."

Once Charley calmed down, she explained what had happened at camp. She didn't tell them that it was Andy. When her mother asked who it was, Charley refused to answer.

The doctor explained that he needed to do a pelvic exam. They wanted to check for sexually transmitted diseases and for pregnancy. This sent Charley into another wave of overwhelming emotions and sobbing.

The exam and urine test confirmed that Charley was pregnant. Her due date was only days from her own birthday. She would be barely fifteen when the baby was born.

246

After several intense conversations with her parents, she finally told them that it had been Andy.

Charley remembered the evening that her parents and Andy's parents met in their living room. She heard them from her bedroom when she left the door open. First, there was a lot of yelling about her being a liar, that his parents would be proven wrong once the baby was born, and finally about whose fault it was. Charley shut the door and turned her music up as loud as necessary to drown out the angry voices. After what seemed like hours, Charley's father knocked on her door. Charley opened it slowly and her father asked her to join them in the living room.

When she entered the room, Andy's mother glared at her through mascara-smeared eyes. Charley looked down and didn't raise her eyes again. Pastor Whalings tried to be kind and pastorly, but his disdain was just under the surface. They informed Charley that she would need to put the baby up for adoption. Having a baby at her age would only hinder her education and happiness. Andy had a fine future in front of him with Seminary College and a church of his own. This transgression would only ruin his future and possibly hers. Pastor Whalings wanted to know if she had told anyone that she was pregnant or that she had had sex with Andy, especially anyone at church. "No, I haven't," she said shamefully.

"That's perfect dear. It is imperative that you don't. We don't need everyone knowing your business, thinking you're an easy young woman." Charley's father, David, rose to challenge the pastor. After all, Andy was three years older than his daughter was. Charley's mother placed her hand on his arm and shook her head no. David sat down slowly and reluctantly.

"Well, it sounds like everyone is in agreement. I'm so sorry this situation arose. I'm sure both of our children have learned a valuable lesson. Will we be seeing you at church on Sunday?" asked Pastor Whalings as he stood in the open doorway.

"No, sir, you won't," Kayla said firmly.

Mrs. Whalings had already walked out to the car.

"I suppose that's best," Pastor Whalings said. "If you need anything, please do not hesitate to call."

No one responded. They shut the door and the Whalings walked away unscathed. But, what about Charley? How would she be able to carry a child without everyone at school knowing? How would she get through this pregnancy and keep any dignity?

Her parents came back into the room and sat down. They were quiet for some time. "Charley, we know that you are a good girl. We know that this was a mistake, but you are the gatekeeper. It is your responsibility to set the boundaries for young men. They will only do what you let them, dear," her father said softly. Charley knew then that she carried all of the blame. Andy was cleared of any wrongdoing because she hadn't guarded her gate well enough.

"We've discussed this situation with your grandmother. When you start to show, you will go to live with her until the baby is born. We'll tell everyone that she is ill and you've gone there to help her with the housework and cooking. You will home school. When you come back, everything will be as it was." Charley's grandmother, a retired teacher, lived in central California, far enough away that no one she knew would see her once her pregnancy was obvious. It would be a well-kept secret.

Charley looked scared and grabbed her mother's arm. "Will you be with me, Mommy? I can't do this all by myself."

"Yes, dear, I will come up as often as I can and when you're close, I'll come stay till the baby is born." Charley looked at her father and he looked away. She knew that he would not be there for the birth of her child. Their relationship changed that year. She was no longer his sweet little girl. He was kind and loving at times, but she was her mother's daughter now.

Charley hated the months with her stern grandmother. They never spoke of the pregnancy, but the larger she got, the more irritated her grandmother became with her. The only saving grace was her mother. She would come and spend weekends with her. They would go to movies, go shopping, and share lunches. People would stare at Charley. She was obviously too young to be pregnant, but she didn't know them and she didn't care what they thought.

When Charley was eight and a half months pregnant, her mother came to stay with her. They celebrated her birthday with ice cream and chocolate cake. Charley's grandmother disapproved and made her feelings known by clucking under her breath. Charley was supposed to be shunned and punished for her circumstances. Celebrating her birthday was pampering a tramp. Her grandmother was her father's mother and she'd never thought much of Kayla. This celebration just confirmed that Kayla coddled Charley and her pampering had contributed to Charley getting herself in a family way. Kayla told Charley to ignore her.

The pregnancy was without complications and Charley went into labor on schedule. The delivery was painful, scary, and something Charley swore she'd never do again. The baby was a boy. He was healthy, smaller than normal, but would be just fine the nurse explained. They asked Charley if she wanted to hold her baby and Kayla told them no. Charley didn't know how she felt. She wanted it over and decided to allow her mother to make the decisions.

After a week of recovery at her grandmother's, Charley returned home. Many things were different. Her parents had moved, they attended a new church, and she was enrolled in a new school. Her parents thought a new beginning was necessary for their lives to be untouched by the birth. The baby was never spoken of again. There were no pictures and no assigned name. It was as if Charley had watched a movie about someone else's life. If she did think about her baby, it was briefly and surreal. There were no emotional connections.

The first time Charley acknowledged any feelings for her child was when Mari was born. The memories of her first delivery had flooded back. When she held Mari for the first time, she was filled with emotions of joy, and yet she felt sad for the little baby boy she had given away. She found herself wondering what happened to him. Her parents assured her at the time of the adoption, that only the most wonderful people in the world were allowed to adopt. They were loving parents who were sad because they couldn't have children of their own. She was giving them the most sacred gift that could be given. Charley believed it. She had to.

Now, Charley was dealing with the reality that her son had grown to be a vicious man, a man who brutalized his son. Her child had died in prison, fighting over cigarettes. The life she'd brought into the world, by not guarding the gate, had contributed to the destruction of his own son, a son that was ruthless, bitter, and tormented others with no remorse, her grandson. Charley felt regret, shame, and sadness well up and saturate every fiber of her being. Why would God play this cruel joke on her? Was He punishing her for her carnal sin those many years ago? Maybe Raider was sent to put her through the hell she deserved. Charley slipped into a dark place, a place without the light of God or hope.

Chapter 54

The lawyer was encouraging. He said that none of the hostages would implicate Charley in the robbery. She was their hero and they were ready to stand behind her one hundred percent. There was nothing that linked Charley to Arthur other than the DNA test results. Her phone bills were scrutinized and the police were unable to prove any communication prior to the robbery. She was no longer under investigation, but he advised her to lay low and not talk to the media.

"Do the police still think I was involved?" asked Charley.

"The chances of being taken hostage by your unknown grandson are beyond consideration. They can't get past the numbers, Charley. That's all."

Mari and Michael were shocked by their mother's revelation about having a son at fifteen. They asked their questions and decided as a family not to bring it up to the grandchildren until Charley was ready to tell them herself. Luckily, the children were young enough that the flood of media coverage didn't touch them. Her kids asked her about her time with Raider, but didn't push when she shut down.

~

Charley was splattered all over the news and newspapers. The public debated her innocence or guilt, after the details of Charley's pregnancy and adoption became public. She was asked to appear on several local talk shows, but declined. She declined interviews and book and movie offers. She just wanted it all to stop. The hospital had to beef up security to keep Charley protected from curious spectators.

Chapter 55
One Week Later

Charley's healing was progressing, but it was slow. The doctors told her children that she lacked the fight to survive. They needed to encourage Charley to recover and suggested that anti-depressants might be necessary. Charley didn't care, she wanted to check out. If she died, she would be with Archie. All this pain and guilt would be gone. She wouldn't kill herself, but she didn't have to help them keep her alive.

While in the ICU, Charley wasn't allowed to have flowers. The hospital had shared her many flowers from well wishers with the other patients, but her room was stark. The grandchildren had drawn some pictures that were taped to the wall and there were a few books on her table, including her Bible. Charley didn't read. She would only stare blankly at the television, mesmerized into oblivion. A nurse brought in a box wrapped with a beautiful purple ribbon. "This came for you today." She handed Charley a box.

"There isn't a card?" Charley asked without much interest.

"Oh dear, it must have gotten separated. I'm so sorry. I'll see if I can locate it for you."

Charley stared at the box and finally pulled the ribbon free. She opened it and her heart leapt. There in soft billowy tissue was an elegant porcelain wolf. It was gray and had deep blue eyes. She pulled the tissue out, searching for a note, some clue to who had sent it. She hadn't shared the miracles that had occurred with anyone, not even her children. She looked at the outside of the box but there were no markings. Usually, a gift shop would have their label somewhere on the box or the tis-

RAIDER'S Vendetta

sue. There was nothing to indicate where this gift came from. Was the card lost or was it from him? Raider would not have sent a note. The wolf would tell it all. But, it was foolish to think that he would waste any effort sending her a gift. Maybe he saw the news. Maybe he knows that she is his grandmother. Charley was exhausted and didn't want to play any head games, but she couldn't get the wondering to stop. No one knew about the wolf but Raider. Why would he send it?

When the nurse returned, Charley asked her to track down the card or find out how the gift had been delivered. She needed to know who sent it. The nurse agreed to try to solve the mystery.

When Charley looked at the wolf, the memories of God's care for her came flooding back. She had forgotten that He had been there for her, providing food and protection through this beautiful animal. The knowledge of God's forgiveness suddenly replaced the shame of her son's conception and death. This twist in her life was not a banner of dishonor; it was a revelation that God loves her through anything. He did not forsake her for her past. The news was a gift, a grandson, a man that she would someday share love and God's truth with.

Chapter 56

Donald was excited. He was finally making the trip to see Charley. He had followed the news regarding her rescue, the robbery, and her relationship with the robber still at large. Donald was a celebrity in his own right. The local news had done stories on his bravery and his efforts to save Charley. When they'd asked why he went to that particular spot, he said it was luck. He was leaving the area for the winter and wanted to check a spot that had provided some wonderful geode samples. It was all fabricated, of course. He wasn't ready to tell anyone else about the wolf or the raccoons. His wife's reaction in his own head was warning enough that he wouldn't be believed. The idea that he would be labeled "looney" didn't appeal to him one bit.

Charley had been moved from the ICU into a private room and when the hospital staff told her that Donald Princeton wanted to visit, Charley almost declined. Then she remembered her dream with Archie. He had told her that Donald would have answers regarding her survival and God's protection over her. Charley looked forward to something for the first time in quite a while.

When Donald came into her room, he hardly recognized her. The woman in the ravine had been near death's door and looked ready for the trip. This woman was vibrant. Her eyes sparkled, even though sadness shone through. Charley reached out her hand to shake but Donald held her hand between both of his and didn't let go. "You have no idea how happy I am to see you alive. I was so worried that I hadn't found you in time."

~

Charley smiled. She had a good feeling about this man. "Well, I'm glad to be alive. Thank you so much for all you did. I understand that it was quite a rescue and you put yourself at great risk."

"If I had been a few years younger, I would've carried you out over my shoulder. Alas, my old bones left me limited."

Charley grinned. "I know how that feels."

"I imagine you do. I've been following the news and I understand that you had a tough time of it. You must lead a blessed life to have survived."

Charley looked at him intently and then asked, "Are you a spiritual man, Donald?"

"I didn't think so before I met you. Now, I'm not so sure. I can't explain everything that happened out there." Charley wasn't sure what he meant and it showed on her face.

"I have questions for you," he said quietly. "Odd things happened, things I can't explain."

Charley nodded to the chair next to her bed. Donald sat down. "Can you explain what you mean?"

Donald looked over his shoulder to make sure no one was close by or listening. "There was a wolf, I think your wolf. He brought me to you."

Charley's jaw dropped. "Dear Bulwark. He didn't leave me."

"No, he was determined to get you help." Donald described how the wolf had blocked him and herded him to her.

Charley realized that she loved that wolf. She felt such gratitude to Bulwark, as well as to God. She suddenly had a thought. "Did you send me the porcelain wolf?" she asked while nodding to the statue on her nightstand.

"No, I didn't. That looks just like him though. I would have if I had seen it."

Charley was even more convinced that Raider had sent the wolf.

"So, Bulwark was your pet?"

"Oh no, he came to me while I was still a hostage. As far as I know, he was a wild wolf that was sent to protect me from Raider."

"Sent? By who?"

Charley looked at Donald and tried to figure out how he would handle her explanation. She decided to go for it. "God. God sent the wolf to keep me safe and alive. I had no idea that he continued to care for me after I fell into the ravine."

"Well, I don't believe in God, but it was obvious that the wolf had been with you before I got there."

"If not God, how would you explain it Donald?"

"I'm not sure. I thought you were Wiccan, you know, a witch, especially after the raccoons. I figured you knew how to speak telepathically to animals and get them to do your bidding."

"Raccoons? What are you talking about?"

"The night we were out there, the temperatures dropped dangerously low. I slept through the night toasty warm and woke to the raccoons. They covered you and me. They had to have been there most of the night. When they left, one smiled at me."

Charley laughed out loud. "Are you serious? It smiled at you?"

Donald grinned, "You're surprised that one smiled, but not that we were covered with them?"

"No Donald, I'm not surprised at all. I have seen unimaginable things since the robbery, things that no one would believe. I have a question for you. How come you can believe that I, as a human, could command animals, but you find it impossible to believe that God exists and would protect us?"

"It would mean my whole view of life would be wrong. I would have to lose my ego and my freedom."

Charley looked at Donald and smiled, a warm genuine 'I Like You' smile. "Well Donald, you're going to have to rethink your explanation. I am not Wiccan and I can't will anything to do what I want it to do, not even my own children." Donald smiled at her. "I think you and I will be good friends. I sense that you'll be searching for the truth now and maybe I can help you find your way. If you think the raccoons are a trip, wait till I tell you about the bunnies."

~

RAIDER'S Vendetta

Donald grinned and settled into his chair. He listened to her story with awe. Had he not seen miracles himself, he would never have believed her. But, he knew that she spoke the truth and he was filled with excitement, this was a God he could consider.

Charley thanked him for coming. It meant a lot to be able to share her story with someone who would understand and believe her. It gave her the encouragement to share the miracles with her children. Donald promised to come again. They exchanged phone numbers and began a deep abiding friendship that brought comfort to them both that lasted for the remainder of Donald's years.

Chapter 57

Arthur was managing. Once he'd left Melinda with her Jeep, taking the three hundred and seventy-five dollars she had on her, he'd paid a traveling farm worker fifty dollars to take him deep into central Mexico. He settled in a small town just south of Mexico City. Many Americans had discovered this sleepy, beautiful area, which allowed him to blend in and find work. Buying a fake ID was easy and he was now Harold Mesker. His hair was cropped short and dyed brown and his beard had grown out. He also wore brown contact lenses to cover his green eyes. He spent his days working at a large brewery and his evenings drinking beer. His legs and arms had healed, but there were scars. His shoulder, however, was still painful and required more time to heal. He was thankful that his job involved driving a forklift and not lifting cases of beer. His rented room was small but clean. Life was doable.

Arthur traveled the short distance into central Mexico City to check out the California papers online at the library. They were a week or so old, but at least he knew what was happening at home. He found several articles about the hostage, miraculously found alive after falling into a deep ravine. She had sustained serious injuries, but was saved by a geologist digging in the area. Arthur was shocked. He had seen the ravine and how far she would have fallen. There was no way for her to survive, but yet, they had pictures. It was Charley. Every few days, Arthur would check the papers for more articles. One article finally gave the name of the hospital where she was recovering. When one of the farm workers Arthur had come to know was heading into San Diego, he promised

259

to take the wolf Arthur had found at a local artist's studio to Charley. He would get it there without any postal stamp betraying where it came from. Arthur knew that Charley wouldn't be sure that it was from him, but who else would send a gray wolf with deep blue eyes?

He couldn't explain why he sent it. It just seemed like he needed to acknowledge her survival. It was that human side of him again, popping out when he least expected it. Arthur had also read that Melinda suffered minor injuries in the crash. He felt bad leaving her there, unconscious, but knew the police would show up and ask a lot of questions. If he didn't know better, he would think these Christians had special privileges, that God did care about some humans. Not all, not him. But then the memories of Bulwark would flood back, how he sacrificed himself for Arthur. The fruit, the meat, and the nurse on a back road. When he stacked it all up, it did favor God's hand in his survival. "No, I know You don't care. It's just a chance for You to show off and rub in your ability to pick and choose, to hear and answer some prayers, but not mine, God. You chose to ignore me for all those years. I don't need You now and I don't want You now. It's too late," he snarled at the heavens.

A week later, Arthur was back at the library to check on news regarding Charley. The last article he'd read said she was still in the ICU, but improving. When he checked the San Diego Union-Tribune, his jaw dropped. His heart began to pound in his chest.

The headline read, *"Grandma Charley Barker? Hostage or Master Mind?"* Arthur began reading the article while his thoughts swirled. This woman was his grandmother? This had to be a joke. They were trying to flush him out. He read on. *The DNA tests had been performed several times and there was no room for error, Agent Megan Morris states. The police have confirmed that Charley Abrams is the paternal grandmother to Arthur Myers, suspected of being one of the murderous bank robbers that hit the Ellisville Bank in Ellisville, California. Mrs. Abrams states that she was unaware of the family connection until the police told her. She, however, admits to an early teen pregnancy and a son that was placed for adoption. Charley was fifteen when her son, Gary Myers, was born. Mr. Myers was killed many years ago in prison. He had been incarcerated for beating a man to death. Her son had a long history of violence and crime. There is no proof of any involvement in her son's life or any connection to his crimes. Police, however, still consider her a person of interest in the bank robbery. The chances of a grandmother being taken hostage by an unknown grandson are too incredible to be easily dismissed as coincidental. When asked if they were pressing charges, Agent Morris indicated that Charley Abrams was under investigation, but that they were not prepared to proceed with formal charges at this time.*

Mrs. Abrams was not available for comment, but her children and friends stand behind this woman as an innocent victim. They cannot explain how the uniting of family would happen in this way, but know that she was unaware of a grandson.

Arthur pounded the desk and caught the glare of the librarian. He continued with the article. *It is believed that Arthur Myers escaped into Mexico and successfully eluded the net of the San Diego police and border patrol. The Mexican police have indicated they will cooperate with FBI and arrest the criminal if he is found in their country. This very public case will make it difficult for Mr. Myers to hide, even in Mexico.*

Arthur was livid. Charley had thrown his whole life into chaos. She was screwing with him even before he was born. She discarded his father, which in turn set him up to be discarded. *You miserable, selfish old woman. You are responsible for all the crap I have endured,* he thought. *You dumped your kid, not worrying what would become of him or your grandchildren. Some Christian you turned out to be.* Not only had this article revealed his heritage, it made him front-page news. He did not need this spotlight on his life or his attempt to flee a botched robbery, a robbery that would have gone off smoothly, without a hitch, if Darrell had not been greedy. And murderous? He didn't kill anyone. He shot a few people, but that was not murder.

Arthur finished the article and saw that Charley had been moved to a private room. She was going to heal and survive, still a servant to her controlling God. Arthur would be able to torment and mess with her till she died. He savored the possibility that they might charge her for the bank robbery. It would be an excellent twist. Arthur was pleased that her God had left her high and dry.

RAIDER'S Vendetta

Arthur left the library filled with confusion and anger. He headed to the nearest cantina. Thus began a night of drinking and fighting, which ultimately ended up with him in a crowded, nasty cell. The next morning, after passing out, Arthur woke up to a stiff neck and aching back. He had managed to snag a seat on the bench against the corner in the drunkard's cell. His jaw and right eye ached. When he felt his face, it was swollen. His right eye felt odd and the lid had swollen almost shut. Ice and aspirin would relieve a lot of the discomfort. He vaguely remembered flirting and dancing with one of the waitresses. Apparently, her husband had come in to pick her up and didn't appreciate finding his pretty wife on the lap of an American man, groping and kissing. Arthur was confident that he had damaged the irate man as well.

Arthur knew the drill. He would give the jailer everything in his wallet and the charges would be dropped. He would go home. He might even know the jailer, since several of them worked shifts at the brewery to support their families.

When it was Arthur's turn to talk to the jailer, he was taken to the barred window and handed a bag with his personal belongings. He wasn't surprised that his money was still in the bag. Some of the men at the brewery had told him that the police wouldn't take it from you, but everyone knew you would be giving it to them anyway. Arthur pulled out the cash and handed it to the man in the window. When he looked up and smiled at the jailer, the man looked at him oddly. The jailer looked at the inside wall of his office and a big grin spread on his face. Arthur knew his goose was cooked, but wasn't sure why. He didn't look anything like he had before. They didn't take fingerprints of local drunkards, so something else had given him away.

Arthur's face flinched when the jailer simply pointed to Arthur's right eye. Arthur realized that his brown lens was no longer in place. It had come out during the fight, which explained the odd sensation he felt. Arthur had one deep brown eye and one bright green eye.

They took Arthur to the station in downtown Mexico City and placed him in a small, single cell. It was the beginning of the end for him. He would lose his freedom and any chance to live his life without any consequences for his actions. The next day, he had a visitor. An attractive woman waited for him in the dingy interrogation room and he knew she was a detective. The Mexican officer cuffed Arthur to his chair while the detective sat there staring at him. Finally, she spoke. "So, Sir, we finally meet. Well, since I have the upper hand now, I figure I can call you Arthur, or Raider, or Harold. Which would you prefer? Just so long as it's not Sir."

Arthur glared at her without responding.

"Okay, Arthur. I am Agent Morris. We talked many days ago while you held hostages in a bank. You remember me, Arthur?" she said with attitude.

"Yes, I believe I do. How are you, *Megan?*" he responded with even more attitude.

"My, you're a feisty little prisoner, aren't you? That's the problem with Chihuahuas, Arthur. They walk big and talk big, but they are still little dogs that can be easily stepped on."

Arthur glared at her. He knew he was average size, but the reference to a Chihuahua made him react in his gut. He had always felt like a small man. "So, Megan, why do you have me chained to a chair? Afraid of Chihuahuas?"

"Oh, not my doing. It's police policy when they have a trapped rat. Keeps them from scurrying under a rock or swimming down a sewer." Agent Morris said with disgust. "Took us longer than I expected to catch you and would have taken even longer without your help. So, thank you for your brash stupidity. Saved us a lot of time and effort."

Arthur dropped his eyes to his hands. His stupidity had put him here.

"Look, we got you, yadda, yadda, yadda. I just need to ask some questions and then we'll be moving you up to San Diego for processing." Agent Morris explained.

"We need to know your relationship with Charley Abrams. Did you know her before the robbery and was she involved?"

Arthur made eye contact. This was his chance to get Charley. Let God pull her out of the mess he would put her in. It surprised him when he heard his own voice say, "I found out yesterday that DNA says she's my grandmother. I didn't know her before the robbery. I figure she didn't know about me either. You can try to make this into something, but you'll

263

be wasting your time. She was a stupid hostage, a pain in my butt. She wasn't involved in the robbery." Arthur didn't know why he spoke the truth. Maybe it was because she might be his grandmother or maybe he didn't want to be known in prison as the bank robber who brought his grannie along. Or maybe he was just done.

Agent Morris looked up after making notes on her large, thick pad. "Some of the hostages say you killed the bank manager."

"You know ballistics show I didn't. The manager shot Darrell with his own gun and Darrell got off a shot before he died. I was on the other side of the bank."

"But you did shoot the woman in the vault."

"Yes, but not to kill her. If I'd wanted her dead, she would be."

"Why aren't you lawyering up, Arthur? Not a smart move for a smart man."

"I'm not telling you anything you don't already know. Plenty of eye witnesses."

"You can sign a confession now. We wrap this up and you get a nice, warm cell to decorate," she said with anticipation.

"Nah, I'll see what my lawyer can work out. Unless you want to know how to find a good donut shop in Mexico City, I'm done talking."

Agent Morris motioned for the guard to return Arthur to his cell.

The next morning Arthur, Agent Morris, and a much larger officer boarded a jet for San Diego. Once seated by the window, Arthur was unable to resist. He leaned over to Agent Morris who was next to the aisle and said softly. "From one Chihuahua to another, how much do you feed your Saint Bernard?" Arthur tilted his head toward the other officer. Agent Morris flinched but didn't comment. Arthur felt some satisfaction that he had stung her pride.

Arthur put his head back and closed his eyes. He should be angry and making this a difficult transport, but he had respect for the big guy, knowing he could take Arthur down in a heartbeat, but that wasn't what stopped him. He was tired, just exhausted. He didn't look forward to prison, but it didn't scare him either. He knew enough cons to know the routine and the games. He would need to be tough, not intimidated, and certainly not a "Punk." Maybe he would be taken out early, like his old man. That would make an interesting circle. He had become the man he hated.

And what about Charley? Could she be his grandmother? Everyone thought so. How conclusive is DNA testing? There was a small part of him that respected Charley, but a bigger part that hated her. If he eventually cared about her, it would mean accepting all of her, even her belief in God. The events in the mountains were creeping in. How did he explain the fruit, the animals for meat, and the wolf? No one would ever believe his story. He didn't believe it and he was there. Arthur slept.

RAIDER'S Vendetta

Chapter 58

California

When Agent Morris showed up at Charley's apartment, Charley was surprised. She had been released from the hospital just that morning. Her daughter drove her home and then left to get groceries and some prescriptions filled. "May I come in?" Agent Morris asked.

"That depends. Are you here to bully me some more about the robbery?" Charley asked.

"No, to discuss Arthur."

Charley let her in and asked her to take a seat. Agent Morris viewed the room, comfortable and unique. She liked more order, but appreciated the creative thinking that went into the decor. Jewel tones of deep blue, green, and purple with accents of gold and leaded glass.

"I wanted you to know that we arrested Arthur in Mexico yesterday. We flew back this morning and he is being held in San Diego. I'm not sure when his arraignment will be."

"Why are you telling me this?"

"I just thought you should know before it comes out in the papers or you start getting calls from reporters."

Charley suspected that this detective was not so accommodating with all her cases. "Why not call? That would have saved you the drive. You want something from me?"

Agent Morris looked at her for a long, few moments. "I don't believe you were involved in the robbery. And, just so you know, Arthur says you weren't either."

Charley was relieved. She had feared that it would be Raider's last chance to punish her. "Is he okay? He was hurt pretty bad last time I saw him."

"Yes, he's fine. It's as if the man has a guardian angel.

A nurse found him unconscious and had antibiotics and pain meds with her. She stitched him up and drove him across the border, at gunpoint. What are the chances of being found by a nurse in the wilderness?"

Charley smiled. She knew God was looking out for him. Even though Raider was fighting with everything he had to kick God in the face, God still loved him.

Agent Morris was curious at Charley's reaction. "You're smiling?"

"Oh, just a big debate Raider and I had. He said God doesn't intervene and I insisted He did! Would love to hear how Raider argues this one away."

"This one?"

Charley felt she had said too much. "Don't mind me, Hon, just dealing with a lot right now. Time for pain meds."

"I'm sorry. I'll get going. I just have one more question for you, if you don't mind."

"Sure."

"Why did you put yourself in harm's way? The hostages tell stories of how you protected them repeatedly. You convinced Arthur to take you instead of them. Why did you do that?"

Charley looked into her eyes. It seemed important to Agent Morris. "Because I obeyed and trusted God. He wanted the people in that bank to survive and He used me. I simply obeyed my Heavenly Father."

Charley saw Agent Morris's eyes tear up. "That is the answer my dad would have given," Agent Morris replied.

"He was a believer?" asked Charley.

"Oh yes. He tried not to preach at me, but he wanted me to believe. Sometimes the pressure he applied was just too much."

"Are you a believer?" asked Charley, gently.

"I'm not sure. Sometimes, I hope that it's real. You know the whole God thing. I would love to be with my father some day. But, then I see the horrible things that happen and wonder where God is?"

"Well, I know it requires a lot of faith. I think that is the hardest thing to accept. Not knowing everything used to drive me crazy!"

"Used to?"

"Well, to be honest, at times it still does. But, it had to come down to this. Do I believe in God? Yes! Do I believe He created us out of love? Yes! So, when I think He's indifferent, I have to remember. Do I trust that He intends the best for mankind? Yes! I do not understand everything He does or allows, but I trust His intent. Does that make sense?"

"In a way," Agent Morris responded.

~

Agent Morris sat quietly for a few moments, oddly finding comfort in this chaotic little apartment. It was as if this woman was a link to her father and she didn't want to leave. Charley looked at her, as if to ask if there was something more, and Agent Morris stood to leave. "Thank you for your time."

"Can I assume that my involvement with the robbery is resolved?" asked Charley hopefully.

"Not yet, but I think soon. I wouldn't be worried, but listen to your attorney and lay low. I know you want to see Arthur, but I'd wait for a while. You don't want to look too anxious to see your captor."

"Why do you think I want to see him?"

"You just found out you have a grandson, a grandson in trouble. Charley, if I've learned anything about you at all, it's that you will see Arthur. If nothing else, you have questions to ask and questions to answer." Agent Morris paused again, feeling drawn to Charley. She shook it off, "I'm so glad you're home and healing. Take care." She stepped onto the porch and stopped. "One last question, Charley. At the cabin, we found items left by you and Arthur. Can you explain where the fresh produce came from? There were items there that couldn't have grown in the area and you couldn't have brought the food with you."

~

Charley tried not to reveal anything on her face, but she was caught off guard. Agent Morris didn't miss her shocked reaction. Charley tried to recover but knew her face had revealed too much.

"You aren't going to believe me, Agent Morris."

"Why wouldn't I believe you, Charley?" she asked.

"It is quite beyond the ordinary and it requires a belief in God that would challenge most Christians."

"Are you saying that God is responsible for the fruit?"

Charley paused and gathered the courage to answer truthfully. "Yes, He was. God performed many miracles after I walked into that bank. He was with me every step of the way and put things in motion that saved my life."

~

Agent Morris looked into Charlie's eyes and saw that she spoke the truth, her truth. She didn't doubt that Charlie believed that God had provided miracles. For a moment, Agent Morris wanted to believe, to stay and hear Charlie's story, get caught up in the fantasy that her father had tried to share. But, just as quickly, her reality flooded in. Charley was a sweet, misguided woman who would discover the horrible truth, that dead was dead and God was a fable. There had to be a rational explanation for the evidence they'd found, but it wouldn't come from Charlie.

~

Charley closed the door after Agent Morris left and headed into the kitchen. She sat at the table with her head in her hands. "Dear God, what am I supposed to do? I believe You have brought this young man into my life, but how do I look at him as a grandson? As family? He has hurt me so badly, Lord."

God revealed his intent so simply to her heart. "I love all my children. I weep for the lost." Charley understood and would do her best to honor her God.

Mari returned with some healthy food and some sinfully delicious treats. They sat down to eat and began their discussion. At first Mari was insistent that she would never accept this man as family and that her mother shouldn't either. But, after hearing her mother's heart, Mari realized that her mother would do what she thought was best. Mari, however, had no intention of forgiving him, let alone calling him her nephew at any point in the future.

"You must know, Michael and I have discussed this and he feels the same way," insisted Mari.

"I understand, Dear. I really do. I don't expect either of you to feel anything but what you feel. I just hope, in time, you will open your hearts and minds to consider why he is who he is."

"Don't count on it, Mom. He hurt you and kept us up many nights, not knowing if you were dead or alive. I hate him, Mother, and I always will."

Charley patted her hand, and changed the subject. She knew this was out of her control. They had their own minds. Charley wasn't even sure how she felt. With time, she figured she would salvage whatever Raider was willing to agree to, but she wasn't driven. God's direction to feed Raider made a lot more sense now. He was showing her Raider's value, so when she did find out who he was, she would know what God expected from her, a difficult request to honor. She had to think of him as Arthur and let Raider go, forever.

A call to her lawyer confirmed what Agent Morris had said. "Stay away from that man. You can't show any interest or any connection to him. We need to make sure you are clear of all suspicion. A visit to the jail would only fuel the media. If you show compassion for him, plan on being drug through a trial," he insisted.

"Okay, I was just asking. It's a little weird finding out you have a grandson, even if he did take you hostage."

"I get it, Charley. You'll have lots of time to resolve all the family stuff later. Just stay away for now! I mean it. You can't allow yourself to get sucked in any deeper."

"Okay, Mr. Alexander. I hear you loud and clear," Charley said, resigned for the moment.

RAIDER'S Vendetta

Chapter 59

The trial was set. Charley obeyed her lawyer and didn't go near Arthur. Over the months of recuperating and waiting to testify, her heart softened for Arthur. A lot came out about his history, his childhood, the murder of his aunt and father, who was her own son. Charley wept tears for her son. She didn't know why he had turned to such a violent life. At times, she blamed herself, but then realized he had made his own decisions.

One evening, she watched the news story about Arthur's military career and the story of Badria. Charley better understood his anger and frustration with God. He had suffered a lot at the hands of religious zealots. The news didn't tell the story of his life with his Aunt Rose, since the knowledge of what she'd done died with her and Darrell. She knew Arthur wouldn't share that with the media.

The day to testify came and Charley walked to the chair with a heavy heart. She was under oath, but she didn't want to be in the position of harming her grandson. The questions started and Charley kept her answers short and to the point. She didn't embellish, offer opinions, or expand on her answers. The bank questions were easy. There were many witnesses in the courtroom, so Charley couldn't lie, even if she wanted to. She would look over at Arthur now and then, but he always averted his eyes. She knew that he watched her carefully the rest of the time. Was he hanging on each word, hoping she wouldn't bury him further, or was he trying to search her face for a resemblance to his own?

There weren't many questions about what she did and why. They were focused on Arthur and Charley was thankful. She didn't want to explain how the Holy Spirit had requested her help to save the other hostages. When the lawyer moved on to the escape and their time in the wilderness, Charley left out the physical and mental abuse. She explained that there were provisions hidden there and that they'd found some fresh fruit. Without any details, she said that Arthur shared oatmeal, canned soup, and water with her.

They asked her about the fall into the ravine and she insisted that it was an accident. Arthur had tried to save her. She described the attack from the wolf, but didn't share that the wolf was there to protect her. It sounded like a random attack.

The District Attorney kept returning to questions about Arthur's treatment of her while captive. He must have been brutal and physically aggressive. Charley didn't lie, but she didn't tell him everything either. She didn't want to compound Arthur's guilt and she knew that she needed to keep the miracles a secret. This was not the proper forum to reveal God's intervention. The media had enough fuel to keep Charley in the spotlight as it was.

The lawyer's final question was about her relationship with Arthur and when she'd found out that she was his grandmother.

"I found out when Agent Morris told me in my hospital room."

"Not until then?"

"No. Obviously, I was aware that I had a son who was given up for adoption when I was a child, but I had no idea what happened to him after that or that he had had a child himself."

The District Attorney thanked her and went back to his table.

Arthur's lawyer was next. She was tiny, but a ball of energy. Her questions were about the release of the prisoners, confirmation that Arthur hadn't injured anyone other than the two people he shot, the teller and the pilot. She also discussed the details of the parachute jump and of Arthur rescuing Charley from drowning. Finally, she questioned Charley about her care while at the cabin, focusing on the sharing of food and the lack of being restrained in any way. Charley again answered the questions briefly and didn't offer any extra information.

When they got to Arthur's efforts to keep her from falling into the ravine, the questions were asked, reworded, and asked again. The lawyer was trying to focus away from the robbery and his brutality and toward his valiant effort to save Charley. "Was Arthur at risk of falling into the ravine with you?" she asked.

"Yes. He was starting to slip through the hole that I fell through," Charley explained.

"At what point did he let go? When did he know it was useless?"

"He never did. He didn't let go. I removed my shirt so that I wouldn't pull him down with me."

"He had you by your shirt collar, correct?"

"Yes, that was all he had time to grab when I slipped through the ground."

"So you were hanging there, suspended over the ravine by your shirt, the shirt he was desperately hanging on to?"

"Yes."

"You are not a small woman, yet he kept you from falling with his injured shoulder. That must have been extremely painful for him."

"I'm sure it was. I was surprised at his strength. He was badly hurt."

"But yet, he refused to let go and let you drop?"

"Yes. He refused to let go."

"You had to, literally, slip out of your clothing to save his life?"

"Yes. He was close to coming down after me."

"Was he angry that you fell?"

"Yes. He was very angry that I allowed myself to fall."

"Why did you take steps to save his life? That was an unusual thing to do for someone who had taken you against your will."

"He couldn't save me and there was no point for him to fall with me."

"So, is it safe to say that you did not want to see your captor dead?"

"No, I didn't."

"And, to clarify again for the jury, you did not know at this point that Arthur was your grandson?"

"Correct. I had no clue who he was."

"Thank you for your honesty. I know this case is complicated for you with Mr. Myers being your biological grandson. Please try to answer these next questions based on your knowledge prior to the revelation that

Mr. Myers was related to you."

"Okay, I'll try."

"Did you fear for your life when you were with Mr. Myers? Or did you feel protected?"

Charley struggled with her answer. She knew that the lawyer was leading the jury away from the fact that she was a hostage. That it became a point of survival and Raider was her savior, not her captor. "I wasn't glad to be in the wilderness with Arthur as a hostage, but I was thankful that he did not abandon me there."

"Did you see Arthur as your protector? Someone who would keep you alive?"

Charley looked at Arthur and he quickly looked down. She thought she saw a glimmer of shame. "I did believe he would keep me alive. He could have left me to die in the helicopter or in the lake. He could have let me drop through the ground and into the ravine. His intent was not to kill me."

"Arthur attempted to save your life on three different occasions?" The lawyer was pushing it now.

"Yes, but he also put me in harm's way so that I needed saving," Charley shot back before thinking about how her words sounded.

The lawyer realized she had misjudged the situation.

"Did you think that his plan was to rob the bank, take a hostage, and escape into the wilderness with someone against their will?"

"No. I think he thought the robbery would be simple and they would make a clean getaway. His partner decided to complicate things. I believe that it became his survival at that point. He did what he thought he had to do to get out of a bad situation that he hadn't planned on. His decision to rob the bank put him on a path that went out of his control."

"My last question, Mrs. Abrams. Do you intend to pursue a relation-ship with your grandson?"

Charley shot a sharp look at the lawyer and then at Arthur. He didn't look away this time. He stared right at her, almost challenging. She knew why the lawyer asked. She wanted to show that Charley's experience was not so horrific that she would dismiss her grandson. But, what was Arthur thinking? Did he want her to say yes? Was he testing her ability to forgive and love as Christ directed her, a Christian?

"I guess that will depend on what my grandson wants," Charley said to Arthur.

"It is a consideration?" the lawyer asked.

"Yes, it is a consideration."

"Thank you. You may step down."

They dismissed Charley and she walked out of the courtroom, followed by her children. She made it out to the parking lot before she collapsed. Michael grabbed her and eased her to the ground. The picture of Charley sobbing, with her children kneeling on each side of her, made the front pages that night.

RAIDER'S Vendetta

Chapter 60

One Year Later

It had been eighteen months since Charley walked into the bank on that fateful day. She was about to visit Arthur for the first time. The trial was over and Arthur had been found guilty on all counts and was sentenced to life in prison. Charley was able to speak at his sentencing and believed that her pleas kept him from receiving a death sentence. His willing participation in a federal crime involving a murder made him accountable for the bank manager's death.

Charley was nervous, but Arthur finally agreed to the visit. Charlie had made numerous requests through Arthur's lawyer.

Once Charley was in the prison, they searched her bag and patted her down. Just visiting a maximum-security prison was intimidating. The guards, the security doors, and the smell made her feel uneasy and anxious to leave. She was led to a visiting divided into cubicles. The cubicles each had a chair, a narrow counter, and a vertical barrier of thick, clear material with a small, metal slotted grate at face level. The transparent wall was marked with fingerprints left by people trying to connect. On the other side, there was another thin counter and a chair. The rules were strict. Nothing in, nothing out, no physical contact, and limited days and hours. She sat in her chair and unconsciously wrung her hands.

A guard led Arthur in. He looked tired and lacked his usual confidence when he sat across from her. Charley wasn't sure what to say or how to start. After a few moments, Arthur began speaking. "I don't know why you didn't throw me under the bus at the trial, but thank you."

"I figured you had enough on your shoulders without

279

me laboring over minor details," she said softly.

"Weren't so minor at the time. You were very angry with me."

"Yes, I was. You were an ass."

Arthur chuckled. "You're right, I was."

"Thank you for saving my life three times," she said with genuine appreciation.

"You're welcome. Sorry I put you in harm's way three times."

His words from her testimony stung. He saw the regret in her eyes. "It's okay, Charley. You were right. I would have put the screws to someone who did what I did."

Charley was finally able to ask. "Did you send the wolf?"

"Yes. It looked just like Bulwark. I had just found out that you survived and where you were. I had some guy drop it off. I figured you would know it was from me."

"I did, but it just wasn't something I expected you to do. It was beautiful, thank you."

Arthur nodded.

"You know, he stayed with me after I fell. He actually herded the geologist to find me."

"Seriously? Papers said he stumbled upon you accidently."

"That's what he's telling everyone. He doesn't want everyone to think he's crazy." Charley told Arthur the story just as Donald had told it to her. Arthur had so many questions. He seemed to enjoy the story as much as Charley enjoyed telling it.

Arthur sat with a knowing grin as she finished the details. "Raccoons? Are you really sure he's not crazy? You didn't see them did you?" Arthur asked.

"No, but if he's truthful about Bulwark, why would he lie about the raccoons? Remember the birds and rabbits? Sleeping is a lot easier to commit to than offering yourself up for dinner."

"You're right," Arthur agreed. "You know that still blows me away Charley. I haven't told anyone."

"I've only told my kids and Donald. I figured after dealing with Bulwark, he would believe me. I wish I knew what happened to him. Donald said that as soon as he realized I was alive, Bulwark took off somewhere fast and didn't come back."

Arthur opened his mouth to speak, but didn't. Charley wondered if he knew something about Bulwark. The guards were ready to escort the prisoners back to their cells.

"Okay if I come visit you again?" Charley asked.

"Why, Charley? Why do you want to see me? I made your life hell."

"I know, but I want to see what God sees in you. He made it clear that you were someone of value to Him."

"Charley, don't start with all of that. Yes, some weird stuff happened, but I'm sitting in prison for the rest of my life, Charley. Where was God for me?"

"You're alive. I'm alive. We saw miracles. He brought us both family. You are in prison because you made choices that ended your life on the outside. Don't put that on God."

The hour went by so quickly and before Charley was ready, Arthur stood and waited for the guard to direct him out.

Arthur looked at her intently, seeming to search her face. "You trust this DNA stuff? You believe we are related?"

"I do," she said softly, with no regret. "Arthur, can I come back?"

"Yes, Charley, if you want," he announced over his shoulder as he walked out.

"I will write. Please respond," she called after him.

Arthur didn't answer her.

Charley followed the other visitors out into the sunlight. She was glad she'd made the three-hour drive to the prison. He was allowed visitors once a month and she was determined to be there. Charley headed home and felt a sense of joy. She couldn't define its source, at first, and then realized that it was God's approval of her decision to see Arthur. She began to hum and sing along with the radio.

~

Charley sent her first letter and waited two weeks before getting a response. It was short and not so sweet. More whys and then a statement that he didn't have anything much to say. Each day was the same.

Charley began writing several times a week. She shared stories about her life, her experience with the preacher's son, and the pregnancy. The letters became a link to catch her grandson up with his family and their lives. His letters came back more frequently and eventually got longer. He asked questions and showed interest.

After some time, their letters drifted to their stay at the cabin and the miracles they had shared. Charley tried not to push, but challenged Arthur to have an explanation other than God's love and grace for them both. She even explained that when he threw her cell phone from the helicopter, it was a miracle. In all that empty space, it shattered a greenhouse! The owner found the phone and gave the police a starting point. Such an insignificant act eventually saved her life. If the detective hadn't been flying over the ravine, she would have died. Donald might have, too.

Along with the letters, Charley went back to visit the next month and cried when Arthur told her about Bulwark. It felt like a friend had died. She was so thankful that he was there for Arthur and protected him from the bear, but sad that he had to sacrifice his life. Arthur had started sketching and told her about a drawing he did of Bulwark. He wasn't allowed to give it to her during the visit, but promised to mail it. When she received it, she saw that it was rough but beautiful.

Charley found herself looking forward to Arthur's letters. He would draw along the edges and his skill was constantly improving. His creative talents were inherited from her, at least that's what she liked to think. They didn't talk much about the grandma-grandkid thing. They were becoming friends and that was enough for now. After nine months of visits and letters, she knew almost everything about his life with his father and his aunt. Charley would go back and reread the details of his abuse and pray for God to heal the brokenness that took over his life. She loved the letters about Badria. He truly loved the woman and she was thankful that he had had the experience of at least one true love in his life.

One afternoon, Charley got a call from a woman who said she was an old friend of Arthur's and she wanted to see him. She had heard about Arthur's misfortune in the papers and couldn't get him off her mind.

Charley promised that she would ask Arthur if it was okay. In her next letter, she told Arthur about his friend Pagne contacting her and asked if she would bring her on the next visit. The excitement in his next letter was remarkable. "Yes, yes, I would love to see Pagne. She is a dear friend from when I was a child," he wrote. His letter was filled with the memories of his time at Langston Hall, a shelter and home for children in the system. Arthur and Pagne didn't have a long history, but it was powerful. They had lost touch when she was sent to a foster home and he was sent to live with his aunt.

Pagne offered to drive and they spent their time on the road sharing their experiences with God. Their stories were so different, but one thing was consistent. Heaven reached down and touched their lives in profound ways.

Once they arrived at the prison, they sat in the car and prayed for Arthur. They prayed for his salvation and his protection in prison. The prayers intertwined and rose to their Father's ears. They asked that Arthur would find purpose, even while in prison.

Once inside, Charley saw that Arthur ached to embrace Pagne. He brought his hand to the window and placed his fingertips on the surface. Pagne brought her hand up and carefully placed a fingertip to each of his. "I can't believe you're here, Pagne. I've thought of you so often." Charley watched as they caught up with their lives. The genuine affection they had for each other was so obvious. Then the stories of their childhood memories began. Charley got to see a bright, loving side to Arthur. She had to fight back the tears. This was who he was supposed to be. Charley saw the hard exterior melt and there was Itchy, a hopeful, loving soul that wanted to love and be loved.

The visit ended too quickly and Arthur was sad to see Pagne leave. They promised to write and Pagne said she would come again, as soon as possible. She had a hectic life, a child with special needs, and her work with an organization that supported children in the foster care and institution system. The distance between them was also an issue. Pagne did not visit again until many years later, however, they wrote to each other. Arthur's walls were covered with pictures sent by Charley and Pagne. Pagne and Charley's walls were covered with Arthur's drawings.

These two women were his lifeline to the real world. They were also prayer warriors who were not going to let him go down without a valiant fight.

Chapter 61

The years rolled by. Mari and Michael each made several visits to get to know Arthur and there was a polite friendship developing. They would never have the closeness most families had, but Charley was so proud of her children for trying to reach out to their nephew. They each began their own journey with Arthur. Even Donald wrote to Arthur. At first, it was to share his story about the wolf, but then they continued as friends. The opportunity to share the events of those two days was wonderful for Donald. He knew that Arthur would believe him. Donald had become close to Charley and to God. After hearing the details about the robbery and her time at the cabin, Donald finally gave in. He was unable to deny the miracles he had experienced and trusted everything Charley shared.

Donald took this newfound truth and let it dust his letters to Arthur. He didn't blast him but simply shared his own journey. Donald and Charley would meet for lunch on a regular basis and pray for Arthur. They prayed that Christians would cross his path in prison and that he would find God.

Charley was patient. Arthur had come to a point where he accepted her prayers and the prayers of others, but he would not allow God into his heart.

~

Charley was almost seventy-six when she made her last the drive to see Arthur. She called him hers now. She knew he loved her when she'd received a hand-drawn mother's day card. The front was a drawing of her, an incredible likeness, and Arthur. She was next to him, under his arm, which was wrapped around her. His heart was drawn outside of his chest and was cradled in Charley's hand. The smile on her face expressed such love. Arthur had drawn himself looking down at her, his face radiating total attection for her. She took it that she had touched his heart. When she opened the card, she read,

Dear grandmother,
I send this to you on Mother's Day because you bring me every aspect of love and nurturing that I could ask for. I love you as my mother, my grandmother, and my friend. Thank you for forgiving me and seeing value in me. I treasure your gift of love.
Your Arthur

Charley didn't hear the squealing brakes or see the oncoming trailer truck as it fishtailed out of control. She was in her own world, singing to her music and thinking about Arthur, his beautiful card, and their visit. Suddenly, the road before her was filled with steel, tires, and no escape. Charley slammed into the semi and then darkness.

~

Charley stood up and heard lovely music. It was their song, hers and Archie's. The room was enchanting, filled with lovely items, Victorian inspired. There was a table set with candles and delicacies for her to taste. As she moved closer to get a better look, she sensed movement behind her. She turned around and Archie was in front of her, young, handsome and grinning from ear to ear. "Dance with me, my love!" He opened his arms and she moved into them. Together they began to move through the room, swirling and swaying as she stared into his face. Their reflection moved across the surface of many mirrors and Charley realized that the beautiful couple dancing was she and Archie. She stopped and focused on her face. She was vibrant and beautiful, in her late twenties.

"Am I really here? To stay this time?"

"Yes, my love. You are here to stay."

"But, I haven't saved Arthur. I don't know if Mari, Michael, and the grandkids have truly committed to God. I have work left to do."

Archie brought his finger to her lips. "Charley, you have planted strong seeds. You have introduced wonderful Christians to water the seeds. You will see the fruit of your efforts, but it will be from here. The Holy Spirit has not abandoned them just because you are no longer on Earth."

"They will be okay? They will find God in time?"

"They each have decisions to make, Charley. You were a shining example before them. Now, it is in their hands."

Charley began to understand that she could not make others decide. She shared truth and love; it was up to them if they believed. Now it was time for her eternity with Archie, deceased friends and family, and more importantly, her Jesus and Father God.

As Archie led her through huge leaded glass French doors, into a beautiful garden, she saw him. Charley dropped to her knees and allowed Bulwark to nuzzle and lick her face. She wrapped her arms around his neck. Her beloved protector, her Bulwark was alive, here with her! The tears of joy flowed freely down her cheeks. "Thank you, Bulwark. Thank you my faithful friend."

Bulwark pulled back and stared at her with his deep blue eyes. "You are so welcome, my sweet Charley."

Charley thought she would pass out, but then laughed, a full, deep, infectious laugh. Archie joined in and they walked with Bulwark, discussing his affection for Arthur and his love for Charley. The excitement continued to build as Charley realized that she was on her way to see Jesus. She let the pain and anxiety of the world melt away.

RAIDER'S Vendetta

Chapter 62

Arthur feared that something was wrong. Charley should have been there by now. She was never late, not in twenty years. She was always the first face through the doors for Saturday visits. Arthur was now forty-five and had spent almost half of his life in prison. He had two realities: The first was prison life, the drama, the hardships and the threats. The second was family, friends, letters, visits, and care packages. Charley had brought life and normalcy to Arthur's cell. He received letters from many people because of Charley and her love. He'd allowed himself to share his fear and the dark side of prison life with Donald until Donald's death. He missed his friend, his Wolf Brother. They had come up with this name for themselves while writing. Charley and her miracles had profoundly touched Donald and he chose to follow God. Arthur didn't hold this against him. In fact, he almost took the plunge several times himself. During nights alone in his cell, there were mental pictures of Charley's arms filled with the fruit, the sacrificial rabbits, and Bulwark. At times, there didn't seem to be another position, except to believe and give himself over to God. But then, the memories of Aunt Rose and the broken body of Badria would slip in, pulling up all the pain and hatred that again filled his heart.

This sadness kept him from a God who continued to protect and love him. The ongoing prayers and God's grace had allowed Arthur to survive the years in prison through divine protection.

Arthur returned to his cell, there were no visitors today. The sense of loneliness overtook him and he cried. Every part of his being knew that he would not see Charley again.

The next day, Sunday, the guards informed Arthur

that he had a visitor. He never had visitors on Sunday. He washed his face, combed his hair, and brushed his teeth. He didn't have to worry about what to wear. That was already decided. When he stepped into his side of the cubicle, he saw Pagne. The look on her face said it all. Arthur's knees buckled and one of the guards grabbed him, preventing him from falling. He sat down and put his head in his hands. He didn't want to break. He wouldn't cry, not here, not where he could be seen.

Pagne leaned forward, bringing her mouth close to the grate and whispered, "Arthur, I'm so sorry, but Charley died yesterday."

"Yesterday, how?" he whispered as he lifted his head to look at her.

"She was on her way here. There was a semi truck."

"No, God. No!" Arthur wailed. "If it wasn't for me, she wouldn't be dead." The nearest guard stepped closer to him, watching, waiting for Arthur to make an aggressive move.

Pagne sat in silence, not knowing what to say. She couldn't say "Oh no, she would have been on that highway even if you weren't in prison." She was where she was because of her choices and her compassion for him. Pagne thought these things, but didn't speak them.

"Did she suffer?" he finally asked.

"No, it was instantaneous," Pagne assured him.

Arthur sat in silence and Pagne shared in the horror with him. She wanted to hold him, soothe him, but she was only allowed to offer her presence.

"I need to be alone, Pagne. I know this was a long trip for you and I appreciate it, but I'm going to explode if I sit here any longer." Arthur stood and moved toward the door. Pagne also stood. Her arms physically ached. She needed to hold him so badly. He blew her a kiss and made an attempt to smile. "Thank you, Pagne," he said sadly. Then he disappeared behind the big metal door.

Arthur walked back to his cell and sat. For hours, he sat. He wanted to rant, to scream, to curse Charley's God, but he didn't have the strength. It was as if everything drained from him and he was just a shell. The fear of how he would survive began to suffocate him. Charley was his lifeline, his hold on anything good and sweet. He wondered about ending it all. Could he take his life and escape the years of loneliness that were going to be his? He considered his options. If he pushed the wrong people, he would get himself killed, if he was lucky. Maybe he would only be injured or disfigured. His cellmate would notice if he tried to use a sheet to hang himself. He could attack a guard, but that would only get him thrown in solitary confinement. If he killed a guard, he would certainly get the death penalty, but how would he pick which guard, when, and with what? His brute strength wasn't a match for a billy club or a gun.

Arthur continued to sit, a shell with morbid thoughts racing through his mind. Then he heard the distinctive squeaking of the book cart. Mouse, an inmate who pushed books and Bibles on the inmates, was coming down the hall. He was frail, pale, and spooky. He always seemed to be smiling about something. No one bothered him or befriended him. The inmates knew there was something lurking under that passive exterior. You felt it. They had a full library in the prison, but Mouse had gotten permission to distribute the books door to door. The administration was convinced that knowledge was the key to the prisoners' freedom. There were posters throughout the prison that said so. The standing joke among the inmates was: No, the key to freedom fits the locks. Give us that key!

Mouse stuck his head in and quietly spoke "Something special for you today, Raider?" The name Raider had stuck when the papers shared the details of the robbery and escape. Once one prisoner had started calling him by that name, it had spread quickly.

"No, Mouse. Just move on. I don't need anything."

"Okay, let me leave this with you. Maybe you'll check it out." Mouse set a flyer down on the end of Arthur's bed. "Sorry to hear about your grandma." Arthur jerked out of his stupor and stared at Mouse. That was the other thing about Mouse. He knew things before anyone else seemed to. It wasn't eerie until now.

"How do you know? She just died yesterday."

"God gives me pictures, downloads I call them. Let's me know who needs prayer," he explained.

Arthur dropped his head and shook it. He was unable to get free of this God nonsense. "Pictures, Mouse? You can't be serious."

Mouse sensed that his comments were not well received. He moved

291

away and headed down the corridor. Arthur jumped up and moved quickly behind Mouse, threatening him. Mouse turned around and just stared into Arthur's eyes. There was a power there, a force that Arthur felt. Mouse was protected from him and everyone else. Arthur backed down and went back to his cell. He saw the bright lime green flyer and picked it up.

It was an announcement for a new support group, which focused on Bible teachings and prayer. Arthur's first impulse was to ball it up and throw it down the hall at Mouse, but the heading stopped him. He stared at the words and sat down in submission. He could not ignore God's presence in his life.

God's Bulwark
Discover Joy, Peace, Protection, and Love

Chapter 63

Charley didn't get to see her garden grow while she was on Earth, but she got to celebrate in Heaven when each seed sprouted and flourished. Arthur couldn't dismiss the miracles and coincidences any longer. At first, he struggled with salvation and his walk with God, but he was on the path that would lead him to Heaven's eternity. Mari and Michael abandoned Arthur for a season. They blamed him for Charley's death, but once the pain had time to heal, they knew what Charley would want from them. He was family and she loved him. The best way to honor her was to honor her commitment to Arthur.

In their visits and letters, Arthur also revealed what Charley and he had shared, the miracles that had occurred at the cabin. Mari and Michael both received God's salvation through Arthur's transformation and testimony. He knew that he had contributed to the most wonderful gift Charley would ever receive; her children eventually with her in Heaven and that gave him intense joy.

Charley's children gave him the porcelain wolf. Arthur valued what it represented, the miraculous outreach of God's grace to Charley and to him. Arthur was eventually brave enough to share the miracles with the pastor and then the group. The stories spread through the prison. Rather than being ridiculed, Arthur became a hero, a disciple. They gave him the respect of a man who has been touched by Heaven. Countless men opened their hearts to God through his stories of supernatural love.

~

RAIDER'S Vendetta

Arthur developed pneumonia and passed quickly at the age of eighty-nine. His family buried him next to Charley.

The members of God's Bulwark held a memorial honoring Arthur, a man that became the symbol of hope to the outcasts of society. The prisoners filled the cafeteria and shared their encounters and memories of Arthur "Raider" Myers. At the front, was a large illustration that Arthur had finished only days before he became ill. It was of a beautiful garden outside of French doors. Arthur, as a young man, was hugging a woman they knew to be Charley, next to a beautiful wolf with piercing blue eyes. This drawing was to be the last page of an illustrated book that Arthur had completed. It told the story of his life, his anger, the miracles, and his salvation. The story of God's grace would continue to reach others. Arthur made sure the good news would not stop with him.

The Beginning

Dedications

Thank you Lord for blessing me
with the gift of storytelling.
I am also thankful for the loving
family and friends you have
brought into my life. Their support
and encouragement is precious.

Another inspiring novel written by

Karen Arnpriester

anessiasquest.com
ISBN-10: 1456504363
karnpriester@gmail.com

Anessia's Quest

Restoration
of a Shattered Life,
a Life Created
with Divine Intent

Karen Arnpriester

Anessia's Quest

ollow the life of a young girl into adulthood. Celebrate the journey and her choices that change a heartbreaking situation into a glorious life of love, truth, compassion and joy.

Pagne finds the love of God and the support of her Heavenly Angel to get her through life's emotional roller coaster. An angel that protects, leads and assures Pagne that she is not alone by using an unusual method of communication.

Pagne shares healing, tears and laughter with a group of broken people that become her family. She discovers the purpose of her life and the revelation of God's destiny for her. Pagne will eventually understand the powerful ripple she created as she lived her life. She was not an accident, she was placed on Earth with divine intent.

FIRST THREE CHAPTERS FOLLOW ....

In the Heavens

Psalms 91:11
"For he will command his angels concerning you to guard you in all your ways;"

Draken walked swiftly through the marble passageway, which was only lit by a warm, golden glow that's source was undefinable. The excitement was building, as he weaved his way through the network of stone halls, intricate stained glass panels, and vines with incredible cobalt and purple blossoms. Each flower's center had a spray of tendrils that shimmered and flickered with light. They pushed their way in through small openings and cracks, covering the ancient stone walls with their winding tendrils. He had the ability to instantly think himself to her, but instead he savored the journey through the tabernacle. As Draken entered the great hall, he sent groups of colorful butterflies scattering. Some of the butterflies were tiny and flashed bright yellow and orange light, while others were massive and moved almost as in slow motion. Their deep-purple and metallic gold wings didn't shine brightly like the others, but had a velvety luster that picked up the room's light with each flutter. The spaces in between were filled with every size and color of these delicate creatures. This room never failed to take Draken's breath away. There were sculptures in exquisite detail, cast or carved from every precious metal and stone, encrusted with jewels and pearls. Above him were strings of glowing orbs that didn't appear to be connected in any way, glistening shades of pink, lavender, blue and green. Beautiful birds of every description dove and soared in the upper dome. Draken would spend hours in this room, simply appreciating its beauty.

As he came upon an area of comfortable chairs, he saw Anessia sitting on the hard floor in her usual position, both legs folded under her with feet twisted out to the sides. She would sit this way for hours.

"When will you ever discover the comfort of these lush chairs?" he teased her.

She just grinned and said, "Probably never." Draken just shook his head. She liked the coolness of the stone floor on her skin.

Draken sat down in his favorite chair, a opulent purple satin with three times the stuffing most chairs would contain. He waited for her to speak, but silence. After a few anxious minutes, he could wait no longer.

"Well, Anessia. You summoned me here. You said you were ready."

She hesitated, she seemed unsure for a moment and then handed him the delicate gold scroll. Draken, a regal man with long white hair and a full beard, took the scroll and fingered it gently, knowing the importance of its content. He took a deep breath and looked into Anessia's eyes. He loved her eyes, so large, so engulfing.

"I am ready," is all she said. Draken felt the contradiction of relief and dread. This would be a difficult quest, filled with many hardships and pain.

"You will have a lot of sadness to deal with, but you were selected with the knowledge that you are capable. You have a strong sense of justice and love."

"Oh, Draken, I want to make a difference, to be part of these miracles!"

"Once you leave, you realize you will not be able to change your mind. The quest will not be recalled," he reminded her.

"I totally understand. I know that I can do this. I know I can make you and our Father proud. I believe I am the one to help fulfill the destiny described in the scroll."

Draken truly adored Anessia and her tender heart, but she was fierce, one of the most committed wards he had responsibility for. He also knew that the quest was a journey filled with love, joy and an incredible outcome.

"I will make the arrangements. Prepare yourself, your time here is short." They both came to a stand, and with a hug and a kiss on her head, Draken disappeared to carry out the necessary details.

Anessia stood alone and waited until she was sure Draken had left the chamber. She could contain herself no longer. She spun around, her hair flowing and gleaming in the light that was radiating down from above. It was wonderful to have a destiny. She giggled and hugged herself. Anessia then mentally willed her beautiful wings to engage, and she flew out of the windows near the top of the upper dome.

She didn't have to fly very far; there, by the glimmering pools, was Ennett. She slowly dropped down behind him, so quietly that he didn't know she was there. Anessia crept slowly behind him and jumped back as Ennett whirled around. But not quick enough, his folded wings smacked her in the face. "Oh Ennett, I thought I got you this time," she said, as she rubbed her cheek.

"Do you forget that I can read your thoughts? You need to work on shutting down that brain of yours when you plan to attack," he pouted at her, while touching her tender cheek. They both laughed and sat down on the cool grass next to the pools of crystal clear water. They slipped their feet in and giggled loudly, as the fish nibbled their toes. Anessia loved the landscape outside the main tabernacle. It had sumptuous gardens, streams, and trees that bore delicious fruits. Flowers of every size, color and scent. Some were deep shades that were fuzzy and glimmered, while others were tucked under the shade of the trees with transparent petals that glowed with pulsing light. The aromas were so delicious.

She couldn't count the different species of animals that roamed through the gardens. Every visit was a new discovery. These unique and exotic creatures would wander the gardens and come when beckoned, allowing her to pet and love on them.

"Well, I am assuming that it is time?"

"Yes, it is," she acknowledged.

"Anessia, it is a different realm there," he warned. "There is darkness, despair and pain."

"I know, I can do this. Draken and our Father do not send me to fail."

"I have faith in you, but please be careful!"

They both sat quietly for a short time. "I need to go prepare," whispered Anessia.

"I love you Anessia, I will be here for you always." They held each other for what felt like an eternity but it was only moments in another time.

Chapter 1

Leah thought she could bear it no longer ... why didn't this baby come out? She had been pushing and writhing here for hours, hurting so bad that she wanted to die. Finally, the nurse came in and said she was ready to have the baby. Leah knew that she would have feelings for this kid eventually, but right now, she almost hated it. They wheeled her into delivery, and after thirty more minutes, the miracle of birth happened. A little, white skinned, red-haired girl with blue eyes. She looked at her and felt numb. She may have connected better if the baby had looked like her. If she had gotten her golden skin, dark, curly hair and chestnut brown eyes. This baby looked like a stray, not her kid.

Leah had endured a difficult life and tried to bury it with alcohol, drugs and sex. During her drunken months of pregnancy, she thought it would be funny to name her baby girl Champagne, after her favorite beverage. Champagne Marie Crenshaw. Champagne would carry her mother's last name since Leah didn't know which John was the proud papa. Leah had considered having another abortion, but this time was different. This baby would change her life, she just knew it. Leah wanted to be loved and wanted someone to love. She convinced herself that she could be a mom. When Leah was in her seventh month, she had stopped hooking and left Los Angeles. She moved north for a fresh start. Champagne was to find out quickly that her mom would fail miserably at being a mother. She also would find out that there was someone watching over her, protecting her.

When the hospital determined that Leah was ready to be released, she was indignant and annoyed. Three days was not nearly long enough if you asked Leah. She figured she deserved and could use at least another week of leisure and strong pain meds while the nurses cared for Champagne. Upon leaving the hospital, she brought the baby back to the disgusting motel room that Leah managed to rent with her assistance checks. Leah figured they would do okay since the amount written on those checks would increase with the birth of Champagne. She might have been able to afford a nicer place, but the majority of her money went for her alcohol and drugs. *How was she going to take care of a baby all by herself?*, she thought. Looking around the room, Leah realized that she should have prepared a little more for the baby. She pulled out a drawer, dumped it, and laid Champagne in it. The strong pain meds were wearing off, and they had only prescribed glorified aspirin as far as Leah was concerned. Luckily she had stopped on the way home to pick up a big bottle of cheap wine.

"Well brat, guess the closest I'll come to champagne for awhile is changing your crappy diapers." She laughed to herself, *"That was a good one Leah … you haven't lost your dazzling wit yet."*

~

Several years crawled by, and somehow, Champagne had survived her mother's indifference. On one summer evening, Leah finally could not take it any longer, the pounding on the door was killing her head. What a hang-over she had. When she jerked the door open, she looked into the chest of a police officer. Behind him stood her neighbor, *Miss Nose Up My Butt*. She could tell this wasn't good by the smirk on Miss Butt's face.

"We got a call that you have a toddler playing unattended on the landing," said the officer.

"Well, I don't see no kid out here, do you?" shot back Leah.

"Not at the moment, but your neighbor called quite concerned. She said that it is not unusual to see your front door wide open and your small daughter playing out here by the stairs. Do you understand how dangerous that is?"

"Well yes, Officer, I do. I'm not an idiot. I am always just inside the door, watching her every move. The kid has gotta have some fresh air and sunshine right?"

"Ma'am, unless you use better judgment and find a safer place for your daughter to play, we will be back out with Child Services," threatened the Officer.

"Okay. I will figure out something."

The officer filled out his paperwork and handed Leah her copy. "This call will be documented." He held the paper for a delayed moment, while making eye contact with Leah.

"Thank you Officer," Leah said sarcastically as she snatched it from his hand.

As the officer moved down the stairs, Leah looked over at Miss Butt as she was turning to head back to her door. Leah smiled a big smile at her and then flipped her off with both hands, followed by slamming the door as loud as possible.

"Thanks Pagne, just what I needed." She glared at her sweet face and grumbled, "Worthless brat." Leah had decided that when Champagne was a year old, she did not deserve the name Champagne. She hadn't improved Leah's life, but complicated it. Leah called her Pagne, which was pronounced as "Pain." The fact that she was showing signs of freckles to go with the red hair from her nameless father didn't help either. Leah hated freckles with a passion. Leah plopped down on the ratty couch that folded out to their bed, and turned on the TV as she filled a tumbler with wine.

Leah's lust for drinking would not allow her to survive on the meager assistance she received, so she began hooking again shortly after Pagne was born. Pagne's childhood was a whirlwind of her mother's customers, late nights, and the consequences of being the child of an alcoholic. One thing was consistent, an anchor that Pagne could rely on, her mother's total disregard for her. Pagne was forced to be self-sufficient. She kept herself clean, got herself ready for school, and made sure the trash in the room didn't pile up too high.

When Pagne was eight years old, Adam Williams was her mother's new flavor of the month ... good looking, funny and he actually had a job. Nice change for Leah. Adam always brought a bottle of quality champagne for her and Jack Daniels for him. A few drinks, some laughs and then .... "Good lovin'," as her mother would say. Leah considered him a boyfriend, so she didn't charge him for her company. Pagne learned to keep out of the way when Adam or other men were there. The close quarters of the motel room made it difficult, but Pagne would lock the bathroom door and climb into the tub, pretending she was in a boat heading to a strange new land.

Pagne would also read with a passion. She loved stories about fairies, far away places, or brave characters who saved the day. She read whatever she could bring home from school. Her mom certainly wouldn't take the time to take her to the library or buy a book. When the tub was too disgusting to get into, Pagne would pile up any dirty laundry on the floor and make a nest. The width of the floor space fit her and the nest perfectly. She wished the walls were more sound proof though. The loud laughing and the noises they made when her mother had sex with the men made it hard for her to read, pretend or sleep. Pagne wasn't sure what they were doing, but she felt uncomfortable hearing them. Sometimes, the men that Leah brought home would hit her. Pagne knew to stay very quiet. She didn't want them to know she was there. Some mornings, Leah's face would be swollen and bruised. When Pagne would look at her with concern, Leah would shrug and say, "Comes with the territory."

Adam never hit her mom. He would always bring Pagne a toy or candy when he came over. He was nice enough but something made her uneasy about him. He didn't do anything bad, but he always wanted Pagne to sit on his lap. She didn't like it, and she wasn't sure why. Even her mom didn't like it. Leah would jerk Pagne up off of him and plop herself down on his lap, while giving Pagne the evil eye. Leah didn't realize how grateful Pagne was for removing her from the awkward situation.

Even at the age of eight, Pagne was independent. She could get her own breakfast and lunch, toaster pastries or cold cereal. It wasn't so bad when the milk hadn't soured, but usually she ate the cereal dry. She did get free hot lunches at school when she started first grade. Leah wasn't hungry until late evening, since she drank her meals during the day. She would throw something together for dinner, but in her drunken stupor, usually burnt it. Pagne didn't eat much. She didn't talk much either, and doctors thought it was because of Leah's frequent drinking during her pregnancy. But, according to Pagne, she just didn't have anything much to say.

One hot summer evening, Leah had drank herself into a stupor and passed out on the bathroom floor, leaving Pagne alone with Adam. He grinned at her and turned on cartoons. Their TV only had three channels. Luckily, one was cartoons ... most of the time. Pagne loved cartoons. She could watch them all day and just pretend she lived in the TV with them where she could fly like a super hero. Adam sat down in the old recliner and motioned for Pagne to come over to him. When she came close, he reached out and grabbed her by the waist and pulled her up on his lap.

"Your mommy is outta service, so maybe Adam and Pagne will have some fun? You wanna play with me, sweetheart?" Her instincts told her that this was not good. Adam's breath stunk so bad from the liquor. She felt his arms tighten around her. Pagne began to whimper and tried to pull away. Adam was whispering and sputtering spit into her ear.

"Be quiet. I'm not going to hurt you. Trust me, you'll like it ... well, I will." She felt one hand slipping between her thighs and the other sliding up her belly, lifting up her t-shirt. Pagne brought her leg up and slammed down hard, kicking him in the shin with her heel. He grabbed onto her even tighter, squeezing her painfully. She kicked his shin again, and this time he let go. As he grabbed at his leg, Pagne was able to slip off his lap and headed to the front door. Adam came up out of the chair and lunged at her, screaming out with anger and pain. He was behind her and grabbed onto her arms. It hurt terribly. She was kicking and screaming. Pagne's screams woke up Leah, and she came stumbling into the room, yelling for Adam to shut the brat up. She was confused when she saw Adam and Pagne struggling by the door.

"What the hell is going on?" She bellowed.

Adam released Pagne and spun around to Leah. "Nuthin, kid just went nuts on me, she tried to run away." It took a few minutes for Leah's drunken brain to absorb the situation.

"So my little Pagne didn't wanna play with you huh?" Leah showed no reaction while she tried to remain standing. She managed to focus on Pagne's face and gave her the most hateful glare Pagne had seen her manage. Pagne pulled open the front door and ran out, tears filling her eyes and clouding her vision. Through her tears, Pagne thought she saw white wings fluttering around her. Then black.

When Pagne woke up, she hurt all over. Every part of her was bruised and sore. Her head was pounding with pain. She could hear voices but she didn't want to open her eyes. She would hear a sweet lady's voice speaking to her at times. She was curious about the woman, but decided it was better to pretend that she was somewhere else. Sleep, she just wanted to sleep. It didn't hurt so bad when she slept. In her dreams she could fly with wonderful white wings, as others flew around her. Laughing, dipping, gliding ...

Pagne woke up to her mother's voice close to her ear. "You gotta wake up. What am I going to do with a brain-dead kid? I can't deal with this Pagne. Wake up now!" Pagne opened her eyes and looked at her mother. Her face was not haggard and worn from worry, but the familiar face of someone hung over. Leah's breath reeked of wine. "Well it's about time. What took you so long ... sweetheart?" Sweetheart was thrown in for the benefit of the nurse who just walked in. "Me and Adam have been worried sick. You scared your mama something awful." As the nurse finished her duties and left the room, Leah moved in really close, so only Pagne could hear. "Pagne, they think Adam hurt you. We both know that's a big fat lie, right? The police are going to talk to you. Mommy can't lose Adam, baby. You gotta fix this."

Later that day, several officers and a very nervous skinny woman named Miss Lament, came into Pagne's room. The officers tried to be friendly and had a teddy bear with them. It was very cute, and Pagne found it oddly comforting to hug. Miss Lament, who didn't smile and had very tiny, beady eyes was trying to ask Pagne what happened with Adam. Pagne decided she didn't have anything to say. She knew that Adam was a bad man, but even at her tender age, Pagne intuitively understood that it was her mother's truth. Leah needed him.

The officers and Miss Lament left very frustrated. Her mother had been waiting in the hall and slipped in. "Good girl. Now we just have to convince the judge. We're going to move in with Adam once this whole mess is cleared up. He's going to take care of both of us. Won't that be nice. We'll be a family real soon!" Pagne didn't respond. "We hit the jackpot, baby," cooed Leah.

That evening, the sweet-talking nurse was on duty. She was taking Pagne's temperature and adjusted her tubing. While she worked, she talked softly to Pagne, assuring her that she would be fine. As she turned to leave, Pagne grabbed her hand, squeezing it tight. The nurse, who's nametag said "Mrs. Greenly," looked into Pagne's eyes. She saw fear and worry in them. She asked,

"What's wrong, hon? You in pain?" Pagne took a deep breath and spoke in a whisper for the first time since waking up.

"What happened?" she asked.

"Oh honey, no one has told you what's going on? Well, I'm not sure why, but you ran out your front door, and then you fell down three flights of cement stairs. You broke your leg, your arm, cracked your head, and have lots of bumps and bruises. You are very lucky that you didn't hurt yourself even worse. I believe you have a guardian angel, dear. Yep, an angel that cushioned your fall. We all have an angel, you know. Talk to mine sometimes, when I'm sad or scared. You should thank your angel for protecting you. They have a thankless job!"

Pagne managed to ask when she would be going home. "You should be able to go home in a few days," the nurse answered. With that news, Pagne began to weep softly. "Oh sweetheart, that's not that far away." She looked into Pagne's face and realized this was something different. "Don't you want to go home?" Pagne just closed her eyes and let go of the sweet nurses hand.

After she left, Pagne whispered quietly, "Thank you." She did see wings, she was sure of it.

Pagne laid in her bed, a cast on right arm, a cast on her left leg, bandages here and there, and a dull headache. Her mom was filling out all the paperwork for her release. Leah looked at the prescriptions for Pagne and was grumbling that nothing was strong enough to do her much good. "The least they could do is give us Valium." Several nurses entered the room and helped Pagne into a wheelchair, Pagne's doctor and a police officer walked into the room. "Now Miss Crenshaw, there are some requirements you must meet to have your daughter home with you," said the officer. "This Adam Williams is not to be within 300 yards of your daughter or your residence."

"But he didn't do anything," Leah insisted.

"That might be, but until the judge makes his determination, the restraining order is in effect," the officer responded.

"Yes, of course," Leah said with attitude.

Pagne's doctor stepped toward Leah and began speaking. "Here is the treatment plan for Champagne's after care. Her therapy is crucial if she is to have a full recovery. I also want to stress that she will need a balanced, healthy diet and a safe, clean environment. Obviously the stairs will present a safety issue, have you made arrangements for assistance?"

"Yes, I have taken care of everything necessary," lied Leah.

"Mrs. Crenshaw, a child services worker will be checking in," reminded the officer.

"Yes, I know, another person up my butt. Can we leave now?"

"Yes, you may. But remember, your court appearance is at three o'clock today. We will remove Champagne from your care if you fail to appear."

"Yes, I know, I know," replied Leah with total disrespect to the officer.

The nurses put Pagne into a cab for the ride home while Leah had a cigarette. Once her nicotine fix was complete, she climbed into the cab next to Pagne. She shot the nurses a hard glare when their faces revealed their disapproval of her indifference. Pagne quietly sat while her mom went on and on about their new life with Adam. Leah talked about how Adam really cared about them, how happy they would all be together, and how Adam would bring money into the house. *She could quit hooking*, she thought to herself. Leah finally shut up and drifted into her fantasy of a wonderful future with Adam.

Pagne considered telling her mother what Adam had done, but she was a smart girl. She knew there was no point, her mother already knew. When they got to the hotel, Leah struggled to get Pagne upstairs, cursing with each step. Once inside the room, Pagne looked around and wasn't surprised to see that everything the doctor had listed was not done. Pagne hopped over to the couch and sat in silence.

"Wanna toaster pastry doll? Know how much you love them." Pagne shook her head and turned on the TV.

A few minutes later, there was a tap on the door. Leah opened it and Adam's head popped in.

"Hey, my two favorite girls. Just wanted to stop by and bring Pagne a get well gift." It was a tin of mints from the liquor store down the street and a car air freshener in the shape of a rose.

"What did you bring mama?" asked Leah with a little girl voice and giggle. Adam slipped a big bottle of champagne around the door.

"Can I come in for awhile?" he asked.

"No baby, not till the court says it's okay. My neighbor next door has big ears and eyes. This should all be resolved this afternoon, you gotta be patient." Leah laughed as Adam tried to grope her through the opening. "We'll all be together soon," assured Leah. Adam looked over at Pagne and winked with a disgusting lick of his lips.

"Okay, but I miss you guys. Good to have you back with us, Pagne." Pagne turned the TV volume up and turned away to look at the screen.

"She'll warm up to ya, baby, just give her some time. I'll call when I get out of court." Leah closed the door giggling. She looked over at Pagne, wanting to share the joy. Pagne could feel her eyes on her, but she didn't respond.

~

Pagne was very nervous sitting in the courtroom, waiting to find out what was expected of her. Everyone was so serious, except her mother. She was whispering insulting comments about everyone. Sticks up their you know what's ... and other such childish remarks. When it was their turn to appear before the judge, Leah bounced up, flicking her hair. Once she was at the front, she realized that Pagne was still struggling to get out of her seat. She smiled and loudly proclaimed … "It's okay baby, Mommy is here." She went back, and very graciously, helped Pagne into the aisle. Pagne was impressed by her performance. Once she made it to the front, Pagne sat at the table facing the judge.

Leah began by explaining that this whole thing was a misunderstanding. She said that Pagne had been throwing a temper-tantrum, and Adam was trying to keep her from running out of the room. When the judge asked if she had been in the room at the time, she admitted that she had not because she was suffering from one of her migraines and was laying on the bathroom floor for relief. "The cool tile is soothing," she explained.

Pagne's doctor was called forward, and he described the extensive bruising on Pagne's thighs, chest and arms. Obviously, a large man's handprints could clearly be seen in the photos they were showing. Leah did not have any explanation for the bruises. The judge looked at Pagne and asked if she had anything she wanted to say. Pagne just looked out the windows at the beautiful blue sky, wishing she could fly away.

The lawyer, representing Pagne's interests, made a good case that the events before her fall were clearly assault and possibly molestation. The judge agreed, and the restraining order was to stand pending further investigation. Adam had been picked up and interviewed after Pagne was admitted into the hospital. He wasn't arrested, but did have a court date.

Leah went into a rage. "This is ridiculous, you are punishing a good man, my man, for something that was very innocent. This isn't fair," she yelled.

"Well, Miss Crenshaw, if you want to have your daughter in your home, you must honor the restraining order. If you disregard the order, Champagne will be placed in the care of the state until this case is resolved," responded the judge with obvious distain.

"Well, I don't think me and Adam should suffer because of this brat. We have a life to start. You guys can deal with her," Leah said as she looked at Pagne in disgust. Leah then turned and walked out of the courtroom.

Everyone stood there in shock, not knowing what to say or do. Pagne hobbled over to the window and allowed one tear to roll down her face, just one. Then she looked to the skies and flew far away.

Chapter 2

The noise at Langston Hall was incredible ... all the screaming, laughing and yelling. But even harder to bear was the crying at night. Pagne had a room with just three other girls. Since she was still recovering from her injuries, she didn't have to stay in one of the dorms. Her mother had been gracious enough to hand the social worker a box of her belongings before slamming the motel door. She had her few items of clothing, some personal papers and drawings, some costume jewelry she had collected here and there, the bear from the police officer, and Adam's gifts: the candy tin and the stinky rose. These last two items she quickly tossed in the trash. The staff said she could go through the donated items to find more clothes and shoes, but she was comfortable with what she had. Pagne settled in to begin a new chapter of life.

This storage facility for broken hearts and dreams was clean, but stark. No softness or textures. Washable surfaces of mustard gold and brown. A local art class had come in and had attempted to brighten the main play room. They had painted a large, underwater mural on the longest wall. It was a good attempt but inconsistent styles and levels of ability made it look second best. Much like the lives of the children living there. The food was good, better than Pagne was used to having, but institutional and a bit bland. The staff were helpful, but Pagne could feel the wall of detachment they had to erect to protect their hearts.

Her healing was coming along slowly and she eventually had the casts removed. Her arm and leg were thin and weak. The facility got her therapy started, and she was thankful that this was not left up to Leah. The county decided that Pagne would receive better care at Langston Hall during her recuperation. There were no attempts to place her in foster-care.

She had been asked several times if she wanted her social worker to try to set up visitation with her mother. Pagne declined. This facility ended up being her home for nineteen months. Pagne looked at her healed limbs. Her leg looked almost identical to the other, except for the scars where they had run a metal rod through her shin for traction. Her arm, however, was a different story. There was scarring and she had difficulty bending it. Most of the time it hung straight at her side. The doctors had to operate to remove bone fragments and repair some of the tendons. The therapist was pleased with the progress Pagne was making, excited actually. This made Pagne realize just how serious her injuries had been.

Pagne enjoyed her time at Langston Hall. She became friends with several of the kids and started to trust them. Her best friend was Bree, who was wild and crazy, compared to Pagne. She had long, blonde hair and pale blue eyes. Pagne somewhat envied her straight hair and flawless skin, no freckles. Bree laughed and giggled at everything, especially if someone farted or burped. Pagne didn't see the humor in these rude body functions, but would laugh with Bree because her giggles were infectious. Bree would sneak into Pagne's room late in the evening, and they'd sit in the dark whispering and sharing their stories. Bree was one year older than Pagne. She also had a lot more to talk about than Pagne. Bree's family died in a car crash several months ago. She didn't have any other family to take care of her. Her years with her family sounded magical to Pagne. Bree had her own room, a little brother to play with, good food, but best of all was her stories about her mom and dad. They were huggers and cuddlers. Bree talked about the stories her mom would read to her. They would snuggle in Bree's bed and use a flashlight to read in the dark. Her dad would take her fishing and hiking. After Bree would sneak back to her dorm, Pagne would lay in bed and pretend she was in her own room with her parents just outside, discussing family plans. She would drift off to sleep .... until Leah would show up at her beautiful house, banging on the door, demanding to get her kid back.

~

Bree ran into Pagne's room early one morning, very serious. This was unusual for Bree.

"I'm leaving today. They found a foster-home for me," she explained.

"You don't look very happy, I thought that is what you wanted."

"I do, but some of the kids have told me how bad their foster-homes were. What if I get a bad one Pagne? What if they don't feed me, or hit me, or worse?" Pagne wasn't sure what to say.

"The social worker said we just have to tell them if something is wrong or call 911," reminded Pagne. "Besides, a nurse explained to me that we each have a guardian angel. So you have one too. You'll think I'm crazy, but my angel wrapped me in her wings when I fell, and kept me from hurting my brain or insides."

"Seriously?" asked Bree. Pagne nodded dramatically. "I hope you're right, I would love to have a guardian angel. I guess I'm just nervous. Kinda weird having a whole new family."

"I'm going to miss you Bree," Pagne said sadly. This was her first experience with truly losing someone that was important to her. She did not miss her mom. Bree left with the social worker later that morning. She was laughing and hugging everyone, as she made her way to the large, front entrance. Bree looked over and saw Pagne, tears rolling down her cheeks. Bree blew her a kiss and was gone.

Miss Renee, the only adult Pagne trusted at Langston Hall, slipped next to Pagne and put her arm around her shoulder. She didn't say a word, and just stood next to her. Pagne appreciated the gesture and leaned into her. Miss Renee was young and had just started working at Langston Hall. She hadn't built a wall around her heart yet. Pagne thought she was beautiful. Miss Renee was tall, her dark blonde hair was cut in a short bob, and she had green eyes that sparkled when she smiled.

Pagne was now left with her one other close friend, Itchy. Itchy wasn't his real name, but he was always scratching. He said it started when he had lice so bad that his skin was raw. They shaved his head, and he had to have baths in really foul smelling medication. When Pagne asked him if he still itched, he said only once in awhile. But it was so bad, he would stop in his tracks and just start scratching everywhere. The bugs were gone, so Pagne figured it was just the memory of the bugs that haunted him. Afterward he would go on like nothing happened. Most of the kids would tease him terribly and act like he had bugs that would jump on them. His real name was Arthur, but everyone called him Itchy. He kinda liked it. He dreaded hearing his name when he was home. He usually got screamed at or hit. Arthur was saved from an extremely abusive dad. His mom abandoned him when he was very small. He lived with his dad for seven years and suffered terribly. At least this was what Pagne thought. Itchy wouldn't talk about his dad or his life at all. If anyone tried to talk to him, he turned bright red, clinched his hands, and locked his jaw. Pagne saw the pain and horror in his eyes.

They had better things to discuss than the past. They didn't get to see each other a lot. Boys and girls were kept in separate sections of the facility. When there was shared time and space, they were stuck like glue. When they did talk, it was about their dreams, their plans.

Itchy wanted to be a policeman, a fireman, and a rock-star. Pagne had decided this particular week that she wanted to be a circus performer. The flying trapeze. She figured this was the closest she could get to flying without wings.

It was Pagne's tenth birthday, and after lunch, the staff brought in a glowing cake with ten candles and "Happy 10th Birthday Pagne" written in bright pink on chocolate frosting. Everyone began singing the birthday song and Pagne actually felt special in those few moments. As soon as the song was done, the kids were screaming "Cake! Cake!" The cake was wonderful ... so chocolaty. Pagne loved chocolate. This was only her second birthday cake, and both were here at Langston Hall.

As the kids moved out to the playground, Miss Renee walked over to Pagne. "Happy birthday, sweetheart," she said, as she kneeled down. "Ummm, this is kind of unusual, we weren't expecting her, but your mother is here. She wants to see you. You can say no, but you should know that she is working with the court to get visitation and parental rights reinstated. It might be a good idea to talk to her. I can stay in the room with you if you'd prefer." Pagne's face fell. Her mother? How can that be? She gave her to the state. So many questions raced through Pagne's mind. Could they really give her back to her? What about Adam? Pagne dreaded the thought of being in the same room with Leah, but she needed some answers.

"I'll see her, Miss Renee," Pagne responded. "Would you please stay in the room with us, at least at first?"

"Of course Pagne." They walked the long hallway, holding hands.

When Pagne and Miss Renee stepped into the waiting room, Miss Renee released Pagne's hand and moved to the chair in the corner. Pagne stood there face to face with her seated mother, the woman who gave birth to her, who was supposed to protect her and love her. Pagne felt nothing but disappointment and an anger building. She then felt a light brush against her cheek. She looked and saw nothing. She just smelled a lovely scent that quickly melted away.

Leah rose from her chair and squealed loudly! "Oh my baby! I've missed you so much!" She moved closer to Pagne and squeezed her in a crushing hug. Pagne pulled away, pretending her arm was still tender. Leah just stared into her eyes and grinned. "You've gotten taller, Sweetie. You're such a big girl. Did you miss your mommy? I sure missed you," lied Leah, as she plopped back down in her chair.

Pagne moved over to a chair on the opposite side of the table and sat down, not speaking or looking at her mother. Leah shot Miss Renee a nasty look. "Whats with the guard honey? You in trouble in here?" asked Leah. Pagne realized that she would have to speak to her mother.

Quietly she confessed, "I asked her to be with me." Leah looked shocked.

"You afraid of me baby? You know I wouldn't hurt you," said Leah, glancing over her shoulder at Miss Renee. "I'm hurt that you don't trust your own mama." Leah had a ridiculous pout on her face.

"What do you want?" asked Pagne, coldly.

"Well, you didn't think I'd miss your birthday did you? I brought you a present. Sorry it looks so messy. The old bat outside had to search it before I could give it to you. Just like a prison in here, huh Pagne? Bet you can't wait to escape!" Pagne looked at the gift bag her mother was holding. Obviously a recycled bag, Pagne didn't think a bag with storks and rattles printed on it was standard for a tenth birthday. The tissue was bunched up, and Pagne could see bright orange knit pushed down in the bottom of the bag. Leah pulled out a sweater, size eight. Pagne thought, *how appropriate Mom. Much too small, middle of the summer and stained*. Pagne figured her mother had found it at the local thrift store or in the lost and found at the motel office. To make matters worse, Pagne hated orange. Her mother looked so pleased with herself and held the sweater up to Pagne. "Looks a little small, sweetie, but sweaters stretch! It's the thought that counts right?" cooed Leah. *This was so ridiculous … there was absolutely no thought*, Pagne told herself sarcastically.

Leah leaned in close, speaking in a quiet voice, thinking Miss Renee could not hear. "I want to bring you home, baby. It's just not the same without you."

"What about Adam? I thought you two were starting a new life," asked Pagne. "Oh Adam. Well, that ended a year ago. Caught him cheating on me with a fourteen-year-old tramp. Not gonna let some slimedog sneak around on me."

Pagne was so angry. *He can fondle and attack your daughter and you keep him, but he cheats on you, and you dump him. Guess it's not cheating if it's your kid*, thought Pagne, but "Sorry," is all Pagne could muster in response.

"Well, I've met several generous men, but no one I can count on. Figured you and me can take care of each other and be two single gals. It'll be fun Pagne. You'll see."

Pagne looked at her mother in disbelief. "I don't want to come home with you!" Pagne said. Leah jumped up, and stepped back.

"I can't believe you … you ungrateful brat. How dare you. I am your mother!" exclaimed Leah. "How do you expect me to live, I need the money your sorry butt brings in from the county. I have rights. You are my kid. No one is going to keep you from me." Leah grabbed the sweater and stormed to the door. "Get used to it Pagne, you're mine and there's nothing you can do to change that. So quit pretending you get a different life. This is what fate dealt you. You're mine, and we're stuck with each other!" Leah quickly stomped out of the room. Miss Renee had moved in closer when Leah jumped up. After Leah left the room, she reached out for Pagne and tried to comfort her.

Things were as usual for the next few weeks, until Miss Renee came into Pagne's dorm early one morning. Once Pagne was through with her recovery and therapy, she had been moved into one of the eight bed dorm rooms. "Good morning Pagne, we need to go see Mr. Phillips in the administration office. We need to discuss your case." Pagne got a lump in her throat. She had been warned by the other kids that when you went to see Mr. Phillips, big changes were going to happen. The courts had decided you could either go home, or be placed in

315

foster-care. Pagne was praying that it was the latter. She didn't know what she would do if she had to go home. She noticed a sweet scent again, the same wonderful aroma that she smelled when she saw her mom. It calmed her, gave her a sense of peace.

"Okay, Miss Renee. Let me put on my shoes." Once she was ready, they headed over to see Mr. Phillips.

When Pagne and Miss Renee got close to the office, Pagne stopped and looked up at Miss Renee. "Will my mother be there?" she asked cautiously. Miss Renee looked at her sweet, freckled face and assured her that she would not. Pagne was relieved and moved toward the office. She had seen Mr. Phillips before, but had not talked to him. He looked like a kind man. "Well, hello there Miss Champagne, please have a seat. That is an unusual name ... Champagne."

"Everyone calls me Pagne, sir."

"Okay then, Pagne, do you know why we are here today?"

"I think so, sir. You're gonna tell me where I am going."

"Yes, dear. We have discussed your case with the judge, your attorney, your mother, your social worker, and Miss Renee. How would you feel about going home?"

"I thought my mom had to do a lot of stuff before I could go there. The other kids said the parents have to take classes and get tests, lots of stuff. I don't think my mom did any of that."

"Well, your case is a little different. The state did not remove you from your mother. Your mother felt she was unable to provide a good home for you, but now she believes she is able to be a responsible parent. Apparently, the person in question, this Mr. Williams, is no longer involved with your mother. The case against him was dismissed, due to lack of evidence." Mr. Phillips paused, "It is the goal of this office to reunite parents and children whenever possible."

Pagne felt her heart clench up. "Sir, do I get a vote?"

"Well, Pagne, we certainly want to hear what you have to say, but this *is* a decision for adults." She wondered if she told Mr. Phillips abut the men coming in all night, the beatings her mother endured, and the drinking, if would it make a difference? She decided it wouldn't, her mother was a good liar. *Who would believe her? She was just a kid.* Pagne leaned back into her chair, deciding she didn't have anything to say.

Pagne went into a deep, dark place. She spent a long time staring out the windows wishing she could fly away into the clouds. She started to wonder why she was even here. What was the point of her life? Was she just to be a yo-yo for her mother to play with? She wanted to know what was going to happen next, but dreaded knowing at the same time. Miss Renee tried to comfort her the best she could. She tried to get her to talk, but Pagne had shut down. One afternoon, Pagne approached Miss Renee. She had to try and reach out to someone before it was too late. "Miss Renee, you heard her. She doesn't love me, she just wants the money she gets for me," Pagne reminded her.

"Oh Pagne, I am sure she loves you. We all say things we don't mean when we are angry or hurt."

"Miss Renee, you don't know my mom." Pagne walked away, defeated.

She moved out to the playground and went to her favorite spot. There was a tree with huge branches that sheltered her from the sun. One branch curved low and was easy to climb onto. From that branch, she could climb way into the bowels of the tree. She felt safe there. She laid back on one of the large branches, staring up into the streams of light that filtered through the leaves. She watched, as butterflies lazily glided through the glittering light. She thought she could smell the flowering vines growing up the trellis close by, but the scent wasn't right. No, it wasn't the vines. She knew this smell, it was the scent that she smelled twice before. The smell of her guardian angel? "Are you here?" Pagne asked. "Is that you?" The scent was stronger, it swirled around her, filling her nostrils with glorious delight. *"It is you … I knew you were real!"* She thought she felt soft feathers brushing against her cheek and arm. Pagne closed her eyes tight and pretended she could see her angel. Then Pagne heard a whisper, "I am here." Pagne almost fell out of the tree. She was so surprised to hear a voice. But did she hear it? It didn't seem to come through her ears. It felt like a thought, a thought that wasn't hers, a blast that shot through her brain. She quickly looked around, thinking one of the kids might be messing with her, but no one was there. It was her and her angel. Pagne smiled and knew it would all be okay.

Several days later, Pagne was taken to Mr. Phillips' office again. Miss Renee was already there when she came in. Pagne was invited to sit, which she did slowly. "Am I going home now?" asked Pagne. Mr. Phillips looked at her quite seriously for a few minutes, and then glanced at Miss Renee.

"Not today, Pagne. We have revisited your case, and we have some concerns about your mother's ability to provide you with a safe place to live."

Pagne was not aware of it, but Miss Renee had done some extensive investigating after their last talk and she had found out that Leah had been arrested three times for public intoxication, and she also had pending charges for prostitution. This oversight by the county was attributed to a mix-up in social security numbers on Leah's police files.

"We have decided to give your mother more time to resolve her issues. Rather than have you stay here while this time is extended to your mother, we have released you for foster-care placement. Miss Renee will explain the process and your rights after our meeting here. Do you have any questions you would like to ask me?"

"No, sir, but thank you, sir."

Mr. Phillips dismissed Pagne and Miss Renee. Pagne felt a huge dread lift, but it was quickly replaced with a new anxiety. What was coming next?

Chapter 3

Miss Renee explained all the rules and safety precautions to Pagne. She would be leaving today. "Pagne, you will love Mrs. Buttonhook. She is an older lady who has been a foster-parent for many years. She is a lovely person, and she absolutely adores her kids. She has three foster-children living with her now. I know she will provide you with a wonderful home." Pagne went back to the dorm to pack up her few belongings. She hugged the girls and asked for permission to see Itchy before she left. Itchy came into the rec room and saw the look in Pagne's eyes. "You're leaving me?" he asked.

"Yep, they found a nice home for me … at least for awhile. I didn't want to leave without telling you goodbye."

"Sure glad you did." Itchy got real quiet and looked down. "I'm really going to miss you, Pagne. Not going to be the same around here without you."

"I'll see if they will let me visit."

"Yeah, that would be cool … good luck, Pagne. Hope they don't figure out what a brat you really are!" He smiled at her with a crooked grin.

"You are so mean." she laughed, as she slapped his arm. Pagne watched as he headed out to go back to the boy's area. She thought she saw him wipe his eyes with his T-shirt.

The social worker delivering Pagne to her new home had a name, but Pagne was too distracted to remember. This lady was really chatty. She just talked and talked. Pagne let her ramble, she was too nervous to try to have a conversation anyway. They pulled up in front of a cute three story house. It was painted bright yellow … banana yellow. Pagne noticed the purple door and shutters. The yard was full of brightly colored flowers. It even had a white picket fence with an arbor to walk under. Pagne smiled to herself and thought, *this is just too cute!* As they walked up the sidewalk to the front door, Pagne smelled freshly cut grass, flowers, and what she thought to be chocolate chip cookies baking.

When they stepped onto the porch, the social worker rang the bell, and Pagne felt her whole body stiffen. She felt a flush in her cheeks. As the front door opened, Pagne saw a young girl, maybe a year older than herself with white powder on her face and t-shirt.

"She's here!" she yelled as she ran back into the other room. Pagne got a strong whiff of her angel, then it was overtaken with the smell of baking cookies.

As soon as they stepped into the living room, Pagne liked what she saw. It was bright and cheerful. Mrs. Buttonhook came in from, what Pagne assumed, was the kitchen. She was older than Pagne expected, and she was very short and just as wide. Her gray hair was styled in very tight curls .

"Well, hello there, my lovely. You are just adorable. I love freckles! My name is Ophelia Buttonhook, but all my kids call me Grandma." Pagne realized that she had never thought about grandmas or grandpas. She didn't even know if she had any. "You can take your time and figure out what feels good to you. I answer to just about anything." Grandma, which was the name Pagne would chose to use, suddenly swept Pagne up in her arms and gave her a big hug. Between the fleshy arms and her full bosom, Pagne thought she might suffocate. "Forgive me, sweetie, I just gotta hug," Grandma giggled. "God built it into my DNA! Nothing I can do about it."

God? Who or what was this God? He built her? This was a very odd woman indeed, but Pagne felt an instant connection with this crazy lady. She felt herself grinning, without knowing why.

After the social worker talked Grandma's ear off for an hour, she finally left. Grandma then focused on Pagne and smiled as she said, "Boy that woman can gab. I didn't think anyone could out talk me. Let me show you around, sweetheart." First she took Pagne upstairs to the third floor. This was an attic room with steep angles on the walls. The stairs came up into the middle of the room. On each end was a window with a twin bed underneath it. There was a small dresser at each end and a large cabinet in the middle. The walls were painted a soft blue with white trim. There were large bulletin boards on each end of the room. One was empty, but the other was filled with wonderful items that all meshed together.

"Well, sweetie, this bed is yours," she said as she pointed to the twin bed underneath the window that faced onto the back yard. "You can put your clothes in this dresser, and you have more room in the cabinet there. Macey will be sharing this room with you. You met her at the door earlier. Let me show you around the rest of the house, and then you'll have time to put away your things while I fix dinner."

They moved to the second floor. There was a large bathroom with a shower and tub.

"We all have to share this one bath I'm afraid. We came up with a schedule that works out fine. In here is the boy's room. They are at softball practice right now. You will meet them at dinner. Tad and Chad are twelve, and they are twins. My room is right here. If you ever need anything, don't be afraid to knock on the door. Be sure to knock nice and loud. I take my hearing aid out at night. If I don't, I end up laying on that side and my ear aches for hours when I get up. Lord knows you'd think I'd roll over." She chuckled to herself as she moved back to the stairs. "Now downstairs is the living room and kitchen. You've seen the living room, so lets go check on how the cookies are coming." Pagne loved the sound of Grandma's voice. So kind, joyful and full of energy.

"Macey, this is Pagne. Pagne, this is Macey."

"Pagne, unusual name. Is that short for something?" asked Macey.

"Well, yeah. My mom named me Champagne after her favorite booze," replied Pagne.

"Well, I like Pagne better; I consider myself a *pain* too!" Macey smiled big and warmly at Pagne. Pagne knew she would like Macey right away.

"Ohhhh my goodness, Macey, lets get this last batch of cookies out of the oven before they burn. You girls can only have one now, because we'll be eating dinner soon. Pagne I hope you're not picky, we eat very simply here."

"I am not picky at all," explained Pagne, as she helped Macey take the cookies off the sheet to cool. "These cookies smell so good! Sure we can just have one?" Pagne asked, as she stuffed one in her mouth.

Grandma just chuckled, "You're gonna fit right in here Pagne."

Tad and Chad exploded into the house as dinner was being put on the table. "You boys go get washed up quick," yelled Grandma. "Dinner is ready!" Tad ran straight to the stairs, and Chad froze, looking at Pagne.

"Who's this?" he asked.

"This is Pagne, you can dazzle her at dinner. Get up there and wash those hands and face, you're all dirty and sweaty." Pagne felt her cheeks warm as she sat at the table.

Seemed like only a few seconds had passed and Pagne could hear the boys pushing and stomping down the stairs. Tad made it through the door first and sat down with the rest of them. Chad was right behind him. He slipped on a sly grin and stood at the table with arms crossed over his chest.

"Why is she in my chair?" he asked. He then tried to look injured and sad.

"Oh Chad, leave her alone. You know you always sit here next to me," Grandma said, while waving him toward her. Chad looked at Pagne and grinned his biggest grin. Once he was seated, Grandma asked them all to hold hands and bow their heads. Macey leaned over and whispered in Pagne's ear, "Sometimes this can take a long time." Grandma started her prayer thanking her God for the food, for the weather, for her health, for all of them and for all the beauty in the world. After about five minutes, she apologized to God for being so short-winded and she promised to make up for it during her evening prayers. Macey breathed a sigh of relief.

The dinner was delicious. Roasted chicken with baby potatoes, fresh green beans, and a wonderful fruit salad.

"Grandma, this is so good," said Tad through a mouth full of potatoes.

"Now just eat, and you can talk later. We got cookies for dessert. Macey made them this afternoon," Grandma announced. Tad and Chad started groaning and grabbing their guts like they were in horrible pain. "Now you boys quit teasing her. She is a fine cook."

Pagne felt comfortable joining in; "I had one earlier and they are good, so if you don't want yours, I'll take them." She smiled at Macey.

"Noooo, we want them!" both boys exclaimed.

With an evil grin, Chad asked "Are you?"

"Are I what?" Pagne asked back.

"You know, a pain?" he asked with a snicker. This started a wave of laughter from Tad and Chad.

Pagne wished she had a dollar every time she was asked this question. She decided Chad was deserving of her sarcastic answer. "No, but I can bring it!"

"Ewwwwwwwww, I'm scared," Chad responded with mock shaking.

"Now, now boys, that's enough. Pagne is a fine name, you leave her alone!"

The boys stopped their teasing, but broke out in giggles every time they looked at each other. After dinner was done, each of them rinsed their plates and set them in the dishwasher.

"Will you kids finish up the kitchen please, me and Pagne need to have a conversation."

"Sure Grandma," they all chimed in.

Grandma fixed two big glasses of lemonade and a plate of cookies. She handed Pagne one of the glasses and moved out the back door into the yard. Pagne never lived anywhere but in the motel and Langston Hall, so a yard was a new experience for her. She looked around at all the flowers, vines, bushes and trees. There was a apple tree and a pear tree. Over in one corner was a vegetable garden.

"We grew those beans you had tonight. We get a lot of our vegetables out of that garden. If you like gardening, I'll let you help tend it." Pagne had no clue if she liked gardening, but she liked the idea of making something grow, especially if you could eat it.

"I'd like to learn, Grandma." Grandma made her way to a little patio of large flat stones. Pretty moss grew in-between the stones with tiny purple flowers. There was a small table and chairs for them to sit. They were made of scrolled metal and the paint was chipped and faded. Grandma had placed brightly colored cushions in the chairs.

"Have a seat, hon, I'd like to discuss the house rules." Pagne listened attentively, while Grandma explained the bathroom schedule, the chore rotation, laundry, and all the daily functions of a family. "I don't have a lot of rules about behavior but the ones I do have are important. Number one is to be respectful of our family. No name-calling, hitting or insults. There is enough of that outside our house, we don't bring it in here. Second, we respect each others personal possessions. Do not borrow or use anything without getting permission. If you need something, let me know, and I'll do my best to get it for you. The last is no lying. We can't deal with the issues of life if we're all lying up in this house. We are a family, and we gotta have the facts if we're going to take care of each other." Pagne agreed to the rules and was happy to be part of this family.

As if they had radar, or they just knew Grandma's body language, the kids headed out the back door as Grandma was finishing. "Can we show her the tree-house now, Grandma?"

"Of course, children. Come in when it starts to get dark. You've got school tomorrow." Grandma took the glasses and headed into the house.

"Come on, Pagne, you're gonna love this!" Macey grabbed her hand and pulled her toward the backside of the yard. As they came around the wall behind the garden, there was an open field. A short distance away was a huge oak tree, gnarled and reaching to the sky. The boys were quite aways ahead and got to the tree first. They scampered up the rope ladder like two squirrels. Macey and Pagne got there as the boys disappeared into a huge wooden shack sitting in the tree. Macey showed Pagne how to climb the rope ladder so that it didn't swing too much. When they got into the tree-house, Pagne was amazed. There were chairs, a table, shelves with books and rocks, dead bugs, and all sorts of treasures. On the floor were huge pillows that now held the twins. "Beat ya again," they taunted.

"So what," Macey threw back. "You had a head start."

"Yeah right," Tad threw in response.

"Stop it you guys. Remember Grandma's rules!" Chad said sarcastically.

"What, you guys don't like the rules?" asked Pagne.

"Nah, they're fine. Grandma is really good to us, and we are all crazy about her, but she didn't tell you the most important rule," explained Macey.

"What's that?" Pagne asked.

They looked at each other and then turned to Pagne.

"Can we trust you to keep a secret?" Macey asked in a whisper. Pagne nodded her head emphatically.

"Gotta promise," Chad said.

"I swear," said Pagne.

"Grandma is bonkers!" Tad exclaimed.

"Tad, that isn't funny. She has some issues, and we help to look out for her," explained Chad.

"What kind of issues?" asked Pagne.

"She forgets a lot, and we just help her."

"Well forgetting isn't that big a deal, right?" Pagne suggested.

The three of them looked at each other and Chad nodded, giving the group permission to reveal the severity of the problem. Macey proceeded to explain. "Well, she forgets what day it is, so we have to be sure to get to school during the week. She forgets to buy food sometimes. She loses everything: keys, her shoes, everything. We try to put things she needs out where she can find them. But the worst thing is, she will forget the stove is on, or food is cooking. She can forget and leave water running in the tub. We make sure her baths are scheduled when we are home; that way we can check the water so the house doesn't flood. We offer to help cook and clean the kitchen so we can be sure everything is turned off. We worry about her during the day, but we can't miss school."

"Why don't you guys tell the social worker?" asked Pagne.

"What! Are you crazy? This is the best place I've ever lived. She is good to us. We just have to look after her, the way she looks after us," replied Tad with such passion. "So Pagne, you can't tell. They will move us out of here so fast that your head will spin off."

"I won't. I already like it here, and I don't want to go back to Langston Hall." The group of survivors pinky swore and Pagne was officially a member of the alliance.

~

Her first Saturday there, the kids were hanging out in the backyard. They were supposed to be weeding the garden, but had gotten distracted with horseplay and teasing. The twins didn't fight or argue much, but they loved to wrestle. Pagne and Macey were cheering them on and would clap when one pinned the other. Pagne wasn't sure how it happened, but she got dared to square off with Chad. Tad and Macey were laughing hysterically, as the two of them stomped around in a circle like sumo wrestlers. This was fun, and Pagne got into her character. She grunted and growled, as she stomped and flexed her thin arms. Chad made a quick lunge for Pagne and he missed, as she jumped and turned to one side. He was up on her again and grabbed her arms from the back. The harder she struggled, the tighter he held. Pagne's emotions shot back to the day in the motel room, to Adam's brutal grip on her frail arms. She remembered his reeking breath next to her face. She began kicking and screaming, and she lashed out at Chad with everything she had. Grandma ran out back and was yelling for Chad to let go of her. He was afraid to, because he was not sure what she would do when he did. He finally released her, jumped back, and tucked himself into a roll. Pagne fell to the ground, sobbing. Grandma shooed the other three into the house. Chad whispered "I'm so sorry, Pagne" when he passed her. Grandma pulled Pagne up and just held her. "You're okay, sweetie. I know Chad wasn't trying to hurt you."

"I know Grandma, I just panicked when he grabbed my arms."

"It's okay, baby" soothed Grandma. She just held Pagne and let her crying slow down, her breathing come back to normal.

They moved to the table and Grandma asked "Would you like to talk about what is so upsetting?"

"I don't know, I'm afraid to say it out loud. I can pretend none of it is real if I don't talk about it."

"I know it feels like that, sweetie, but you know it's lurking in your memories and heart. You know if you don't want to talk to me about it, God will listen."

"You keep talking about this God. I have never heard about him before. Why would I want to talk to him?"

Grandma took a deep sigh. "Well, this is gonna take some time, why don't you go get us a piece of that rocky road cake we made and a big glass of milk. Let the kids know you're feeling better; they are worried."

"Okay, Grandma, I'll be right back." After reassuring the others she was okay, especially Chad, she prepared a tray with two big slices of cake and cold milk. Pagne made her way carefully out to where Grandma waited for her.

As they ate cake, Grandma chatted about insignificant things, encouraging Pagne to join her in conversation. It didn't take long for Pagne to become comfortable, and to trust Grandma. She realized that she ached to talk about the years with her mother, the men that frequented their house, and how unloved she felt. She told Grandma all about Adam, the attack, her injuries, and how her mother picked Adam over her. Pagne revealed how afraid she was that the courts would send her back to her mother. Pagne shed so many tears and reduced the tissues in Grandma's apron to pulp. Grandma sat quietly and listened, frequently squeezing Pagne's hand until she was able to get it all out. Once Pagne was calm and had said everything she felt in her hurting heart, Grandma knew she was supposed to say something wise. Something that would help make sense of this young lady's heartbreak. She had to weigh her words carefully.

"Pagne, I don't know your mama, but she sounds like a broken spirit to me. Most of the time, when people are hardened and selfish, it has come from needing to survive. You say you have never met your mama's family? Maybe she suffered great harm in her life, and now she is doing the best she can. I am not saying that it is acceptable or fair, but when someone is broken, they do unspeakable things. That is why God is so important. He can mend broken spirits, and he can change who we are and how we live."

"But Grandma, who is God?"

"That's a big question hon, and I'll do my best. God is a living power that rules, and He created Earth, our universe, and all universes. He created man to be his companion. He is love and compassion, and he hates sin, because sin destroys his creations. He will remove all sin someday."

Grandma could see the confusion on Pagne's face. She decided one brief conversation would not be enough to explain what men have struggled with for thousands of years. She hugged Pagne and continued to her favorite part. "Once our lives are done here, we will dwell in Heaven for eternity with him and all the angels. We only have to believe and accept his son, Jesus, as our Savior", explained Grandma. She saw Pagne's face light up with recognition.

"I have heard about baby Jesus before. His birthday is Christmas, right?"

"Yes child, that's right. God is his father, and He also wants to have a relationship with you. To help you get through life and the troubles we all will have to endure. God loves you, Pagne, you are his daughter."

"I guess I don't understand why God gave me to my mom. She doesn't love me. Why didn't he give me to someone wonderful, like you?"

"I don't know all the answers, sweetheart, but I do know that he has wonderful plans for you and me, for everyone who will follow Jesus. I know he helped bring us together, and that he wanted us to know and love each other."

"Grandma, you mentioned angels. Do you really believe in angels?" asked Pagne.

"I sure do. I believe everyone has a guardian angel that helps them through life."

"So do I. Grandma, would you think I was crazy if I told you I can smell mine, and sometimes I can see her wings or feel them brush against me." Pagne wasn't sure how much to share but felt safe with Grandma. "What if I told you she talked to me?"

"Why, child, I don't think you're crazy. I just think you are a special young lady that has an open mind and heart and this allows you to see beyond other folks. You are blessed. "

"Grandma, it is okay if I talk to my angel?"

"I think your angel would like that very much. Must get boring hanging around all the time, and no one talks to you," Grandma said. They talked awhile longer and saw that the sun was setting. "Next time Pagne, I'll share my life with you. It's longer than your story and a little sad in parts, but it is my story and I wouldn't change it for anything."

"Okay, Grandma."

They walked into the house holding hands and feeling like this moment in time changed them forever. Pagne stopped Grandma just inside the door with a question. "How would God fix my mother?"

"Well, he knows what is in her heart and what she has endured. He also wants her healthy and in a loving relationship with you. I would say praying for her is the best way to start." Pagne gave Grandma a squeeze and ran off to find the others.

The next three years were wonderful. Pagne really came to love this crazy family of hers. She believed that eight eyes could certainly look out for one old lady. She liked her school and her teacher. They went to church on Sundays as a family. They all shared the work, laughed together, and grew closer and closer. Macey told her that she was going to be a dancer when she grew up. The girls would crank up the music in their attic and dance for hours. Grandma would take out her hearing aid, and the boys just got to suffer. Sometimes Tad and Chad would come in to laugh at them and would end up joining them.

Tad wanted to be a baseball player. He hoped he could go pro when he was old enough. Chad played because Tad wanted to. He enjoyed it, but that wasn't his passion. He was a science geek. Chad would talk for hours about microscopes, chemistry and bugs. He loved bugs. He would tell them about every bug in their yard, what they ate, how they multiplied. He would drive them crazy, until they ran away screaming ... no more ... stop! Chad would eventually give in, and they would play endlessly.

The tree-house was their sanctuary. They spent hours up there playing games, teasing, laughing, and debating. It was their place, where they were in control and set the rules.

Pagne loved that she could put her past behind her. It was all about now. No one talked about why they were there. They just were, and they were happy.

Each of the kids would make sure Grandma had lunch for the day before they left for school, so that she wouldn't cook while they were away. The kids always made sure someone came right home if the others had after-school activities. Several times, they found the stove on or the freezer door left open, but it wasn't anything they couldn't handle. It was a good life, loving and caring for each other.

~

While sleeping , Pagne was having the most beautiful dream. She was in a lush garden filled with flowers, butterflies and birds. The birds were singing beautiful songs, and one flew up and sat on her shoulder. There were also angels flying and fluttering about. Pagne realized her angel was near; she could smell her. The scent was so amazing ... it got stronger and stronger. Pagne kept turning and twisting, looking around for her angel. "I know you're here, I can smell you" she yelled in her dream. Then she heard her angel's voice.

"Pagne, wake up, now!"

Pagne sat up and realized the lovely angel smell had turned into stinking, choking smoke. Now that she was awake, she heard the smoke detectors wailing. How did they all sleep through them? She jumped up and woke Macey,

"Get downstairs now. Wake Grandma. We have to get out of the house." Pagne saw her little, white Bible from Grandma on her nightstand and stuck it in the waist of her pajama bottoms. They both ran to the second floor. Macey threw open Grandma's door and woke her by jumping on the bed. Pagne ran into the boys room and jerked them from their deep sleep by screaming their names. Grandma and Macey were first into the stairwell, heading to the first floor. Pagne was close behind, and the boys were following her.

As Macey and Grandma reached the bottom step, Grandma lost her balance and fell hard. She screamed in terrible pain, then whimpered "My hip is broken, my hip." Tad pushed ahead of Pagne to help Macey pull Grandma out the front door. Pagne looked back to tell Chad to hurry and he wasn't behind her.

"Where's Chad?" she screamed.

Tad looked up, confused, "I don't know. He was right behind me."

Pagne ran back up the stairs, screaming for Chad. The flames had now made their way up inside the walls and were breaking through into the hall. Chad was in his doorway with his microscope and an armload of papers. "What are you doing you, idiot?" screamed Pagne.

"I can't leave it behind," he screamed back. As Chad moved toward Pagne, a portion of the ceiling fell, pinning Chad to the floor. Pagne moved in and began pulling the debris off of him. Feeling the heat and finding it harder and harder to breathe, she was struggling not to panic. She finally got him free, but he didn't appear to be breathing. Pagne had no clue how to do CPR, and there was no time. She could feel the heat becoming unbearable. She drug Chad to the top of the staircase and pushed. He rolled down and landed at the bottom of the staircase with a loud thud. Just as Pagne headed down the stairs, the flames broke through the wall, and engulfed her. She had no idea what to do, so she ran down the stairs not realizing that she was feeding the fire that consumed her clothing and skin.

Pagne was in such a panic that she tripped over Chad on the floor and rolled across the room. As she tried to sit up, she saw several firemen enter the living room. "Chad! Get Chad! He's right there." One of the fireman swung Chad up and disappeared out the door. The second fireman quickly reached Pagne and wrapped his jacket around her to smother the remaining flames. He then lifted her up and carried her out of the house. Soon, she was lying on the neighbor's front lawn. Pagne looked over and saw their lovely home crumbling in the flames. She knew that she was burned, and wondered why it didn't hurt more than it did. She closed her eyes and smelled the lovely scent of her angel, then she heard someone screaming, "She's in shock!" as she went back to her lovely dream. She would not understand the importance of her selflessness that night for sixty-seven more years.

Pagne woke up in a strange room, it was brightly lit, and she was disoriented. As her eyes and brain focused, she realized it was a hospital room. She could hear the equipment beeping and quiet voices in the hall. She realized that her chest hurt, and it was very difficult to breath without making the pain worse. She found the buzzer on her bed and summoned the nurse. As the nurse entered, Pagne tried to sit up, but found it very painful. She hoarsely whispered, "Where is my family? Are they okay?" She saw movement in the corner of her eye. Leah leaned in next to her head from the chair by her bed. "Why, I'm right here honey. All the family you need." Pagne wanted to scream in despair, but she didn't make a sound.

Over the next few days, she found out that everyone survived the fire. Grandma had broken her hip alright, and was placed in a nursing home. It would take several months for her hip to heal, but her foster-care days were over. She had gotten up in the middle of the night to make a cup of tea and left the burner on. Unfortunately, a dish towel was close enough to the stove to ignite and start the fire in the kitchen. The firefighters said that Chad barely survived, but that rolling him down the stairs saved his life, as it got him below the worst of the smoke. He was bruised and had some smoke inhalation issues, but he would be fine in a few weeks. Pagne, however, was not so lucky. She had suffered third degree burns on her neck, chest, arm and shoulder. They would heal with painful treatments, but the scarring would be extensive. She thought about her rotten luck; *of course it was her perfectly fine arm that was burned.* Pagne would fluctuate between self pity and anger. Sometimes she would smell her angel, but ignored her or told her to go away. *"Where were you? Why didn't you protect us? Why didn't you protect me?"* Then she would cry softly.

Pagne was so sad that her time with Grandma and the kids was over. She had never felt so loved and connected in her life. She tried not to blame God, to wonder why he let her be so happy to just take it away. But there was no one else for Pagne to blame.

To make matters worse, Leah was an every day annoyance while Pagne was in the hospital. She was so rude and demanding of the nurses. Ordering extra food and drinks for herself while she sat in Pagne's room, going on and on about how she was going to sue the county. What were they thinking? Letting an old, deranged woman care for her precious baby. This should be worth quite a bundle. All the pain and suffering she had endured, all the days in discomfort she had spent sitting by her child's bed. The embarrassment she would endure when everyone stared at her disfigured child. It was just unbearable, the burden she must now carry. The local news and paper were willing to give Leah a very public soapbox to vent her rage and suffering.

Pagne almost looked forward to the painful water treatments for her burns. Her mother wasn't allowed in the treatment room. The nurses were kind, and Pagne could see they truly felt her pain - physical and mental.

One afternoon, while still in the hospital, Pagne heard some familiar voices in the distance. She looked up and saw Chad and Tad standing in the doorway.

She squealed in delight to see them looking so healthy and here to see her.

"How did you get here?" she asked. They moved close to her bed.

"Our new foster-parents brought us. After all, you saved Chad's butt. You look good Pagne, for almost being a crispy-critter," Tad said with relief. Chad stayed very quiet and just kept looking at her arm. Tad talked excitedly about their new home and filled Pagne in on all the great details. Pagne was happy for them, but her regret and pain from her own circumstances showed on her face and in her smile. Then, there was that awkward silence, the one you could cut if you had a knife. Pagne didn't have any good news to share and she felt Chad's discomfort. Chad cleared his throat and asked Tad to give him a few minutes alone with Pagne. Tad headed out of the room, making kissing sounds, as he went looking for a vending machine.

Pagne knew Chad needed to unload his feelings, and she patiently waited for him to speak. After a long, painful delay, he finally spoke. "Pagne, I am so sorry. We could have all gotten out of the house in time if I didn't go back for my stupid stuff." The tears began to roll down his cheeks. "I should have been the one burnt, not you." Pagne looked into his sad face and felt her own eyes tearing up.

"Chad, I am just glad that we are all okay." He reached over and gently touched her bandaged arm.

"Does it hurt much?"

"Some," she lied. It hurt a lot.

Chad stood there in more painful silence. They were both relieved to hear Tad coming back in. "Get the mushy stuff over with?" he asked, with a mouth full of chocolate candy. Chad turned and jabbed Tad with his elbow.

"Shut up, Tad."

"Pagne, it was good seeing you alive but we gotta go." Tad leaned in and gave Pagne a soft hug and moved to the door. Chad was trying to hold back more tears.

"I'll try to come again," he whispered, but this would be the last time they would see each other. Chad reached for Pagne's copper curls and gently twirled them in his fingers. He mouthed, "I am so sorry, please forgive me." The pain in his eyes mirrored the pain Pagne was enduring. Pagne took his hand with her good hand and squeezed. She smiled and nodded at him, knowing that if she spoke, it would release fountains of tears. The boys left as quickly as they emerged. Pagne laid back and shut her eyes, trying to close out all the pain. She then heard the unmistakable screech of her mother's voice coming down the hall. *"God, if you are there, please take me now,"* Pagne prayed to herself.

Eventually, Pagne was released from the hospital into her mother's care. She guessed that her mother's threat of a lawsuit was being taken seriously, and the county didn't want to aggravate the situation further. Leah had played the outraged and concerned mother very well on the five o'clock news and acquired a high profile lawyer.

Pagne was surprised to learn that her mother had gotten a job as retail clerk nine months earlier. Leah's drinking and lifestyle had taken its toll on her looks, and she found it difficult to find men willing to pay her what she thought she was worth. Leah pretended that she left the business while she was still on top, on her terms. This new job gave Pagne some grace of time without her mother around. With the small income her mother was making and the assistance she received for Pagne, they were able to move into a small, one-bedroom apartment. Pagne slept on the couch. It was some time before she could return to school. The pain medications she needed kept her groggy and unable to focus.

She was a local celebrity for a short while because of her heroism. The city and the local fire departments established a college fund for Pagne. Luckily they made sure no one had access to it unless used by Pagne for college tuition. Her popularity was short-lived because a local politician was caught buying drugs from an undercover cop. Pagne was no longer the main attraction for the local news or newspaper and the media had tired of Leah's rantings and her battle now would be fought in the courts.

anessiasquest.com
Kindle available on Amazon

Reviews

Get your box of tissues ready, sit in your favorite chair, swing, etc. and begin a journey that will stay with you long after you've finished the book. Karen Arnpriester has definitely been blessed with the gift of writing. ... The characters could be anyone around you whether you know them or not. They are well defined. You get to know them and their hearts. Your heart breaks for them and rejoices with them. The situations are so realistic. They are situations you see or hear about each day. Some of them may be experiences you have dealt with yourself. For this reason the book stays with you. You will always see yourself in this book in some way. I look forward to reading more from this author. Her book most definitely blessed my heart and spirit.

Sandra Stiles - 5 Stars   www.goodreads.com

This story is one of joy and sadness, triumph and tragedy, love and forgiveness. I laughed, I cried, I found myself wanting the story to continue at its end… to know what lies beyond for Pagne as she continues turning pages in God's unending story. Truly inspiring, Pagne's journey is an amazing reminder that we each have a destiny and role to play in God's eternal plan. Needless to say… I'm a fan! Looking forward to the movie!!!

Pam Rich

This book was surprisingly refreshing for me, since my favorite type of reading is learning manuals or true stories. I read a lot but took time out to read Anessia's Quest. It came with me on a vacation and I just could not stop reading it. I felt emotionally attached to the characters and was feeling their joys and their pains. I even thought about them later wondering how they were doing. The author has a real knack for keeping your attention. I hope there is more to come from this author, she is on to a great start! Two thumbs up!!!

Ava Peterson – Amazon 5 Stars

I Loved this book! I did not want to put the book down. The author did a great job at catching my attention. I definitely laughed out loud with some of the funny moments in this book. Most of the characters in this book really touched my heart. To sum it all up it is a great heart warming, funny, and inspirational book. I hope to see more of Karen's books in the future.

Crystal Quiro – Amazon 5 Stars

It is a very powerful book that points out God is in our lives. It is a book of redemption. I could not put it down!!!

Trisha Timosh – Amazon 5 Stars

I read this book in two sittings. Up to eighty pages the first time, then took an entire morning to finish the rest. And I did need tissue. The story is an emotional ride, the characters are real to you – you care or you hate them or you have hope for them. The author is a natural story-teller.

Jennifer Locke – Amazon 5 Stars

A novel of real-life trials and triumphs, "Anessia's Quest" is an inspirational, well-written, magical story of God's love. Spanning over an entire lifetime, we get to know these characters so deeply. We share their pain, joy, excitement, and shame… but their faith shines above it all. Karen Arnpriester expresses the power of healing as each endures to be the person they want to be, rather than the person they think they are. I am captivated by Anessia's strength and compassion. Truly a book I didn't want to put down…. And when I finally did, I found myself wanting more from this author.

Jana Adams – Amazon 5 Stars